LUCKY SCORE

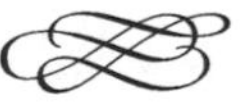

LUCKY SCORE

LUCKY O'TOOLE VEGAS ADVENTURE: BOOK 9

DEBORAH COONTS

Published by Chestnut Street Press

eBook ISBN: 978-1-944831-62-2
Paperback ISBN: 978-1-944831-64-6
Hardcover ISBN: 978-1-944831-63-9
Audiobook ISBN: 978-1-944831-52-3
Large Print ISBN: 978-1-944831-45-5

Cover design by Streetlight Graphics
(www.streetlightgraphics.com)

Formatting by Kate Tilton's Author Services, LLC
(www.katetilton.com)

CHAPTER ONE

THE BARREL of a gun pressed to my temple stopped me mid-stride.

"Put your hands up." A female voice forced to a deeper timbre echoed in my ear, her breath hot on my cheek.

Adrenaline surged through me. My anger spiked.

Saturday night. Vegas. My hotel. A crowd packed in.

Over my dead body.

I grabbed the gunman's forearm, pushing upward. Then I reached up twisting the pistol out of her hand. She yelped in pain as I wrenched her arm behind her, dropping her to her knees.

My knee was poised to pop her elbow should she even look at me cross-eyed. I stared down at my newly discovered cousin who was more like a half-sister.

Bethany.

Only seventeen, she was all arms and legs, big eyes, and bad judgment. "The gun's a fake. I was just…" she stammered then stopped as the error of her joke washed over her a moment too late—I could see it in the widening of her eyes, the flush of her flawless skin. Her youth mocked me. Yesterday, I'd been just like her—well, not quite as stupid I hoped, but a teenager without a home, without a father—her mother was in an asylum and mine should've been.

I'd been the Big Boss's problem and Bethany was mine.

Life had spun full-circle.

At twice her age, common thought said I'd traded time for wisdom, though most days, nobody could prove it by me. The kids had it lucky—with time they could mitigate stupidity. But, for the rest of us with so much time behind us and the past being the only immutable, our stupidity plagued us with the hope for a cure dwindling.

I cranked her arm a little harder, forcing home my displeasure and maybe a bit of a lesson.

"Ow!"

The crowd milling in the lobby had moved back, giving us a wide berth. Thankfully, nobody had panicked at the sight of the gun. We all were a bit twitchy about that sort of thing right now, all things considered. When I tucked the pistol in my waistband, securing it at the small of my back, the crowd clapped. "Party's over. False alarm."

A few folks snapped photos. Should one of them show up in the *Review-Journal*, it would teach my cousin a lesson, but I shut down the shutterbugs with a glare. "Don't even think about it. Privacy concerns trump your right to gain followers."

A weak threat in this viral-crazy world.

Pay-per-follower—the latest get-rich scheme. Thank God I had aged-out of the digital marketing department. If the millennials took over, would they kill us all on our thirtieth birthdays? Fiction becomes reality, thereby consuming the old adage? The way my life normally went, anything was possible. Great, something else to worry about. As if a hotel full of NFL players and their fans, newly-found relatives without enough sense to know firearms in public spaces were rather incendiary, a mother who still hadn't named her months-old twins, a father who was taking his sweet time recovering from a bullet to the chest, a fiancé who personified perfection, and a former love who didn't, but who still had a place in my heart—not to mention the scabbed-over bullet wound to my calf that was making me slightly less than my normal impatient self.

A month after New Year's and a birthday that sank me further into my fourth decade, and I was hardwired to pissed-off. And I wasn't sure why. All of the foregoing was nothing more than a whine, none of it anything more than business-as-usual. But something had kidnapped my smile—not that that was all that unusual either since I'm doing all this soul-baring and all.

My job was Vice President of Customer Relations keeping the Babylon, Vegas's primo Strip resort casino hotel, in a non-viral space, at least that's the job they paid me for. Family was a cross we all bore, some of us better than others. Given that my mother, Mona, would try a saint's soul, and I would never be considered for canonization, I probably fell at the apex of the bell curve on handling familial relations. I could live with that. When it came to my family, resisting homicide was a huge victory. The men? I don't know. It's like the adage writers followed me around. Grass is greener? Check. Love is blind? Check. Any port in a storm? Well, not exactly, but close enough considering the green grass analogy. I hadn't taken the plunge, but the fact that it was tempting was so out of character for this serial monogamist. When it comes to love…women are clueless? Okay, not an adage, but, if it were, I'd prove it, too. And that part about telling myself that fermented fruit juice is the same as eating the fruit when it came to keeping the doctor away? That was getting to be a problem—one I admitted only to myself—but I felt it dogging my heels, waiting to take a chunk out of my butt.

Do I need to say I'm not handling the vicissitudes of life well?

Didn't think so.

People drifted back into what they had been doing: ogling, drinking, chatting, looking for the next Vegas conquest—normal activities on a Saturday night.

Don't let them forget.

Immobilized by her arm at a painful angle and my hands applying the leverage, Bethany hadn't moved. Her long hair hung across her face. She wore fatigues and boots, with a hint of face paint still lingering behind her ear.

I didn't ease up on the pressure. "That was about the dumbest stunt in the history of mankind." Only a few months ago, a boil on the ass of humanity had opened fire from the Mandalay Bay Hotel, a horror that tore the fabric of humankind. And no matter how carefully we stitched life back together, the cloth would never be whole again, never be as it once was.

None of us would be.

Bethany angled a wide-eyed look up at me. "I just wanted to get your attention."

"That was the most insensitive, asinine, juvenile…" The inadequacy of words stopped me cold. "Do you know how many people died?" The horror of that night, the outdoor concert, the bullets flying, people dropping, screaming.

"You're right, seriously stupid. I wasn't thinking. As a joke it—"

"A joke! A gun is never a joke. Nor are they toys! What the hell is everyone thinking these days?" Treading the line between protecting the right to own a gun and keeping guns out of the hands of psychopaths and idiots required a balance the country had yet to find. "Where the hell did you get a gun?" I growled, my anger spilling over, dousing rational thought.

"It's not real. Ow!"

"Not real?" Sure looks like it." I gave her arm another tweak, less than I wanted but probably more than I should have. The reciprocal pain of her stinger raced up my arm. "There are consequences to every stupidity. You put a gun to my head; you're lucky to be alive. Had a security guy been close by…" A security guard with a twitchy trigger finger and a crowded lobby —dear God!

After releasing her arm, I helped her to her feet.

"Do you need assistance, ma'am? We've been monitoring," a voice sang out from the phone in the holder at my hip.

"Speaking of security." A voice I didn't recognize and a breach of protocol. He should've scrambled a team the minute he saw a gun, fake or not.

"O'Toole here." Yes, my name is O'Toole—which doesn't match either of my parents'. My mother had yet to explain, but, to be honest, an explanation would border on a confession, a confession I didn't need to hear. That's how it was with Mona—she hid secrets with obfuscation. She had, however, provided an explanation as to my first name, Lucky. My given name had been her sister's, Bethany's mother's, nickname. I still fully processed that as Mona carried a load of guilt over her sister and what had happened. "Stand down. I got this. False alarm."

"Roger that." He sounded bored.

"Who is this?"

"Fox, ma'am."

Fox. The guy Jerry, our Security Head, had been grousing about. "I'm writing you up, Fox. First sign of a gun, you should've sent a team."

"It's my first night on the desk, ma'am."

I rolled my eyes and let out a heavy sigh. Where the hell was Jerry? A rookie was the same as no one minding the store—and with the hotel full and the NFL in town! "It'll be Jerry's call." Jerry's toes were safe from me stepping on them, but he'd sure as hell hear about it.

"Security?" Bethany looked at me wide-eyed as I holstered the phone. Only a few weeks into being a Vegas resident, Bethany had yet to learn that, in a hotel like mine, with cameras everywhere, no movement went unwatched.

"Somebody walks into a casino with a gun, people get their knickers in a serious twist." I pointed to some of the cameras hidden among the hummingbirds and butterflies taking wing across the lobby ceiling—millions of dollars in Chihuly glass.

"Somebody's always watching. We can never be too careful." Had I ever been stupid enough to put a gun to somebody's head and not meant to pull the trigger?

After the recent shootings, we'd started x-raying every bag that went up to a room—not one guest, no matter their rung on the food chain, could carry a bag to their room. All of them went through our bell staff. Stuff a couple of rifles in a golf bag and hoist it on your shoulder like you just enjoyed a quick eighteen holes. Nobody would've thought anything of it. Now, we lived in a new reality where crazies killed for their fifteen minutes and the news outlets gave it to them.

Amazing how after one shot of adrenaline I was right back to that night. I rubbed my hands together to keep them from shaking. Of course, putting them around my cousin's neck would also do the trick. Instead, I pulled the pistol from my waistband. Its heft was slightly lighter than the average handgun with a full magazine "What's with the commando gear?"

She brushed down her fatigues. Her Timberlands still had sand on them. "School doesn't start until the fall, so I got a job." Shoulders back, she tried to reclaim some dignity. Folks wandering past gave her some serious side-eye and a wide berth, which she tried to ignore.

"As a mercenary?" I glanced up from my examination of her gun. Nicely balanced, it felt good in my hand. "Before you start at Cornell, I suggest you grow a brain."

Lacking even a gossamer-thin comeback, she wisely conceded.

The end of the barrel had an orange ring around it. "What is this?"

"Indicates it's an air gun. I'm working the field at War Vegas."

"The new place west of town where everyone dresses up like a Marine or something and pretends they're retaking Fallujah?"

"Yeah." The girl looked proud, so I kept my derogatory thoughts to myself.

Maybe I was getting old, but I couldn't see how running

around shooting people would advance society. Silly me, but I thought that was the sort of thing we were working to put a kibosh on.

"It's so realistic," she said, her enthusiasm growing. "The guns look real but only shoot plastic pellets—they sting when they hit, but no lasting damage—just enough to know you're dead."

"You do know this conversation is super-alarming, right?"

I tucked the gun back in my waistband.

"I need that back. I wasn't supposed to take it. With it strapped into my leg holster, I didn't realize I had."

"Pretty pricey, I bet, to get all that looks-like-the-real-thing. Don't they check their inventory in and out?"

"With the players, yes. The workers are assigned their own pieces."

"All handguns?"

"No, we get to choose. Why are you asking?"

"Oh, no real reason." I grabbed her shoulder and dug in my fingers until she looked at me. "Other than a bunch of lightly-trained loonies running around town with weapons that look so much like the real things, it'd be hard for a Marine...or a cop to tell the difference at first glance. And a fraction of a second is more than you normally get when you point a gun at somebody who has a weapon of their own." I shrugged and readopted a light but scathing tone. "I mean, think about it: What possibly could go wrong?"

As she opened her mouth to answer, a scream echoed over the crowd in the lobby.

People stopped, glasses half-raised, their mouths open, their posture frozen as if The Ruler of the Universe had hit "pause."

The scream came from the direction of the front entrance. I couldn't see anything through the crowd, so I started pushing my way in that direction. Bethany dogged my heels.

One scream fell short of sufficient inducement to run. Through the years, I'd learned women have this weird habit of screaming when they see people they know, or, better yet, people they recognize.

To be honest, running would have been a bit optimistic. Limping along like Igor, I was a far cry from fluid form. My leg didn't exactly scream, but the muscle grabbed, demanding attention. Nothing like having a balky body part that still wanted to whine at being perforated by a bullet. Pain brought me to a momentary halt, and I danced around on one leg while I massaged the offended extremity. A month should have been plenty of time for healing, or at least enough to run out of whine. But I couldn't be so lucky, could I? A weak play on words, but, simple as I am, it made me smile.

"Are you okay?" Bethany asked from right behind my left shoulder.

"Never better." With my ego on the line, I launched off again with renewed vigor. Foregoing my Ferragamo heels for matching flats had been a wise choice. Hemmed for heels, my brown tweed lightweight wool slacks were a tad long, but the fashion police were the least of my worries tonight. The pants were new, along with the harvest-gold cashmere sweater set. The fire had consumed everything to the point that I almost believed it had reduced me to cinders as well.

Taking my weight only on my toe, I could hobble without whimpering. Still, I nearly took out two children who had no business being in the lobby of a Vegas hotel at this time of night—not that it was terribly late, but kids and a Saturday night in Vegas just screamed wrong. I will admit to often being in the minority on that, though, which made me wonder, if you started life in a casino, where would you finish up?

Rhetorical question—I was the walking, talking answer. Well, actually, I started life in a whorehouse in Pahrump, but only geography separated the two experiences.

Bethany, showing a curious flash of wisdom, stayed behind me and didn't try to rush ahead.

I hoped the screamer was nothing more than a drama queen low on attention. We had those in spades in Vegas…and it was Saturday night. Probably a full moon, too—the crowd had that kind of vibe. I'd maxed my Fitbit running from one crisis to another. I glanced at my phone. Four minutes to handle the screamer before I was needed elsewhere, not even a challenge for my superpowers.

Right.

The NFL memorabilia signing event would end in five minutes, and I'd been on my way to help the former greats of the game make their way to the after-party when I'd been waylaid by a stupid teenager, to the extent that is not redundant.

A quick dodge around the future wards of the state, I grimaced as my leg let me know what it thought of that, then I bounced off a wall of solid human flesh. Two men, sausages in suits. They didn't even register my blow.

"Sorry."

Part of the NFL contingent in town to celebrate the San Antonio Marauders becoming the Las Vegas Marauders, or whatever name some marketing firm chose in the future. Given the over-blown morality of the NFL, a big win for Sin City.

But one that came with a whole new set of problems.

Completely unaware of my presence, the men stared over my head.

Bethany tugged on my arm, "Do you know who that is?" Breathless, she stared, big-eyed, at one of the players. I was half-surprised she refrained from drooling.

"Yeah, I do. Beau Boudreaux."

At the sound of his name, Mr. Boudreaux, a mountain of muscles and arrogance, glanced first at Bethany, then leveled a gaze that held a just-try-to-protect-her in his small dark eyes.

I might not be able to take him by myself, but I could recruit an army to help if I needed to.

A bruise bloomed across one cheek. Trouble had already

found him. And, judging from the sand that clung to his shoes and the hem of his pants, the trouble hadn't found him here.

One small blessing in a night completely devoid.

But, even though he probably wasn't on property when he'd gotten crosswise with someone fool enough to take a swing at him, I hoped the trouble didn't involve the Babylon. The hotel that had released tapes of him laying out his girlfriend with a left jab had just filed for bankruptcy to avoid the litigation costs of going public with the tapes. "No hero-worship here, kid. He's just another future has-been who can't refrain from hitting women. NFL is all over him."

Boudreaux shrugged as if to say there were lots of stupid women in the world willing to go to the mat for him. He wasn't the denying type.

Several months from her eighteenth birthday, Bethany was still jailbait, so I had a little time to figure out how to make her listen to all I'd learned the hard way. "Can we get through, please?"

Boudreaux didn't budge. Instead, he turned back toward the front doorway and widened his stance and held his arms out, blocking our path.

While I considered a swift kick to the back of his knee, another scream echoed over the crowd.

Okay, not a normal screamer. One scream could mean anything. Two screams narrowed the scope of possibilities to serious.

I tugged on the sleeve of the NFL guy closest to me, the one who wasn't Boudreaux. "Can you see anything?"

"Nah. A bunch of looky-loos in the way. Probably some female all bent out of shape."

Ya' think? That much was obvious, but pointing that out would probably not be in my best interest. I ducked around the two players. The time for measured calm over, this time I picked up the pace.

She screamed a third time.

I fought the urge to run.

The humans teeming in the lobby, their heads on swivels, moved toward the sound.

Working my way through the thickening crowd, I still couldn't see anything. At least the surge of humanity was moving with me. I grabbed my phone and hit a familiar speed dial. "Security?"

"Security." The new voice again, deep with an edge. I'd been hoping Jerry had returned from a sit-down in the can or wherever he had run off to. Only a serious threat to life as we knew it or the Siren call of Mother Nature could make him leave his post on a Saturday night.

"O'Toole here. Is this Fox again? Who the hell are you?" I didn't bother to keep the hard out of my voice—nice took time I didn't have.

"Jack Fox, acting security head, ma'am."

I'd never seen anything on this kid and Jerry had given him temporary control of Security? "And Jerry? Where is he?"

"On a break, ma'am."

Jerry didn't take breaks, but now was not the time to argue. "Okay, Fox, we have a screamer by the front entrance. What's happening? Can you see?" One of the security cameras ought to give them a bird's-eye view.

"Yes, ma'am. Bringing up the feed now." The kid was in love with the word "ma'am." I couldn't tell why, or how he meant it.

Actually, I'd made my peace with the whole ma'am thing: I chose to see it as a sign of respect rather than age. A pyrrhic victory and probably delusional, but delusion was my only escape from reality.

I eased through an opening in the crowd and darted ahead past a couple clutching each other with one hand and a flute of Champagne with the other. The girl's tiara identified her as the bride. Ahead of them, a gaggle of young men looking for mischief formed a wedge to part the crowd. I fell into trail behind them.

"What do you see?" I shouted into my phone to be heard above the excited murmurs around me.

"Holy shit!" Apparently, Mr. Jack Fox was as young as he sounded. And not particularly helpful.

But his response did tell me one thing: I was going to need help with this one. "Send a detail NOW!"

"Yes, ma'am." The young voice sobered. "Ms. O'Toole, he has a knife."

A guy with an automatic weapon and several full magazines was our worst-case scenario. A man with a knife, a distant second, but still a major problem in need of a quick solution. My heart rate climbed until blood pounded in my ears. "Is he…?"

"No, ma'am. He's just standing there. There's a lot of blood. Should I make the calls?"

"Put someone between him and the crowd and get the crowd back. I'm seconds away if someone would get this wall of humanity out of my way."

"Do you need help with that?"

"No, just keep the knife guy from hurting anyone until I get there. Can you see any victim?"

"Negative."

"But there's blood?"

"All over him."

"There has to be a victim somewhere. Find him!" I used the masculine generically, but a man with a knife? In all probability, the victim was a woman. So many men came to Vegas with a need for sex and with no respect for the women who provided it—one of those ethical swords men regularly threw themselves on. But the women were the ones bloodied.

"Roust the doc out of bed, but wait on the paramedics." The media stuck to the EMTs like remora on sharks. "Security is on its way, right?"

"Yes, ma'am."

"After they've secured him, have them fan out. Given that he's covered in blood, the guy couldn't have wandered too far from the scene of the crime. We need to find his victim STAT."

Snaking through the crowd, I took a moment to think. The crowd was interested, calm not panicked. An odd commentary on modern life that a man with a knife was viewed as a curiosity and not a threat. But, then again, this was Vegas where everything was part of the show.

Until it wasn't.

Jack Fox jumped into the silence. "But the blood. I think it best to call the EMTs." The kid had balls—not one of the best attributes for a young security guard, but usually the kind attracted to this kind of work. I bet he even wore his shirts two sizes too small to show off the size of his biceps.

"My job is to do the thinking, Fox. Your job is to do as you're told."

"Roger." One word slid in like a lethal blade between two ribs.

Guess I wasn't a ma'am anymore. So much for the whole respect thing. "On second thought, you're right." I so wanted to avoid the spectacle of flashing lights and sirens but, on the theory that where there was horseshit, there was a horse, we needed to be prepared to find a victim in need of serious medical attention. "Rally the EMTs, and find Jerry and have him call Metro; tell him to keep it on the down low. We don't need the cops screaming in here, too. He'll know who to call. You start working through the video feed. Track the guy with the knife. I want to know where he came from and how he got to my lobby. First priority is to immobilize him. Second priority, find who donated all that blood. I can't stress the urgency of that enough." I disconnected then called my office. Miss P, my Number One, answered on the first ring. "I need you to sub for me at the signing." The NFL legends, past and current, would be signing memorabilia in the Golden Fleece Room. Someone from my staff needed to be there. "Escort them to the party at Babel." Babel was our *über* cool rooftop lounge and club.

"On my way." Miss P rang off. Ours was a long and close corporate marriage where verbal shorthand sufficed.

The crowd thickened as I drew closer—human concrete setting up from fluid to impassable. My plow of young men now became a wall.

"Everybody back!" I shouted as if anyone would listen.

Nobody even glanced my way.

I wedged a shoulder between two more big guys, these two blocking my way. "Excuse me. May I please get through? I'm with the hotel."

One glanced at me. "No way, lady."

I elbowed him in the ribs hard enough to make a point but stopping short of breaking anything. As he cringed, I moved through.

"Shit, lady, I think you broke my rib. All you had to do was ask." He put a hand on my shoulder, jerking me back.

"I did." I met him eye-to-eye, mine slitty, his bloodshot and wide with surprise. Most bullies didn't expect a woman topping six feet with some bulk behind her punches. "Let go. If you don't, next it'll be your nose."

Wisely, he let his hand drop.

"That was so cool," Bethany said from behind me as she rubbed her shoulder.

My definition of cool and hers were separated by seventeen years.

People around us muttered, their excitement growing.

I could read that murmur—someone recognizable.

Shit.

Cellphones held high, folks snapped unobstructed photos.

"Everybody back! No photos."

Nobody moved. Phones remained high.

Finally, I shimmied through a crack in the human wall into the open and drew a deep breath.

A man, covered in blood and holding a knife, and a pretty

decent blade at that. Twelve inches, a serrated edge, it had a black plastic handle, a coating of blood and a military look to it.

Bethany gasped when she saw him.

I put out an arm, keeping the girl back.

"I know that guy," she whispered as she clung near my shoulder.

"Yeah." I knew him, too. And my heart sank.

This was so not good.

CHAPTER TWO

NOLAN PONDER—the owner of the Vegas-bound NFL team, with money to burn and a lifestyle to match wore a dazed expression and wobbled on unsteady legs. The knife seemed forgotten as he took in his surroundings with a vacant stare.

He'd been making big promises, stepping on more than a few toes to coerce the approval of the team owners, the league, and apparently the Almighty herself, to bring the San Antonio Marauders to Vegas. The whole thing hinged on a unique money deal. A deal requiring a significant state investment. A deal lacking support from those who were scraping by and in need of state assistance. A deal orchestrated by the man holding the knife.

Blood coated Mr. Ponder's hands and most of the rest of him. The only way I'd keep this out of the news was if he'd been on a hunting trip and had decided to gut an elk in our lobby. The tux he wore pretty much shot a hole in that theory. Covered in dirt, he looked like he'd been in close hand-to-hand combat and rolling around in the desert.

"No," Bethany insisted. "I *know* him. Like, I saw him tonight."

I didn't have time to draw her out. Ponder needed to be deweaponed before he perforated a guest. “Stay right here,” I barked as I rushed toward him with a security detail a few steps behind me. At least the new kid in security had known serious when he heard it.

Given Ponder’s higher-than-most profile, I was glad I’d arrived first.

Stopping in front of Mr. Ponder, I waved the security guys away. “One of you, get rid of the crowd.” My eyes left Mr. Ponder for a flash to make sure the security guys understood my order was not a suggestion.

They both gave me the bug-eye. Easy to interpret: Saturday night, the crowd our normal level of epic. But I was the boss. One of the security dudes, I assumed the least experienced of the two, peeled off and started moving the crowd back.

I gave our main attraction my undivided attention. “Mr. Ponder, are you hurt?”

Nolan Ponder, his shirt red with fresh blood, his tux jacket showing wet, dark stains and a white powdery substance that covered his left shoulder and arm and most of that side of his face, looked right through me. He wove on unsteady legs. “Hurt?” His eyes flicked to mine.

“Want me to take him?” The remaining security guy hulked at my shoulder.

“No, I got this. Just wait. Step back a little. Keep the kid here.” I nodded at Bethany, then inched closer to Mr. Ponder. I couldn’t see any pulsing wounds, but truth exceeded expectation—there was way more blood than I thought possible. He breathed heavily, deep, tortured lungs full of air. The whites of his eyes were visible—did that mean I could shoot him? I forget.

But all I had was Bethany’s air gun. I couldn’t kill him, but I could start a stampede that might.

Panic was setting in. I felt the glare of the cameras. My every move would be recorded and then shredded by lawyers and the vast public for eons to come. Okay, overstating, but at least for my lifetime, which was all that mattered to me.

Pink tinged his skin—not the pale of someone losing a lot of blood. He blinked as if trying to focus and occasionally shuffled a foot to maintain balance. Blood splatter stitched across his face—a well-dressed, garish Frankenstein. I couldn't imagine where he'd been, what he'd been doing, and what he'd seen.

Visuals tended to implant themselves in my gray matter and torture me in the wee hours.

He reeked of back-alley fear mingling with the metallic tang of blood, but no alcohol. I wondered what kind of drugs he'd been doing. Or maybe he'd had a total psychotic break. Wealthy, handsome, influential, with the requisite arm-candy wife—number four if I remember correctly—he didn't seem the type to have any sorrows to drown, but I'd been surprised before.

I'd leave the why for the cops. But I'd sure like to know the who.

"Mr. Ponder. It's Lucky O'Toole, Albert Rothstein's daughter. The V.P. of Customer Relations here at the Babylon." I searched for a glimmer of recognition.

Nothing.

When he raised his hand, I took a step back, even though he seemed confused by the knife he held and not particularly intent on burying it in my chest.

"Lucky, can I help?" A familiar voice sounded behind me.

Jerry! Finally!

A trim black man, pressed and proper in khakis with the sleeves of his starched shirt rolled up and a flash of gold at the wrist. The perfect Head of Security, his tone and manner invoked calm but demanded compliance.

"No." It came out a bit harsher than I intended. "I got this." Problems were my thing, and Mr. Ponder was the very definition of a huge problem. Besides, he knew my father—not a friend, more a respected adversary—but still, this was Vegas and relationships were currency. "Is Romeo on his way?" I asked Jerry. I didn't want to say "police." Experience taught me that particular word makes knife-wielding, blood-covered folks a bit twitchy.

I so needed a new job.

Jerry tried to cover a hint of anger with concern. He needn't have bothered. "Yeah. I told him lights off. No need to attract an even larger crowd."

Detective Romeo was my ace-up-the-sleeve with the Metropolitan Police Department, Metro to us locals. Through the last year or so, the young detective and I had forged an easy alliance.

I glanced past Ponder to the front doors where, for the moment, a phalanx of valets barred entry and exit. Jerry once again ran the show—for that I was thankful. I wouldn't have to lead him by the nose as I would Fox. "While we're waiting on him, get some of your men to ask out front how Mr. Ponder arrived here."

Jerry motioned to his men who had been close enough to hear. They filtered away through the crowd, which was now well back, alleviating the claustrophobic crush but giving the camera bugs better shots.

For every action, an equal and opposite reaction. Yin and yang —one of the immutable rules of existence.

Jerry inserted himself between me and the knife. "Let me," out of the side of his mouth. Translated, it meant "Stay out of my way." Possible threats to my health and physical well-being brought out the Papa Bear in Jerry—he'd been my mentor long before I'd earned partner status.

Technically, now with the recent promotion, I was Jerry's boss, but neither of us stood on that bit of corporate fiction.

Mr. Ponder raised the knife. Alarm flashed across his face.

Instinct gave me a sharp prod. I leaped at Mr. Ponder, pushing the knife down. Jerry stuck a leg behind him, then shoved Ponder backward. He landed with a thud on his back, the air leaving him in a whoosh. Jerry went with him, landing on top, using his weight to hold Ponder down. The knife clattered across the marble. Not wanting to disturb any evidence or add any trace of my own, I left it where it fell. Instead, I grabbed a gun out of the holster of the security guard standing next to me. "You haven't gotten to the part of the course where they tell you what this is for?" I asked, not expecting an answer, which was a good thing as he gave me a forty-watt stare. I trained the gun on Ponder. "I got him, Jer."

Jerry crawled off Mr. Ponder. He brushed down his khakis and shirt as he stepped away, giving me a clear shot if I needed it.

"Why didn't you let me handle him?" Jerry let his irritation show.

I worked to control my tone. Few things pissed me off more than some man thinking I couldn't handle my job. "Why didn't you let me? You don't need a penis to handle a man with a knife, only some balls."

Jerry either didn't have a comeback or was smart enough to keep it to himself.

"Where have you been, Mr. Ponder?" I resisted the urge to grab his lapels and shake the truth out of him. "Where'd all the blood come from?"

He lay on the floor staring at the ceiling. The blown-glass hummingbirds and butterflies mesmerized him. He giggled. "Pretty. Why don't they move?" He cocked his head. "Oh, there they go."

"The guy is stoned out of his mind," Jerry stated the obvious.

"Where'd the blood come from, Mr. Ponder?" I kept asking on the misplaced theory that if I kept wailing away, at some point, I'd get the answer I wanted.

He giggled again and shrugged, then wiped his palm down his pant leg as he pulled in another deep breath. "They shot him."

Okay, not what I expected, but it was something. "Who?"

"I don't know who shot him. Too dark."

"No, who did they shoot?"

"Pain in the ass."

"That really narrows it down," I said out of the side of my mouth to Jerry.

The lobby had grown quiet, the crowd hanging on the edge of a collective inhale. Curiously, the only sound was the omnipresent piped-in music. Right now, it was Bobby Darrin singing *Mack the Knife*.

Laughable irony—the soundtrack of my life. I didn't laugh.

Ponder was totally out of it like the wheels were still turning but the hamster had died. He scratched at his arm, then rolled over and pushed himself to his knees.

Jerry grabbed an arm to steady him as he staggered to his feet. "Mr. Ponder, if you're not hurt, you've got a lot of blood there. Maybe someone else needs our assistance? Can you help us out? Where were you before you showed up here?" Since I'd been singularly unsuccessful, Jerry took up the cause.

"I don't know." His brow creased with effort. "Game. Kids."

"Okay. Close to here?" I asked.

"Lake."

"Near a lake?" This being the Mojave, lakes were not plentiful. The first glimmer of hope. "A big lake?" If he meant Lake Mead—searching there could take awhile, but it'd be a start.

"Asshole," he muttered. He shrugged out of Jerry's grasp.

Jerry moved back but only a step or two.

Ponder's non sequitur momentarily rocked me back on my heels, then the bolt of lightning seared through my pea brain. *Shit!* "Lake? You mean Senator Lake? This is his blood?" I tried to keep my voice calm, but it didn't work. Even to me it sounded screechy and tight.

Ponder looked at me, panting as if he'd sprinted to where he stood. For a moment, I thought I saw clarity and horror, then his knees buckled, and he crumpled. Jerry and I both jumped. He caught his left arm, I the right; then we gently lowered him to the floor.

"Where the hell is the doctor?" I growled, wishing somebody, anybody, would show up.

"Busy with a bleeder in Stairwell Fifteen," Jerry said. "A guy took a header. Split his skull. Doc'll be here as soon as he can."

I keyed Security again and got the same kid, Fox. "Any luck on figuring out where the knife guy came from?" I didn't feel the need to explain the man was Ponder. Experience had taught me it was best to give only the information needed and nothing more.

"We're not finding him on any of the feeds."

"Okay. Check with the front desk. Find out if Senator Justice Lake is registered in the hotel. If so, we need to check his room. Better yet, we need to find him. STAT. Break the rules, do what you need to do. I'll shoulder the consequences. Just find him!" I tried not to shout—I didn't want the closest bystanders to hear, but damn! Senator Lake!

Granted, Lake was a worm, and a particular thorn in Ponder's foot—they were on opposing teams in the NFL in Vegas battle, but Ponder had won. And knifing Lake wasn't even close to an ideal solution to the bad blood between them—a good one maybe, but not ideal. I'd met Lake once. He was the kind of guy who put the justifiable in justifiable homicide. But I couldn't see the point in testing that theory if one had already won.

"Where am I?" Ponder whispered, his voice hoarse.

"The Babylon," I answered. "Mr. Ponder," I let a hint of demand into my voice. "We need to find Senator Lake. Where is he?"

Flashes popped as the crowd pressed in, eager to record every word.

"Lake?" he spat the word. "You find him; I'll kill him."

Bethany moved in close. Leaning in, she whispered, "I know where you can find him."

CHAPTER THREE

"WHAT?" I whirled on her. "How would *you* know?" I didn't mean it quite the way it came out. Fear was doing the talking—how could my kid cousin be caught up in a murder or assault, or something bad with a whole lot of blood?

"See those welts?" She pointed to red marks peppering the right side of Ponder's face and his neck and torso where his shirt gaped open. "I know what caused them."

In a blinding bolt of clarity, I did too.

"Ponder was at War Vegas tonight?"

Bethany nodded, her eyes dark in a pale face.

I snagged my phone from its place on my hip and dialed.

Romeo picked up before it even rang on my end. "Almost there. Shit, you'd think there was a demonstrators' convention in town from the number of folks out here with banners and placards."

"If you don't have a cause, a bullhorn, and a closed mind these days, you can't get any press. I need you to change routes." I gave him the lowdown on our theory, keeping my voice low and my hand cupped over my mouth—last thing we needed was a bunch of interested spectators going along for the gruesome ride.

"You think somebody shot Senator Lake and his body is somewhere at War Vegas?" Romeo didn't sound surprised. In fact, he sounded world-weary and stretched so thin he twanged. Tires squealed in the background.

I could picture him wheeling his lumbering Metro-issued vehicle through a tight U-Turn, the shocks sagging, the whole thing leaning against centrifugal force. "Nobody here can find Ponder on any of the video feeds which means he likely wasn't in the hotel when he got all that blood all over him."

"Okay, I'm en route. I'll send a couple of officers to hang on to Ponder until I can get there."

Somebody else could come arrest him or take him in for questioning, I felt sure. But I didn't want anyone handling Ponder and my hotel other than Romeo and his kid-glove treatment, so I didn't suggest it. "I'll stash Ponder in my office. The doc should give him a once-over—he's higher than a three-year-old on a Tonka truck overload."

"That bad?"

"A kite on a very long string."

"You never run out of those things, do you?"

"What?"

"Never mind. I'll call you if I find anything."

Mr. Ponder slumped in a chair by the window in the front vestibule of my office. When I'd designed the windows overlooking the lobby below, privacy of a potential murder suspect hadn't been front and center. His back to the glass—we'd drawn the shades to keep zoom lenses and grainy news footage at bay.

Breathing a bit easier now, he kept his head bowed.

"Asshole!" A voice sang out from the corner.

I laughed; I couldn't help myself. Leave it to my foul-mouthed Macaw, Newton, to correctly sum up a situation in one word.

"Can't you train that bird any better?" Jerry and his man had half-carried Ponder to the mezzanine.

With a hand to my chest, I feigned insult. "Please. He nailed it."

"You got the EMTs coming?" Jerry asked, even though he knew the answer.

"Of course. Our job is to keep him alive until they get through the crazies out front." The NFL, once America's pastime—or was that baseball? Anyway, one of our defining sports had become polarizing. Factions squared off over a neutral zone patrolled by the police, everyone shouting obscenities across the divide. Kneel or don't kneel? Offense so easily taken where none was meant.

Closed minds, open mouths. A sign of the times.

I wanted my magic back…and maybe some civility and appreciation for differences and the learning possibilities inherent in them. Yeah, I'm a dreamer.

But Vegas, the land of misfit humans, was good at that melting-pot thing. Maybe we could lead the nation into a kinder and gentler world. The thought, so out there, struck me as a real possibility. New York City knew how to break down fences as well.

"I'd say Narcan as a precaution." Jerry was one step ahead of me on the same trail. Ponder looked like just another opioid overdose. We'd seen so many lately I could recognize them at a hundred yards.

We had two kits stashed in the kitchenette—somehow that seemed like a good place for an antidote to narcotic poisoning. I handed the kit to Jerry and he did the administering—blood wasn't my thing, and Mr. Ponder had bathed in the stuff.

Almost immediately, Mr. Ponder's breathing eased. If only something could bestow the same effect on me. But I couldn't stop thinking about who had donated all that blood. Where was he? Yes, I had everyone beating the bushes and if the victim was in my hotel, we'd find him, but I needed to *do* something. Nothing worse than being at the starting line, engines revving, waiting…

Pretty soon my head would explode, or I would.

My assistant, Miss P, all polished perfection in her Dolce, cascades of gold chains, and spiked golden hair with matching attitude, rushed through the door only a few minutes behind us.

I skewered her with the spear of my frustration. "Aren't you supposed to be keeping the former NFL greats, and the current ones, from misbehaving by offering them supervised VIP treatment?" That sounded a lot like handling teenagers, probably for good reason—though young humans were not my forte, nor in my job description, thank God.

Although, Christophe, my fiancé Jean-Charles's five-year-old son, and I seemed to be getting along. Probably a reason for that, too—maturity wasn't my strong suit.

Miss P raised an eyebrow—something she'd learned from me, which didn't necessarily mean it was an appropriate response. "Brandy's handling it." Brandy, young, beautiful, and Detective Romeo's main squeeze was the youngest member of our Customer Service Inner Circle.

Miss P, ever the hostess no matter how unseemly the gathering, poured Champagne for Jerry and herself, Wild Turkey 101 for me.

Mr. Ponder got water. He didn't seem to care. Instead, he'd crinkle his brows and glance around, taking us all in, each time as if seeing us for the first time. Sweat ran in rivulets down the sides of his face. Periodically, he'd hike a sleeve and scratch at his skin—it was almost raw. One leg bounced, powered by nervous energy; yet, he remained curiously removed from the blood.

To have words with Jerry, I turned my back on the room and stepped closer. "Where were you?"

Circles of sweat darkened his shirt under each arm. With his fingers, he touched at the sweat dripping down his face, then he studied his fingers as if expecting blood, and then he wiped them on his khakis. "We'd gotten a call. Disturbance in the Bungalows." The Bungalows in the Kasbah was our private enclave reserved for only the most worthy patrons which, by casino definition, were the ones keeping the most money in play on a very regular basis.

"And?"

"False alarm."

"Who made the call?"

He pursed his lips and shook his head. "Fox took it. Haven't had a chance to dig out the details." His hand shook as he pulled a handkerchief out of his pocket and mopped the sweat.

"You okay?" I squeezed his arm and he flinched.

"Sure." He didn't sound convinced. "Ran to the Kasbah. Then to the lobby when I heard your call. No time to catch my breath."

"Still smoking?"

"This job eats a hole in you." A hackneyed excuse.

"If you're looking for an easy way out, lung cancer isn't it."

The door burst open, interrupting his glare.

My father, his face pinched in pain and worry, his beard a dark shadow on unusually pale skin, strode through. While he lacked his normal bravado, he radiated enough pissed-off to attract everyone's attention.

Great. Who invited drama to this party?

"Lucky! What the hell? Why do you want to find Senator Lake, that asshole?" His eyes bugged when he got a look at Mr. Ponder. "Nolan? Shit! Who shot you?"

"Nobody," I managed before being drowned in the shriek of Sky Ponder, the current Mrs., who rode in on my father's wake.

Ponder flinched. Hell, we all did.

One step too slow, I almost caught her, but before Jerry, who was slower still, and I could stop her, she flung herself across the room toward her husband. We needn't have worried that she'd deposit her trace on him as well—she stopped at the sight of him, leaving a foot between them. "Oh, Nolan!"

Jerry took one arm, and I took the other, making her a human wishbone. "Give me an excuse, Sky. We'll make a wish."

Tiny and emaciated in the current style, Sky was no match for my bulk, even though she tugged and twisted and clawed at my grip on her arm. So much for my threats. "Sky, pull yourself together. This isn't helping." A bad tack, I know. Telling a crazed person to pull herself together usually backfired and this time was no exception, but I was all out of clever.

She turned on me, talons at the ready and going for my eyes. Cocking my elbow, I waited for a clear shot. One blow to her jaw…or maybe her nose—putting a kink in its surgical perfection would be striking a blow for us unaltered heathens.

Just as I coiled, lining up on a target, Jerry grabbed her from behind, pinning her arms to her sides. He picked her up, saving me from myself. Stellar character that I am, I graced him with a glare.

What was it with me tonight? I was itching for a fight and couldn't figure out what was spurring me on.

Of course, being railroaded into plans to meet my fiancé's mother might have something to do with it. Shouldn't I be the leading lady of my own life? Right now it seemed everybody else got the plum parts and I had only a minor speaking role.

With her feet dangling, Sky Ponder flailed backward at Jerry, but only landed one glancing blow, losing a shoe—a Lou-bou, of course. I kicked it aside. How did such a classless woman come by classy taste? Imitation, according to my mother, but that would mean the woman had a modicum of intellect, which was impossible to detect.

I could've told her fixing up the outside never upgraded the inside—that took way more work. Not that she would understand or care.

Jerry plopped Mrs. Ponder unceremoniously in a chair, catching her as the chair threatened to tip over backward. "Be still or you'll be spending the rest of the night in the drunk tank in the basement." Beads of sweat glistened on his bald pate. Far from his normal pillar of strength, he looked a little wobbly, his gaze darting around the room. From her chair, Mrs. Ponder lashed out. Her remaining shoe connected with Jerry's shin in a bone-bruising thunk. He didn't even flinch.

"Sky! I'll have you arrested." I barked the words like a rabid dog, thankfully without the frothing mouth. "Now, sit and shut up."

That seemed to do it. She squirmed in her chair like an overactive child but she stayed put.

Threats—a major arrow in my quiver of control—were having only limited success.

"Arrested for what?" Cowed, she still could throw some attitude.

"Being supremely irritating."

Miss P hid her smirk at Sky's acceptance of my bullshit.

I watched Jerry. Something about him looked off. His breathing was shallow, his face haggard as he leaned against the wall behind Mrs. Ponder. Maybe he was tired, as he'd said—he sure looked it.

My father loomed over Nolan Ponder. "Are you hurt?" He looked around the room, then glared at me. "Why haven't you helped him?"

"We've done all we can. EMTs are on their way. The doc, too, though he's handling high volume tonight."

"He's not hurt?" Some of his bluster leaked away.

I shook my head. "High as a kite, but the blood is somebody else's."

He whirled on Ponder, who was still taking all of this rather casually, even as stoned as he was. "What the hell have you done?"

"Don't answer that," I ordered Mr. Ponder. Apparently, I was the only one thinking down the road to incarcerations and courtrooms.

But, to be honest, I was half-inclined to throttle the truth out of him. I had no idea how to balance his interests with the blood donor's. Romeo hadn't called, so I assumed he hadn't found a victim—not that he'd had much time.

Amazingly, Ponder clamped his mouth shut, leaving me in my precarious ethical dilemma.

"Father." I could do pissed off, too. "You know better. He's whacked out of his mind. We've got enough problems right now without encouraging self-incrimination, our largest being the person who's missing all that blood." I think I might have yelled that last part.

"Seems Ponder could shed some light on that." His growl matched my bite.

"He can't remember jack," I said, hoping a lack of information would shut down his bluster. "We're turning over every rock we can think of, hoping he slithers out. I got this one, Father." My father on the warpath would be more than I could handle tonight. Old-school Vegas, he was used to handling problems in his own style, which often not only flouted the law but beat it into submission.

He backed down. "This whole NFL thing has the world on tilt."

"No shit." I took a deep breath. There was nothing else to do but hold the lid on until the EMTs and the cops got here. "Mr. Ponder," I asked all casual-like, "without saying more, would you happen to know where Senator Lake might be?"

"Lake?" My father tensed. "What does that snake have to do with this?" His eyes widened. "You think the blood is—"

I silenced him with a slitty-eyed look, then turned back to Ponder. "Senator Lake? Have you seen him?"

Ponder wove a little in his chair as he tried to hold eye contact. "Dark. Shot. Blood." He shivered.

Sky pressed her perfect pageboy into place, then tucked her hands under her thighs. Everything about her set my teeth on edge. The forced concern. The histrionics. And wasn't there a law about wearing Lilly Pulitzer outside of Florida or after midnight? Her dress was perfect for a yacht in the Med but not so much for after-hours Vegas in January. And neon orange nail polish was trying way too hard. "He's not talking until our lawyer gets here."

"Sky?" Ponder perked up like a puppy responding to his master's voice. "What the hell are you doing here?"

From his tone, it was hard to tell whether he was happy or not. Confusion was what came through the loudest.

"I just got in." She gave me a measured glance, not even bothering to veil the challenge in it. "I was looking for my husband, then I saw the videos go up on YouTube. I grabbed Albert, and here we are." Her voice, high-pitched with a perpetual whine, reminded me of a five-year-old—even though you could crush them, they lied to you anyway...just to see what would happen.

"You weren't expected?"

She plucked at the hem of her skirt, drawing the attention of every male in the room to her legs—a strategy as old as time.

"Mrs. Ponder?"

"My husband, I thought I'd surprise him."

"Damn party," Ponder growled. "I told you not to come."

I glanced back at him. His head hung forward, his chin on his chest.

"A party?"

Sky answered for him. "It is a big celebration moving the team to Vegas." She shrugged a bony shoulder as her gaze skittered from mine. "Nobody wants to be left out of the biggest party of the year."

I wanted to disagree—I'd be more than happy to be left out. "Where'd you come in from?" I asked.

She ignored me for a moment as if trying to figure out who was the Alpha dog in the room. Her gaze swept the room, then reluctantly, like a puppy looking for love, sniffed in my direction. "L.A. I have a suite at Chateau Marmont," she said as if I surely should know that. "What happened here? What have your *goons* done to my husband? Why is there all that...that...*blood*?" She gave a shiver of revulsion worthy of an Oscar, but a tiny tear trickling down her cheek would ice it. I kept looking for it but it never came.

"Shut up and sit down, Sky." Nolan Ponder waded into the fray; his voice weak but filled with conviction. The drugs were losing their effect.

"First, Lucky, could you have someone escort my wife to our suite?"

Now, that was an unexpected turn. So, the current Mrs. had only need-to-know status. Interesting.

Sky stomped her foot—she'd reinstalled the shoe after shaking some sand out of it. "Nolan!"

He waved her away.

She reached for his arm, but I grabbed her before she touched him. Enough of us had donated to the trace evidence on the man already.

"You call me, Nolan, if you need anything." With a quick move, she bypassed me and pressed a cellphone into his hand.

He dropped it, and it clattered to the floor.

I retrieved it—an iPhone, its case emblazoned with the new team logo in red and gold.

He took it, stuffing it in an inside jacket pocket, then his face closed and he nodded to Jerry. "Get rid of her."

Jerry opened the office door and motioned to his men who waited in the hall. One of them stepped inside.

My father jumped into the silence while we waited for Mrs. Ponder to gather her things and her dignity. "Do you think the victim could be in the hotel?"

I took my father's elbow and led him out of the middle of the action to the chair behind the desk. "I have Security and Housekeeping scouring the property, surreptitiously, of course."

"And?" My father settled in the chair, his face ashen underneath the flush of anger.

"Nary a drop of blood."

Miss P moved in beside him, holding the chair with one hand

and handing him a Wild Turkey with the other. "Here you go, sir. Just what the doctor ordered."

He accepted her peace offering with a glare. He'd been out maneuvered—he didn't have to like it; he just had to live with it.

Miss P sidestepped my displeasure. Bourbon was *not* what the doctor had ordered—my father's recovery from a bullet to the chest had been slower than anyone was comfortable with, and spirits, no matter how emotionally medicinal, were not on his permitted list. But I was in no mood to quibble. I'd lose anyway. This was one relationship in my life that eluded me.

Okay, not true. In fact, they all did. At sea in an emotional dinghy, every seam leaking, I hadn't a clue what ocean I navigated nor where I'd eventually drown.

I turned back to Ponder. He'd been rooting in his pocket. Extending his hand, he opened his fist to show a casino chip. It looked like ours.

"I have this. Not sure where it came from."

"Nolan!" Sky stopped on her way through the door. Her foot stomp carried a veiled warning.

"Get out of here, Sky."

She didn't budge.

I pulled my father's pocket square from his pocket, then flapped it open, and Mr. Ponder placed the chip in the center. Our chip, for sure.

Mr. Ponder moved to wipe his eyes but stopped at the sight of the blood. "One of the players, he said something about a more interesting game. I went with him. I must've found it."

"Player?"

"Yeah, the kid, Boudreaux."

"Nolan!" Sky screeched.

I gave a nod to the security guy, and he pulled her toward the door.

Once the door closed behind them, I turned to Jerry. "Any private games tonight?" Security monitored all non-casino games in the hotel. For obvious liability reasons, we didn't have many.

If he heard me, it didn't register. Sweat poured off of him and he'd started to shiver. His gaze wandered—a bee tasting the flowers but not finding any to his liking.

"Jerry? Are you okay?"

His hand shook as he swiped at the sweat on his brow as he finally looked at me. "Tired, I guess."

"Any reports of someone running a game in the hotel tonight?" I asked again, and I shucked and jived a bit, trying to catch Jerry's attention and keep it.

"No, but the loonies are running the asylum." He gave a silly, choked laugh. "Fox can handle it. He's Senator Lake's man."

For a moment, I didn't know what to say. Very out of character for Jerry, who wore decorum like a Boy Scout merit badge.

"Is he okay?" Miss P got the same vibes I was getting.

"Fox works for Lake? Some politician's lackey is on our desk tonight?"

"I coulda told you that," Ponder chimed in, still not quite himself but looking better by the minute.

"I was kept out of the loop, why?"

Jerry shrugged, then gave my father a pointed look. "Like I said, the loonies."

My breath caught. Was my father messed up in this? I wouldn't brace him in front of these people, he deserved that much, but when I had him alone…

"Boudreaux? Doesn't he play for your team, Nolan?"

"After that fiasco in the elevator, I told him this season just over would be his last."

"Fiasco in the elevator?" My father gave me a quizzical look. Normally on top of stories like this, he'd fallen behind, not only in the news but in his recovery as well.

"He dropped a girlfriend with an elbow to the jaw. Caught on tape, he copped to an alcohol abuse problem. Local boy, he's from

Ely. His daddy's some sort of bigwig up there. Beau played at Reno before making the leap to the NFL." Probably more than anyone wanted to know. "We need to find him." Conversation stopped as I got on my phone—this time a call to the front desk.

Sergio Fabiano, our front desk manager, answered with his trademark effusive tone. He was our resident babe magnet, or whatever they called too-beautiful men these days, and he loved to infuse his voice with a sort of breathless quality—something I found totally off-putting...along with his too-long black hair that he was constantly flipping out of his eyes. "It's a great night at the Babylon, where the world comes for fun. Sergio Fabiano here to help."

That wasn't our official tagline, but it also wasn't a battle I wanted to fight. "Sergio, I need to know which room Beau Boudreaux is registered in."

"Yes, Ms. O'Toole." His voice dropped the effusive. "One momentito."

I felt all eyes in the room on me while I waited for him to return. I didn't have to wait long.

"We don't have anyone by that name on the register."

Of course, this couldn't be easy. "He's famous in some circles. He might have registered under a different name. He's one of the NFL players here for the big announcement. Call his team, any players you can find, and see if you can find him, okay? Last I saw him, he was in the lobby."

"Yes, Miss, Sergio will find him for you."

I disconnected and pocketed my phone as I looked around my office. "He's working on it."

Mr. Ponder seemed to be better able to focus, so I kept with the questions, dancing around my previous advice to everyone else. "What kind of game?"

Shivers wracked his body. "Man, what did they do to me?"

I leaned to the side, trying to see his eyes. "Mr. Ponder? You okay? You need help?"

Frankly, to me, he looked the best he had all night. "What kind of game did they lure you in with?"

By some incredible force of will, he pulled himself more upright. "I assume Baccarat, high stakes. That's what I play."

"Is that what they said?"

"They said a different kind of game. I was playing Baccarat, so I assumed they meant a different version of that game. That was their implication."

"Where?"

"I don't remember." He turned tired eyes on me, but they looked clear.

"Did you go by car?"

"I don't know."

"Jerry, do your folks have any new information?"

No response.

Jerry tried to answer, then his head lolled onto his chest and his knees buckled.

Bethany, who'd been holding up the wall in the corner, lunged for him.

"Don't!" I barked.

That single syllable hit like a jolt from a Taser, and she stopped as if frozen.

In slow motion, Jerry slid down the wall, landed on his knees, then fell forward.

I cringed when his face hit the carpet.

"He's going to kill you," Bethany said.

"Not if he dies first." I dropped to my knees by his side. His breath was rapid and shallow, but he was breathing. Blood oozed from his nose that angled a bit off center—hard to tell with it still mashed into my carpet.

Bethany eased down opposite me, Jerry between us. "Dies?" the smirk in her voice had vanished.

"Don't touch him," I said in the same tone, but now with a sense of urgency. I rested my hands on my knees to keep from grabbing Jerry and doing anything I could to help him. But I couldn't. Not yet. "Miss P, get the other Narcan kit. And hurry." Then I turned back to Bethany. "I'm going to roll him over. Don't you touch him." I'd seen the white powder on his right side after he'd grabbed Mr. Ponder. Jerry had brushed it off with both hands.

Reaching inside Jerry's shirt, I grabbed the fabric from the inside. Then, with my forearm for leverage and bracing him against my knee, I eased him over. "Jerry?"

No response.

With two fingers, I gently opened his eyes. All white.

Miss P disappeared into the back office then reappeared with the requested drug in a nasal squeeze bottle. "I thought I'd seen it all," I said as I administered the antidote. But I'd never seen my Security Head OD-ing on opioids. "Call the paramedics. Find out where the fucking hell they are."

"Bad girl. Very bad girl," Newton sang out.

"And somebody shoot the fucking bird."

"Asshole." Newton gave it his derisive inflection normally reserved for me, his version of eating crow. Not that parrots were omnivorous.

"Jerry's heart is racing off the charts along with itching, sweating, weakness, losing consciousness. He wasn't like this in the lobby." I sat back on my heels and prayed for my friend, my business better half, to stabilize.

"What's going on? You're freaking me out," Bethany said, her eyes wide.

"See the white powder on Ponder's jacket, left side and sleeve?"

"Yeah."

"Jerry got that all over him, then brushed it off with his bare hands."

"You think *touching* it did this? What the hell is it?"

If he'd encountered the stuff in my hotel, that put not only all of us but all of my guests at risk. "Fentanyl, a new form of super potent opioid. Romeo told me he almost lost one of his men to it last week—the stuff can kill you even if your only exposure is dermal. You don't even have to ingest it. The State has petitioned to use it in the cocktail to execute the Death Row guys." I loved irony, but this tidbit stuck in my throat.

"They've been cutting heroin with the stuff. Amazingly lethal," Miss P added.

"Man, what happened to the days when having a few drinks and dancing the night away was considered a good high?" This first sign of getting old was pining for days gone by as somehow better. With that as a metric, my age was showing.

"Your age is showing." My father gave me a hint of a smile, as if reading my mind.

"And my wisdom." I sat back on my heels. "This explains the opioid haze he was in. Not sure why it didn't kill him, though."

"You didn't touch it?" Bethany's voice turned breathless and she grabbed my arm. "It could've been you."

"No. Luck of the draw."

"If you had, I wouldn't have known what to do."

"Jerry would have. And Miss P. And now you know, too. Metro issued every member a Narcan kit. Hell, they even carry one for the dogs. They sniff it out, and it kills them. Lost two dogs before Romeo got the department's okay for the kits. We have them all around the hotel. Security carries them. Hell of a world."

"Where do you think Ponder ran into this stuff, and, if it's so potent, why didn't it kill him?" my father asked.

If this stuff was in my hotel…

"Miss P?" I communicated my horror with a look.

"I'm on it."

For some reason, that flipped my pissed-off switch. "Hell, everybody's *on* it. We need to find it. Find Boudreaux. Find Lake. Find *something!*" My voice rose with each word, riding on my anger and my fear.

I looked down at Jerry—the man who had been my rock for

decades and had saved my ass more times than I could count. "Don't you dare die on me."

My phone rang. "What?" I didn't even look at the caller ID.

"We've found something," Romeo said, his voice a monotone. "I could use your help."

CHAPTER FOUR

WAR VEGAS.

The name alone gave me chills as I piloted the Ferrari through the masses teeming along the Strip. Night had deepened, providing the perfect backdrop to the miles of flashing neon.

Loose Slots! Girls! $9.99 Seafood Buffet! Nude for you!

Each a bright lure tossed into the sea of humans in an attempt to get a bite.

That last one I liked the best—nude what, exactly?

As I hit the Fifteen and goosed the five hundred horses, my mood darkened, not that it was even close to bright, to begin with. The car leaped forward, pressing me back.

"Cool," Bethany whispered, overcome with awe—fast cars and murder, a typical Saturday for me, but a bit outside the girl's previous normal. But she was part of my family now; she'd get used to it. Some folks were born to money; we were born to murder…or solving it, at least.

I'd let the girl talk her way into coming along—she was my resident expert in all things War Vegas. Shooting people for fun and profit—that whole thought seemed so spectacularly horrid, so

I didn't brood on it. Life in Vegas operated at the very periphery of imagination. People came here looking for that unique, pushing-the-boundaries experience.

We either got them out of it, called a lawyer, or notified their next of kin.

Tonight was shaping up as a next-of-kin kind of night.

I wondered who would grieve for Senator Lake. Not many, if scuttlebutt could be believed, but surely even the worst among us had someone to cry over their grave. Maybe I was wrong; maybe life wasn't benevolent like that, but I didn't want to believe it, so I didn't.

The lights of the Strip faded to a glow behind us, leaving space for the darkness to fill around us. The flash of passing streetlamps strobed, pushing aside the darkness for a moment, then plunging us back in—a dizzying, disco-ball light show. I concentrated on the expanse of concrete stretching in front of me as it gently curved around the north, then the west side of town. Periodically, I cast side-glances at the kid, wondering what she was thinking. Those of us responsible for creating the Vegas fantasy, for sweeping the darkest bits of reality under the fantasy carpet so others could ignore them, paid a heavy emotional price.

Hence the disassociation, the compartmentalizing, and the Wild Turkey and Champagne. It wasn't a future I wanted for the kid. She'd seen the worst, and now she deserved better.

For the rest of us who had to live in this spook show, I wanted the fantasy we created to be our reality.

"If you live it, you will be it." I heard my mother plain as day as if she were there to whisper her mantra in my ear.

Unfortunately, Mona wasn't always right. In fact, she was rarely right.

"You see enough bad, you learn to mistrust the good," I admitted to Bethany—maybe the cover of darkness made the admission less of a confession. "Go to Cornell. Get away from here. Make a happy life as a vet in some fabulously bucolic place. And make sure you have a guest room for me, preferably padded."

Bethany, her face serious, her eyes straight ahead, said nothing as she gripped the edge of her seat, but a grin lifted the corner of her mouth. "You said you see everything here. Now I know what you meant."

This wouldn't be her first dead guy.

But walking where death had so recently visited always instilled a sense of ominous reverence. Not dread exactly, but the uncomfortable reality of confronting something that will come for us all whether we are ready or not.

I didn't want to tell her it would get worse before it got better. Seeing a killer's handiwork was horrible.

Confronting the killer was so much worse.

Growing up involved the acceptance that human depravity was real and so much more horrendous than a mind could imagine. That realization had changed me in ways I could never fix; it had killed the child who'd played inside, or at least made her so much more wary.

The Christians got it wrong: Original Sin wasn't the burden we bore.

We bore the ongoing sins of our brothers and sisters. Maybe it was the same, and I just missed the whole allegory. Maybe tonight the horror of what we all had become had finally broken me.

We looped around to the west side of town, peeling off at Charleston and heading west into the dark, unyielding landscape of the Mojave, an animal barely domesticated, jerking at its leash of water and cultivation, desperate to be freed to reclaim its own. Just beyond the light, I sensed its looming, hungry presence. As a child, I'd gotten to know the desert well and learned to respect its dangers.

A sign flickered in the distance. Neon, half of it dark, it said simply "WAR."

The end of the road.

"And here we are." I took the turn too fast, sliding the Ferrari in the dirt. Fishtailing, I slammed the wheel over and slid to a stop in front of the trailer that served as an office—or at least the sign hanging by one corner over the door indicated as much—as a cloud of dust enveloped us.

"Classy." I let it go at that. As first jobs went, this one was a far sight better than my first paycheck. I'd earned a whole two bucks an hour as a greeter in a whorehouse...my mother's whorehouse. So I really couldn't call dibs on hurling the first rock.

Floodlights illuminated a couple-acre patch of land behind the trailer. The fence seemed superfluous as there was nothing of any value to protect—just slabs of concrete and cinder blocks erected to mimic shells of buildings, a few burned truck skeletons, and piles of stones and bricks as if a mortar had imploded a building.

Another seven-foot chain link fence topped by three rows of barbed wire circled a windowless brick building to our left.

"What's in there?" I asked Bethany when we met in front of the car. "It looks like it was built to house enough ammo to start a small revolution."

"We don't have ammo. The guns are air powered; the pellets, if you will, are hard plastic. But the guns look real, as you know—we have some that are used in military training and really mimic the real things. And we have a shitload invested in camera equipment."

"Cameras?" I perked up. Video could be helpful.

"Each gun has a camera so you can see in real time the path of the bullets."

"And when someone is hit?"

"Honor system. They're supposed to raise their hands to indicate they are dead."

A game of life and death. Was I the only one who saw the inevitability? I raised my hands.

"You're not dead." Bethany gave a little snort.

"Little do you know." I nudged her toward the gate into the

gaming area. "Let's go find Romeo. He said he was at Building Ten. Does that mean anything to you?" The rolling hills, the bombed-out shells of buildings, the darkness and the shadows, a place Death would hide.

"Yeah, follow me. It's at the far edge of the stadium."

"Stadium?" I let her lead, following a step or two behind. "Like gladiators?"

"That was a coliseum."

"Whatever." I resorted to the teenage word I hated the most. Being corrected by a teenager—such fun. "If it's a stadium, where are the spectators?"

"Watching digital feeds."

"In real time?"

"Yeah."

"Is any of it recorded?"

"No." Bethany shot me a glance over her shoulder. "No one saw any need."

"An oversight. I mean, who would ever think anyone might actually be hurt or killed at a place where the goal is to shoot to kill."

"It's all a game."

"Am I the only one who sees any irony here?" We shuffled through the sand, which held the footprints of those who had run this gauntlet before us. My toe connected with a brick or rock, something hard in the shadow. "Damn."

"Hence, the boots," Bethany said as she grabbed my elbow. "It's just around here."

On the other side of a pile of bricks so tall I couldn't see over it, Detective Romeo stood looking down at a body covered in blood. Thin to the point of needing an IV, Romeo was now down to being a human hanger for his ubiquitous Columbo raincoat. Even the cowlick at the crown of his head had gone limp.

"A game, you say?" I stepped aside. We all grew up sometime—tonight was her night. I put a hand out to keep her back—we both stayed well away from the body. Maybe the M.E. could glean something from all the footprints in the sand—we didn't need to muddy that with our own.

Bethany swallowed hard. "Holy shit."

Taking in the whole scene, I reevaluated the wisdom of bringing the kid and my cavalier attitude toward "growing up." This wasn't growing up—this was tantamount to child abuse.

"I can't believe someone didn't find his body before we came looking for it."

"Few of the players come this far." Bethany's voice cracked, and she cleared her throat. "Out here, things get too spread out. Shooting people is much more fun in tight quarters."

"The fact that you can say that in all seriousness and from personal experience strikes me as a bad thing."

"The earlier you learn human nature, the better off you are to protect yourself from it." She tossed out the grown-up line like she owned it.

"Assuming all this knowledge doesn't leave you in the fetal position, locked in a padded room."

"Offense is the best defense. I learned that from you."

"You're just trying to make me feel good."

Neither of us could smile through the horror in front of us.

Romeo motioned us closer. We stood back, behind him, as the three of us stared down at the body of Senator Justice Lake. He stared back through unseeing eyes. Blood saturated his shirt—drying, it had started to darken at the edges, the red losing its brightness. A large pool stained the sand underneath him to a dark muddy brown.

A shirt had been tugged over his head—some sort of football jersey bearing the number 88. If it was an NFL jersey, it was a prototype I hadn't seen. Gashes in the shirt, dozens and dozens of them, shredded it like a teenager going after a pair of jeans.

"How many times?" I asked, barely able to force out the words.

"Forty, but that's just on the front. Some are shallow, some deeper. Some angled. Lake's hands show defensive wounds. Hell of a battle." Romeo sounded distant, far away, as if retreating from reality.

I knew the coping mechanism. I felt myself retreat along with him, but the shivering teenager who clung to my arm kept me in the present, grounded in a parental way. "You shouldn't be here." I patted Bethany's hand, consoling myself. "I'm really sorry I brought you."

"I invited myself." She squeezed my arm tighter. "I'm cool."

The lies we tell ourselves.

Blood splatter hit everything I could see, rocks, sand. It stitched up the side of a concrete wall nearby. Streams of it. Dots. Dripped dots. Rivulets. A bloody handprint on his chest.

I breathed in and out, in and out, wishing for a paper bag. "Somebody had a real hate thing going on."

"Or they were whacked out of their mind," Romeo, said, his implication clear. The young detective had decided this case was a slam-dunk.

"You think the handprint is Ponder's?" I asked although I could tell he'd made up his mind how all this was going to go—never a good thing in police work.

He shrugged. "Makes the most sense."

"Doesn't prove anything. You're supposed to be the dispassionate observer, the champion of the truth. Hard to uncover the truth when you've already decided what it is." What was up with the kid? Jumping to conclusions had never been his M.O.

"Aren't you the one who always says experience is a great teacher? If the handprint is his, and he had the murder weapon…" He left me to draw the obvious conclusion.

"I know, a case a prosecutor would salivate over." For some reason I felt like clutching at straws. "Beyond a reasonable doubt, though? I don't know…"

"What, you want a video?" Romeo couldn't help the mock.

I resented it. "This is not the time to play good cop, bad cop. I don't have to tell you how to do your job."

"Why do you have so much energy for Ponder?"

"I don't. I'm more invested in the process, which protects us all. You have to prove he did it; otherwise, he gets a presumption of innocence. Besides, if the good guys all go to the bad side, where does that leave us?"

"With job security."

"Detective, you are getting on my last nerve." I snapped my fingers as a thought flew across the synapses. "Video! Speaking of."

Bethany stared side-eyed at the body. I had to tug on her arm several times to get her to look at me. "I know the video from the guns isn't archived. But presumably there were people watching the game tonight?"

"Are you kidding? With all the football dudes here? Primetime kinda numbers."

"Wait. There's live video?" For the first time tonight Romeo sounded hopeful.

I waved him to silence. "With all the sports celebs, maybe someone recorded the video feed?"

"They aren't supposed to." Bethany looked doubtful.

Ah, to once again have that innocence. "They aren't supposed to stab people either."

"That's equating killers with video watchers."

"Rule breakers. Sometimes we put them in jail; sometimes we need their help. Black and white fade to gray. Can you access who signed in to watch?"

She thought for a moment, then nodded. "Yeah, I think I can."

"Over my dead body!" a man growled as he stalked in our direction. Several of Romeo's men restrained him. "That's proprietary information."

With a sweeping gesture, I directed his attention to the former Senator Lake. "You can live with this on your conscience?"

The guy did lose a bit of his bluster when he saw all the blood.

"Let me guess. The owner of War Vegas?" I asked my cousin.

"A franchisee, but yes." Bethany dug a toe in the sand as she refused to look at him. "My boss, Bogie Wilson."

"Bogie?" I mouthed to her, making her choke back a laugh.

Romeo pushed himself to his feet, taking his time, his motions slow. He dusted off his pants where he'd knelt in the sand. "A warrant is nothing more than a formality here. A state senator was killed on your property during a game which you run. Any judge on the planet would sign my request in a heartbeat." He turned and leveled a gaze at Bogie Wilson. "Wouldn't it be better, all things considered, if you were seen to be cooperating with the police?"

"Seriously? My fans are the 2nd Amendment crowd, the NRA, those dudes."

"Any cooperation with authority might be perceived as weakness," I added.

"You're not helping." Romeo looked like he'd like to clap a set of cuffs and a muzzle on me.

I got it—the last thing he needed was to chase around unnecessarily. In a murder investigation, time was often the most important commodity. "I thought you guys worshiped at the altar of the police," I said to Bogie.

He shrugged, giving me the point. At least he knew to retreat in the face of overwhelming odds. "Our computer equipment is in the building behind the fence along with all the gear." He lowered his head and gave Romeo a semi-glare. "You'll want to check all of that as well, I presume?"

"Of course. I presume that won't be a problem." Headlights arced across the grounds. "There's the Medical Examiner now."

Bethany and I stepped back to give the M.E. and his techs room.

The M.E. wore white coveralls, covers over his shoes, gloves, and a frown. He kept his gray hair military short and his manner all business. His techs set to work without instruction, each with a job to do. One to take photos. One to collect trace. One to analyze footprints.

"Jesus," the M.E. growled as he glowered in my direction. "Coroner's going to have a coronary." The Coroner was the PR front man; the Medical Examiner did all the heavy lifting. As the mouthpiece, the Coroner would have to handle the hot potato of a dead legislator.

"He's a showboat. I doubt he'll begrudge the airtime."

"He may even go national with this one. That'll give him a total hard-on." The M.E. gave me a hint of a smile. "Your take?" He lifted his chin toward the body.

Our normal game, but I was never sure why we played it. "He was shot, once in the right shoulder. Not sure from where. I'll need your trajectory analysis. But the shot didn't kill him. His heart was still pumping when he was stabbed multiple times." I pointed to the blood spatter on the nearby rocks. The same kind of stitching of droplets that I'd seen across Nolan Ponder's face and shirt. "If his heart hadn't been pumping, I don't think you would have that kind of pattern."

"What about from the knife as it was being raised and then lowered to stab him again and again?" Bethany asked.

"It wouldn't look like that, and there wouldn't be as much blood. That spray definitely looks like the knife nicked an artery. What do you think, Doc?"

The M.E. surveyed the scene. "I agree."

An attaboy I needed tonight. I gave him the quick and dirty about the video feed. He motioned to one of his techs. "Shasta?"

A woman, blonde, and much too young, responded to his summons, joining us. "Sir?"

"Bethany here will guide you through the computer to find a list of log-ins for the game viewing last night. Document all of it."

Bethany gave me a look over her shoulder as she left with the tech. "I need to talk to you."

"Later. The list of voyeurs is more important right now."

She shot a glance at Romeo's back I couldn't read.

EVERYONE AT THE CRIME SCENE HAD A JOB TO DO, SO I LEFT THEM to do it. Romeo said he'd round up Bethany and bring her home. The kid was bunking with my parents, which I thought would be good for all of them—or would be a disaster of epic proportions. The jury was still out on which way it would go.

With my mother, all bets were off.

The police had me blocked in, so it took a bit of maneuvering to get the Ferrari free. Once freed, I let the horses run as we galloped back toward the beckoning beacon of the Strip, where magic lived. From my vantage point in the foothills on the far west side of town, the Strip sliced across the horizon in front of me, beckoning me home. Downtown clustered on my left, the lights thinning as I followed them across to the right until I reached the intersection of Sahara, where the lights exploded as the density increased and the hotels grew taller. The Babylon, Wynn and Encore, two sisters clustered together, Mirage, Palazzo, Caesar's, Bellagio, the green glow of MGM peeking through the buildings of New York, New York, then terminating in the beam of light shining from the tip of the Luxor to the gold shimmer of Mandalay Bay. Aria, The Cosmopolitan, they tucked in among the cluster but didn't stand out on the skyline, at least not to me. The newest addition was Cielo, my hotel. A gem among larger stars, as I intended. It sat just across from MGM, nestled in next to the airport.

Home. My two hotels bookending the magic as if capturing it, holding it.

At the 215, I wheeled to the left and hit the onramp, then settled in to make some calls.

Miss P answered on the first ring. "EMTs took Jerry to UMC

for further eval. He's fine, not to worry. Cops are sitting on Ponder, not literally, of course. They are still here, but the CSIs have processed him."

"Processed him?"

"Took his clothes, the knife. Got blood samples from everywhere. Collected trace. I think they combed every hair and probed each orifice."

I shuddered at the visual, but I wouldn't give her the satisfaction of a reaction. "I'm assuming he's not hanging on your every word."

"Lying down in your office. Door closed. The officer with him sitting at your desk."

Another jab I wouldn't respond to. Like the three bears, I hated someone sitting in my chair. "And the doctor?"

"Still waiting on him. Ponder refused to go with the EMTs, but they seemed satisfied he was out of the woods."

"The media attention would be a bit of a disincentive." If he were arrested, I doubted his money could buy his way out of at least a version of the perp walk, but this was Vegas where money could buy anything. "What's he wearing?"

"One of the Babylon's velour tracksuits. Your father brought it down for him."

"Our logo emblazoned on his chest in that candid perp walk photo and printed above the fold on the Sunday *Review-Journal.* My family is intentionally trying to kill me off early, aren't they?"

"Despite appearances, I'm not sure that's their goal."

"Trade places with me, then say that with intention." I glanced at the clock on the dash. Shift change an hour ago. My timing needed vast improvement. "Can you raise Mr. Fox in Security and ask him to meet me in my office?"

"Where are you?"

"Ten minutes out. I'll hold."

In less time than it took to choose a song from the playlist, Miss P was back. "He's on break."

"Since when did everyone in *Security* go on break?" I took a breath, then rushed on. "Rhetorical question. Get ahold of him when he returns and arrange a meeting somewhere, I don't care where."

After I rang off, I wondered at the wisdom of allowing her such latitude in light of her recent passive-aggressive streak. But, given the relative magnitude of my current problems, I doubted she would add overmuch to my burden with her choice, so I let my bet ride.

Everybody had been riding my tail lately, each in their own way. I wasn't sure what that was about, but since I was the common denominator, I'd bet a significant portion of my net worth that all of it had to do with me, my attitude, my shortcomings, my choices or my inability to make them, or any or all of the above. Although I knew they meant to incite positive changes, all the "help" left me feeling under fire and adrift…and pissed, to be honest.

With my toes curling over the edge of the abyss, I was doing the best I could. And being reminded that my best wasn't good enough was way too demoralizing for me to own right now.

So I settled back into the relative quiet, lulled into a happier glow by the growl of a perfectly tuned, well-engineered, high-performance machine. My love for cars went all the way back to a need for freedom.

I'd saved every dime from every tiny, menial, disgusting job my mother foisted upon me from the time I was twelve to buy my first car at the age of fifteen and a half. A fire-engine-red Cutlass convertible. Used, of course, it had been born long before I had been, but love had been lavished upon it. The old man who sold it to me had made me promise to do the same. The car had belonged to his wife. She'd died a year before. It seemed to me, even as young as I was, that parting with that car was more difficult for him than hacking off a leg would've been.

To know such love…

Even though I'd never met her, I had honored my promise and her memory. In my book, promises were immutable. Maybe that's why I took so long and gave each one so much angst before offering my hand in a handshake.

Other things, though, weren't as indelibly imprinted on my value construct. I'd forged my mother's signature on my hardship license application.

And freedom had been mine.

Until, two weeks later, I'd been sent to Vegas to work for my father. Of course, no one had bothered me with that little tidbit. I'd just recently learned the truth when my father thought he was going to die and admitted his paternity and his and my mother's subterfuge.

Still processing all of it, I wasn't sure how I felt other than I usually wanted a drink when those thoughts tortured me.

How do parents do that? Not being a parent, I didn't have an answer.

And I didn't want to ruin my comparatively stellar evening by diving down that rat hole.

So I didn't. Instead, I leaned my head back and listened to the tunes of Luis Miguel. Latin music resonated in my soul. Someday, I would explore why that was, but for now, I let the music and his smooth vocals soothe the worry, at least until I made it to the Babylon.

It took me fifteen extra minutes to weave my way through the phalanx of protesters. One even spat on my car. Spitting on a Ferrari! If that wasn't a felony, it should be.

I tossed the keys to a valet and shrugged back into my life, sagging under the weight.

As I strode into the lobby, people still chattered excitedly, some pointing out the spot where Ponder had fallen as if the blood still marked it with a red X. Thankfully, that was not the case—the clean-up had been thorough; the recent past erased. We're good at that in Vegas.

And maybe, if I paused and clicked my heels three times while repeating "There's no place like home," life would return to normal and none of the previous three hours would have happened.

Fantasy: the snake-oil dream peddled in each come-on flashing over the Strip and appearing on televisions around the world.

But I'd seen behind the curtain.

I pushed through the door to the stairs, banging the door off its stops, then bounded up the stairs two at a time, ignoring my screaming calf. At the top, my breath tore through my chest, my heart hammering. The Lucky O'Toole Self-Improvement Plan put on hold by life, now reared its nagging little head. Only in my early thirties and I was feeling like Death might be welcome.

Not a good sign, but daunted, I felt powerless to make the changes, to give up my coping mechanisms and strip myself bare. Everything about that made me want to curl up into the fetal position. Years ago, that alone would have launched me into self-betterment. Apparently, I was no longer that person. I didn't know whether that was good or bad; it just was.

"Ms. O'Toole?" The voice emanated from my pocket—my in-house push-to-talk. Security calling. Sounded like Fox had returned to his desk.

The call came on the heels of the doctor as he stepped through the office door, beating me by a stride.

"Where is the patient?" the doc asked.

For a moment, I was stymied as to which question to answer first, then I grabbed my phone. Before I pushed-to-talk, I lifted my chin toward Miss P, "She can tell you." Then I pressed my phone to my cheek and stepped around him. "O'Toole. Please tell me you found Boudreaux."

"We've got panty pushers in elevator eleven." Fox kept his tone even, something I doubted even I could do. "And negative. Still looking. If the two men you mentioned earlier are here, they are buried deep."

Not the best analogy, but I shook it off. "You and I, we need to talk."

"We are talking."

Newton and his perfectly inflected "asshole" would have been appropriate here, but alas, someone had muzzled the bird by covering him for the night. And, despite my low standards, quoting a bird somehow seemed beneath the me I aspired to be, so I didn't give in to the temptation. "Delilah's, thirty minutes."

"No can do. My ass is in this chair for another three hours. Bought and paid for."

While I worked through a list of responses, none of them appropriate, I half-listened to Miss P with the other ear as she told the doc that the EMTs had taken Jerry to UMC, our nearest hospital, and "the other gentleman" had refused a similar trip. Her decorum made me smile as I returned to my security guy. "*I* bought and paid for you, so *I* call the shots. Vivian Rainwater can sub for you—if you don't know her, find her, then call me. I'll take the ladies in elevator eleven. Double our security presence at the party in Babel and keep the staff looking for the player. We found the other guy." Unused to people milling around my office, I took a bit more circumspect approach when speaking about the now-deceased senator.

"You found Lake?" The question sounded casual, but I sensed a serious undertone.

"Yeah."

"What'd he say?"

"Stick to your job, Fox." I cut off any reply by severing our connection. Too late I remembered Fox had worked for the senator. Better to deliver the news in person—rock Fox a bit, then call his bluff. The guy was working an angle. I knew it; I just couldn't prove it or identify it. But Death had come visiting, so it was time for the thumbscrews before he found another victim.

Before leaving, I turned to the doc. "Even if Mr. Ponder refuses your services, insist."

He gave me a tired nod as he turned sideways to slip past me—him moving in, me heading out.

I ignored the irony there.

Panty pushers. Silly amid the serious—normally I welcomed it. Tonight, I found it an odd inconvenience. I needed to find my father and pull his story out of him. First the panty pushers, then murder—solving or committing it; the jury was out.

I let irritation and worry lengthen my stride as I made my way down the stairs, then burst through the door and into the lobby.

Panty pushers. I worked to focus on the problem at hand. Blood, a lethal topical opioid, and a dead senator fought for every brain cell, but I'd done all I could. Had Ponder done it? Was there a killer loose in my hotel? And the Fentanyl? Who would be next?

But Security and Housekeeping hadn't been able to find anything amiss. Not that Fox was serious about manning the helm or anything.

Fox—was he covering up or uncovering? I had no reason other than loathing to remove him from his perch—the decision to put him there had come from higher than my corporate rung, so I needed more before I crossed my father, who had had a hand in Fox's hiring, I was sure of it. There was no other explanation for a rookie playing sides to be manning the helm.

But one problem at a time.

Almost apoplectic with worry, I was actually glad to be handed a bit of mischief I could solve.

The young women in elevator eleven were playing way out of their league.

The key was catching them in the act.

I needed bait.

Across the lobby, Chase Metcalf nursed a soda as he signed autographs.

Perfect.

If Beau Boudreaux was the black hat of the NFL, Chase was the white hat. Many likened him to Steph Curry who, despite being undersized and leaving the pro scouts somewhat underwhelmed, had taken the NBA by storm. Chase even had the beautiful wife and cute kids to match. He also was that curious coloring that defied racial labels, so no one owned him, and everyone felt he was theirs. A man of the world and they loved him.

So did the women.

A small herd of them in all shapes and sizes, ages, and races, and in various stages of dress and undress fawned around him. He handled them each in turn with a smile and the aloofness of the unavailable.

Using my size and a scowl, I waded through the throng, ignoring the muttered "wait your turns" and the "you can't have him, he's mines." Wishful thinking knew few limits.

But, if we couldn't have our fantasies, the homicide rate would skyrocket.

My theory, and I had no proof…well, only me, but I still would bet my reputation it would hold water.

"Chase," I touched his elbow to get his attention. He turned impossibly green eyes my direction. I ignored the fact that we were the same height. I gave him the weight advantage as he was probably solid muscle and I…wasn't. "Lucky O'Toole. We met at the cocktail party yesterday."

"Yes, ma'am. Good to see you again."

"I hate to drag you away from such adoration, but I could use your help if you have a minute."

His eyes lost their glint. "Sure. How can I help?"

CHAPTER FIVE

I STATIONED Chase at the door of elevator eleven along with one of our security personnel, Temperance Tremont—a truly stunning young woman who trained for the MMA on the side. All red hair, buff biceps, and a shy smile, she was climbing the pound-for-pound rankings, or so I'd been told. To be honest, I had no real idea what that meant other than I should be nice to her when at all possible.

Leaving Temperance and Chase with their instructions, I stepped into another elevator for the trip to the top public floor, the fifty-second, on the east wing of the hotel.

I figured the panty pushers would consider Chase Metcalf worth the full ride.

Several young couples joined me in the elevator as the doors closed, cocooning us from the noise and mirth of the lobby. The piped-in music was rather dull. I made a mental note to tell the staff that, if they wanted to go retro, the Rat Pack was their only choice. There ought to be a law against instrumental-only tracks of old pop songs. Without the words, there'd be no Kumbaya moment of shared history, so, what was the point?

I keyed Security, anticipating Vivienne on the other end. "You've got the eye in the sky on in elevator eleven, with audio?"

"Yes, ma'am." Fox again. "Monitoring it now."

I didn't even know the guy, and he was worming a hole through my carefully constructed executive veneer. "And Ms. Rainwater? Isn't Vivienne supposed to be subbing for you and you're going to give me a time and a place that's convenient for you?" Sarcasm, my voice of choice.

"Been busy."

The guy was avoiding me. Hadn't someone warned him that with time I only get worse? "Keep your feed rolling until I say otherwise."

"Yes, ma'am."

I sighed as I disconnected, careful to keep my frustration from echoing through the line to Fox's satisfaction. He was a bit heavy-handed with the ma'am thing right now. Off and on, like a lover's affections. Not literally, of course. That thought nauseated me. But, even for me, it was a weird analogy.

Ma'am. That one word made me feel old where most other more obvious reminders didn't do more than dent my shield of self-delusion.

Knowing the noise would only increase once the elevator deposited me into the fray in Babel, I unwound my earbuds, connected them to my phone, put one bud in my ear, and let the other one dangle as I dropped my phone back in my pocket.

When I glanced at the reflections in the elevator doors, the young people with me snapped to attention like recruits before a drill sergeant. These days, I guessed anyone with a walkie-talkie and a hint of authority was one of the oppressors. Most days it didn't bother me to be included in that group. Today wasn't one of those days.

Today I really wanted to be young, in love for at least the next few hours, in Vegas, and on my way to one of the best nightclubs in town—Babel, the Babylon's rooftop Party Central.

But that train had left the station.

I stared down my reflected glare. My shoulder-length hair had been recently returned to its natural shade of light brown from bottle-blonde. I still wasn't sure which was the real me, but that was consistent with my vacillation about everything. Jutting out below wide blue eyes, my cheekbones were the only thing about me that hadn't been whittled and rounded by time and indecision. Confidence built on that. Throwing my shoulders back, I went to work on my badass. Already there, I needn't have bothered. I was pretty sure the kids in the elevator with me had stopped breathing.

Once the crack in the doors was wide enough, they squeezed through like cattle desperate to avoid the branding iron.

I waited for a more dignified exit. As I drifted through the opening, catching a side view, I realized I was smudged in blood in more than a few places—transferred when I'd grabbed Ponder, I suspected. No wonder the kids had hung on the verge of apoplexy.

With my badass complete, I strode into chaos.

Backdropped perfectly by the lights of the Vegas Strip, writhing bodies danced to music at a decibel level just short of violating the United Nations Convention Against Torture—yes, I'd measured it to be sure, making our lawyers happy. Thousands of strands of twinkle lights wound around every vertical post, pole, and tree, and draped over the swimming pool in a shimmering blanket of light.

While not a private event, with the NFL types in town and mingling with the rest of us, we'd jacked-up the cover charge to keep the numbers down. By the looks of it, we hadn't jacked it up enough.

The well-dressed and the well-funded stood five deep at the bar to my right with only inches to maneuver—the hotel executive in me rejoiced. Well, except for the niggling worry that we'd blown right through fire safety limitations. The private tables ringing the pool and roped off from the riff-raff, who only paid five hundred a head rather than ten-grand for a table seating four, were either occupied or sported a sign with "reserved" in three-inch red letters. The real celebrities rarely showed up before midnight, so the next few hours would be a bit light on the photo ops but long on the hook-up opportunities. And the NFL types would provide some eye candy in the interim.

The Average Joe part of me shuddered—too much noise, too many folks trying too hard to be hip, trendy, important, and desirable. All that was way too much trouble for me anymore—all I wanted was a night of uninterrupted, very sound sleep with someone who loved me wrapped around me like a swaddling blanket. To have any real hope of that, I'd have to add it to my job description.

Magical thinking for sure.

Bartenders darted and dashed—how they kept from having a major collision always confounded me. Good training and flawless execution were the reasons our head bartender, Sean, always told me with a smile. Peering over and around the crowd, I saw him in the thick of the fray, guiding his staff as he fielded drink orders. With a ready smile and a quick quip, Sean's story was that he was Black Irish with the hint of an accent to back it up. New Jersey was really home, but, like everyone in Vegas, Sean had embellished his story to add to the magic. At least that was his story. Personally, I figured embellishing improved his odds of getting laid, and that was his real motivation, but call me cynical. I didn't care what line he fed the ladies. He was a master of mixology earning a cult following among our regulars.

Recently, the good citizens of Nevada added another variable to the party quotient by legalizing recreational marijuana. Good thing or bad thing, for those of us in the people and party business, it was a real thing.

The smell of pot rode the breeze and swirled around me, so strong I hoped for a second-hand high.

"Welcome to Babel," a deep voice greeted me.

I looked up into the bright smile of our resident head bouncer, Ralph. "Wow, the boss is in the house. I thought you could delegate this sort of craziness to one of your understudies." I had to shout to even come close to being heard.

Even still, he stared at my lips, reading the words. "I could. But, man, some of my teammates are here signing stuff. I like goin' around with the young guys. These are my folks. Makes me remember the best times, you know?"

I'd forgotten Ralph had played in the NFL. His size should've been a constant reminder, but I'd met him after that. Funny how we meet people and we take them from that point forward. Only the ones we let in open their past to us in return. Ralph's resume mentioned the NFL, but we hadn't...until now.

The elevator beside me, elevator eleven, opened, disgorging a couple of men running on the high octane of hollow promises made by our panty pushers as they ascended to the party. I could read that look. With sixteen thousand hookers roaming the four miles of the Vegas Strip, lots of empty promises swirled and lots of men wore that same hopeful, chagrined, elated, and dazed look. Should they or shouldn't they? A here-hold-my-beer question made worse by the excesses available in Sin City.

As the men high on the fantasy brushed by me, I tugged at a bit of silk peeking from a back pocket of the one closest to me. Panty Pushers pushed exactly that. And most invitational lingerie was made of silk. High cost to attract a fat wallet. No doubt, the girls would call it quality presentation, but I'd always had a problem with quality as a concept when speaking of the bartering for sex, but apparently, I was alone in my delicate sensibilities.

As I held on and the man moved toward the bar, the fabric trailed out of his pocket. A lacy, delicate G-string. Black and white, it had Fancy French in every square millimeter, and there were precious few of those.

Given that my mother had imparted her philosophy of the

Power of the Undergarments when it came to love and seduction, I considered myself to be a bit of an expert.

French and fancy, for sure.

I didn't even have to look. A phone number and fake name would be stitched to the inside—like those cloth labels mothers used to sew into kids' clothing before sending them to camp. But I looked anyway, a quick glance.

I was wrong. Not a phone number, just a name.

Billy the Boilermaker.

A guy. Now that was unexpected, and I struggled with the appropriate interpretation.

As the fabric pulled away with the final tug, the guy turned, then had the decency to color when I held the G-string looped over a forefinger in front of his face. He reached to grab it—a flash of gold encircling his left ring finger.

"You know better." I sounded like the Moral Police, which made me throw up a little, figuratively speaking. To me, passing judgment on others was, at best, asking them to do the same. The last thing I wanted or needed was some stranger casting stones. I wasn't about to start the fight. I balled up the tiny bit of silk and stuffed it in a pocket.

He drew up in offense, but he didn't ask for the bit of lace wedgie-maker back. "It's just a party. Consenting adults and all that. My wife will be there, too."

"A party? With hookers handing out the invites? Your wife will be there, too?" For once, words failed and I was left gulping like a guppy. Finally, I managed, "You expect me to believe that?"

He gave me a slow once-over. "I don't give a rat's ass what you believe."

I'd asked for that. "Who's Billy?"

"Don't know." He clearly wasn't interested in cooperation.

I didn't blame him—we all knew to offer little, especially when criminal self-incrimination reared its ugly head. Short of thumb-screws, I wouldn't get any info out of him. But I didn't believe a word he said. *His wife would be there!* Right. Cheaters would cheat. And I couldn't imagine the temptation bombarding the players. While I respected a woman's right to make a living as she saw fit, I still rebelled at the anyone-is-fair-game mentality. Personally, I didn't play in somebody else's sandbox, and I thought no matter whether personal or business, the rules should be the same.

The crowd at the bar swallowed the man and his friend in a flurry of back-slapping and high-fiving. Guess he was somebody I should've recognized.

Shoulder to shoulder, Ralph and I absorbed the mix of scantily-clad women, suit-bedecked football players, and the assorted lesser luminaries who had ponied up serious green to rub shoulders with the has-beens, the wannabes, and the current flavors in favor. Sports stars and Hollywood celebrities—oil and water, but they filled the house.

My youngest associate, Brandy, filtered through the throng. Still young, still willowy with long legs that drew long stares, still pretending to be oblivious, she was a former stripper I rescued from earning easy money the hard way. She'd taken to the corporate life, despite the serious pay cut and longer hours—respectability the thumb pressing on that scale. Her worried look made me think perhaps I hadn't done her any favors.

And I knew who caused the worry. Romeo.

Her gaze passed over me twice before I bled through the gauze of her distraction. Without a smile, she shifted course and strode toward me. Standing on her toes, she shouted in my ear. "I got all the players here and all set up with table service, bottle service, and pretty much every other kind of service. We had to make a detour through the Bungalows. Mr. Whiteside forgot something at his bungalow. But now they are all here."

I nodded my thanks but didn't ask how all-inclusive she'd been. She knew providing an illegal service, and prostitution was curiously illegal in Clark County and thus in Sin City, wasn't allowed. But, making something illegal didn't make it unavailable.

The war on drugs had proven that beyond argument. The illegality simply removed the income stream from the taxing authorities. However, providing either would land the hotel in a heap of hurt, so it didn't hurt to check on staff occasionally. Everybody had their price.

Brandy's lower lip quivered, offsetting the anger in her eyes. She grabbed my arm with both hands, anchoring me in place. "You talk with Romeo?"

A question with ample latitude for prevarication in its answer, thank God. "Nothing of substance. Why?" Cocooned by the noise, I was certain our voices wouldn't carry more than a few inches, so eavesdroppers weren't a concern.

"He's been acting weird. I can't put my finger on it, but something bad is going down. He doesn't want me to know, but he's been hanging with Reynolds."

My eyebrows lifted in displeasure. Detective Reynolds! I'd loathed the man when I'd met him. One of the bottom feeders. I couldn't prove it, of course—he was too clever by far. But I was letting him run with the line, hoping one day soon I could jerk him up short.

I stared into the worried eyes of my assistant, then put my lips close to her ear. "And you're worried Reynolds will lead him astray?"

Brandy leaned back and gave me a measured look, then leaned in close again. "No. Reynolds is an ass, sure, but there are lots of them."

Given her stripping thing and my working-my-way-up-through-the-ranks thing, we'd both seen more than our share.

"He doesn't hit my two-bit-hood meter," Brandy continued.

We had differing opinions. Perhaps her youth shaded her view. "Why is Romeo slumming with the detective?"

Brandy pursed her lips, making most of the men within eyeshot go weak-kneed. If she was aware, she hid it well. "Something screwy about this whole NFL thing." A tear trickled out of the corner of her right eye. She ignored it. "I don't have any specifics, just a gut feeling, you know?" She waited for my nod before continuing. "But Romeo has his ass in a vise. Not sure how, or who's turning the screws, but I know it as well as I know my own face."

I'd felt it, too, but I wasn't going to add fuel to her fire—she was worried enough. And, with a black belt in some obscure form of mortal martial art, she didn't need encouragement to run around town busting kneecaps or something.

"You've got to help him."

And therein lay the problem: he hadn't shared. If he wouldn't let me in, how did she expect me to right this wrong and save my young Galahad, who had saved my bacon more than once? I'd returned the favor a time or two, but I think I was still on the short end. "When I catch up with him, I'll tie him down until I get his story, okay?"

The tear had made its way to her chin where it clung, a shimmering drop catching the multicolored lights. She swiped at it with the back of her hand, then gave me a weak smile.

My offer wasn't much, but it was all I had.

Saving someone who didn't want to be saved wasn't one of my superpowers. My inadequacy washed over me, pissing me off as I watched my assistant ease her way toward the bar. I didn't watch long enough to identify her target.

Ralph had moved a few steps away, giving Brandy and me room to shout at each other in peace. I rejoined him to once again to survey the crowd. I tilted my head slightly toward the ear with the earbud, as if that would help me focus through the noise to hear Temperance when she let me know our trap was set. Nothing so far.

Owing to their size, the football players stood out, clumps of trees in a swamp of people. I could picture Ralph as one of them. Same size, same fearlessness.

I nudged him with my shoulder. "Who's the class out there?"

He took a moment—perhaps to walk down memory lane. "I'm an old guy, so I know them best. But I'd say no one out there is classier than Marion Whiteside. He was the meanest, toughest middle linebacker on the field. He'd just as soon put you in the hospital as anything. But off the field? A good man, you know? Lost his wife last year to breast cancer. Not really back with us yet, if you get that."

I *so* got that. "Which one is he?"

He lifted his chin toward a man who looked like he was having words with another man half his age and half again his size.

Funny how loss could shrink a person.

Black on white. The thought surprised me. I'd never differentiated people by race or creed. By gender, for sure. The men had the upper hand in that game, so I leveled the playing field when I could. Every now and again, I used to wonder what it would be like to be a man in a world built for men—not that I'd ever have that chance, but it was fun to dream.

But the current PC dictate of being über aware of race had filtered through my consciousness, and it pissed me off. The fact that we had to be aware because of racists and bigots and horrible things appalled me.

To me, people were people—good, bad, or indifferent. Race had nothing to do with where you fell on that spectrum.

When the younger guy turned, the light caught his face. "Beau Boudreaux. Once an asshole, always an asshole." Even though I couldn't hear them, it was easy to tell who was messing with whom. The asshole wore his dirty blond hair long and his anger raw. His eyes, set too close together above wide high cheekbones, closed to slits. The bruise I'd seen before was already darkening to purple from fresh red.

"Boudreaux. Yeah, he thinks he's all that. My man Marion has been all that and ended up being so much more."

Boudreaux. Out in the open causing a ruckus. Why hadn't Fox been able to find him? Or Sergio for that matter. But players became unrecognizable once they no longer had a number on their backs.

Hiding in plain sight. Interesting that was the thought that tugged for attention.

"Your man's name is Marion?" A Boy-Named-Sue kind of indignity. "Tough gig." I vaguely remembered stories from his playing days, but he was before my time.

Ralph gave me the side-eye. "That was the Duke's given name."

"Yeah, I know. And they changed it to John Wayne."

"Well, in Marion Whiteside's case, he didn't need to hide behind a pansy-ass Hollywood name." Ralph's grin ran headlong into my scowl.

This whole night had me itching for a nose to break—not a good thing for someone who was paid to *de*-escalate. I so needed to get over what was really bothering me, if I could only put a finger on what it really was.

I needed to grow up. Well, maybe not grow up—that wasn't hard; it was inevitable. But identifying as a grown-up—now that was the kicker. I was a walking, talking prolonged adolescent, or at least I was acting like one. But identifying the problem didn't mean I knew how to fix it.

With both hands, Boudreaux shoved Whiteside in the chest, rocking him only slightly, but not moving him off the bit of real estate he'd claimed. Whiteside raised his hands but didn't give ground. I couldn't hear what he said, but Boudreaux flushed scarlet.

That's all I needed. Ralph was one step behind me when I pushed myself in between the two men.

"You've got my stuff," Marion growled.

"CTE got you, old man?"

Marion reached across me, and I knocked his arm to the side. "Enough."

Being the gentleman I was counting on, Marion Whiteside pulled his punch. Beaux Boudreaux wasn't cast in the same mold.

His punch glanced off my jaw.

Without thinking, I cocked my elbow, aimed for his nose, then threw my bulk behind it.

I caught him expecting me to cower at his manliness.

His nose exploded in a mist of blood.

Shoulders hunched, he cupped his nose in both hands. Blood oozed through, small drips dotting his white shirt. His eyes slits, he glared at me. "You hit me."

"Restating the obvious. Not the brightest bulb, are you? What, a forty-five watt?" Marion stepped in on one side, Ralph on the other. "I'm coming for you, asshole."

"One against three," Boudreaux muttered, his words muffled by his hands and his failing courage.

"Two old guys and a woman." I tossed that threat into the three feet separating us. Stupid, I know. "You ought to be able to take us." Somewhere in the dark recesses of my empty skull, a bell of warning sounded: humiliate a bully and they'll come for you when the odds are more in their favor.

His hands raised, Marion stepped forward.

Boudreaux stepped back.

I hid my smile as he teetered on the edge of the pool. Some of the crowd around us realized what was going on and had stepped back, out of the way, to watch. The music pounded. The dancers danced. Boudreaux took another step, his heel finding air. He flailed his arms, fighting for balance. Blood from his nose ran down his face.

Marion leaned forward, giving him a push with his index finger.

As large as he was, Beaux Boudreaux made a huge splash.

Not the kind he wanted, I felt sure, but the one he deserved. His Brioni tux would never be the same, but several-thousand-dollar bespoke tuxes were consumables for these guys. Hell, since it was part of the NFL required uniform, the League probably paid for them.

Boudreaux popped to the surface, gulping air. He flapped his arms like a wounded bird, beating the water into submission. "I can't swim." He disappeared under the surface. The pool was just deep enough he couldn't stand and breathe at the same time. But he could bob up and down like an apple at Halloween.

The crowd laughed as they recorded his humiliation. Life had been a lot more fair before iPhones and their megapixel cameras. In my day, we could suffer humiliation but not have to have it shared with the world.

My glee over teaching him a lesson evaporated—this had crossed the line.

The player popped back to the surface. "Help me!" His voice held the high-pitched whine of true fear.

Ralph reached in and grabbed the player. Fisting one hand in the front of his shirt, he pulled him out of the pool.

"Impressive," I stepped in next to him to make sure the kid wasn't going to die of apoplexy in his embarrassment or something and to keep Marion from coming for him right now on my turf.

"I keep in playing shape," Ralph explained. "Not that I want to play again, you understand. I like my job. Just habit. Part of who I always was."

No matter how much we want to change, we are always who we were.

Marion Whiteside gave me the once-over—not in an ugly, aggressive way, but in a more you-just-broke-his-nose kind of way.

A curiosity I was used to.

Teddie used to tell me it was my way of keeping the world at arm's length.

Teddie. He so got me. Then he left.

Maybe he did me a favor—he knew me better than I did. His absence gave me time to catch up and maybe glue the broken bits of me back together. But that didn't change the fact that my heart still hurt. Over time, not nearly as much, but still...

"Ms. O'Toole, we've got the elevator," Temperance's voice echoed in my ear, saving me from a brutal turn through the past. When I grew up, I'd been expecting to leave self-doubt in the rearview. But little about being an adult was as I expected. "Everything is in place. They're on their way up."

With one finger, I pressed the bud in tighter to my ear and held the little mic in the wire up to my lips, cupping it in my hand. "All as I asked?"

"Affirmative."

"Roger. I'll take it from here, but make sure your friends in Security keep the video and audio rolling." Ralph didn't ask any questions when I turned and left him to handle the fallout between the ghosts of football past and football present.

That's my life, nothing but a voyeur in a Dickens novel with a modern twist.

Yeah, pun intended. I was on a roll—not a very good one, but at least I had a bit of me back.

I cleared a semi-circle around elevator eleven, diverting a few folks to the other exits—not that there were that many takers this early in the evening. Mostly folks hovered around the elevators as a way to carve out a bit of breathing room while strategizing their dive into the melee. Those, I encouraged toward the bar. In an effort not to be looming when the doors opened, I decided to hold up the wall next to the elevator opening.

Even though I'd done this sort of thing a million times, my heart beat a bit faster than normal. Was it the upcoming confrontation or simply being hardwired to the pissed-off position?

Would be good to know, but I didn't have a clue.

An eternity passed before the doors slid open and I pounced. Feet wide, I blocked the doorway.

Chase Metcalf, clutching a gossamer thread of a black and

white G-string, gave me a shit-eating grin. "Always wondered what doing this sort of thing would be like. I've been married since like forever." The way he said it left no doubt as to his supreme joy in that fact.

"Thanks."

He handed me the G-string. "Wouldn't want to explain that to the Missus. She has a jealous streak." With a wink, he slipped past me, staying within earshot.

The girls moved to join the party.

I cut off their exit. "Not so fast." I joined them in the elevator. I held up the bits of lace that passed for underwear these days. "Fancy."

The girls had the same look: impeccably groomed, sheathed in designer from boobs to butt, with stilettos that had me drooling. They were beyond beautiful—the stuff of male fantasies worldwide. But high-end hookers usually didn't troll in elevators. Their hourly rate alone was sufficient to rule out all riffraff except the high-roller riff-raff. High rollers were usually high profile. They didn't troll for fun in elevators either.

Big eyes gazed at me, widened in pure innocence. Well, maybe not pure—their skirts barely peeked out from under the hem of their jackets. With no shirts, their lovely light pink lace bras were on full display along with the assets they held, ripe and presumably appealing. This season's Valentinos with silver spikes and five-inch heels added a bit of class.

The taller one, a world-weary brunette with duckbill lips and a wind-tunnel face, sized up the situation quickly. "You mean this was a setup?" She gave Chase a look that would turn most men to stone, and not in a good way. "Honey, you don't know what you're missing." The words held attitude, but her eyes held anger and a hint of fear.

"No offense intended, ma'am, but why would I want hamburger when I have steak at home?"

An impressive use of the derogatory inflection of ma'am.

"I think he just insulted us," the taller one who'd been doing the talking said to her partner in crime. The blonde hadn't said a word—she looked like she knew the score.

"You think?" I hid my laughter, which wasn't hard as pissed-off took over. With everything else on my plate tonight, I didn't need two hookers challenging my word and testing my resolve. "Ladies, let me escort you to your appointment with Metro while Mr. Metcalf avails himself of the festivities."

"Oh, man, Ms. O'Toole, you're not going to turn us over to Vice are you?" The blonde finally found her voice. She even worked in a whine—a whine I remembered.

What was her name? We'd met before, here in the hotel. *Stella!* Of course. She'd upped her game and her attire. While unfortunately still in the business, at least she'd moved up the food chain from giving blowjobs in the men's room.

"You know the rules, Stella. I told you before I didn't want to see you back plying your trade in my hotel. This isn't baseball. Two strikes and you're gone."

The brunette whirled on her partner. "You were caught here before?"

"Nice try." I gave her points for trying. "Don't be so hard on her. I've seen you as well—threw you out for tag-teaming in the casino. What's your name?" She clammed up as I snapped my fingers while I searched the dark recesses. "Olivia!" She didn't confirm or deny, but she did flinch. I'd hit the target. "Both of you, you need to come with me."

Chase had joined the party in Babel, and I was alone on the descent with the two ladies. I fought with an idea for a few floors, then dove in. "You two want to make a deal?"

A glance passed between them. "We're open," Olivia said. "If you take us out of the action tonight, we lose a month's worth of income. We both teach school in Iowa. We come in for the big weekends. Our take this weekend could make our year."

A sob story that fell on deaf ears…sorta. As a champion for the underdogs, I loved a good sob story.

The blonde put a hand on her friend's arm. "But we weren't—"

A lasered look from the brunette shut her down.

"You weren't what?" Two Iowa schoolteachers. I couldn't quite get that to fit comfortably in my pea brain. I'd been around long enough to know their second job wasn't unusual, but I still felt a bit conflicted. Most would be shocked to know how many women traveled to Vegas to engage in our oldest profession for a big weekend—fight weekends were the best. Then they would go back to normal lives, their friends and co-workers none the wiser.

I wanted to keep them off the streets, to yell at them to go home, but who was I to judge? For sure, I hadn't walked a mile in their shoes, and my mother always told me I couldn't even evaluate someone's choices until I'd done that. She never told me how to pull that off, though, which perhaps made her point—you gotta let people be who they are.

And part of being free, adult, and American was the ability to make our own choices, good, bad, or indifferent.

I twirled the G-string on my finger. "Where's the party? Tell me about Billy the Boilermaker." Just saying his name conjured thuggish men armed with baseball bats, long on intimidation and short on smarts.

"Billy? He's some wet-behind-the-ears kid from Purdue. The older players are running him around. Rookie hazing, they said."

"And what is Billy supposed to know?"

"Who's in and who's not," Stella said after a pause.

"He's the doorman?"

"Yeah, nobody knows where the party is except him. It's all part of the secret thing. The organizers like to keep it that way so nobody can crash the party or call the cops." She stopped, her face coloring at perhaps giving too much away.

I raised an eyebrow. "The cops? Is the party in my hotel?"

Under the glare of her compatriot, she gave me a hesitant nod.

"I need more." As the doors started to open, I pressed the stop button. "Your choice, me or Metro?"

Stella caved. She leaned in. "Beau is hosting it. It's in his room here at the Babylon, but he said he's running under the radar—no one would know where to look."

"When's the party start?"

"Tomorrow night, ten thirty. Fun gets rolling around midnight; doors will be locked, masks come off."

"Masks?"

"You better be there before midnight," the brunette said with surety and a don't–you-know-that attitude.

"Boudreaux is staying here, you're sure?"

"He's hosting a party here," Stella said.

A subtle distinction. "Under the radar?" The girls nodded as my finger hovered over the stop release. "One more thing. Where are you two staying?"

"The French Quarter."

Of course they were. My pseudo-aunt, Darlin' Delacroix's, hotel. They say everyone has one of *those* relatives—I had two, my mother and Darlin'. And her hotel gave me the creeps as much as she did, but for the ladies, I'm sure the price was right.

"If you're lying to me, I'll hunt you down and take you to Metro myself, got it?"

"Yes, ma'am." Stella proffered her room key.

Satisfied I'd gotten some of the straight skinny and had given them a good dose of scared, enough to maybe get their attention, I opened the elevator doors.

"He's going to kill us," the brunette said to Stella as they shouldered past me.

"He won't know. I got your backs on this one."

Their looks of disbelief presented a Kodak moment. "Be careful; I might live down to your expectations."

They looked like they didn't understand.

"You're welcome at the Babylon as patrons, but no transacting business here, no soliciting business here. My last warning."

Lost in thought, I followed them off the elevator, relinquishing it to a huddle of players and their hangers-on.

Their story sort of hung together but something niggled at me. My gut told me there was more, that they had lied by omission or deflection or both.

A party in my hotel? A secret place? Under the radar? No one would know where to look?

The two-by-four of realization hit me between the eyes and I sagged under my own stupidity.

CHAPTER SIX

MAKING LIKE a salmon, I fought my way upstream through the crowd in front of Registration. Leaning over the desk, I flagged down one of our trainees. Young, stick-thin, perky, strawberry-blonde, she ignored me at first, focusing on the guy in front of her. Tall, wide, blonde, and unhappy, he leaned slightly across the counter trying for subtle intimidation. Poised to intercede, I paused to see how our gal would handle him. All our front desk reps had to learn how to deal with the angry and the privileged used to getting their way. True to Babylon form, she stood her ground with a smile and an open, accommodating stance. When she pushed something across to the guest, the situation defused and he shouldered his way through the rest of the folks waiting their turn. She motioned for another clerk to take her place, then darted over.

I lifted my chin toward the guy who was winning friends and influencing people as he pushed them out of the way on his way to the elevators. "You handled that well."

"He just needed a key. Some folks get angry when we ask them to prove they are indeed registered in the room for which they want a key." With flawless skin, no dark circles under bright eyes, she didn't look old enough to get a hardship driver's license. Either we were flaunting the child labor laws or I was getting old. I couldn't remember being that young. Scratch that; I could remember *being* that young, I just couldn't remember *looking* that young. For the first time, I wasn't jealous. After years spent earning a Ph.D. from the School of Hard Knocks, I wouldn't trade problems with anyone.

Was that part of being a grown-up? Or just not being stupid? Were they synonymous?

The guy brought back memories of my time on the front desk —a long time ago and a different property, but a similar experience. "Most of them are just angry you don't recognize them. I'm sure the NFL types are worse than most."

"He's more of a wannabe." For a moment she looked worried as she glanced at his retreating back, then she rearranged her features into a smile as she refocused on me. "They're the worst. What can I do for you?"

A glance at her nametag. "Ginger, I'm Lucky O'Toole."

"Yes, ma'am, I know who you are." She managed to stifle a slight eye roll.

"You do?" Despite the years in my job, I never ceased to be amazed when employees I'd never clapped eyes on somehow knew who I was. Of course, numbers were in their favor—thousands of them and one of me, but still. "Okay, I need your help."

She stepped closer. "Of course. I'm in the management-training program. You addressed our class last month."

"I remember." Sort of, but I didn't remember her, not that I would have unless she'd tripped me or punched me in the stomach or something. Young people with their bright-eyed optimism and unbridled exuberance were imminently forgettable. The ones harboring hurt and fear—those made an impression. "I don't remember you at the front desk."

"I just rotated from Security. This is my second day on the desk. My rotations are six months."

"Are you aware of the Secret Suite?" Most of the hotels in Vegas had a Secret Suite—an exaggeration of a silly trend that started with secret menu items and ended with hidden hotel rooms. Like the off-menu food, the Secret Suite had to be specifically requested by someone in the know. We didn't advertise it. It wasn't on our website or our list of rooms and rates. As one might suspect, one had to pay dearly for that kind of cool with back hallways and secret entrances.

"Yes, ma'am."

"Have we put anyone in that suite for tonight?"

Ginger and I waited until a desk clerk finished a transaction, then Ginger pounced on the computer, her fingers flying through the menus. She gave a slight downturn to her mouth as she read the monitor. "That's odd."

"Let me guess. No name but there's a hold on the room."

"Yeah."

"Check the keys." We had real keys, big old-fashioned brass keys, but unlike the old ones, ours were embedded with digital chips. They hung on two-foot braided silk ropes ending in pom-poms, ensuring no one would pocket the thing and go home with it. Straight digital keys that could be duplicated didn't provide the kind of privacy that gave the Secret Suite the requisite cachet to be worth serious five figures a night.

While Ginger disappeared into the back, I pulled the nearest computer around and entered my ID and password. Ten seconds and I'd changed the passcode for the Secret Suite, locking it down—no one would be going in or out without going through me. Then I returned all to its original position and turned around to survey the lobby.

After all the years in the business, I could tell by the crowd gathered what big event pulled them in. Fight weekend drew the beautiful people, human sharks attracted by the hope of blood. Conventions had their own personalities: the clothing crowds all dressed to the nines. The Olympia crowd, barely dressed to show off rippling muscles. A special concert—well, that depended on the performers, but each had crowds with personalities as unique as their own.

Knowing my clientele was critical to anticipating needs and problems.

The NFL crowd was new. They were reminiscent of the monster truck crowd and the NASCAR crowd, but with a dash of the pocket-protector geek vibe of the card counters and March Madness odds-players.

Still trying to get a bead, I watched everyone milling around. Despite the cool weather—it was January after all—men wore team gear as if, despite dad bellies and receding hairlines, they were ready to jump off the bench and join the game at the raise of an eyebrow from the coach.

Men and their fantasies.

I didn't begrudge them—God knew fantasy beat the crap out of reality most days. But I sure wished they'd get the memo that no matter the state of your physique and the wad spent on laser hair removal, sleeveless shirts with huge armholes were never a good idea.

Questionable fashion choices aside, the men I could handle. The women were more problematic. Herds of over-done and under-dressed women salivating over the possibility of rubbing body parts with NFL millionaires sashayed their exaggerated hip swivel—hell, exaggerated everything—through the lobby, their antennae on high alert for the next target. While I empathized, I thought, as women we often sabotaged our own battle cry to be taken seriously as sentient beings.

But each of us has her own path.

"Ms. O'Toole?" Ginger had returned.

I took a deep breath before absorbing the bad news her tone promised. Coward that I am, I decided against the face-to-face thing. "Bad news?" A word grenade lobbed over my shoulder.

"Not sure. Of the four keys to the Secret Suite, I can account for three."

I processed her particular choice of words while I watched a young woman thread her way through the crowd. In a business suit, decade-old Ferragamos with a kitten heel, a silk camisole, and a serious expression, she carried a briefcase, also Ferragamo, and held a phone at the ready. I could just make out the logo on the back. The Las Vegas Marauders, silver and red. She appeared to know what she was looking for but had no idea where to find it.

I could so relate. Although, right now, what I looked for was a bit of a muddle as well, but I chose to ignore that in the interest of pretend sisterhood bonding.

Of course, looking for anything other than a stiff drink and a stiff…never mind…was a waste of time. This was Vegas—whatever you were supposed to find usually found you. Not that I'd tell her, but she should probably grab a bottle of righteous Champagne, sit back, enjoy, and wait for the curtain to rise on the shit show.

A life strategy I could get behind.

"Tell me where the keys you can account for are." I still hadn't turned back around, and I let the words drift over my shoulder. Ginger's breathing had escalated. And her verbal obfuscation only piqued my interest.

"Two are in the back." Her words were measured, her tone noncommittal.

I waited, tensing to absorb whatever she was working so hard to hide. Was she covering for someone? Hiding fault? Or simply deflecting possibility? I watched the gal I assumed had some association with the football team. She looked tired, worried, and more than a little irritated as she stopped under the Chihuly glass and pirouetted slowly as she scanned the crowd.

"Mr. Fabiano has apparently taken the third one."

"Sergio?" I had asked him to find Lake and Boudreaux. If he

had the scent of a trail, I wondered why he hadn't called me. "And the last?"

"I don't know."

I reached back and Ginger deposited a key in my hand. My hand closed around cold metal as I pushed myself off the registration desk and launched into the crowd. I made a beeline for the gal in the suit. The skin in between her eyebrows bunched in a frown as she scanned over the crowd. She looked right through me as I approached.

I touched her lightly on the arm, drawing her disinterest. "May I help you?"

Despite spotting me several inches, she had the bearing and presence of someone taller. "I can't imagine with what," she said after giving me a cool once-over. She shifted her briefcase from one shoulder to the other. The logo said Ponder Enterprises.

Ouch. "Suit yourself, but if you're looking for Nolan Ponder, you'll have your troubles getting to him."

That earned me a sharp stare. "Why is that?"

"He's in a bit of legal trouble at the moment." I gave her an overview, hitting the high points but skimming over the detail.

Pressing a hand to her chest, she lost the haughty pinched look. A softening of concern replaced it. Her nails sported a perfect, squared-off youthful French manicure, but her skin put her closer to my age, at least by my calculation. Dark smudges of mascara shadowed the skin under her eyes.

"There must be some mistake."

"I was there." I wanted to give her something positive to hang onto, but my encouragement tank was pegged on empty. "If you have anything that might shed light?"

"I just got here. Mrs. Ponder had the Citation. It took longer than anticipated to come get me in San Antonio. This is the first I've heard of all this." She visibly pulled herself up by her metaphorical bootstraps.

"You came from San Antonio?"

"I manage some assets for the Ponders. Their house closing was this evening. I've got some calls to make. Do you know if they've contacted our legal staff?"

"No, I'm sorry."

She looked over my shoulder, then around the lobby, then refocused on me. "I need a room. This trip was last-minute."

"We're sold out. The NFL is a big draw." I took her measure as she deflated a bit. If I pulled a few strings for her, maybe she'd feel obligated to return the favor. Who knew when I might need some insider insight into this whole mess? "But perhaps I can help you with that?"

GINGER ASSURED ME SHE'D TAKE CARE OF MY NEW FRIEND, SAVING me precious time. I dove into the open maw of elevator eleven as the doors were closing. The group inside wasn't too happy—my bulk forced them to invade each other's space in a big way. Of course, that was most likely their hope for the evening, but usually some verbal foreplay and liquid lubricant helped vanquish the inhibitions. Not that I much cared about the discomfort I caused.

Why had Sergio gone to the Secret Suite without me? As far as he knew, I was looking for both Senator Lake and Beau Boudreaux. So, why leave me out of the loop?

What did he hope I wouldn't find? My cynicism disappointed me. Sergio had been a stellar and trusted employee for a long time. But that degree from the School of Hard Knocks taught me no one was above reproach, not even me.

Lost in thought, I felt the elevator doors close behind me. I keyed Security and got the same young, male voice. Fox. The guy was worse than a bad penny. "Give me Jerry, please."

"Yes, ma'am, but didn't you send him off with the EMTs to UMC?" The kid lowered his voice. "Something about a drug overdose?"

Feeling eyes on me, I glanced up from my phone. Six pairs of peepers, wide peepers, stared at me. No one said a word as they shifted uneasily. Facing the back of the elevator and my co-riders face-on clearly made everyone nervous—I wasn't following the unwritten social protocol.

Rules.

With my profound authority issue, half of me wanted to stay that way just to see how twitchy everyone would get during the short ride. But the other half of me, the half that won, didn't have time to play silly mind games...although the temptation was almost overwhelming.

"Fox!" I barked into the mic—I still had my earbud in place. I never knew how useful the hands-free thing could be.

How I wished Jerry was on the other end to help me. I felt my self-control evaporating. At my adrenaline threshold, my brain had started taking circuits offline to protect them from the overload...or that's what I told myself.

"Let's get one thing straight, Fox." As I paused, reaching for the right words, I felt the elevator slow. "Jerry didn't ingest any drugs; you got that? Fentanyl. If you don't know about it, you need to. Touching it can be lethal."

"I know. We had a briefing on it last week. But protocol calls for him to take a leave while all is worked out."

Nothing I loved more than some *kid* quoting verse from a chapter I wrote. "We'll see."

"I'm in charge here."

Oh, grace be to the Powers that Be, I got the fight I so wanted. "I'm afraid you are misinformed, Fox. You work for me." Cursed once again by an idiot with a Y-chromosome, I filled my tone with lethal. "Don't you forget it."

What the hell quirk of one-upmanship got him hired over Jerry's opposition? And why the hell was he so friggin' cocky? I mean, other than being young and male, which meant that whole judgment thing had yet to be wired into his thought processes—an explanation, not an excuse.

I so wanted to rip him limb from limb. But while I lacked the necessary self-control and could overlook the serious downside, I lacked the time.

Priorities—an adult concept that took the fun out of everything.

First, find the party room, and then dismantle Fox.

The doors opened and the noise of the party ramping way up hit me with the force of a straight-line wind. The storm had intensified in the few minutes I'd been gone. Rooted to the spot where I stood, I didn't move and the inhabitants of the elevator eased around me on either side.

Without Jerry, I didn't have a go-to guy in Security. No, I had a kid with an overblown ego reveling in an Alexander Haig moment.

"I'll fly solo on this one, Fox. You are out of the loop." I disconnected before I heard him not call me ma'am one more time. I guess I'd reached that limit, too. The thought that I'd cut off my nose and all of that raced through the tiny bit of functioning gray matter I had left. Tonight, more than most, I needed Security. No, I needed Jerry; but, absent a miracle, I'd have to settle for an ally.

I keyed Miss P. "Get me somebody in Security on the Q-T who I can trust."

She didn't even hitch. Barely a pause. "How about Vivienne?"

"Rainwater? Perfect. We'll need a secure channel."

"Of course. Wait a moment." I could hear her talking in the background, and then she came back. "Channel 77."

"Double sevens, I like it. Remind me to give you a raise."

"The ink hasn't dried on the last one. But, when you're feeling magnanimous, I could use some time off."

"Had you asked for a Ferrari, your odds would've been way better."

"If you don't ask..."

"I believe the more accurate line would be, if you don't dream..."

Her laugh as I disconnected reconnected me to my normal, and this was it.

Ralph held open the elevator doors and peered in. "You coming out or just riding up and down for fun?"

"Wasn't there a kid's story where a boy would get into an elevator and it would transport him to a different world?"

"I believe it was a tollbooth." Ralph gave me a sympathetic look, or maybe it was gas, I didn't know.

Key in hand, I stepped out of the elevator. "Tollbooth? Where the hell does anyone find a tollbooth these days?"

"Most of them are gone, so, I'm afraid you're screwed. You need a new fantasy."

"You have no idea how right you are." I punched him in the arm because I needed to punch something and I couldn't hurt him if I wanted to, which I didn't. "You got a bead on one Billy the Boilermaker?"

"Have you come back to knock some sense into more players? What you want with the kid?"

"The kid?" I gave Ralph a slitty-eye. "Why? Does he need some sense knocked into him?"

"I got a soft spot for the rookies. Him in particular. But he's been sliding around with Boudreaux, not exactly a stellar influence in my book."

"Understandable. Tell me about Billy."

"Runt of the litter. Got the talent. A bit weak on the physical presence if you know what I mean, but the heart's what's got him here."

If Ralph wanted to worm anyone under my skin, that was the exact way to do it. The runt with a big heart, against all odds, and all those clichés. I tried to resist. "The *kid* has some information I could use."

Ralph had been in my employ long enough to know he'd put a

toe over the line by asking, and he didn't step any further. Instead, he motioned for me to follow him into the party. A human speedboat, he cleaved through the sea of people. Thankful to follow, I rode his wake. Normally happiest as the lead dog, I pondered the lot of the follower staring at the butt of the ones in front. That was a bit of change I'd never accept.

Lead or die fighting my way to the front—a motto I should have tattooed on some visible body part, but I refused to do a Mike Tyson.

As I launched once again into the fray, the music wasn't quite at the level that would turn my brain to Jell-O and dribble it out through my ears, but close. Or maybe it was at that level but I didn't have a brain left—a more probable theory. The bass thumped through my chest until I couldn't breathe.

Billy the Boilermaker wasn't what I was expecting. He was a skinny white kid with acne scars, all legs and arms with hands that belonged on someone twice his size.

"Let me guess, wide receiver?" I had to lean into Ralph to be heard.

"No points for that guess." He clasped the kid on the shoulder, making him jump—he hadn't seen us coming. "Best prospect at that position in a decade." Ralph leaned into Billy.

I couldn't hear what they said, but Billy turned to me with a tentative smile. He moved closer. "How can I help, Ms. O'Toole?"

I held up a finger. "Ralph, I've got something I need you to do," I shouted into his ear, then watched him weave his way back toward the bar. Then I turned my focus to the young man in front of me. "I'm here to make sure you have the key." A shot in the dark, but I needed to prove my theory without showing my cards.

He pulled one to match the one I had out of his pocket.

Bingo—a rare win tonight for which I was grateful.

"So old school. And what the hell am I supposed to do with this rope thing? Jesus!"

The kid had no appreciation for tradition. Maybe that was

part of being a kid or a football player. In an effort at solidarity, I showed him mine. "If you need another."

"Nah, I got it covered. Boudreaux wants me to let people in at ten-thirty tomorrow night." He eyed me in an odd way. "You're coming to the party?"

"Wouldn't miss it."

"You got an invite? Rules is rules."

"Is they ever." I managed a straight face as I patted my pockets. "A bit of lace. I have it somewhere." I shrugged as I searched, then my fingers brushed the silk I'd taken off the guy stepping from the elevator. "Here you go." I held the delicates up for him to see.

His surprise registered. "You being with the hotel and all, I never would've pegged you as the Privé type. Remember, the costume is black and white only. Masks must be worn but can come off at midnight when we lock the doors."

"Is that to keep everyone in or everyone out?"

"Huh?"

"Never mind." Locked doors invited a challenge, but I had a key and the code, which stacked the deck in my favor.

"We meet here, and I'll let you in." He glanced at his watch. "But you need a costume." He eyed my attire—hardly lack-of-color appropriate.

"Black and white, I know." My brain raced as I tried to figure out where to get a black and white costume. With twenty-four hours, I felt sure I could produce the pope's robes if that's what the evening called for, so I wasn't worried. "What's Boudreaux got to do with the party? I'm new to the whole scene and not sure I understand completely."

"Each party, the boss chooses a celebrity to host it. Adds to the cachet, or so I'm told. It's not my scene. I'm running interference for Beau cuz—well, you know."

"He has a reputation to uphold?" Breaking Boudreaux's nose would cost me; I'd known that when I'd done it. But now I realized how much. He had info I needed, and my skill set, limited as it was, didn't include groveling.

The kid looked like he thought Boudreaux was as nuts as I did, but he was wise enough to realize staying on Boudreaux's good side enhanced his longevity.

I wasn't that smart—not that that was an alert-the-media tidbit or anything.

This time, when I turned to follow Ralph, he was long gone and I had to fight my own way through the bump and grind crowd. I didn't have far to go, but it took me a bit longer than anticipated.

Through a doorway hidden behind a row of thick bamboo on the far side of the bar and down a longish hall, I let my eyes adjust to the relative darkness—I guessed the cave thing was meant to enhance the whole secret thing. Personally, I thought it a bit irritating. But, not my circus, not my flying monkeys. The Secret Suite was the product of our Operations brain trust. I couldn't take the blame—I'd thought it a bad idea from the get-go. When our Operations Head told me we needed the suite to keep up with competition...well, it hadn't been my best moment. I remember saying something about the Babylon never "kept up" but rather set the standard.

Awkward, but true.

You'd think it'd be hard for me to talk with my foot in my mouth, but not so.

Up ahead, at the end of the hall, I could see Ralph scuffling with someone. "Ralph. What are you doing?" I narrowed my eyes as if that would help me see in the darkness.

"Ms. O'Toole! Ms. O'Toole. Get him off. He will kill me."

He'd found Sergio Fabiano, as I'd hoped and feared—I'm not good with disappointment.

"Kill you? No. But make you suffer? Now, there's an appealing idea," I said, trying to feel it.

Ralph lifted Sergio up and set him on his feet. He looked at me with big eyes as he shot his cuffs and marshaled his dignity. I waited for it. I didn't have to wait long. He flipped his dark hair out of his eyes then gave me his patented pout.

My eyes rolled so far back I could see my brain, or the empty space it had occupied. Games. I hate games. "Hold him. Do not let him go or talk with anybody," I ordered Ralph, who accepted with a nod as he pulled Sergio away from the door.

For some reason, the word "Private," stenciled in red letters, held an ominous warning. I was just looking for a party, so I wasn't sure why I was so jumpy.

Of course, the perforated body of Senator Lake had tilted my universe.

Using a knuckle, I keyed in the new code I'd put in place. I'd been careful not to include any common number with the previous code, the one anyone accessing the suite in the past twenty-four hours would have used. That way, I felt sure I wasn't obscuring any useful fingerprints.

The music thumped, or was that my heart?

I tested the door. Still locked. Inserting the key in the lock, I turned it to the left until I heard a click—a double validation lock that enhanced the whole privacy thing.

A light push and the door moved inward with a whoosh worthy of the stone guarding the entrance to King Tut's treasures. That was by design—an effort to conjure Babylonian riches hidden beyond. And it wasn't too far from the truth. Several million dollars had gone into the finish-out of the suite. Crammed full of high-end electronics—so many that the equipment to run them needed a climate-controlled closet—the suite even had a Japanese toilet that came with a clicker. Depending on the setting, the toilet would invade your privates in more ways than you could imagine, cleaning every crevice. The only thing it wouldn't do is hand you a hundred when it was finished and ask if it could see you again sometime. Personally, I thought that was a huge missed opportunity.

Inapposite of the rest of the hotel, the Secret Suite was a contemporary oasis. While my father preferred the panache of calling the twenty-five-hundred square feet of sunken couches, Italian marble, and big-screen TVs, the Secret Suite, I, in my call-a spade-a-spade style simply thought of it as the playroom where wine could be spilled and no one would cry over a hand-knotted silk Persian carpet…or be billed for it. The noise-dampening construction was also a selling point—when the privileged set partied, things could get out of control and often did. The key was making sure the rest of our guests slumbered peacefully or partied on without alerting the media.

The foyer was dark, illuminated only by the light filtering in with us, which was minimal—just enough to light overactive imaginations but little else.

"Lights. Dim," I said with an authoritative tone—maybe I couldn't order around the people in my life, but I'd be goddamned if I couldn't command a bunch of electronics. The lights responded, easing in the brightness. I had a reason not to brighten them further—a wall of glass separated the Secret Suite from the swimming pool in Babel. And it was dark tonight. Bright lights inside would not only attract attention from the partygoers above but also would allow them to see inside.

An undulating green light, ghostly and iridescent, waved along the walls. Two-way mirrored glass formed one entire wall of the great room, providing a view into the crystalline waters of the Babel pool. Voyeurism at any other pool, but at Babel few took a dip, not willingly anyway. I rounded the corner into the great room, leaving the lights off. The weird light through the pool was enough…more than enough.

As the lights eased on with the subtlety of the rising sun, I crept down the hall.

A hand clapped over my mouth.

"Coming to spy, are you?" A low, gravelly, angry voice growled in my ear.

CHAPTER SEVEN

SENSING THE power of the presence behind me, I stifled the urge to fight.

"Are you going to scream?" he asked, a hint of expectation in his voice.

Boudreaux. Great, a guy who got his rocks off hurting women. And I'd find out just how long he held a grudge.

I wanted to tell him screaming would be ineffective, but as my mouth was covered and sharing that bit of info would not be in my best interest, I decided to bite him instead.

"Ow!!" He let go.

I whirled on him. "Shit, Boudreaux! You knew it was me."

He took two steps back until out of elbow range. "Self-preservation. Last time you got this close, you broke my nose."

For a tiny pinpoint of time, I thought about apologizing but didn't think I could overcome my insincerity. And, quite frankly, pretending I had hat in hand, my groveling would have a hollow ring that even Boudreaux would recognize. "You deserved it."

He gave a little laugh...a very little laugh. "Not gonna argue. Just didn't expect some girl to deliver it." He took a step back, shielding his nose, which had a twist of tissue extending from one nostril. Blood still crusted around the other nostril and the whole proboscis angled off-center. "Are you still looking for a fight?" With that tissue and probably blood and swelling, his voice sounded all nasally.

He struck me as the kind of guy who would say that with a leer, but he didn't. "Yeah, but rebreaking your nose would be redundant."

"Good to know." He let his hands drop, but remained wary.

"I'm not going to hurt you." I almost smiled at the absurdity—me against a pro football badass. As long as I remained wary and saw it coming, I felt sure I could hold my own, or at least run fast enough to stay ahead until I could call for help.

"Don't lie." He motioned toward one of the couches. "Take a load off. I assume you're here for a reason. You found me. Let's compare notes. Can I pour you a beverage? I hear this place comes fully loaded."

No way was I going to show him mine, but I could play along. "Primo juice, epic bubbles, and top-drawer distilled spirits. Only the best." I settled on the couch, then leaned back and watched the lights dance, and marveled at the odd figures silhouetted through the pool water—like tripping but with no psychedelics involved.

"Pick your poison."

"Champagne." I justified my choice to myself—lower alcohol content, not as large a sin. The double-edged sword of self-delusion.

Boudreaux returned with a glass, then took a position by the window. "Don't worry about the nose. It gets broken twice a season at least. You were right; I deserved it. Life's a little out of control."

"I can identify." Bonding with a rebel footballer—I wasn't sure how to process that. "Being put on the chopping block couldn't be good for your career."

He lasered me with a sharp look, then turned back to the

window. "Where'd you come by that information?" He dropped the play at being collegial.

A sore spot…and maybe not common knowledge—if I read the subtext right. I blew at a lock of my hair that tickled my eyes. "I have no idea. Probably just assumed given all your recent trouble, the suspension, the lawsuit, all of that. You're a big distraction for the Marauders right now." I paused as a thought hit. "And you were the kind of bad the team didn't need when trying to present its good face to the citizens of Nevada."

His shoulders hunched up around his ears.

The sucker-punch of truth.

"Ponder wanted me out." Boudreaux's voice vibrated at the lower register of hate. "He didn't care about my value to the team. Told me he had it on good authority that I had more than a drinking problem, which I don't. I've been trying to figure out whether he was making it up or somebody was out to get me."

I didn't point out that he'd played into their hands beautifully. "And?"

"I don't know. I got a lot of haters, I won't lie."

"And Ponder?"

"Like all the robber barons, the guy's a snake. If it lined his pockets, he'd be all over it."

"No matter who got run over in the process?" I asked, not that Boudreaux had the inside skinny on Nolan Ponder's ethics, but his opinion would be interesting. He certainly had a beef with his boss.

"Collateral damage, he calls it." He turned to face me. "Look, I could really use your help here," he said before I could think how to play this.

I sipped the bubbles for a moment, delighting in their tickle, then the warmth as they delivered the alcohol punch. Bottled happiness. So why wasn't I happy?

I needed friends and I needed answers, so I jumped into the snake pit. "Maybe we can help each other. Want to tell me about the party? How'd you get sucked into all of this? Seems you've got a lot to lose at this point."

He turned his back, preferring to stare into the shimmering pool waters and at the party above. "It's not what you think."

I wanted to tell him that nothing was what I thought it should be, but that sounded overly dramatic and self-indulgent. The fact that it was true made it so much worse. "So, what is it?"

"The NFL knows, but you can't tell anyone."

"They know about a party you're throwing in Vegas while on probation and they're cool with it, but I can't tell anyone?"

"Pretty much."

Convenient. However, the bigger the lie, the more truth it held—one of those clichés with a kernel at the heart of it. This one had a ring to it. "Must be a big fish you're after."

This time, he gave me a different kind of stare. "You didn't get to be Vice President of this hotel group by nepotism alone."

It was sort of hard to look beyond the tissue hanging from his nose and see the intelligence behind it, but I knew suck-up when I heard it. "If you're looking to sway me with undue flattery, you'll have to do better—Vegas is the Bullshit Capital of the Universe. You wanna tell me what's going on? I can shut down this party." The suite had been subtly altered for a crowd—furniture moved back, an extra bar added at the far end of the room. I couldn't see through the doorway to the bedroom, not that I would expect that would be part of the entertainment area, but this was Vegas and nothing shocked me anymore.

"You won't." He gave me a complicit smile. "You want to see how this whole thing turns out almost as much as I do."

Damn, I hated it when someone read me right. "Who has your ass in a crack? The Ponders or Senator Lake?"

"An interesting ménage, don't you think?" He stepped to the bar to pour himself another drink, leaving me to dangle on that hook. "I'm really not sure exactly what is going on between those three, but it's some weird shit."

"And how did you end up in the middle?"

"Mr. Ponder's money gal. Long story, her marriage is on a fast track to nowhere. Her husband's an idiot who can't keep it zipped. She and I, we're friends."

The tumblers fell into place. "Is she here in the hotel?"

A side-eye from Boudreaux.

Easy to read—how much truth did he have to feed me to keep me on the hook, or something to that effect.

"Just arrived."

So he knew. Had she called him or had someone else put the bug in his ear? And I was also wondering why he felt the need to exonerate her in some fashion. "Is this money gal brunette, pretty with a haughty disdain to match?" The gal in the lobby looking for someone or something, holding the phone with the Marauder's logo on the back.

"Yeah, but once she gets to know you, she's cool."

"You guys working together?" I didn't tell him I'd scored her a room and she owed me.

"More like me working her."

Men! When it came to women, even dogs had a leg up in figuring them out. The woman had fifty IQ points and light years of evolution on the footballer, but he still thought he was running the offense.

"What's your angle?"

"She's in tight with Ponder." He kept his voice flat, his insinuation cloaked. He took a sip of his drink. It looked like straight cola. His grimace confirmed it. Painted by the odd flickering light, he stood at the window and stared up at the party. The tissue in his nose fell to the ground. He hardly noticed it. "Something's going down."

"What?"

He looked at me like I needed an infusion of IQ points.

"I know. You don't know. But any ideas?"

"Got something to do with Lake. I've been trying to find him, but he's gone radio silent."

He didn't know Lake was dead—or he wanted me to think he didn't know.

"Tell me about that bruise on your cheek." The angry red rectangle was starting to purple-up. "Where'd you get it?"

He touched the spot. "Some dude went all postal."

"Why?"

"Said I was hitting on his wife." Boudreaux stumbled a bit over the words.

"Were you?"

He flashed the leer I knew he was capable of. "Maybe."

I stifled the urge to wipe it off his face. His emotions, his personality, could turn on a dime. "What beef would the Ponders have with Lake? They won."

"So maybe it's all nothing."

Enough of nothing to kill a State Senator. "NFL seems to think it's something if they're giving you a long leash."

"You know how Jerry Jones started the war with the front office over the Elliott suspension? Well, the Commissioner is fighting back."

"If he can't fight fair..."

"Fight dirty." Boudreaux's smile told me why he'd been chosen as the front man.

"So, the front office thinks the Ponders are mounting a mutiny?"

"They force-fed the move to Vegas to everyone involved. Probably broke some kneecaps in keeping with the venue. NFL just wants to make sure nothing dirty went down and it's a clean deal."

He was pretty naïve for a bad guy, but I didn't feel the need to educate him. Right now, I appreciated folks who didn't see the whole world painted with the gray of cynicism. "So, if you take Ponder down, then you get to stay with the team?"

"Something like that, but you didn't hear it from me. And if you tell anyone, I'll deny it. Nothing's in writing. NFL won't claim me either if you're thinking of checking."

Like I said, convenient. "Tell me about the Ponders and the Privé thing?" When he turned to look at me, I showed him the G-string.

That got a little snort and a head shake. "Yeah, well, the Mrs. is involved anyway. But the Boss, not so much. He indulges her, which would be way beyond my tolerance…way beyond. Not really a party someone like Nolan Ponder who spends his time courting buttoned-up suits would want to be affiliated with."

"You think money would run if some of them knew?"

"That's what my source says."

"The money gal?"

"Yeah."

"She got a name?" I hadn't asked her. Something about her made me think asking questions would shut her up. With feigned indifference, maybe I could gain her trust.

"Goes by Brinda. She'll confirm everything I've told you. Not about me staying on the team, of course, but all the rest. You coming to the party?" Boudreaux kept his voice flat, his reason for asking hidden.

"Wouldn't miss it."

He raised an eyebrow. "Didn't peg you as the type."

That was the second person this evening alone who'd said the same thing, piquing my interest. I should run, leave the party to the pros, but when those particular smarts were passed out, I was behind the door. Kept life interesting—at least that's how I justified it. "You'll be there?"

"Here. Yes. I'm hosting, but it's not my scene." He gave me a look I couldn't read. "You know what you're getting into?"

His paternal tone made me bristle. "I can handle myself."

He winced as he touched his nose. "I got that."

His expression turned hard, and a tick worked in his cheek as he stared up at the partiers writhing to music we could feel but not hear.

"What's your relationship to Senator Lake?"

"The Coach?"

His pursed lips took a downturn. "Coach?"

"Yeah, high school. Ely."

"Was your number eighty-eight by chance?"

He snorted. "No. That was Fox's number."

"Fox?" I tried to keep my voice even, my interest casual, but my heart pounded at the gift straight out of left field, not to confuse the issue with mixed sports analogies.

"Yeah, we were friends back then. Both of us considered top prospects to take it at least to the college level and most likely beyond."

"What happened to Fox?"

"He got several concussions. Came back too quickly." Pain from the memories hunched his shoulders and tightened his voice. "Forced it. We all did. You only get one shot. There're so many hotshots, you can't even have a whiff of something wrong with you."

"How do you force coming back from a concussion?"

He turned away from the window, moving to refresh his soda. "You want more?" Anticipating my response, he took my glass.

With my Pavlovian hotelier instincts, I couldn't resist casting a critical eye around the place. Everything looked in order—housekeeping was doing their job. On the second pass, I spied something sticking out from under one of the legs of the chair closest to me. Semi-circular, it looked like a chip. After a quick glance over my shoulder to see that Boudreaux was occupied, I bent to retrieve it. I was right—a chip, indeed. Emblazoned with the Babylon logo and denominated in five hundred dollars. Boudreaux's voice sounded behind me.

"Knowing your tastes, I brought you the bottle."

I stuffed the chip into my pocket and rearranged myself back to casual.

He loomed from behind me, then bent to fill my glass. If he noticed my chip stealing, he didn't show it. "It was a different time, not so much attention on CTE and all of that. But still, we were kids so folks paid more attention. Fox's parents were concerned and got involved. They wanted to make sure he showed no signs of anything ongoing."

"Did he?"

Boudreaux leveled his gaze, capturing mine. "No. Coach saw to that."

"Coach? Like Lake?"

"Yeah. He gave him some drugs to mask the symptoms, but they made you a little wonky. Not hit-in-the-head wonky, just not quite yourself."

"Fox played?"

"Broke his back. He's lucky to be walking. Everyone was amazed he recovered completely, but he could never play again. His spine is unstable. One hit could turn him into a paraplegic."

"And Lake?"

"Fox blamed him, which was stupid. Things went south when Coach shepherded me all the way through college to the NFL."

"Fox now works for the man he blamed for derailing his career."

Boudreaux slugged his soda, then filled his glass with high-octane bubbles. "Fox works for Ponder. He's got nothing to do with Lake that I know of, but I don't count either of them as a friend."

I was so confused, but Boudreaux wasn't the one to untangle that knot. "Anything about you and Lake that you wouldn't want anyone to know?"

He gave me a veiled look, then pursed his lips and shook his head. His gaze drifted from mine. "Man, he's the guy who got me here."

"Tell me about that if you don't mind?"

"Nobody recruits from a high school in Ely, Nevada. Hell, back in my time we didn't have enough kids to fill out both sides of the ball. Most of us had to play offense and defense. Coach made sure I got some college looks."

"I get that. Anybody besides Fox have an old score to settle with the coach?"

"Why?"

I had his attention now. "He's dead."

Boudreaux reared back like he'd taken another blow, this one bloodless but emotionally lethal. "Who?" That one word held murder in it.

"Somebody with a grudge strong enough to drive them to do something horrible."

"Tell me." His voice was low, the words riding on a threat.

"You don't want to know."

He grabbed me by the shoulders, picking me up until my toes barely touched the floor. Despite my heart hammering and my mouth suddenly going dry, I didn't cave. "It won't help."

With a shake of his head, he set me back down. Nobody I'd ever met could pick up my bulk in a straight-arm lift. Beau Boudreaux deserved a wide berth. I'd underestimated him, preferring comfort in the dumb-jock cliché.

Beau Boudreaux was anything but.

The effort to contain himself showed only in the tic working in his left cheek and the darkening of the bruise to a blood red.

"What'd that guy hit you with?"

"Cold cocked me with the butt of a rifle."

That piqued my interest. Even though Nevada was an open-carry state, very few wandered around flaunting their rifles. "You know him?"

"Never seen either of them in my life."

~

"WHAT WERE YOU DOING HERE?" STILL SHAKING FROM MY encounter with Boudreaux, I stared down Sergio as I joined him and Ralph outside the door of the Secret Suite. I considered locking Boudreaux inside, but he'd be more fun to follow. I considered firing Sergio, but he'd be more fun to kill. I gave my future former front desk manager the slitty-eye. "We have a lobby full of folks ready to stampede if they don't get their rooms soon and you're here? Why?"

His pout disappeared as some other emotion tugged his lips into a thin line. Fear?

"Weigh your answer carefully."

"What did you find in there?" Ralph asked me. "You look a little pale under the pissed-off. You good?"

"Trying not to think about it." I'd flapped a red cape in front of an angry bull—anything could happen, and I had no doubt it would. I also had no doubt it would be my fault and I'd have to live with it.

I shivered. All the blood. The anger. The viciousness. Did Ponder really do that? Seemed out of character for a guy who had everything. But appearances were nothing more than clever disguises. But why? The buzz saw of that tiny little word sliced through my focus.

If Boudreaux could be believed, Fox had a good why.

I wondered where Fox was at the time of the murder. But Ponder was still the one covered in blood, stoned out of his mind, holding what I'd be willing to bet turned out to be the murder weapon. And, if Fox worked for Ponder, what did that mean?

Mr. Ponder had just beaten Lake at his own political game. What winner would kill the man he'd vanquished? Made no sense. If Boudreaux could be believed, his own beef was with Ponder, not Lake. Were his lying skills as finely tuned as his athletic ones? And Mrs. Ponder? What was her angle here?

With too many suspects, or potential ones, I focused on Sergio. Tonight, he'd been working the mid-shift and, even assuming he was up to his tight little ass in alligators, he hadn't had enough time to perforate a State Senator, even on a manager's break. "You are going to tell me what's going on, every ugly little detail beginning with the who, moving on to the how, and ending with the why. I'm pretty sure I know most of it, but I'd like to hear it from you. And, Sergio, this is one time where the truth really will set you free...to a degree. My jury of one is still out—convince me why I shouldn't kick your ass all the way to the border." I played to his fears, knowing he wouldn't call my bluff. "Tell me the truth. You know I will do all I can to help." But stupidity is hard to overcome, greed as well. I didn't say that, of course, but damn. Even without his confirmation, I felt sure he was guilty of at least a moral lapse. Did death make it worse? Deserving of a more harsh punishment? Or was the crime separate from the result, unforeseeable and unintended? If a moral lapse was a crime, I would've been shot at dawn decades ago as a habitual offender. So hard to punish someone for something I myself had flirted with.

Judgment: something we all did too much of and something I was ill-suited to.

"Come on, Sergio, give me something. You know I want to be on your side. Well, unless you are a knife-wielding madman, which I don't think you are."

Hand to his chest, he reared back. "Sergio? A killer? Never!" Even though way overdone, at least he was consistent. "Is somebody dead?" He took a deep breath and blew at his hair. It didn't move, stuck as it was to his forehead. Clearly, Sergio felt a bit warm while I was chilly in the January air.

My silence told him all he needed to know and he paled.

"How much, Sergio?"

"Money? You think I sold the suite on the side? I would never!" Either his offense was real, or he was a far better actor than anyone believed.

"What then?"

He waffled, clearly caught in one of those awkward places. "Okay, I took the money from Mr. Boudreaux..."

"How much?"

"Ten thousand."

At least it wasn't chump change. His go big or go home earned a smidge of respect. Clearly the corporate side of me was losing her grip.

"But, I took it to the police."

I narrowed my eyes as if his aura would appear and tell me whether he was lying or not. It didn't. And threatening him with jail wouldn't do any good. Hell, the guy would figure out some way to make an orange jumpsuit into a fashion statement and incarceration into a profitable bit of unpleasantness. Visual as I was, I stopped myself from diving down that rat hole in the nick of time. "An odd way of throwing yourself on the mercy of the court." And extraordinarily misguided—I was the one whose money he'd pilfered—well, technically not me but the Babylon. However, where one ended and the other began was impossible to tell.

Yes, I needed a life, but for the foreseeable future, this was it.

"The police..." He averted his eyes.

A cold shot of dread hit my heart. "Yes?"

"Your Detective Romeo. He told me you knew."

CHAPTER EIGHT

"WE'VE BOOKED Ponder on Murder One," Romeo remarked rather casually as he slid onto the barstool next to mine.

Focused on my Wild Turkey and trying to drown the visuals of Senator Lake's body, I hadn't seen him coming. Of course, I was sitting at the bar and facing the wrong way.

Romeo.

I still hadn't figured how to play this and now he had forced my hand.

Delilah's was our main watering hole in the middle of the casino. On a raised platform, with trellises wound with trailing bougainvillea and the waterfall, it was a nice oasis in a sea of blatant Vegas. The baby grand, a lustrous white, gleamed in the corner, but the keys were covered. Nobody played it much anymore.

Not since Teddie.

We'd often meet here when I had a late night. He'd play; I'd unwind. I wasn't sure whether I missed him as much as I missed the feeling we'd be fine.

I'd been a fool. Once a fool, always a fool?

With the wounds scabbed over, my heart had chosen Jean-Charles, my fiancé. But could a heart that had fallen for Teddie be trusted?

Problems for another day, but they niggled at me nonetheless, a relentless itch that couldn't be scratched.

Romeo watched me as if he knew what I was thinking, which he probably did. While I was tired of being an open book, I'd decided to own it as I turned to face the bar, ignoring Romeo's knowing reflection.

Coward that I am, I decided to take a circuitous route with the young detective. "I'm assuming Ponder was holding the smoking knife, as it were?"

"M.E. confirmed. The knife had been wiped. Only prints on it were Ponder's."

"That seems suspicious." I twirled my glass enjoying the light reflecting in the lone ice cube. As my father always said, any more ice than that bruised the bourbon. "What's with your jaw?"

"A hook I didn't see coming."

Romeo and his glass jaw. "How long were you out?"

"Long enough the guy was gone."

"Not Brandy?" With her black belt, she would more likely kill him than knock him out.

"She would never."

"Agreed." I savored a sip of 101, letting the fumes work their way into my sinuses. "Don't you think it's a bit pat that the knife had been wiped before Ponder grabbed it?"

"Only if Ponder wasn't planning on getting away with it, which would be beyond stupid. The M.E. also said the handprint matched Ponder's. He'll test the blood, but it's looking bad for Mr. Ponder."

"Looking bad is hardly an airtight case." I wrapped my hands around my glass—one ice cube to avoid bruising the bourbon. Bourbon was one of those lovers your mother warned you about. The kind you sought solace from after a particularly odious day.

The kind who warmed you up but left you feeling worse. The kind who stole a key to your place and kept showing up until one day you came home and everything was gone. I took a sip, flirting with disaster. I was okay. But a voice deep in the recesses of my soul whispered, "I was fine until one day I woke up in a gutter and couldn't remember how I got there or where I belonged, or even who I was. That person I was had moved on without leaving a forwarding address. A long road back, Lucky; start now." I took another sip and ignored the whisper of truth. "Did the M.E. have a time of death?"

"You know those guys won't swear to anything other than a several-hour-window unless they have a stopped watch or the whole thing on video."

"An hour before Ponder showed up in my lobby? Less?"

"That fits the window of opportunity."

Not exactly what I wanted, not that that was unusual or anything. "Did you get any more out of Ponder?"

"Same song; he doesn't remember much but swears he was at some private game." Romeo's disbelief was evident. "The guy was stoned out of his mind. But he had the murder weapon and half the world has heard him swear to kill Lake."

"But why? Where's his motive?" I took a sip of my firewater and relished the burn all the way to the warm explosion in my stomach. Closing my eyes, I could feel the warmth spread through me, banishing the chill of reality. "He had the murder weapon, but he didn't have a gun. When were you going to tell me Lake had been shot before someone finished him off with the knife? Or were you hoping I'd just skim over that part?"

"I don't like your tone."

"Ah, that's a page out of my playbook—offense is the best defense. It's the only tack when you don't have one."

"I figured you saw it."

I wanted to believe him, but this wasn't how we normally did things. In fact, nothing about this was normal in any way. "And the Secret Suite? Did you think you didn't have to tell me about that either? Why, because I'd find out about it eventually? What the hell have you gotten yourself into?" My voice splintered like tempered glass taking a blow. As I said, I don't deal well with disappointment, and I deal even less well with being intentionally cut out of the loop.

Romeo motioned to the bartender. "One just like that," the detective said as he pointed to my drink. "But make it a double."

"That is a double." The bartender wiped out a glass with a bar towel and set it in front of Romeo.

"Then make it a double-double." He darted a look in my direction. "I don't know what you're talking about."

I counted to ten. That didn't even begin to put a dent in my anger, but it was all I had so I counted again, this time to thirty, then I gave up.

"How far'd you get?" I knew he was chasing something or someone, even if he wouldn't tell me.

"Not nearly far enough."

Curiously though, I had gotten pretty far. Romeo wasn't doing an end run. That was not who he was, not what we were. And the endgame of that line of thinking had me even more worried—the kid was in way over his head, and he was trying to handle it on his own.

But I'd have to be clever to get the truth out of him. He was still a guy and suffered from the Curse of the Y-chromosome. "Sergio says you asked him to comp the suite for a party—a very special, private party. What's going on?" I also wanted to ask him why he hadn't asked me for the suite, but I knew the answer. He didn't want me to know. "Did you ask Sergio to do that?"

"Yeah."

"Why?"

"To see what happens and who shows up."

"That's not an answer."

"It's all I've got."

"You mean it's all I need to know."

"No. Unfortunately, it's all I've got—a few loose ends that, when I tug on them, they lead me here and to this party. All I can do is stir the pot and hope something jumps out."

"Terrific. Will you be there?"

"I'm not sure. I can't figure a way to work it. Cops aren't exactly welcome at the hippest parties."

"Ah, Grasshopper. No man is an island." He did me the courtesy of smiling. "You must rely on your friends." I pulled the chip out of my pocket. "I have an invitation."

"No way are you going by yourself. Lake was killed. This isn't a game."

"Sure it is, just with higher stakes. But I'd never go by myself. I'm smarter than that. I'm bringing reinforcements."

"Jean-Charles?"

Both eyebrows shot toward my hairline. "I don't know what this party's about, but I have a feeling it wouldn't be his crowd."

"True." Romeo kept his expression passive.

Even still, I was getting a glimmer as to what I might be in for.

"Who's going with you?" he asked casually as he took a long draw on his drink.

"Teddie and Jordan."

Romeo threw back the rest of his double-double, then signaled the bartender. "More, please."

"How much more, sir?"

"Enough."

The bartender started to comply, then retreated at my scowl. "You've already had enough, Grasshopper."

The fight left him, his shoulders slumped, and he looked like the kid he'd been a week ago. "Lucky, I gotta play this out. It may all end up taking me out, but I have no choice. I'm not going to take you down with me."

I was a bit player in a B movie. I knew it!

Being at the party put me in the crosshairs more than him, but

I didn't point that out. And arguing him off his lofty perch of martyrdom would be impossible, so I switched gears. "What about the Fentanyl? Just like Jerry, Ponder could've gotten into that and not known it."

"And it should've killed him, but by some weird quirk of fate, it didn't."

I didn't believe in quirks. Instead, I accepted them as a challenge.

"Jerry's only alive because we were there to intervene." Romeo stared down into his empty glass as if divining wisdom.

"That's not where you'll find what you're looking for."

"You should know."

I winced at the sting of the truth.

His face crumpled. "Sorry."

I laid a hand on his arm. "Don't be. Friends are good for the truth. I'm still confused as to what the drug thing was about." I wanted another hit of joy juice, but Romeo's words stopped me, for a moment. Tonight wasn't the night to draw my line in the sand. I took another hit.

"It's a way to kill somebody that might look self-inflicted and accidental." Romeo trotted out his flair for the obvious.

Or at least, I considered it obvious, though I wasn't one to rub salt in wounds. "True, but it doesn't feel right. Ponder had won. Lake lost. Why kill him now?"

"Ego."

I swiveled my stool so I could face the young detective. I thought about calling him out on his drink choice, but I didn't live in that pulpit, even though he apparently did. "Ego? You're shitting me, right? Men are really that..." At a loss for the perfect adjective, I let it hang.

"Some are."

A reality two-by-four to the forehead I could've done without. "How does one live in a world where half the population is still struggling to overcome Neanderthal tendencies?"

"Not half. I said some were. Not sure of the percentage, but alcohol, drug use, and women dramatically derail a male's thought processes; and no, before you ask, that is not oxymoronic." Romeo motioned the bartender over.

At his questioning look, I shrugged. Maybe a liquored-up Romeo would tell me what I wanted to know.

"Moronic, for sure," I groused. Men as a whole were at the top of my shit list.

When the bartender filled Romeo's glass to within a hair of the lip, he stared at it in rapture; then he shook his head. "Why do I get the feeling we're self-medicating and that can't be good?"

"Because we are, and it isn't. But it keeps my head from exploding."

"There is that. But, for the record, something's got to give or it's going to get ugly."

I didn't have a rejoinder. He was right, not that I would admit it, not out loud anyway—that would make it real. I had more than enough real right now.

He rooted in his inside coat pocket and retrieved a plastic bag, which he set in front of me. "Recognize this?"

I didn't touch it. Touching it would make it mine. Stupid I know, but I really wanted to get stupid drunk tonight so another kind of stupid didn't slow me down. I stared at the disk in the plastic bag. A chip. One of ours. A thousand-dollar denomination.

Ponder had one just like it, or at least I thought they were the same. "Is that the one Mr. Ponder had?"

"No." He pulled out another bag labeled with Mr. Ponder's name.

I added the one I'd found to the mix. "Found this second one in the Secret Suite." At his quizzical look, I filled him in, and then put my chip back in my pocket. I pointed to his new one. "Where did you get this?"

"One of the techs found it at War Vegas." Romeo took greedy gulps of his Wild Turkey.

"Ponder could be right about being at a private table."

"Or somebody is spending a bunch of money to make us think so."

I couldn't argue. "Go easy. That's 101; it has a bite." I should know.

"Shut up" was easy to read in his look. "It makes it all seem like a bad episode of CSI or something."

"That party is getting more and more interesting. You really are taking a stick to a nest of snakes, aren't you?" My maternal instincts stirred. He'd been my protégé. Now he was my equal... more or less...but I still felt protective. And I felt like giving him a good spanking. I saved us both the embarrassment by following his lead and draining my glass. The bartender was ready with the bottle for a refill.

Part of me wanted to say no, the part with no voice. I watched as he filled my glass as he had Romeo's. A serious amount of booze. I stared into the amber liquid in my glass, divining the wisdom it offered—precious little. I should take that as a warning. Instead, my phone dinged, saving me from a fleeting prod of virtue.

A text.

When will you be coming home? Should I pick you up?

Jean-Charles. A man most women would kill for. I looked at the rock on the ring finger of my left hand. Why did it feel like a ball and chain rather than a ticket to a happy life?

What was wrong with me?

Not sure when. Up to my ass in alligators.

Be safe. Love you.

So simple, yet so hard. I pocketed my phone.

Romeo shook his head.

"What?"

"Nothing."

I knew that inflection of *nothing* and its subtext. "Don't go there."

"What?"

"Beating someone senseless with advice about their love life is usually a minefield best avoided."

"Never stopped you." He took another greedy gulp. "Mixed metaphor, by the way."

"Now look who's the critic. Do as I say, Grasshopper, not as I do."

"Convenient."

Witty repartee eluded me at the moment, so I sidestepped.

I wanted to assure him that we all had choices, but, to be honest, that wasn't always true. And the kid was smart enough to know the angles, the options. And I wasn't even in the game, so it was hard to give advice that would mean anything. "What can you tell me about Senator Lake?"

"He's dead."

"Cute." I fixed the kid with a stare, which he avoided. "You going to tell me what's eating you? What game you're playing?"

He shook away my question. "I can't. Not now anyway."

I could tell he wanted to, that he needed help in the worst way. If I managed my pushiness correctly, I could get it out of him. Problem was, I wasn't sure I had any finesse left. "Lake was wearing Fox's jersey from high school." I filled him in on Boudreaux's story.

"The fact that you make those weird connections before the ink is dry on my notes has stopped bothering me," Romeo said, his tone saying the opposite.

"That's why you're here. You need me. We need each other."

He shrugged in unwilling acceptance. Experience had taught me how to read his non-verbal signals.

"So, who killed Lake?"

"I'm just digging into all this, Lucky. Why don't you just consult your magic crystal ball?"

I knew better than to grab that fight-bait—we were both having a bad night, so it would get ugly. I didn't do ugly anymore.

Drama. I was so over it.

Ely was cropping up too often to be ignored—and, trust me, Ely was so far from anywhere it was easily ignored. Was this all about something that happened in Ely a long time ago? Or did someone want us to think it was? If it was, then what was the Ponders's connection to Ely, Nevada, a place neither of them would be caught dead, I felt sure.

I needed boots on the ground. Who did I know in Ely?

Daisy Bell. My aunt's illegitimate daughter who'd gained some cachet, couldn't remember what. An expert at laying low, she'd be impossible to find without my aunt's help. Last I'd heard, Daisy Bell was turning tricks in the local watering hole. Her mother had paid off the constabulary, saying Daisy needed to wake up in the morning with a purpose. From my interaction with her, I was pretty sure she started each day with a hangover. Probably not the purpose her mother intended.

Romeo gave me a half-grin. "Don't take the trip to Doomsville with me. You wouldn't like a place where life is gloomy and the future uncertain."

"True that. Lake could've set it all up."

"Except for one small fact." He sounded pretty pleased with himself. And it was just like him to hold the best for last.

"Yeah?" I used my feigned disinterest as a goad in case he had visions of milking this.

"Ponder called Lake from his cell about an hour before the beginning of the M.E.'s time-of-death window."

The case against Ponder was stacking up like a bunch of form-fitting bricks. A bit too pat for my taste. "But, if he knew Ponder was gunning for him, why would he meet him in the dark where everyone was carrying a weapon?"

"Maybe Ponder gave another reason for the meet? Questions with no answers, right in your wheelhouse."

"If I could get Jerry back in-house, I know he could sniff out a private table, even if they worked hard to hide it."

"Whose job is it to monitor that kind of stuff? I'm sure the Gaming Commission is totally anal when it comes to outside gaming."

"Security. Then it's supposed to be passed up to me."

His eyes met mine. "I can see why you're concerned. Is Jerry a suspect?"

Every fiber in my soul wanted to scream "no," but there were rules and I'd have to play the game to exclude anyone. "I can't rule him out right now."

"Man. Sucks, you know?"

Everyone I counted on was under suspicion or outright attack. "More than you know."

"A thousand bucks. A lot to lay on the table." Romeo pushed at the chips through their plastic covering.

"For you and me, maybe. But you'd be surprised how many people toss this down without thinking about it."

"Win big or go home."

Or jump from a tall building. I didn't say that, of course. He probably knew better than I the exact count of the gamblers who lost everything, then sacrificed the rest. Gambling addiction—as bad as all the others. Maybe worse as it sort of flew under the media-attention radar, so nobody knew the extent except those of us who lived with it.

"What do you know about Mrs. Ponder?" Romeo's question sounded casual, but I knew it was anything but.

"Mrs. Ponder." I gave him a long look. "Seems she has the most to lose in this game."

He squirmed and chafed. "She wasn't even here. I checked McCarran. No record of her plane taking a landing slot. Not at North Town either."

"Really? Okay." That wasn't okay. She was here. I saw her. But how and when did she arrive? "She's got your nuts in a vise."

He flicked a look at me, then looked away as color rose in his cheeks. "Harsh."

"Am I wrong?"

He shifted, looking uncomfortable at my analogy.

Men and their parts.

In my younger days, I thought it would be interesting to spend a day as a guy with balls the size of oranges and a penis of equal magnitude. When I noticed there seemed to be an inverse relationship between penis size and IQ, I thought the price would be too high for the experience. Apparently, the ancient Romans agreed—that's why all their statues of great men have relatively unassuming junk. There was a lesson there for all the swordsmen. "Would you rather have a twelve-inch dick or a 160 IQ?"

Romeo gagged as a sip of mash went down the wrong way.

His face turned red as I pounded him on the back. "Sorry, my timing sucks."

Finally, he was able to pull in some air as he glared at me.

"What?" I said, working to hide the self-consciousness I felt. Not wanting to give him a glimpse of the gutter I'd been mentally traversing, I didn't look at him. Although my avoiding it was stupid—I'd sorta let the cat out with my question.

"Where did *that* come from?" His words were a tad choked as he dabbed at his eyes with a cocktail napkin. "Where'd you go?" he pressed.

"Rome."

He spluttered a bit. "What?"

"Someone told me I needed a new fantasy. I'm trying a few on for size." I hazarded a sideways glance.

"Your fantasy life would be an annuity for some shrink."

As would the rest of my life, but I wasn't about to agree. To deflect uncomfortable questions, I segued back to the topic we both were working hard to avoid. "Mrs. Ponder?"

He sighed and shrugged, shifting a weight. "I can't say a whole lot, okay? But since it's you and we're partners and all."

I shooed the bartender out of earshot. With empty stools on either side of us, we were insulated. "Won't go any further."

"I know." He grabbed the sides of his stool as if to move it closer, but the thing was bolted to the floor. Not sure whether having the drunks falling off was better than having them fall over, but the lawyers wanted it that way.

"It's Reynolds."

That almost knocked me off my stool.

Before I'd been unofficially promoted to Romeo's sidekick, Detective Reynolds had been the kid's partner. Of course, Reynolds had had official partner status with Metro. Me? I was a freelancer; something Metro wouldn't approve of. I didn't approve of Reynolds, so I figured we were even. "The man is a scandal begging for an above-the-fold headline in one-and-a-half-inch type. What's he doing?"

"Dealing."

"Like drugs?"

Romeo nodded.

"And you ratted him out."

"No. I wasn't that smart."

"You confronted him." Romeo was a good detective, bordering on great, but he lacked the bad-guy gene—didn't think like one, couldn't be one. That made him easy fodder for those who did, especially if they were donning sheep's clothing and hiding behind a badge.

"Yeah." His mouth turned down with defeat. "I figured I could save him, you know?" He finally looked at me.

"My middle name is Pollyanna."

"Maybe I learned it from you."

"It's not a bad thing, kid. You just gotta be a tad more cynical. You can't save everyone if you don't save yourself first."

"When are you going to take your own advice?"

"This isn't about me."

"You don't watch your step, it will be."

I probably should heed his warning, but I knew I wouldn't. Saving my own ass wasn't part of my skill set. That fell to Jerry and Romeo, but now, with each of them compromised, I was feeling a bit exposed. "So what'd he do to you?"

"The usual."

"Made it look like you waded through the mud, not him." Partners, by definition, knew too much; they had to. And you had to trust them with it. But when that trust was misplaced…that must've been something else I'd inadvertently taught Romeo.

"Yeah, but he's holding it over me. Got me on a short leash."

"Extortion."

"But if I report him, then I gotta fight for my own job, my reputation. Right now, he's got the goods on me or made it look that way, and I don't have squat. I'm such a fool."

I laid a hand on his arm. "No. You were being a good guy. I'm assuming you didn't have him cold?"

"Enough to ruin his career maybe, but not to send him up. Your buddy the D.A. would've laughed my case out of his office. Reynolds is two years from retirement."

"I get it."

That perked him up a bit. "You do?"

"Of course. Don't stop being you." I took a sip of my drink as I tried to process Romeo's pickle. And how to wise him up when this was over but not turn him into a hardened cynic, which I'd already seen signs of. "So, where did you step on toes, Reynolds's and Mrs. Ponder's?"

"I was just chasing it. The drugs weren't your normal street drugs. That's not what this is about—well, some of them were painkillers, but that only started showing up recently. Before, the drugs were performance enhancers, stuff banned by professional sports. Packaged with other stuff used to mask the usage, of course."

"And Mrs. Ponder?"

"She's got an interesting past. Even did some time."

"Let me guess, for dealing."

Romeo didn't insult me with the answer I already knew.

"Where'd she get nailed?"

"Ely."

"Wow, it's like that tiny town is the Epicenter of Darkness."

"Convenient and coincidental. We need more."

The young detective was reading from my playbook. Reaching out to Daisy Bell surged to the top of my list. "I'll get more. I can't help thinking that it's quite a step from being a dealer to being Mrs. Nolan Ponder. A lofty perch someone would do almost anything to protect."

"It smells to high heaven, but I haven't been able to nail her, not yet anyway."

"Mr. Ponder and the Fentanyl. Any connection there?"

"The M.E. is testing the stuff. It's street-made, so maybe we'll get lucky and the formula will be like a signature or something."

"And that will lead us back to her. I'm willing to bet a large wad on it."

"I've bet my career on it," Romeo whispered.

With my thinking already fuzzy and my attitude so low even a connection, a theory, a bit of hope in the darkness, couldn't elicit a sign of life, I pushed my drink away. "Buck up, kid. We're making progress." Bourbon—it was also the lover who did a lot of talking for you. "Is there a football connection?"

"Yeah, I had a chance to talk with Mr. Ponder about it on the QT."

"And he mentioned it to his wife."

"He said he didn't, but I got the feeling he was covering his ass as I'd made it clear we were off the record and he was to tell no one."

"After that is when your life imploded. Mrs. Ponder protecting her piggy bank. And Mr. Ponder doing I'm not sure what."

"Pretty much."

"That's actually a good thing. Narrows our scope. All we have to do is find the toes you stepped on, and Ponder is a starting place."

"He's in my custody."

I slumped under the weight of that. "Awkward."

"Looks bad, doesn't it?" Romeo threw back his drink. A bit of the amber elixir escaped and dribbled down his chin. He wiped it away with the back of his hand. "I can hardly wait for their demand."

"That'll be a pretty tough one to expect you to maneuver."

"Somehow I don't think that's one of their concerns."

"Yes, but what exactly they ask for could be enlightening."

"If you say so." Defeat took the starch out of his posture and the fight out of his words. "There's another twist." Romeo glanced around to see if anyone was paying any attention to us. They weren't.

"Fire away." I lowered my voice out of respect to his paranoia.

"Most of the guys didn't want the risk of a direct payment in cash or that sort of thing."

"Darn, not the episode of Stupid Criminals I was hoping for."

That didn't get even the wisp of a smile. "How'd the deal go down?"

"They paid with memorabilia."

"A black market for memorabilia. This is sounding way too O.J. Isn't he in prison for trying to steal some of his back, or so he said?"

"Not sure about O.J.; his wasn't one of my cases. But I do know that these players with all their contract provisions and money riding on playing time and all of that, and the risk of being medically discharged from the sport if you have multiple concussions and all of that, they'll do almost anything to mask symptoms and keep playing. Especially the ones who blow everything they make."

"And then there are the ones who can't imagine either being out of the spotlight or they have nothing to fall back on if football is taken away."

We sat cocooned in our own thoughts for a moment.

"That probably covers a very large percentage of the current players."

"And then there are the former players who need to blunt the pain and all to just to make it through the days."

"So, down-on-their-luck icons of Super Bowls Past can mortgage their history to fund their future." Even though I got it, it still made me sad.

"Or their habit." Romeo piled it on. Blowing your life was worse than blowing your fortune by many magnitudes. "Hey, it's tough to go from King to nobody. Some turn to substances to dull the pain. Or they got a lavish lifestyle way outside of their retirement income."

"Or women used to designer clothes and important jewelry."

Romeo winced. "Back to Mrs. Ponder, what a peach. She doesn't really fit the mold—she's married to the money. Man, he owns the friggin' team. But somehow, she's involved. He might be, too, for all I know and she's just a screech owl protecting her turf. I sniffed around. Found some evidence that folks were stealing or blackmailing or something. I didn't get that far. But somehow stuff appeared on the market that had no business being there." He threw back the last of his drink then motioned for another.

I put my hand over his glass and shook my head at the bartender.

"Mother, you're pissing me off." Romeo tried for mad but ended up sounding sad.

"It's my job. I'm your partner."

He didn't argue.

"What does Reynolds have on you?"

"A tape, some eyewitness accounts."

I could write the next chapter. "The video showed you in a compromising situation. Easy to prove it had been tampered with."

"It hadn't."

"What were you doing?"

He clamped his lips tight for a moment, pursing them, then shook his head. "I can't say any more other than they saw what they saw; they just interpreted it wrong." He reached over and squeezed my hand. "I didn't do anything against the law—well, I might've skirted it just a bit. And remember, just like a snippet of a conversation taken out of context, innocent video clips can look damning."

"And Mrs. Ponder?"

"Time served for dealing. A long time ago, but you taught me zebras never lose their stripes. And once I started pulling that string the parachute closed and I started hurtling toward oblivion. But this is my problem." Romeo lifted his glass to drink, then realized it was empty. Regardless, he tilted his head back to drain the last remaining drop, sticking his tongue out to catch it like a drop of poison.

I'd been there. I knew how it felt. And I'd kill the person who did that to Romeo. Okay, kill was overstating...but a payback from the Seventh Circle of Hell sounded like just the thing.

"And I'm your partner, by your own admission, so no arguing."

He backed off his stool. "Well, I have a murder to solve."

"Mrs. Ponder isn't going to be any happier with you now that you've arrested her husband."

When Romeo didn't answer, I turned to look at him.

"I don't know. There's something going on there. The Ponders aren't exactly the epitome of the loving couple."

"Money, the great divider." I'd felt it, too. "Listen, if you need anything from Security, you need to go through a young lady named Vivienne. She's my contact with Jerry out. Go through her for everything, okay? And keep a guy named Fox totally in the dark."

"Same Fox?"

"Yep."

"You have problems in Security?"

"None proven, but my gut is trying to tell me something."

"You listen to it. Far as I know, it hasn't let you down yet."

I watched Romeo as he walked away. All the jaunty was gone and my gut was screaming.

I missed life as it used to be. Where had this train left the rails?

I turned back to my empty glass and motioned for a refill. Romeo couldn't drown his sorrows, but nothing stood in *my* way. "Fill it again," I said to the bartender, "and keep it coming until I don't feel anything."

CHAPTER NINE

"OH." PAIN seared through my head. "Turn off the light; it's so bright."

"Sorry. The sun doesn't have a dimmer switch." A male voice that sounded a lot like Teddie.

But it couldn't be Teddie. Please, don't let it be Teddie. An epic hangover was problem enough. Teddie being here would be cataclysmic.

A rustling. The light dimmed.

"Better?"

Teddie!

Why did life take delight in hitting you while you were down, presenting your worst fear at your worst hour? A huge cosmic joke that was cruel—and, no matter how you spun it, cruel was never funny.

I bolted upright and instantly regretted it. A spear of pain stabbed me through the left temple. Everything ached. The world was fuzzy, my memory even fuzzier.

A weight settled next to me. A familiar fragrance—Old Spice—triggered emotions on a level I didn't know existed. The comfort of the familiar, the warmth of connection, the hurt of deep loss.

Amazing that a simple smell could conjure all of that in an instant. His touch would take me the rest of the way, back to depths of feeling I didn't want to feel again. Not with him. Not now. I shifted away from him—an act of self-preservation.

After stuffing pillows behind me, which I felt rather than saw, he said, "Lean back." He didn't touch me—perhaps he was protecting his heart, or maybe mine—with Teddie, it was always hard to tell. Extraordinarily perceptive, achingly self-absorbed, he always left me to guess his motives. Not the foundation of a lifetime. "Here. Drink this."

I eased my eyes open, blinking rapidly against the dim light and the pain.

This wasn't a bad dream. Damn.

Teddie sat next to me—I hadn't imagined him, not that I would have. Well, not without copious amounts of alcohol. If memory served, I had that part covered.

At least this was my bedroom, my apartment at Cielo, my boutique hotel on the south end of the Strip. But I'd started at the Babylon...at least, I was almost sure I had.

That whole piece between then and now was missing.

Wait. *My home? My bedroom?* "What the hell are you doing here?" A verbal spear to keep him at a safe distance.

"Helping a friend."

I angled a glance at him as I pushed at the hair hanging in my face. "We didn't..."

A flash of wistful softened the blue of his eyes. Yeah, I could see that even in this light. That sort of nuance was imprinted on my heart. Spiked blond hair, chiseled features, lush lips, and kind blue eyes, he would always have a piece of my heart. He wore the tattered blue jeans that were just tight enough—my favorite pair. Thankfully, he'd traded the Harvard MBA sweatshirt with the cutout neck that I'd been so fond of wearing for a light flannel shirt in a royal blue, which set off his eyes nicely. Yeah, I could see all that, too.

"No," he said, his voice carrying only a hint of his smooth tenor. "To quote a very, very dear friend, low as they are, I still have my standards."

"I think I'm thankful for that." Drunkenness and inhibitions rarely lived in the same human. Inordinately human, I doubted I was an exception.

"Morals are a bit of a bother, aren't they? Something else you taught me in spades."

"What happened to us? For a moment in time, it was so great." I'd never articulated that, not to Teddie anyway, even though I knew he knew it. "I really hate you for ruining that."

"I know."

"Why?" Unsure as to whether I wanted an answer, I whispered the word. "She wasn't worthy."

"No, she wasn't you. Not even close."

That much I knew. I waited for more—something I needed, whatever that might be.

"I had lessons to learn. I never fully appreciated you or what we had. Life wised me up."

I got it, but logic pales in the blinding light of an emotional fire. "I know. But I'm not sure I can forgive you."

"I'll wait." He pushed a glass at me. "This will help."

The world spun a bit. Cotton lined my mouth. And my head…any sudden movement would split my skull at the very least.

Catching a hint of apple, I eyed the glass. For some reason, I trusted him.

"Jordan's famous hangover cure," he said, anticipating the question. "He made it, if that lowers your resistance any." That did it. Jordan would never rip my heart out and leave me for dead—or poison me in the morning.

Suddenly greedy with hunger, I grabbed the glass and drank the concoction down, not stopping until it was gone. "Even better than remembered." Jordan had made it for me before. That I'd needed it before probably should bother me. And it did…but not enough.

A long road back.

He handed me a napkin, and I dabbed at my mouth. "Apples, ice, sugar, lemon juice, and a healthy dose of the hair of the dog, in this case, brandy. What's not to like?"

I thrust the glass at him. "More."

"Okay, but when I tell you to, put your hands over your ears. The blender on the ice-crushing setting will turn what's left of your brain to liquid."

There wasn't anything left of my brain, but I didn't mention it. Instead, I watched him amble toward the kitchen. Still had a nice ass. A sparkle on my left ring finger stopped my heart.

Jean-Charles!

The ice-cold slither of total panic raced through me, freezing everything. "I've got to go." Brittle as ice, I moved carefully, peeling back the covers and shifting my legs toward the edge of the bed.

Teddie peeked through the doorway to the kitchen, the blender in one hand. "He knows."

"What?"

Teddie disappeared. Knowing him, he figured retreat was the better part of valor here. "He knows," Teddie shouted.

"All of it?" I shouted back, then held my head in a vise between the heels of both hands to keep it from exploding. I sucked in air between my teeth against the pain. "Don't ever let me have another drink."

"What was that?" Teddie again poked his head through the doorway.

"Shut up and stop grinning at me like a rabid hamster."

He disappeared. God, he was worse than a Whack-A-Mole Game. Where was my bat? "So what does Jean-Charles know exactly?"

"Not sure…exactly." A bit too much lilt infused his response.

"I'm very glad you are having so much fun at my expense." I eased my legs back under the covers, then leaned back, careful to keep my head balanced over my shoulders lest it roll away.

"It's not as bad as you think. Okay, some of it, maybe, but not the Jean-Charles part."

I didn't pursue that because, right now, I needed to believe him. "Are you going to tell me what happened, how I ended up here?" My pain threshold long exceeded, I kept my voice slightly above a whisper—apparently, Teddie could hear it.

"You had…an episode."

The buzzsaw of the blender sliced through my brain making words impossible. I yelped then clapped my hands over my ears. My pissed-off switch still flipped, my anger flared. But my head would most likely explode if I threw off the covers and stalked into the kitchen in search of a knife, so I opted to dream about homicide rather than commit it at the moment. But I was conflicted: kill Teddie or just shoot myself?

The truth, like emotional road rash, stung with a fire. I wasn't mad at Teddie, not really, not anymore. I was mad at myself. But, swine that I could be, I felt like taking it out on Teddie.

So incredibly, embarrassingly human. My superpowers were nowhere to be seen.

Maybe he deserved it, maybe not, but most of the time when we didn't get what we deserved, it was a bullet dodged rather than a windfall. I tried to take solace in that.

The blender flicked off.

I eased my hands off my ears, keeping them poised in case I had to slap them on again. Moments of silence and my confidence bloomed. "I thought I was going to get a warning."

"Sorry."

So passive-aggressive.

I guessed that also was something I'd taught him in spades. Reflecting on my recent treatment of him, I felt the prick of shame. The high road had always been the one I wanted to stay on. Apparently, I'd drifted to a lower path…much lower.

Holding a full glass, he wandered back in. With one hand, he hiked up his jeans. He'd lost weight. It didn't look good on him. For a moment, he hesitated.

I patted the spot he'd vacated.

Back where we were, he handed me the glass. "A bit slower this time. Hair of the dog is a good thing, but there is a limit."

"Limits. Apparently, I'm pretty good at blowing through them." I took a sip of the drink, then another for good measure. The pain muted a tad, but stayed just sharp enough to give me a pointy-end-of-a-stupid-stick poke.

"You said Jordan made the first glass."

"I lied to get you to drink it."

Yeah, he so got me. I both hated that and loved it. "How did I get here?"

"You don't remember?" Teddie looked like he was enjoying this.

I opened my mouth, but it was Jordan Marsh who answered as he breezed into my bedroom. "That's the problem with going toe-to-toe with a bottle of 101. You don't remember, but everyone else does." Jordan, in town to rehearse a show he and Teddie would be performing in the Babylon's theater, was my de facto roomie, staying in the second bedroom in my owner's suite.

"Well, aren't you a breath of fresh air."

He waved a paper sack at me. "Be nice. I've brought provisions."

"Ice cream?" The words came out with a reverence I felt from the tips of my toes.

"Please, a concrete from Neilsen's." Concretes were the latest things in Vegas. Just extra-frozen ice cream, but oh they went down easy. "Paolo had me believing that limo really was a performance vehicle moonlighting as a stretch. But what you don't know…"

"Will land on my desk tomorrow." As our head chauffeur, Paolo answered directly to me. A casino was nothing more than a small town, and everything Paolo did ended up in a memo to me as his corporate parent.

I took a moment to drink Jordan in, watching him as he pulled three tall cups out of the bag and peeled off the lids.

Dark, tall enough, handsome in a way that put him in Cary Grant rarified air, swoon-worthy in every aspect, Jordan was the top of the A-List ladder in the movie universe, the stuff of female fantasies the world over. In a cruel twist of fate, he was also gay, a fact I'd hidden for the better part of two decades. Thankfully, as of a few months ago, that little secret was common knowledge. Jordan and his partner, Rudy, now lived in the open, happy and content.

Nothing like living one's true life.

I'd love to do that…if I could figure out which variation on the theme of my existence was the valid one.

"Vanilla for me," Jordan said with a wink. "Because I'm such an ordinary Joe. Peach for Teddie, because he's a real one. And coffee for you." He eyed me with a hint of serious. "Because you come with a kick."

"Cute." I accepted my cup and tried not to drool. It slipped in my hand a little from the frost coating the outside. Teddie handed me a spoon. I didn't look at him, and I was careful not to touch him. If a scent could take me so far back, I didn't want to feel what a touch could do.

"I do try to entertain," Jordan said with a wink as he settled opposite Teddie on the other side of the bed. "But last night, you stole the show."

I didn't press, opting instead to enjoy the last few moments of blissful ignorance as I spooned in, then savored, the first cold dollop of lusciousness. "You spoil me." The words were muffled by the cold creaminess I held in my mouth like a kid hanging onto the last days of summer.

Flanked by two such handsome, kind, fascinating men, I should be over the moon. But not even an overabundance of male pulchritude could mask the sordid story they were trying to deflect me from pursuing. "Tell me."

A look passed between the two men.

Finally, the not knowing trumped the self-loathing to come. "Somebody man up. I'm going to find out anyway, but I'd really like to do some damage control, if possible."

Jordan shook his head. "Probably beyond even your formidable skills."

My heart sank. "Did I remove any clothing?"

Again a glance between the men, but no ready answer offered.

"Seriously? I took off clothing?" I screeched a bit, but the pain brought my decibel level back down.

Jordan patted my leg through the bed covers. "Don't worry. Your singing voice is really quite nice. I never knew."

"I *sang?*"

He bit down on a laugh, which earned a glower from me. With no real information and fear taking root, my stomach clenched and my mood, teetering on the edge of abysmal, took the final plunge. *What had I done?*

The muffled peal of my phone saved me from speculation or at least distracted me enough for me to find some emotional balance.

Nobody moved. I glanced under the sheets. No way was I parading around in my skivvies to find my phone. "Somebody get my phone before the world as we know it is forever altered."

"Somebody has an overinflated opinion of herself," Jordan muttered as Teddie jumped to do as I asked.

I bristled—apparently my skin was a bit thin today, but I had no one to blame but myself, which wasn't helping. "I believe I held your life in my hands for the better part of two decades." Snarky and a desperate attempt at collecting the shards of my self-respect, but as a tactic it was a good one.

"You did." If he felt remorse at his jibe, it didn't show.

"Now that you don't need me anymore, the gloves are off, is that it?"

"Of course not, but you need to lighten up on yourself. We're all human, Lucky, even you."

Human. That sounded like a severe case of underachieving.

"It's in here somewhere, but I can't find it. Why do women wear so many clothes with hidden pockets?" Teddie pawed through a pile of cloth that I was alarmed to recognize as the clothing I wore yesterday. At least it seemed as if I'd made it home with all of it…I thought.

"Pocket of my pants, right side."

All he had to do was lift my pants and find the weight. How hard was that? But that simple calculation seemed beyond him—proof positive the Y-chromosome lacked the finder gene.

With phone in hand, he passed it to me. Somehow, through all of that, I was able to answer before the ringing stopped. "O'Toole." My voice sounded like me, even though I was light-years from feeling like myself. And I'd traveled all that way in less than twelve hours. A new low…or an alternate universe I'd found by diving through a wormhole of self-immolation. A parallel reality, that's what this was. It had to be as everything was not quite right, a movie reel projected at the wrong speed.

"We have a problem." Miss P's whisper evaporated my hopes that this all was the aftermath of bad fish for dinner or something.

"Why are you whispering?"

"I thought you might have a headache." Her voice returned to normal modulation and normal attitude.

"You know." A statement, not a question.

Jordan gave me a know-it-all look I tried to avoid. "The great thing about getting shit-faced: you don't remember, but everyone else does."

"You said that already." I stuck out my tongue at him, then returned to Miss P. "I'm all ears."

"Break-in last night. Bungalow 7."

"Anybody hurt?"

"Thankfully, the guests were at Babel until well after 2 a.m. They didn't recognize they'd been robbed until they sobered up this afternoon."

"Afternoon?" I'd just gotten up. I'd assumed it was morning. "What time is it?"

"Three."

"In the afternoon?" I shouted that last part then ignored the stupid-stick jab of pain behind my left eyeball.

Silence greeted my outburst.

I tried to focus on the job I was supposed to do. If I could do that, then maybe I could find me again. Somewhere between last night and this afternoon, the me I used to be had gone missing. "What did they get?"

"Sports memorabilia."

I started breathing again. "Okay, not too bad."

"Four-million dollars' worth."

"What?" My voice screeched like a violin in the hands of a two-year-old.

More silence. Miss P knew I processed bad news slowly.

"How'd they get in?"

"There's the kicker. No sign of forced entry, no windows unlocked."

"Door was locked?" My thoughts scrambled for a toehold.

"Lucky, it locks automatically. Key card is super secure after we had that hiccup with the software."

Hackers had discovered a flaw in the software of all the high-end keycard locks in hundreds, if not thousands of hotels. Worse, the manufacturer hadn't built in a way to update the firmware, so all the master boards in the locks had to be individually replaced. We'd just completed the entire retrofit. Talk about taking decades off my life. Our insurance guys almost stroked out. The lawyers produced a flurry of hot air and paper. And, when the dust settled, we had new boards in all the locks and no huge claims to pay or litigate. We'd gotten off light.

"You double-checked the board was replaced on the locks on Bungalow 7?" Even though we'd been anal about the replacements, with over three thousand guest rooms alone, we could've overlooked one. The odds would be infinitesimal, but nothing was one hundred percent—not even me.

"Affirmative. It's showing as replaced and checked. It passed the last security check done four days ago."

"Shit." I swung my legs over the side of the bed as I eased myself to a sitting position. The pain was tolerable. I'd inhaled half my concrete, which calmed the hunger beast, at least for the moment. I put my hand over the tiny mic on my cell phone. "You two scram." I shooed Teddie and Jordan away.

"You don't want the down and dirty about last night?" Jordan asked. Still in the doghouse, Teddie wasn't that brave—or perhaps was that wise.

From the Cheshire-cat grins on the two of them, I knew the knowing would be worse than the not knowing. "No, I can't change it so I'll live with it, whatever it is." I took my finger off the mic and returned to Miss P. "Romeo?"

"My next call."

"Jerry?"

"He's fine. Doctor will release him maybe later today, but we have to work through the drug protocol in-house."

"That's absurd. He didn't take anything willingly. I'll handle it." We both knew that could be problematic, but I wasn't going to admit that just yet. The rules had yet to be rewritten for the new reality that included Fentanyl. All previous drugs had to be ingested or injected. I wasn't sure I was ready to live in a world where readily available drugs could kill on contact. Thirteen-year-olds could buy the stuff on the Internet, and I had no idea what to do with that.

"Your call, but I agree. It'll just be a dance with legal and the insurance guys, mainly legal though."

Yeah, having the Head of Security suspected of drug use could cause all kinds of blowback.

"How do you think they got in?" Miss P asked, knowing anything I said would be raw speculation.

I knew she, too, was worried we'd overlooked something, something big. A possibility, remote, but there—a taper to light the worry wick. "I don't know. Have Vivienne meet us there."

"Got it." A pause. "Do you think our burglar is back?"

"If he is, I'll kill him myself." I disconnected and tossed my phone on the bed.

Teddie and Jordan both paled at my blooming smile. "You two are coming to a party with me. Tonight. Ten-thirty. Black and white. I need a costume, too. Now scram. I've got to take a shower and get back in the game."

JEAN-CHARLES DIDN'T ANSWER THE THREE TIMES I CALLED ON MY way down in the elevator, not that I blamed him. At this time of day, I figured he'd be upstairs in his eponymous restaurant—well, marginally eponymous. JCB Prime had been a compromise. His mother—yes, I'd called in the heavy artillery—had been the deciding vote. I'm not sure he'd forgiven me, and I didn't blame him. But his choice, JC Prime, sounded to me like a New Age Evangelical Eatery. In a moment of weakness, I'd dug in my heels at the thought of denigrating a deity. Not my usual blasphemous approach. Not sure what that was about, not that it mattered.

Anyway, thoughts of unimportant things distracted me from worry.

It took years of maternal brainwashing to keep me from riding up to the top floor and finding my chef and smoothing things over, if possible.

"Let them come to you, Lucky." If my mother had said that once, she'd pounded it into my head with her verbal hammer enough times to soften my skull. Maybe that was my problem.

Besides, *mea culpas* often stuck in my craw and went no further. The importance of fixing it would determine the level of groveling I would resort to. The only way to know that for sure was to face it.

And the jury was out on that.

But I couldn't fix it if I couldn't get him to answer his phone.

Conflict wasn't my best thing—unless it could be solved with an elbow to someone's nose. I didn't think that would be a wise choice with Jean-Charles.

Something was wrong with me, and I didn't know what. So I did what I always did: I ignored it and dove into the deep end of my job, a great hiding place that would suck me under if I weren't careful.

The elevator spit me out in the lobby of Cielo. Subtle fountains and waterfalls, walls of growing grasses, furniture of natural and humane fabrics and wood responsibly harvested contributed to the overall Zen vibe. The place had been feng shuied by the masters.

An oasis in a city of crazy.

At least that was the theory.

My choice to forego a casino had prompted derision from the old guard. I compensated by having the most indulgent spa in town. So far, the occupancy rate supported my gut feeling this would work, but the proof would be in the long term. Right now, we still had the new-hotel smell, but Vegas denizens could be notoriously fickle. We needed to cultivate cool to stay.

My staff nodded to me as I walked through the expected quiet. A few folks relaxed in the bar. Everyone else was either at the spa or drinking in all Vegas had to offer before they rushed back to the peace.

But the bottom line wasn't my priority right now.

A burglary in Bungalow 7. The outside security experts had assured me it was an impenetrable fortress—a requirement for the kind of clientele we charged very real five-figure money to stay there. We'd made that promise, and we'd failed to deliver.

And I had no idea how.

I pushed through the front door and immediately cringed against the assault of the sun. Tears hit my eyes. Pain stabbed. Eyes closed to slits, I rooted in my Birkin—a ridiculous gift from the Big Boss and, as such, something I both loved and found too showy.

As usual, caught between two versions of me.

How do you reconcile the yin and the yang? I felt like one of those theater masks with one face smiling, one face tragic. But straddling the fence could get downright uncomfortable, not to mention inflict serious damage to soft parts. However, doing something about it would come only when the discomfort exceeded my very high tolerance for pain.

But Jean-Charles might force me to one side or the other.

Momentarily blinded, I squeezed my eyes tight. Rooting through the detritus of my life that had found its way into my startlingly cavernous bag, my hand finally closed on my sunglasses. I stuffed them on my face and tentatively opened my eyes. Tolerable. Like I said, high tolerance for pain. And for humiliation, if Jordan's and Teddie's insinuations could be believed.

Through the years, I'd taken my share. I'd live through this—few died from embarrassment.

The valet had my ride waiting. Young, eager, and way too chipper, he waited by the open driver's side door of a red Ferrari, top down, engine idling at a low growl. Not my car—I'd borrowed it from the dealership at the Babylon. They'd been nice about the extended loan, but I knew I was perilously close to exceeding my corporate privilege. I had a brand-new vintage Porsche, a gift for my very recent birthday from Jean-Charles, but I couldn't bring myself to hand her off to the valets. So she stayed in the garage at Jean-Charles's house, safe from a car-loving kid who couldn't resist a quick joyride. Jean-Charles only pretended to understand. He felt slighted. I could see it in his eyes when we spoke of the car: one of the rarest Porsches available, a 1953 356 American Roadster. The car of my dreams. I should drive it, but I couldn't bring myself to drop it in the ubiquitous potholes all over town.

My shortcomings were stacking up like floodwaters behind a dam.

At some point, physics would exert her power.

I handed the kid a twenty and was rewarded with a smile.

The traffic on the Strip moved at slightly more than its normal glacial pace—midafternoon was the best time to cruise. Not in the mood, I wove in and out of the gawkers, the hopefuls, and the lost.

The neon faded under the assault of the afternoon sun. The city always seemed muted to me during the day, missing its magic. Not my favorite time. Yet I felt the anticipation building.

A true Vegas rat, I loved the magic of the night.

Expecting to run the gauntlet of protesters, I was amazed to find them but a bad memory. But that was the way with protestors—all fire and brimstone that quickly burned itself out. Tooling up the curved drive of the Babylon, I entered a different world where energy only slightly ebbed, gathering strength as day eased toward dusk. A steady stream of cars kept the valets running. I tossed my keys to one who darted in my direction, then strode through the entrance.

Today I barely noticed the Chihuly overhead or the indoor ski slope behind a wall of Lucite to my right. To my left, Reception was busy but not overwhelmed, and a nice crowd moved toward the entrance to the Bazaar, where everything from a frozen daiquiri to a high-end wedding was available for a king's ransom.

I followed the bright tile mosaics in the white marble floor, which formed a subtle yellow-brick road leading all to Emerald City, the casino. Crossing a bridge over the waterway that wound its way through the lobby, our version of the Euphrates, replete with reeds and grasses, waterfowl, and glimmering golden fish, I had to dodge a couple taking wedding photos. At least that's what I thought they were doing. The biker attire complete with leather bustier, chaps, no pants underneath, and lace-up boots made me doubt my guess until I spied the tiara with a mini veil. The guy wore leather pants, a vest, and so many tattoos they sorta ran together in a Where's Waldo bit of mashup craziness. They had matching tattoos on their necks—something about bikers and bitches. To each his own, I guessed, but I didn't like it. Although it wasn't hard to figure which common interest brought them together.

What commonality did Jean-Charles and I have?

That thought lasered me out of left field. Since no answer sprang readily to mind, I parked the question for another day.

Water behind the dam.

Right now, I needed to know if our thief was back.

And, if so, the odds of me not becoming a guest of the state at some maximum-security facility were dwindling by the second. He'd out-clevered me once. I'd choke the life out of him before he did it again.

The shouts of joy, the energy of the crowds ringing the tables, the smell of money did little to lighten my mood as I strode through the casino, although I did notice a stain on the mosaicked carpet and one of the wall sconces was sputtering. Barely slowing, I bent and retrieved two empty longnecks from a potted plant, then tossed them in the bin and kept going.

Down a long, almost hidden hall, a nod to the security guard who wisely recognized me, I burst into an immense glass-domed atrium. Tall plants climbed toward the soaring ceiling. Trailing tendrils of flowering plants hung from the metal latticework supporting the glass high above. Bungalows nested together, a babbling stream slipping between them. Most of the bungalows had several bedrooms and a great room—a private oasis, some with a tiny dipping pool in back, others without.

Bungalow 7 was by far our largest with five bedrooms and a private pool large enough for a bit more than dipping. Miss P waited by the door. She didn't look happy. Guess it was contagious.

Kneeling beside her, one of the CSIs from the Coroner's Office dusted the door lock. Vivienne stood to one side looking nervous but calm. If I could get a cup of whatever Kool-Aid she was drinking, I'd slurp it down by the bucket. Short with skin the color of a very dark tan and the jet-black hair and high cheekbones that telegraphed her heritage, Vivienne looked like she'd stepped out of a sepia-toned photo from the past. Regal, that's what she conveyed, and I both liked it and envied it. Smart and unflappable, she was essentially Jerry's right-hand man. Whether he considered her that or not, he should.

I deviated for a quick tête-à-tête with her. "Have you had a chance to review the tapes of Mr. Ponder's Knife Show?"

A wisp of a smile. "He just showed up. Appeared in a crowd of people that quickly dispersed when they noticed him."

"I bet. I'm surprised someone didn't get trampled to death. Was he on any of the feeds from outside?"

"No. It was dark and one camera coming up the driveway was inoperative. We had a guy working on it, but it was down when Mr. Ponder would've walked by, assuming he walked."

"Given his state, he couldn't have walked far. And Fox? Is he on duty today?"

"His shift starts at five."

"When he shows up, let me know. Thank you."

I moved to loom over the CSI as he worked. "Anything?" I asked.

"Wiped clean." The youngster didn't even glance up at me.

Of course, it was.

"He's back," Miss P whispered.

Our thief had cut a wide swath across the West disappearing into Canada. As far as I knew, he'd never been caught. "How could he get past the lock? The electronic board has been replaced, the vulnerability fixed."

"Got any other explanations?"

"Of course, I do. The guests handed out keys or didn't keep care of them. Somebody could've let the thief in. They could've left a window open and temptation in the open."

"They were at the party at Babel."

"So they say. You lose millions of dollars' worth of stuff, you're going to lie about it. Have you pulled the tapes?" It was one thing to lie, another altogether to fool the omnipresent cameras, not that it couldn't be done. But to do it, one generally needed help. I tapped the CSI on the shoulder. He rose from his crouched position to tower over me. "Can you pull the lock? I'd love to know how somebody waltzed in here and stole some serious swag."

"Sure. I'll give it a shot. Between you and me, I've seen a lot of these locks. The manufacturer got complacent, making the hackers unusually arrogant and sloppy. Fifty bucks and they could piece a device together to open these things that would fit in a lipstick tube."

"You're not making me feel better."

A smile lifted one corner of his mouth—so quick if I hadn't been looking for it, I would've missed it.

"Only thing you can do is change out the electronics inside."

"We've done that."

"Then I don't know." He set to work taking off the lock. Set into the door, the lock and its removal took lots of dismantling and more than a tolerable level of noise.

"Can you open it up and tell me what you find?"

"I'll have to put it through some tests back at the lab. Things that look right might not be right."

"Boy, I'm living proof." Everybody gave me the wide-eye.

"Didn't mean like that. My experience has proven his point; that's what I meant."

"Nice recovery," Miss P said. "Maybe you really are you even if you haven't been acting like it."

My eyes grew slitty, but that was the best I could do. She'd seen enough of my act, so I didn't scare Miss P anymore, not that that put me off trying.

The whole criminal enterprise was growing in front of my eyes like a super-virus or something. And, like antibiotics, my superpowers no longer worked.

Was Jean-Charles my kryptonite?

Focus, Lucky, focus.

Wild Turkey 101 was a more likely culprit. Anything to excess exacted a price.

My head throbbed. The spindle of my life was spinning out of control, wobbling and on the verge of toppling. Problems I'd solved were coming back to haunt me.

I'd never felt more lost.

"Okay, let me know what you find about the lock," I said to the CSI, then I grabbed Miss P by the elbow and moved her away from the noise. "Who was the big loser last night?"

She swallowed hard. "Stanley Lipschitz."

"Great, a sleazy pawnbroker." If today could get any worse…

"I heard that." The voice came from the bowels of Bungalow 7—a pouty, medium-high whine. "You're into me big time, Miss Big Shot."

The Stanley Lipschitzes of the world made all the rest of us look like shining examples of pure virtue. We'd had a few run-ins through the years, especially when I worked at the Big Boss's properties downtown closer to Stanley's shop…it had been his father's then. Stanley, Senior, they'd called him Big Mo—don't ask me why—and he had been a shrewd businessman. He'd been gunned down in the parking lot of the Desert Dunes before they imploded it, so maybe he wasn't as shrewd as I remembered.

Anyway, Stanley had inherited his mother's Cadillac and his father's twitchy trigger finger. If he had any other assets, personal or otherwise, they remained hidden. Big Mo left his shop to his brother Sonny with the proviso that Stanley be paid a salary for the rest of his life. He could be paid to work or to stay away; I hadn't a clue. But, if I were his uncle, I know which I'd choose.

The grapevine had been buzzing a few months ago about Sonny passing on. Something about his death being suspicious. Guys like Sonny, with his old Vegas cachet invited that kind of water-cooler talk. I hadn't heard anything further, so I figured it was one of those rumors that would be buried with the body. Nobody said who'd gotten the shop, or I hadn't heard, not that I cared...until now.

"It gets worse," Miss P said, her voice the harbinger of Worst Fears Realized.

"Let me guess. Okay, we have a pawnbroker, so there must be a fence. Am I getting warm?"

Miss P gave me a withering look that did not have the desired effect.

"Okay," I tapped my chin with my forefinger and stared up at the glass dome above me as if thinking. In truth, I didn't need to think. Bad seeds like bad apples tended to find their way into the same basket. "Murray Godwin."

Miss P deflated. "How'd you know?"

"This kind of gambit has his stink all over it. I swear deceit is built into his DNA. The NFL, money, players paid to test their strength rather than the limits of human intelligence, is fertile ground for the shysters of the world. Murray Godwin is the pretender to the throne. I'd be shocked if Murray wasn't in this right up to his gold chains, open-necked polyester shirt, cheap suits, and MJs older than the kids shooting each other for them. In fact, if he wasn't, I'd be sort of disappointed."

"You'd be the only one."

I'd been itching for a fight. Looked like I'd found one.

"Be careful. Jumping to conclusions can be lethal."

"Warning duly noted." I softened my tone. "Thanks." I appreciated her concern and cherished her friendship. The older I got, the more I realized how truly valuable friends who hung around in spite of me were.

And Murray Godwin was the enemy who wouldn't go away, proving my theory of yin and yang, balance to the Universe. Frankly, I could handle a little wobble to the world spinning on its axis if he'd just disappear.

Murray would not go quietly into the night. Admittedly, he wasn't exactly the battle I was looking for, but he'd do.

"Who's inside?" I motioned toward the dark maw of the doorway to Bungalow 7.

"Stanley, Murray," she paused, taking a deep breath, "and their lawyer."

Three against one, pretty even odds, if I did say so myself.

I dove through the doorway, then paused to let my eyes adjust to the darkness. "Lucky O'Toole here, Stanley. May I come in?"

"In the great room," Murray answered.

"Why don't you turn on some lights?" I asked as I felt my way down the hall and around the corner, the world slowly coming into view.

Two men sat in opposing chairs, their feet on the vintage Danish midcentury coffee table, in knotty chestnut, long extinct. They leaned back, balancing on the spindly legs of the Neils Moller side chairs. A third man, presumably the attorney, stood silhouetted in front of the plate glass window. The water in the swimming pool fractured the light into thousands of dancing diamonds, mottling the walls, the furniture, and the man in front of the window. His back to me, he painted a familiar outline.

When he turned, I masked a gasp of recognition.

Squash Trenton stared at me, his mouth set in a hard line, his eyes cold.

Wavy brown hair, stocky but solid build—I'd seen him in

skivvies and a Superman apron when we'd traded repartee in his kitchen—he was the personification of pugnacious. We'd connected with an easy banter, a friendship beyond the lawyer-client relationship, or so I'd thought.

Apparently, I was wrong.

He fired the opening salvo. "It's just business. Don't take it personal."

"Business is always personal," I said, a bit confused by his presence. He'd been on my payroll as recently as a few weeks ago. I didn't know our current status but finding him on the opposite side of the fence reeked of an ethics violation at the very least. "What are you doing here?" I asked the obvious because I needed to hear him say it.

"What I always do, representing my clients."

Murray and Stanley gave me shit-eating grins.

I wanted to tell them they hadn't out-maneuvered me as I didn't know I was in the game, but I wouldn't give them the satisfaction of knowing they'd shifted my world slightly.

"Nothing but a hired gun, is that it? So the whole lecture you gave me about being at a point where you could pick and choose?"

He squirmed, which gave me a moment of satisfaction—not much, considering evisceration was the lightest sentence I'd consider appropriate, but it was something in a miserable day of nothing.

"But seriously?" I made a sweeping gesture with my arm to include the two no-loads threatening to break my chairs, damage my furniture, and push me over the edge toward homicide.

"Their money is as good as yours." He stepped toward me as he pulled a paper from his pocket.

"Aren't you still working for my family?"

"Here's your final bill."

When I didn't take it, he laid it on the coffee table.

"You're not still tying up loose ends for the Big Boss and Mona?" Seventeen years of care and feeding on both sides.

Didn't that count for anything? In my book, for sure, but I wouldn't grovel, especially in front of the low-rent peanut gallery watching each verbal thrust and parry with ill-concealed glee.

"All done. Your parents have released me from their indenture."

Subtext there, for sure, but I had no idea what it meant. "From lofty heights to bottom-feeding, how the mighty have fallen." My emotional footing was sinking in the quicksand of disbelief and, to be honest, a feeling of betrayal.

Lawyers, a bad reputation well earned.

I'd thought Squash Trenton was different, given family history and all. My mistake.

"Innocent until proven guilty."

"Oh, those two are guilty. Long track record to prove it."

Lipschitz grinned as he hefted his glass, an exquisite cut-crystal Steuben tumbler in a classic style no longer made—easily seven hundred for two. He held the glass between his thumb and forefinger with an irreverence appropriate for a two-dollar purchase from Crate and Barrel. "This little lover's spat is so much fun. I wonder who jilted who?"

"Whom." I snapped off the syllable like a knife-thrower releasing his blade.

"Ah, must be the missy who's getting the boot."

I could do without the commentary, but I wouldn't give him the satisfaction of a forceful "shut up."

"I don't know." Murray Godwin eyed me through his round-rims, looking like a human owl, blinking against the light. The only hair on his head were tufts growing from each ear. His Coke-bottle lenses magnified his eyes to cartoonish size.

"The lawyer is licking a wound, seems like."

That brought me up short. Was this payback for a personal rebuff? Men could be stupid—I was engaged for Chrissake! Could Squash's manly sensibilities, to the extent that isn't an oxymoron, be so delicate? So…misguided? Did he really want to poach from someone else's herd? So not cool.

Men could be so disappointing.

But they didn't have a lock on it. I'd been a huge disappointment to myself lately, so who was I to cast the first stone?

Squash darted a look at Murray.

"Seriously, Trenton? This is *personal?"* I asked.

"Nothing like a lover scorned," Lipschitz said with a knowing nod.

"Woman," I barked.

"What?"

"Woman scorned."

"So it was you who got squashed?" Murray chuckled at his own cleverness.

Note to self: give up puns this instant; they are demeaning.

"No." Icicles hung from the word. "The quote. You got it wrong."

Lipschitz shrugged as his feet hit the floor and he reached for the bottle of Wild Turkey hiding behind the flower arrangement in the middle of the coffee table. "Seems right to me," he said as he filled his glass.

My stomach roiled as the bourbon smell hit me. The stab of pain behind my left eye pulsed. My mouth held not one hint of moisture. "Water."

Nobody moved, so I helped myself at the bar, plucking ice from the sterling silver bucket, and then drinking with the relish of a lost man stumbling onto an oasis.

"My clients have suffered an incredible loss at your hands," Squash intoned as if pleading to the jury.

I drank, washing away the cotton in my mouth, then I set the crystal down with precision as I marshaled my thoughts and my composure. "Did your clients put their valuables in the safe provided?" I turned to the group of men whose gloating I considered a bit premature.

Squash deferred to the two men whose smiles vanished.

"Did you?"

"We thought the room was secure."

"I'll take that as a no." I turned back to their hired gun. "Your *clients* did not secure their property as per our hotel policy, which they agreed to when they registered. If you don't believe me, read the fine print on the check-in forms. I'll need an inventory with photographs if you have them, and proof of value."

"You'll file the claim with your insurance?" Squash asked.

"No, but I will make them aware of the missing items. If you wish to be compensated, the liability is on your clients. I suggest they contact their insurance carrier."

Godwin and Lipschitz squealed, but Squash silenced them with a raised hand. "The fight is just beginning."

"Bring it on, but I'd be careful if I were you. Letting a personal slight guide a professional endeavor is a quick path to self-destruction." If only I could learn to walk that walk.

As I turned my back and left them, I made a promise to myself to heed my own advice. Life was hard enough without letting emotion lead you into a battle you couldn't win.

As the pain still thrumming through my head reminded me.

And I wondered just how much of my life I'd screwed up.

CHAPTER TEN

JEAN CHARLES still wasn't answering, which allowed me to avoid all the stuff I didn't want to face in my life and in myself. This was a good thing—I was in no shape to face consequences today. Ensuring the avoidance by running away seemed in order. I just needed a target.

My father actually answered his phone.

"Where are you?"

"Trying to bust Jerry out of the hospital."

"Stay put. I need to talk to you. I'll be there in ten minutes." I didn't give him time to answer.

UMC, our main hospital on Charleston Boulevard, was close enough that the engine temp in the Ferrari barely got off the peg. The valet—yes, even hospitals had valets in Vegas, where the economy ran on tips and other under-the-counter cash incentives—looked bored. Of course, this being Vegas and with our recent influx of Silicon Valley kids with a different exotic car for each day, I guess the valet saw more than his share of fancy iron.

My father would've stashed Jerry on the top floor in the primo suite. I didn't even bother to ask the perky gal manning the information desk.

As I knew he would be, my father, hands on his thighs and his expression serious, sat by Jerry's bed. He glanced up when I walked through the door and gave a tight smile. "We've got one hell of a problem." Yes, the Rothsteins used offense as a weapon.

"What? Not even a hello to your favorite daughter?" I looked for a vessel for the flowers I'd grabbed from the kiosk downstairs, settling on the water pitcher. "Don't try to cut me off at the pass. You need to tell me about Fox."

"Thanks." Jerry seemed touched as I set the pitcher with its riot of flowers on the window ledge where the flowers could drink in some sun. Sitting upright, he looked a bit weak but showed his normal level of pushback at life, which did a lot to restore my balance. A large bandage covered his nose, and a bit of blood had leaked under the skin forming a dark half-moon under his right eye. "Fox wasn't supposed to be on the desk last night," Jerry said, taking the lead.

I couldn't wait to hear what my father didn't want me to know, but we'd get there. "Doesn't surprise me. And then there's the issue of the bogus call to get you to the Kasbah. I haven't tied that in yet—not sure if Fox took it, then doctored the log, and then with a break-in last night that I'm following up on."

"Where were you last night?" my father asked as if he knew.

"Sleeping off an overindulgence." I stopped his recrimination with a glare. "Not my finest hour. I failed. But I guess too much booze was a better choice than jumping from the fifty-second floor."

And that was the closest I'd get to a cry for help. And I needed help. My performance in all facets of my life was dismal, and I saw no way out. Solving everyone else's problems was the place I hid. I lacked the skill-set to solve my own.

"Life's not that hard." My father sometimes chose tough love when a hug would do. Normally, I accepted it. Right now, I wanted to break his nose—another sign I wasn't myself, as if I needed one.

"Romeo give you anything on the murder?" Jerry asked, clearly surfing over the undercurrents.

Too antsy to sit, I leaned against the wall. Shucking off a shoe and wiggling my tired foot and stretching my angry calf, I decided to let him run with the line before setting the hook. "The knife was the murder weapon. No prints but Ponder's. The handprint on Lake's chest, that was Ponder's as well. A phone call from Ponder's phone summoned Lake to his death, or so the brain trust thinks at this point. The scene was a mess." I couldn't hide my shudder. "Lots of blood. Lots of anger turned Senator Lake into a human colander. I'm sure the Medical Examiner is still working the scene. He did take Ponder in, that much I think I remember."

"Enough to bury Nolan," my father said, putting a point on it.

Both men eyed me. "I'm sorry," Jerry winced. Death was part of the job in Vegas where folks often came to bet their last dime. But murder? Really, really ugly murder? Not the norm, at least since the Mob got steamrolled.

"I had a rough evening."

"I'm guessing now is not the time to mention AA?" My father gave me a half humorous, half-serious, under-the-brow fatherly look.

"When I'm down is probably not a great time to hit me."

"Hell, yes, it is. It's the only time you probably won't hit back."

I looked to Jerry for support but he shrugged and nodded his agreement.

Normally, I would've lobbed back my father's "suggestion" with a verbal hand grenade of my own. Today, I didn't have the energy to argue. And, to be honest, that bit of truth in every bit of wiseass hit me between the eyes. I was probably long past needing a twelve-step program. I wondered if they had one that would pull me out of the whirlpool of my life. And I was almost ready to admit it. "Your concern is so noted."

That seemed to surprise them both.

Always keep them guessing, my motto. That and live it until you become it. That one cut both ways.

"How're you doing?" I resisted reaching out to smooth the blanket covering Jerry—a bit intimate for a colleague, but not so for a friend. Negotiating the current climate of harassment and inappropriate breaching of personal boundaries had me totally tied up.

Before he could answer, his wife, Clair, darted in like a dog sniffing dinner. "Oh, hey." Tall, trim, her face pinched with worry, she seemed to relax as she fussed, smoothing blankets. "I'm glad you're here. Your father is a bad influence." Then she spied the flowers in the water pitcher and gave me a look; one hand on a hip added attitude.

"It was all I could find." I skewered my father with a slitty-eye. "Tell me about it."

"At least now she has something to do," Jerry teased.

Clair moved next to me, resting her head on my shoulder. "Lucky." That one word captured all her fear. She breathed it out as if expelling the devil.

"I know." I squeezed her hand. Fear and anger coiled through me like a live wire snaking and sparking. Even after last night, I wanted a drink—a double I could throw back to dampen the rage. One to toss on the fire lit by the one I'd thrown back in Bungalow 7. Self-loathing welled up, and another kind of fear, this one not so easy to douse.

Clair looked between the three of us—conversation had ground to a halt when she walked in. With Jerry's recent brush, talk of death wouldn't help.

She took the hint. "I'll just go find another water pitcher." She backed toward the door as she said it, then turned and bolted.

Jerry watched long after she'd disappeared. "Came close, didn't I?"

"Close enough for all of us." I shook away the memories of him struggling to breathe, of falling.

"I made it. I'm alive. Thanks for that." Jerry smoothed an invisible wrinkle in the blanket.

"I'd heard of Fentanyl but never seen it in action. Not like that. Scary stuff. Romeo told me they were cutting heroin with it now; that's what's killing so many."

"The world is getting meaner."

Jerry stated the indictment I lived with. Not too long ago my worst problems were a guy with an anaconda and a hotel full of porn stars with libido overload. Talk about circling the drain and then getting sucked down.

"Speaking of Romeo, he's not looking so good." As the Head of Security, Jerry added a bit of fatherly to his job.

Did any of us look good? If I looked half as bad as I felt, then the next nurse to walk through the door would take one look and scramble a code blue. "He's in a bind. Can't share, but I'll fix it."

"You can't do it all, Lucky."

"For my friends, I will, or I'll die trying."

"That's what I've been trying to warn you about." My father chose this moment to jump back into the fray.

"Beating a dead horse, Father. You got any ideas? I'd love to hear your take on our little exercise last night."

"You mean about who Ponder perforated?"

"No, about whether the Patriots will win another Super Bowl this year."

He pulled on the cuff of his shirt, arranging it exactly one-quarter-inch longer than the cuff of his jacket. Then he worked on the other one. Finally, he looked up and met my gaze with a weak smile. "Cute."

"Cute is about all I can hope for—clever is well beyond my current capabilities. So, who did Ponder have a beef with?"

"I wasn't part of all of this NFL political ball-tossing."

I caught my reflection in the mirror over his shoulder. My reflection stared back at me. At a fully filled-out six feet, even in flats, I always looked bigger than I felt. Somewhere inside there was a normal-sized person shouting to get out. She might as well give it a rest—absent carving off a limb or two, this was the me I was going to be. The blue eyes staring back at me looked like me. So did the high cheekbones and thin-lipped mouth that wanted to curve into a smile. But the light brown hair, not so much.

Teddie had changed things.

Some people come into your life and mix it all up, leaving it different—different, but somehow better. The hair wasn't the only thing he'd changed. I was only beginning to realize that.

My father, shorter than me, had always somehow seemed so much bigger. Not tonight. A bullet to the chest, marriage to my mother, and the recent birth of twins had all taken their toll. Tonight, I couldn't see any of the normal bullshit and bluster that had been his trademarks. For as long as I'd known him, he'd been bigger than life, immortal.

I was beginning to see the fallacy of that as well.

Growing up sucked.

To avoid myself, I pulled up a chair next to Jerry's bed, putting him between my father and me. "You might not have been scrambling for the ball in the middle of the scrum, but I know you. You know everything that has gone on, every argument, every political power play, every marker that was called in or given, allegiances made and broken. Give me your take. If there was ever a time to pony-up the inside skinny, this would be it."

My father shifted in his chair as if weighing words and consequences. He started slowly. "Everybody knows that Ponder and Senator Lake are on opposite sides. They loathe each other. Last month in Carson City, security at the State House had to pull them apart."

"Lake is a snake oil salesman, a malignant narcissist with little interest in the truth. I can see why a self-made man such as Ponder would want to squash him like a bug."

"Ah, Lucky, there are so many folks like Lake in the world. Paying attention to them, giving emotion and time to them, just gives them power. Patience, persistence, and truth are the only weapons that work, and it takes time."

"But Ponder didn't think he had time?"

"When an NFL team wants to move, it telescopes time."

"But Ponder had won."

"Only the first battle, but the war continues. Concessions, real estate, construction, permits for alcohol sales, you name it, Lake held most of those strings, if not directly, then through markers he holds…held."

"A multi-layered onion. Why can't one of these things be easy to peel?" I turned back to Jerry. "Why don't you tell me about Fox?"

Jerry's expression closed. "Ask your father."

"Really?" I leaned back, bracing for a good story. "And? Are you holding back on me?" I raised an eyebrow at him as I crossed my arms.

My father shot Jerry a daggered look. "He's one of Senator Lake's security personnel."

I wasn't sure whether my father was pissed Jerry had made him look bad or whether he really was holding out on me. "Did you confirm that with Lake?"

"Of course. Lake wanted him installed." My father grabbed his knee with locked hands, pulling it toward his chest. He winced but held on. "Why?"

"I heard he had a huge beef with Lake from long ago and that he actually works for the Ponders."

"I told you something was off about him, Albert," Jerry blurted the accusation at my father, who waved him to silence.

"What was off?" I directed the question to Jerry.

"He is. A loose cannon." Jerry ignored my Father's daggered look.

"He's Lake's man," my father insisted. "I've spent a lot of time with Nolan lately, and I've never seen him around."

"How'd he end up on the desk? As Head of Security, that's your call. You have the latitude to ignore me or my father—anybody, really."

"I never returned to Security. I went from the Bungalows to meet you in the lobby and ended up here. Fox is a big dude long on bullshit. Vivienne would've been the right choice to take the helm, but she'd defer to him until she could reach me. And I haven't been available."

All that made sense. "Do you remember what time he came on duty last night?"

"Sure. He was late." Jerry shot my Father an I-told-you-so look. "Came rushing in all excited over the disturbance in the Bungalows. Said it involved several of the NFL players at Bungalow 7, specifically—"

"—Marion Whiteside and Beau Boudreaux," I said, stealing his thunder. "And when you got there, no one was there."

"How'd you know?"

"They took their fight to Babel where I interceded. But, to be honest, I was connecting very loose dots. Marion growled something to Boudreaux about having his stuff. Brandy had said they'd made a detour through the Bungalows on the way from the signing to the party. And I found a couple of unsavory pawnbrokers in Bungalow 7 claiming their stuff had been stolen. Somehow, and I don't know how I'll prove it, but I'm willing to bet we are all talking about the same stuff, if you will, memorabilia worth a small fortune."

"And what time do you think Fox showed up, more or less?"

Jerry thought for a moment, probably thinking through the scenario and how it went down. "Six or seven minutes before Ponder staggered into the lobby."

As I suspected. "So he wasn't on post at the time of Senator Lake's murder. Interesting."

"He worked for Lake," my father reiterated as if this were exoneration enough.

"So, employees get a free pass?" Like I said, sarcasm fluency was something I often flaunted.

"Of course not." And my father had a lock on indignation.

"If Lake was as awful as they say, I'm sure working for him provided motivation enough." I turned back to Jerry. "We can add Fox to the suspect list. I'm checking his motive, but if it plays out, it's a dilly."

"If Fox killed Lake, he did the world a favor." Only my father could view murder as an appropriate solution.

I let it go. "Why is he here? And why has he mutinied and seized control of Security?"

My father winced as he shifted to cross the leg he held over the other, pulling his foot closer with a hand on his shin. Pain still pulled on his features and I wondered if the pain would ever go away. "It's part of the dignitary protocol."

"He's a state senator not a head of state. You forget who you're talking to—I wrote that protocol."

He sighed. "I know. I don't want to admit it, but I've lost a step. When I push, people push back. They wouldn't have dared in the not-too-distant past. I'm an old man. I don't like it."

"There aren't any other good alternatives. Besides, people are assholes. You took a bullet to the chest. The assholes see an opportunity."

"Lake." My father shook his head. "Back in the day, his bones would be bleaching in the sun."

"Well, somebody shot him in the shoulder, laying him out, then probably slowly and methodically tenderized him with a blade, keeping him alive long enough to feel it, know it. Would Ponder do that?"

"We never know what people are capable of when they have everything threatened."

"He owns an NFL team."

"He's leveraged to within an inch of his life. And he just delivered the fatted cow, the one he hoped to slaughter to fill his coffers again, to Lake."

"How so?"

"The real money here is in the merchandising rights and the concessions at the new stadium. Lake was after a large chunk of that."

"Stealing money from his constituents, so politics as usual." That whole angle didn't surprise me. These days, personal profit was the only motivation I could see for the idiots jumping into the political game. "And Fox?"

"Lake's eyes and ears on the NFL while they're here."

"Any idea what he was looking for?"

"Knowing Lake, leverage."

"And you? You were playing both sides?"

My father didn't seem bothered by that. "Been doing it all my life. The key is to be the last man standing."

"Given Lake's current residence laid out on a slab in a cold locker, I wouldn't let the police in on your theory." I felt a cold chill. I knew the game, but most days I wondered why we had to play it. Couldn't we meet in the middle, divvy up the pie, and all go about our business?

One thing stood in our way: greed.

"Well, Fox is up to something still. He's still manning the fort as far as I know, even with his boss silenced."

"Any idea who Fox is spying on?" Jerry pushed himself up, then hit the button to raise his bed up.

"Probably everyone and anyone, looking for leverage, just as his former boss taught him."

As we digested that, Clair rushed back in with a new water jug as if she'd been standing outside the door waiting for a sign she was needed. "You okay?"

Jerry's smile filled with love and patience. He took her hand and squeezed it, waiting until her gaze settled on him. "I'm okay. We're okay. Try not to worry."

She visibly relaxed. “Okay. Okay.” She set the jug by the sink. “I’m going to get some coffee.” She glanced around our small huddle. “Anyone want some?”

We all nodded, probably for the same reason: something warm and familiar to ease our pain, although we each suffered from a different kind.

I leveled a look across the bed. “There’s more to this. What’s the NFL angle?”

My father settled back. “They’re a wee bit skittish about allowing a team here in Vegas.”

“Yes. Vegas will strip their lily-white players of their innocence and corrupt their souls.”

“Something like that.”

Visions of Beau Boudreaux and his panty-pushing partiers, all of them flouting the rules, danced in my head. At the confluence of youth, Y-chromosomes, too much money and over-the-top adulation, mischief and mayhem, and down-right lawlessness were part of the program.

Jerry cleared his throat. “And then there’s the security side of it.”

“We’ve got a bunch of players, perhaps behaving badly, and Fox is in the henhouse.” Yes, I enjoyed saying that. I’m simple. What can I say?

Jerry pursed his lips and nodded once. “He can spy on anybody.”

“Do I need to point out that you guys have totally jumped the rails on this? Talk about leaping to conclusions.” My father actually sounded serious. “You’ve no proof he’s doing anything underhanded.”

My eyes rolled on that one but I refused to dignify his righteous indignation. “I’m assuming if Lake won, the Ponders would be the losers?” My father nodded, but I didn’t need his confirmation. “So, if Lake is as big a scumbag as you say, what did he have on them?”

My father shifted his gaze out the window as if the view toward the Palms was mesmerizing.

"Give it up, Father."

For a moment I thought he'd get his back up, but finally he wilted. His eyes were bloodshot when they met mine. "Nolan told me this in confidence. He's divorcing Sky."

"Now, there's a shocker. But if that provided legal grounds for the NFL to jerk chains, the league would be gutted. Perhaps Nolan found out about her arrest for dealing?"

My father shook his head. "How do you know this stuff?"

"You pay me serious six figures to know this stuff."

"You are an exasperating daughter but a terrific employee."

For some reason, I was insulted by the distinction. Shouldn't a good child also be good at her job? Even when her boss was her father? Why could I never get a bead on what any male in my life expected of me?

"I play to my strengths." I didn't know what else to say, although tipping his chair over backward looked promising.

"No, it wasn't about her arrest, not directly. A man in his position would be a complete fool if he didn't run a very thorough background check on anyone he was going to get into legal bed with. Nolan Ponder is a lot of things, but a fool is not one of them."

I wanted to beg to differ. The man had staggered into the lobby, covered in blood, holding a knife, and drugged out of his mind, but we all knew that. Shoving my father into the gaps in his logic wouldn't get me anywhere I wanted to go. "What was she convicted of dealing?"

"Little stuff. Pot, cocaine, the stuff all the rich kids used back in the seventies."

"No opioids?"

"They didn't have those then."

"Heroin?" At his look, I continued. "That's the stuff I wish I didn't know."

"I don't know the particulars, but you should be able to find them." My father rubbed his chest where the bullet had entered. Whether it hurt or itched, I couldn't tell. "Nolan is divorcing her because she had a torrid affair with Beau Boudreaux."

For once, words fled. Mr. Boudreaux had left that little factoid out of his story. Thankfully, my thoughts settled and it hit me—everybody in this little farce had a viable motive to kill Lake—well, almost everybody. "So, Mrs. Ponder would lose everything if her husband succeeded in divorcing her?"

"Yeah, but she couldn't have killed Lake. She arrived after you'd carried her husband up to your office—well after Lake was killed."

"And Romeo had said the Ponders' plane didn't land at McCarran or North Town, the two fields we have that can handle large jets. I'm still not convinced, but I don't have an answer. There are plenty of ways to arrive in Vegas."

"Pissing in the wind." I inherited my love of a well-turned phrase from my father, not that I thought his comment was that well-turned.

"Every stone, Father, every stone. We've got a motive for Mrs. Ponder; an opportunity has yet to be determined. What about Mr. Ponder? What does he have to lose that he doesn't already want to get rid of?"

Even though it pained him, my father leaned even closer, lowering his voice. "He's addicted to painkillers. He told me he's working to get off the stuff, but it's been a huge struggle."

That pushed me back in my chair. "Wow, okay. Is he getting some help with that?"

"No, he couldn't afford to, not with the team moving and all. Everything hung in the balance. If his addiction came out…"

"He'd lose his team." This time Jerry stated the obvious.

"Well, somebody damn sure found out."

"Lake?" We all said in unison.

"The pieces are fitting together." I rubbed my hands. "I love it when things come together."

"Do I need to remind you that you can't prove any of this?" my father cautioned.

"At least I have an inkling of who may be doing what to whom." I wasn't sure how the memorabilia thing tied into all of this, or if it even did, but I had at least five hundred pieces of a thousand-piece puzzle—enough to start seeing the big picture.

"Where's Fox now?" Jerry asked.

"Last I heard, pretending to be you."

My father eased his foot to the floor, then leaned forward. "We need you back on the job, Jerry. And soon. When you feel up to it, of course."

"I'm fine. But I doubt that when I return will be up to me." Jerry's attitude took a swan dive from displeasure to the depths of despair. Vacation was not part of his lexicon.

"What do you mean?" My father's interest sharpened.

"Drug protocol," I answered, knowing he'd understand the shorthand.

"That's absurd." Red flushed his checks.

"Your blood pressure." I waited for the flush to fade. "As Security Head, Jerry comes under even more scrutiny than most. Insurance and legal will confirm. Even I don't have any wiggle room. We're going to have to jump through each hoop on this one. Your Mr. Fox insists."

That little stink bomb had the desired effect.

"You don't know Fox's target. Hell, you don't have anything against him other than he's by the book."

"And sat at the feet of someone who flouted it." I didn't mention I had more suspects than Fox. My father knew it and chose to focus on Fox. Understandable, I guess. None of us wanted to believe someone like us was capable of the depravity necessary to do what they did to Senator Lake.

"What can you do?" my father asked with more than a hint of skepticism.

"Jerry, you feel up to chasing a few things for me, on the QT, of course?" He brightened. "Thought so. You know the Security Head at Chateau Marmont in L.A., right?"

"Yeah, she was one of Clair's bridesmaids."

"Cool. I've got several things for you."

CHAPTER ELEVEN

RETRACING MY steps to find where I'd left the car, I jumped when my phone buzzed in my pocket.

Jean-Charles!

Finally.

A text.

Meet me in your office?

At least he was still "talking" to me. The choice of my office put a pall on everything, though. Neutral ground? No witnesses? Time spent trying to read anything into his choice was time wasted. But preparing for the worst was the only disappointment-avoidance ritual I knew.

Jean-Charles waited in my office when I breezed through the door. Brandy and Miss P were playing scarce.

Cowards.

"Hey." I tried to sound normal, whatever that was. As if nothing had happened, I guess. I gave him a kiss when he rose to greet me. Thankfully, he returned it, and with more warmth than I deserved, which made me feel like slinking away to look for a rock to crawl under.

Suffering from a high tide of self-loathing and a low ebb of courage, I put the desk between us, settling in my chair which groaned under the assault. I so needed to get the thing fixed or turn it into kindling. My ego, delicate as it was, could only take so much.

"I am sorry I did not take your calls," Jean-Charles started with a soft lob, his delicious accent covering any hint of displeasure in the French way. "That was small of me, but I thought we ought to speak in person." Dressed in his chef whites, his soft brown hair curling slightly over his collar, his blue eyes dark and serious, he looked delish as always, but he also looked like he had gas. Or something painful to say.

"Talk in person? A classy version of the we-need-to-talk text?"

He looked confused. I didn't explain. If he came here to call our engagement off, then he wouldn't appreciate the smartass. My heart constricted. Faced with the thing I thought perhaps I wanted, I realized I hadn't a clue. Every choice came with a compromise, and I'd been working to keep it all.

And therein lay the problem.

"You are feeling okay?" Jean-Charles was usually kind, except when he was angry.

In desperate need of an emotional life preserver, I took his kindness now as a good sign. "My stomach's on fire. Someone put a hot poker through my temple. I can't seem to drink enough water. And my self-loathing has soared past previous levels. Other than that? Fine."

He didn't smile, but the color of his eyes lightened and the tick that had been working in his cheek disappeared. "According to Jordan, you had a rough night."

"I'm glad you didn't witness it." I brushed the hair out of my eyes and summoned my courage. "They called Teddie. He stayed with me."

"I know. He called me."

That surprised me. Given how Teddie had treated me recently, I thought any hint of gallant was gone. "He did?"

"He loves you." Jean-Charles clearly didn't like the idea, but he'd accepted it. "He loves you enough not to help you sabotage what might be a stellar future because you are afraid to listen to your heart."

I wondered which future he referred to. The one with him or one with Teddie…or maybe even my job, but I'd have to do a whole lot more before someone higher up wanted to scour the jails looking for someone who would even consider taking my job.

"I am not afraid of my heart." The problem was my heart was having a bit of trouble giving me clear guidance.

"I will not argue or parse words. That is right, *non*?"

I nodded. When the pressure was on, he got the English right—more evidence he pretended not to know American idioms or high-level vocabulary for my amusement. One of the many things he did for me.

He pressed himself up from the chair. "You must take some time. Figure out what it is you really want."

"I know what I want, but I'm afraid I don't deserve it." The words tumbled out on a whisper before I could stop them.

He opened his mouth to speak, and then clamped it shut, pausing while he searched for the right words. "Can you explain?" He lowered back down slowly.

"I've never admitted that to anyone, least of all myself, and you want more?" My world reeled. Deep dark secrets I'd only heard whispers of in the darkest hours when defenses were sleeping and courage low. Everything I'd felt and heard as the daughter of a town pariah hammered me. Then my mother sending me away and my father not admitting I was his for two decades after I showed up on his doorstep looking for a job, any job, finished me off. I'd been fifteen—a hard age made more difficult by my family. Jean-Charles had heard the story, or the abbreviated one that skipped along the surface like a rock thrown at the perfect angle.

Now we'd both mine the damage. "I have never been quite sure I deserved love, was worthy of it."

"That is absurd." Even with the French flair added, the words were still demeaning in their dismissal.

"It is how I feel. Denigrating my feelings is not the path to understanding." I didn't move, barely drew a breath; if I did, I would shatter.

He knotted his hands in his lap as he leaned forward, emotion pulsing through him. "You are so confident, yes?"

"In my work, yes. People don't have to like me. I don't risk myself; I just have to be good at it."

"You hide behind your competence, no?" He leaned back, relaxing into the chair. "I understand these things."

If he was going to give me a lecture about "just fixing it," I wasn't sure I could be responsible for what might happen. The truth, long buried, fought to rush through the fissure I'd created. I wanted to stop it, and yet I wanted the relief of saying the words, expressing the anger. More than anything, I wanted him to understand.

"You are strong on the outside. People see that and assume you are not a little girl on the inside. We are all the children we used to be. Yes, with time and help and understanding, we can glue some of the broken pieces back together."

"How do you do that?"

He rose from his chair and extended a hand. "Come."

He led me to the couch where I snuggled in beside him, absorbing his comforting warmth. "Your parents, they think only of themselves."

Blasphemy to a little girl taught to please, but it had the ring of truth.

"You care for them, yes, but they didn't care for you. Oh, they kept you safe, but they hurt you when you needed them the most."

Afraid to speak, I nodded as tears welled. I swiped at them

with an angry pass. I had cried enough for the me I used to be. Now it was time to fix it.

"I am angry." There, I'd said it. I was angry at my parents, *both* of them. Mona, my mother, kept me in a perpetual pissed-off position. My father, I cut him some slack, not sure why. Maybe because Mona had lied about being underage when they'd met and conceived me. Everything snowballed from that little lie.

"They deserve your anger." Jean-Charles pulled me closer. "But you can't change what has happened."

"A few "I'm sorrys" would go a long way to healing the hurt." That really wasn't true. I'd gotten the best apologies I was going to get from each of them. What I really wanted was to make it all different.

"Have you told them?"

I waffled on that one. I thought I had. Maybe I hadn't, not truly or honestly. "It's hard to share the things I'm keeping secret even from myself." I'd been avoiding myself for so long now I wasn't sure I knew how to get acquainted—it was like the worst blind date imaginable. My hands shook with the need to dull the edges with a shot of something, anything above eighty-proof. I wove my fingers together, my knuckles white as I gripped against the urge to pour myself a dose of the Wild Turkey in the cabinet. A few feet away. I was entitled. No one would judge me.

No one except the most important person…me.

Jean-Charles smiled as I looked up at him. "What's the first step to solving a problem?"

His words brought a smile. "Joining the long chorus of quoting me back to me, are you?"

"And?"

"The first step to solving a problem is admitting you have one." I parroted a line I'd said a million times.

"The first step is always the most difficult."

Okay, a bit too paternal, but he was trying. Points for that.

One more thing welled up, dark and evil, shaming me. My

hands still shook, so I dug in my nails—the pain gave me focus as I tested myself. One toe over the imaginary line into total honesty which, at this moment, I was thinking might be highly-overrated. All in or get out of the game, right? I pulled in a deep breath, then another. Before I started seeing stars, I leaped. "I don't think I can forgive them." The words came out strong and unafraid, surprising me.

Jean-Charles gave a Gallic shrug, which I felt rather than saw since I didn't have the courage to look at him. "It is not about forgiveness."

"It's not?"

"Forgiveness is an emotion; you feel it or you don't. It is no matter. To live with the hurt, to heal, requires understanding. Before you argue and say that is nothing more than an explanation, it is not an excuse. Yes, another of your best phrases and one that is most true in many cases."

"But not now?"

"No, in this case, you cannot ask people to be who they are not. If you wish to move past the hurt they gave you, then you must understand who they are and accept they did their best."

"Even though woefully inadequate?"

"If it was their best, that is all you can ask."

I didn't want to accept that, even though the peal of truth clanged around in my empty skull. With both feet on the floor, I leaned forward, leaving the shelter of Jean-Charles's arm. "Okay, say you're right, I'm not quite there, but for the sake of argument, okay?" I glanced at him.

Not even a hint of a smile to mock me. Raw, vulnerable, shaking with need and fear, I couldn't handle anything other than sincerity.

"I know I should know this, maybe even have owned it, but give me the whole skinny. How exactly would all this go?" I unwound my hands, then placed one on one knee, the other on the other, and willed them to stillness. The shaking had stopped. I still felt all tingly inside, like I'd had a near-death experience.

"Thoughts, you can control."

He had much more confidence in me than I did, but I chose not to interrupt.

"You must know they did their best, know they did not mean to hurt you. Then you can understand."

"Okay, then what? Understanding is acceptance and all of that?" Skepticism—one of my best deflection tactics, second only to sarcasm.

"Not in the way you mean. Then you can understand what happened, that it was not meant in meanness. After that," he tapped his heart lightly, "after that your humanity will heal your hurts, and you can have a new kind of relationship with those who did these bad things to you."

"If they really did it out of meanness?" I knew my parents didn't, but I wanted Jean-Charles's complete theory so I could either prove it or abandon it.

Once again, he surprised me. "If they did this on purpose, then they should be shot at dawn."

A laugh burst forth, breaking the tension and my melancholy mood. "I don't trust easily or well."

"Yes, this I see. You must allow time for those of us who love you to prove we are trustworthy. Do not cast me aside just yet because you are afraid. You have a big heart. It has been cracked a few times, I know, but hearts heal. Tell your parents what you hold inside."

"What if they react poorly?"

"You will have the peace of having been heard."

"Will it be enough?"

"You will accept it."

Not exactly the answer I wanted while he was reading from his crystal ball and all. Nobody could assure me life would be perfect, but I could promise myself I would make it better.

The drinking. The anger. The pushing people away. I'd been running from the hurt and hiding from myself.

And just when I'd hoped being an adult would be a smoother ride.

"You have seen me in my life, my story. In that way, you get to see behind the curtain, if you will. Shouldn't I get to see you in the same light?" Not only fair, it was imperative if I was going to build a future with this man.

"Indeed. You must see me in the place of my heart. We will go to France."

"To Provence?"

"No, to Paris."

"Paris?"

"Yes, when I was a small boy, my parents sent me to live with my grandmother. She lived in the Marais, which wasn't nearly as fashionable then. We are an old family. We have much property but for a time, very little money. My parents could not bring the vineyards back to life and raise my sister and me. They kept my sister with them."

The little girl inside flinched—a similar story to mine. "How old were you?"

"Seven." He patted my knee. "But it was Paris! In the Marais, there are many different shops, one for the meat, one for the cheese, one for the wine. The vendors, the ladies with their baskets haggling, debating the merits of one cheese or another, whether it was a good season for that cheese. I was mesmerized."

"There's a season for cheese?"

"*Mais oui*!"

"I never knew."

"Most days I would not go to school, and I would spend the day learning from everyone. My favorite was baking. From there, I fell in love with food preparation and presentation."

"And your grandmother?"

"She would beat me, but I would not stop. Finally, she threatened the baker. He made a deal with her. I would go to school in the morning and then apprentice to him the rest of the day. He paid me in food, a deal my grandmother could not turn down. It is where I grew up and became me."

"You will show me these places?"

"*Oui.* The baker, he is old now. His son runs the *boulangerie.* His daughter, she has a *patisserie* one block down. The cheesemonger is still there fighting with the Jewish ladies who want the best cheese for pennies." His face lit up at the memories.

"And your parents?"

"They had no choice." A message lingered in the words.

Perhaps my parents hadn't had a choice either. "I have a few things I need to wrap up here."

"When do you not?" His smile rounded what could've been an accusation into a tease. "But the senator, he is a problem, no?"

"Well, not personally."

"Yes, he is dead. I know this. I am sorry."

Even with only a few hints into Lake's game, I thought perhaps Jean-Charles was one of a handful who might feel that way. "There are a few complications."

"Murder. Emotion. Always complications. When do you think you might be able to go to France, then?"

Right now! The little girl inside me screamed. I wanted to run away from all the unpleasantness I had to face. But the running had to stop, right here, right now. If Jean-Charles and I didn't work out, it wouldn't be because I was running away from things that scared me, that had hurt so much in the past, a raw wound Teddie had ground salt into. "Hard to say. A couple of weeks?" With all on my plate and Romeo and Jerry both on the sidelines, I thought that a bit optimistic, but hope springs eternal. Was I already sabotaging the trip? I thought about that for a moment. If I was, I was hiding it from myself. Knowing me, not out of the realm of possibilities. Despite best-laid plans, I was still a work in progress…and would be for a long time, I suspected.

"Sure."

He stood, then pulled me to my feet. "I need to go argue with a meat purveyor and the cheese man; both are trying to rob me blind."

And I need to…what? Catch a killer? Catch a thief? Save a friend? Save myself?

My priorities were proving to be a bit problematic.

Jean-Charles folded me into an embrace. Was he drawing strength from me or the other way around? I hoped it was mutual —that sounded like a good balance. One thing I did know: If he turned out not to be the one, I'd sure miss his touch.

"How is Christophe?" I whispered against his skin.

"He is desolate. I cannot make your happy face pancakes the way you do."

I couldn't imagine breaking the boy's heart. But I couldn't imagine living a life other than the perfect one for me either.

As if Jean-Charles could read my thoughts, he whispered, "We will both be fine, in time. You must do what is right for you."

WITH A SIXTH SENSE THAT WAS AS SPOT-ON AS IT WAS disconcerting, Miss P walked through the office doorway, side-stepping Jean-Charles, who dipped his chin and smiled as he walked out.

"Been having fun?" Miss P's snark couldn't quite hide her concern. She thrust a familiar white bag with a red-and-yellow palm tree logo at me. "Double-double. Animal style. Two orders of fries, extra crisp. And a diet soda. No joy juice until your liver is back in the pink."

My knees threatened to buckle. "In-N-Out, the best hangover cure known to man. I should double your salary."

"Just give me a hug." She pulled back the bag and started

unloading the contents, spreading them on an unfolded napkin on my desk. "It's not about money. We never have been."

I did as she asked, squeezing her tighter and holding her longer than necessary because I felt like it.

She went back to unwrapping my hamburgers. The aroma alone took away the pain. The food filled the void. One comfort for another—not always healthy for the body, but sometimes the only thing that would heal the soul.

"You got some for yourself?" I asked with my mouth full. My mother, Mona, would be appalled, which made me proud. Mona, with the heightened sensibilities of a reformed hooker, knew Miss Manners backward and forward. My father grew up in the Mobbed-up Vegas and made a name for himself in the corporate-run rendition. My family—quixotic to be kind. Batshit crazy to be more accurate. And me, where did I fit? I didn't know, but I felt right at home.

Home.

Maybe that's what Jean-Charles threatened.

A girl was supposed to leave her father's house. I'd just found my father. And it dawned on me that I had never left his house—I'd just made it mine. Was that the same as leaving or staying? Who knew?

Miss P perched across from me and retrieved a much smaller sack from the bag for herself.

In the comfort of friends, we both said nothing as we shared the fine repast.

Curiously, even though my stomach hurt as I pushed away from the desk and leaned back in my chair, all the other parts that previously had been filled with pain had quieted. "We've got one hell of a mess."

"By my count, we have three, maybe four." Miss P meticulously folded the paper wrapper from her hamburger, a dainty single, no cheese, and then flattened the box her fries had come in before slipping them back into the sack—her way of forcing order out of chaos.

That sort of OCD thing made me nuts, but it seemed to help her find calm.

I cocked one eyebrow at her, which she studiously avoided. "Are you ready now?"

"Quite." She pulled the pad on my desk around to face her, then found a pen under the unsigned papers, corporate memos, and other time sucks that had found their way into the pile.

"Jeremy—" I began.

"On his way."

Jeremy was Miss P's much younger husband—an Aussie hunk that set many hearts swooning. But she had won his, earning my eternal appreciation. Miss P was the poster child for the be-yourself-and-your-life-will-find-you cult of modern living. I'd love to be an acolyte, but their teachings eluded me.

"Okay." I wadded up the detritus of my feeding and tossed it over Miss P's head at the waste can across the room. Some of it made it. Some didn't. A few fries landed in her lap. "Sorry."

Miss P plucked at them as she muttered, "So passive aggressive."

"I heard that."

"I hope so," she said with a grin as she tossed the fries at the can. They went in…all of them.

Clutching at straws, I tried not to find irony in wayward French fries. "Thank you for the meal. I feel much better. And I know we're not about money, not totally. I'd be lost without you."

Warmth filled her smile. "I like you much better when you're a grown-up."

"Me, too, but I'm still a work in progress, so going all adult is still championship stuff. You can't expect it all the time."

"Aren't we all?" She must've seen my surprise as she continued, "What you see on the outside doesn't always mirror what's happening on the inside."

"Fake it until you become it?" One of Mona's favorite lines. She'd lived it, and she'd made it real. Miss P had also manifested her happiness. Maybe there was something there.

"Exactly. So, Jeremy will be here any minute. You can tell him what plans you have for him." Along with being Miss P's squeeze, Jeremy was Vegas's primo private investigator. "What else?" She held her pen poised over the pad.

"Has Vivienne been able to track down Fox?"

"No. And his shift started an hour ago."

"A no-show?"

Miss P nodded, her lips a thin, tight line.

Any way I looked at that it came out as so not good, but there was nothing I could do, not at the moment anyway. "Well, have her keep looking and keep us posted. Right now, you and I need to track down some missing baubles."

"Oh! Fieldwork."

Her conspiratorial tone made me laugh, then sobered me up. "We're not the goddamn FBI. This will be an information-gathering expedition. Do I need to remind you someone has already died?"

That didn't even dim the wattage. "Where are we going?"

I glanced at my phone. "It'll be dark soon. I'm thinking we need to do some shopping." I had hours until the party. What could go wrong?

For a moment, confusion crinkled her brows, then the light dawned. "You can find such interesting things at a pawnshop these days. Especially in Vegas."

"Indeed. Even, perhaps, some baubles that might have been reported stolen. Send some food and high-end wine to Bungalow 7."

"How high-end?"

"Enough to convey a bit of suck-up and my sincerest apologies for the break-in. Make the whole presentation sufficient to keep them gloating for a bit."

She practically vibrated with excitement. Personally, skulking around dark alleys in shady parts of downtown wasn't on my top ten of cool things to do, but I had been awfully short-sighted recently.

"Beau Boudreaux paid Sergio under the table for access to the Secret Suite."

She finished taking notes before she looked up. "How much?"

"Ten grand, according to Sergio, but once you breach trust, everything you say becomes suspect."

"A tenth of his salary."

"Less."

"Does he need the money?"

"Not that I know of." I paused, which sharpened her attention. "He said Romeo asked him to do it."

That caught her flat-footed. Her composure returned quickly. "Have you asked Romeo?"

"He confirms."

"Going behind your back, it must be serious."

"That's what I thought—well, after I thought about killing him."

"I applaud your restraint."

I was feeling better by the moment "He's involved in all of this somehow, and he's up to his eyeballs and sinking fast."

"An explanation, not an excuse."

"He's young and stupid, and it's our job to see he gets an opportunity to grow older and learn the error of his ways."

She snorted. "You just want the chance to rub his nose in it."

"There's that."

"And Sergio?" she asked.

"Romeo lied to him. He told him I knew."

"You're his boss. He should've cleared it with you."

I shrugged. Romeo, known to all as my friend, had led him astray. I got it.

Miss P looked at me askance. "You're getting soft."

"Stones and glass houses. The more you live, the more human you become."

Life: I suspected learning was really just growing tired of fighting.

For a moment, I let my brain rest. As long as I could remember there had always been another rung on the ladder to climb to, something else to prove, although now I wondered who to. I'd never learned to vacate, to relax.

A singularly American affliction.

Jean-Charles could lose himself in a glass of fine wine and a performance of classical music.

Balance.

I could identify it even if I couldn't attain it.

"We've got to save Romeo."

Miss P, her cheaters perched on the end of her nose, her classic Chanel jacket and Katherine Hepburn slacks looking a bit creased after the long day, looked up from her sheaf of papers. "Maybe he doesn't want or need to be saved."

"And that would make me irrelevant, so I'm not even going to entertain that possibility."

"Oh, honey, you don't need to save everyone to be relevant."

"For now I do, and our young detective has gone Lone Ranger."

"I see." She nodded once to hide a sigh. "And this time you are Tonto."

"I'm his friend."

"One he probably doesn't deserve. None of us do. Have you seen this?" she asked, diving back into the sheaf of papers she clutched.

At least she'd let me step on my own landmines. "I have keen powers of observation, but I'm not clairvoyant."

She raised an eyebrow, nonplussed. "A simple no would suffice."

I opened my mouth to argue I couldn't say yes or no since I

had no idea what "this" was, but I was too tired even to sniff the bait. So I waited. Good things coming to those who wait and all. Yes, to pass the frustration, I played cliché games with myself. I found that was far less risky than saying them out loud for people to scoff at.

"This is a copy of the insurance claim Lipschitz and Godwin have filed with our insurance company."

I snapped my fingers as I held out my hand. Rude, but my veneer thinned under stress.

I scanned through the list—they'd even included pictures. "Somewhere in this list is a clue as to who stole all this stuff. Did they leave anything behind?"

"Interesting question."

"If they did, it won't be in the hotel room. They'll have taken it back to the pawnshop."

"We *are* going undercover, aren't we?" Her voice held a breathy tone.

"No," Jeremy said as he strode into the room. "You are Head of Customer Relations. You do not slide under the radar." He silenced Miss P's argument with a kiss…a really good kiss from the looks of it. If his wavy hair, golden-flecked eyes, strong features, and soft manner didn't turn a female's knees to water, his accent would melt the hardest heart. "You tell her," he said to me, catching me mid-fantasy.

"Tell her what?"

He settled on the couch, his legs stretching for miles in front of him. He pulled Miss P to his lap, but she chose a safer, more dignified position next to him. "Never mind. You're the leader of the foolhardy and fearless. You'd be no help."

"Was that a compliment or a cut?" I raised my hand and closed my eyes for a moment to refocus. Enough fun and games. "Romeo has a problem. I can't tell you what exactly, but I need you to follow someone, let me know who he meets with, where he goes, where he takes a piss or buys drugs. You know the drill."

"Stalking, spying, and not being discovered. I'm your guy."

"You don't know how happy that makes me feel," Miss P deadpanned.

"Nobody'll mess with you, love." He patted her knee.

A hint of humor passed between us. In Vegas, everybody messed with everyone else, especially in a hotel. If Jeremy preferred to ignore that obvious nugget, I'd leave him safe in his delusion.

Pretending made life less scary. Great love came with great risk. Yin and yang dogged my every move.

I knew it, but that didn't mean I had to like it.

"This tail will be different than most."

"How so?" I'd managed to wrest Jeremy's attention away from his bride.

"He has serious training in how to spot a tail. One misstep and he'll…" Frankly, I didn't know what Detective Reynolds would do. I loathed him as a human, so I ascribed all sorts of moral corruption and criminal leaning to him, but I had no proof one way or the other. "Well, you be careful."

"Who's the bloke?"

"Romeo's former partner, Detective Reynolds."

Jeremy's smile grew wider. "You want me to follow a cop?" He sounded like he'd salivate if it wouldn't be undignified.

"It's Metro, so I wouldn't ascribe a high level of competence to the detective. From what I've seen, the department has done its best, surprisingly enough, to limit the damage Reynolds can do."

"Typical. Give him enough rope, then wait for him to drop the noose over his own neck and then step through the trap door."

"Hopefully, Reynolds has done just that."

"You have any more than that?"

"No. I don't want to influence your perspective. Just give me the facts, and I'll figure out the importance."

"Can I roll Dane into this? It takes more than one to run an effective tail, especially on a pro."

"Sure." Paxton Dane, a long tall drink of Texas moonshine with a rattlesnake's bite. We'd had a troubled history, one I still hadn't put to bed. Never one to be cowed by an unfortunate analogy, I forged ahead. "But, first, can you have someone check at the airport and tell me what time the Ponders' plane landed the night of the murder? It's a Citation, I think. Don't have the tail number." Even though Romeo said he checked, I needed confirmation of what he found.

"Not public info. I may have to wait for my contact to come on duty. I'm not sure."

"Dane's been to the McCarran tower with me before. I'm sure he remembers my contact there. If not, have him call me." Lost in thought, I reached for the phone as it rang, without checking the caller ID. "O'Toole."

"Lucky?" Mona. My mother.

Her tone immediately killed any forward momentum. I slammed my feet to the floor and leaned forward. "What's wrong?"

"It's Bethany. She's gone. Wouldn't listen when I told her to wait for you or call Romeo. Said something crazy about not trusting him."

"Not trust Romeo? Why the hell not?"

"She's seventeen. Who knows what she's thinking or why?"

Good point, but the fact that Romeo was making friends and fans far and wide didn't help my *joie de vivre*. "Have you tried her cell?"

"She left it here. Said I could track her."

Okay, what started out as a bit of Mona drama now turned serious. "Any idea where she was headed?"

"She's looking for a gun."

"Of course she is. I guess chasing boys like any normal seventeen-year-old would be too much to ask."

"You're not helping."

"Bear with me here. I won't be any good to you if my head explodes."

Her sigh barreled through the line. I could picture the foot-stomp that usually accompanied it. "A rifle, I bet?" It dawned on me the better question was not what happened to the rifle, but how it got into War Vegas in the first place. Curiously, Romeo hadn't voiced his concern.

"Why did the kid have to go off chasing a killer?"

"It runs in the family."

"It wasn't a question."

"Lucky, even *I* know questions begin with why."

Rhetorical would not be a concept she would understand, or at least admit to understanding. "So this is *my* fault?" I didn't even take a breath. "I'm sure you're right, Mother." I'd pushed the lid off, but I had no intention of leaping into the dark void, even though my mother seemed curiously divorced from the pitfalls of running after folks who don't want to be caught and who are armed with weapons. Perhaps Mona never truly understood the maternal thing.

Was that sort of personality disorder hereditary?

I shook away the excuse to run. "Did Bethany say anything about War Vegas?"

"What's that?" My mother: an endless stream of disappointments, curiosities, and viable justifications for homicide.

"Where Bethany works?"

Mona didn't miss a beat, proving once again that being a narcissist, or at least mildly psycho, had its upside. "Oh, no, not there." She breathed into a pause.

I waited. The other shoe could kill me, but at least I was alive while waiting for it to drop. Finally, my lack of patience won. "You going to give me a hint?"

"Somewhere downtown, that's all I know. You'll find her before anything bad happens?"

"Of course." I didn't promise something bad wouldn't happen

to her *after* I found her. Frankly, this family had more than its share of hardheaded women.

Downtown.

If she was meeting someone in particular, all bets were off—she could be anywhere, in any one of countless thousands of hotel rooms. She was young and exuberant, but surely, she wouldn't be that stupid?

Wishful thinking aside, all bets were off. Science had proven the judgment centers of the brain weren't fully functional until age twenty-five, which was optimistic in most cases by my way of thinking. But if she was that damn dumb, she'd self-select herself right out of the gene pool eventually and there wasn't a damn thing I could do about it.

Have I mentioned how much I hate being out of control?

I abandoned the totally stupid course of action and focused on two of the lesser insanities—okay, three. I dismissed meeting someone in plain sight. Even in Vegas, carrying a rifle around attracted attention, whether the gun was real or only designed to look lethal. So back to the two possibilities: a gun store or a pawnshop.

Pawnshop. A bit of coincidence hard to ignore.

Miss P waited, her pen once again poised over the pad. I hung up the phone as I thought through the plan. "Check all the gun stores downtown; there aren't more than one or two. See if they're open now and, if so, for how long."

"Be right back." She launched from her perch on the edge of the chair and disappeared into the front office.

"Bethany gone wandering?" Jeremy gave me a little smirk.

"Not you, too? This is so not my fault."

"She follows you around with dogged affection and adulation."

"Your point is noted." I let my fear trickle into the silence while Jeremy made notes on the list of names I'd given him. A couple of times he asked for clarification—a distraction I was grateful for.

Miss P returned before I had time to work myself into too much of a lather. "Gun shops all closed." She glanced at Jeremy.

An easy to read glance that told me, in the interest of her family harmony, we should keep our upcoming escapades under wraps. For all his forward thinking, Jeremy could be stifling when it came to protecting his wife—one of those ties that bind, then choke the life out of you. My perspective, of course. Miss P seemed to be able to handle what I knew I could not.

Jeremy levered himself out of the chair. "I'm off then." He gave us both the eye. "You're not going to do anything stupid, are you?"

Miss P and I both shook our heads, but like kids caught in a lie, we studiously avoided looking at each other.

He rolled his eyes. "Don't even bother." His smile vanished when he speared me with a look. "Bring her back in one piece."

"I promise."

Miss P grabbed a lingering kiss, then we both watched him go and waited until the outer door shut. Miss P made sure he'd actually gone through it and wasn't lingering out of sight but within earshot. "We're good to go." She sounded like a kid on Halloween ready to make a killing in the trick-or-treating business.

With more experience, I didn't share her enthusiasm. I needed a vacation. Even with all its potential pitfalls and emotional landmines, Paris sounded curiously appealing.

"Okay, put in the food and beverage order for Bungalow 7, grab your secret decoder ring and ray gun, and we're off."

CHAPTER TWELVE

"YOU DO have the list, right?" I asked Miss P, who sat next to me lost in a *Starsky and Hutch* fantasy that included an attitude and an itch for blood. This whole "field operative" idea of hers was getting out of control. She'd morphed into a loose cannon in designer duds.

We were gliding along in the Ferrari, halfway to downtown, and I'd just thought of the list. Somehow, it had slipped through the steel trap. Of course, a wayward teenager wandering the dark streets alone looking for a gun had me a bit distracted.

"You mean that bit of fiction Tweedle-Dum and Tweedle-Dee slapped on us?" Totally into character, she'd even roughed up her tone a bit.

I wanted to laugh but she'd probably shoot me. Good thing she wasn't packing or this could get dicey with her fixation on this whole role-playing thing. Why did we all seem to want to be somebody else, even when we had life knocked? She mimicked my moves, my tone; hell, she was even starting to use my vernacular, which she'd always found a bit base for her liking.

If I'd wanted a mini-me, I would've bought one.

What I wanted was a drink, in the worst way. To be honest, I wasn't sure I could face reality without my vision obscured by the gossamer cloth of slight inebriation. And right now, I was as sober as a judge on Monday. "Yes, the insurance claim."

"I have it."

"Thank you." How many balls had I dropped recently? I tried to avoid the answer and the obvious conclusion. "Do you think anyone else is in the killer's sights here?"

"If there's someone who knows his or her identity, maybe. But for now, I'd bet the killer thinks they solved their problems and got away with it. So, they're laying low."

"Until we rattle their cage."

"Would you stop being me?"

"It's a bucket-list item. A real fantasy."

Determined to live down to her expectations for herself, she smoothed her pants and adjusted her pearls as if heading to high tea. "You need a new fantasy." Guess I wasn't the only one.

Two blocks from Stanley's pawnshop, I wheeled to the curb and killed the engine. The car alone would announce our arrival, or, at the very least attract the wrong kind of attention. I hoped to be a bit more if not stealthy, then circumspect.

I keyed Vivienne—along with looking for Fox, she was watching Bungalow 7. "Any movement?"

"A couple of girls went in. Nobody has left."

I almost hung up—girls were a penny a dozen in Vegas, blending into the expectations enough to go unnoticed. "Can you take a still of the women and text it to me?"

"Already did. On its way."

Everybody exhibited the competence I felt slipping away. "Awesome. Thank you." I sat for a moment waiting for the ding. One glance. Yep, our panty pushers. "The plot thickens."

Miss P rewarded me with a smile as I showed her the photo. "The girls in the elevator?"

As I said, everyone was passing me down the stretch. "A connection, but I haven't a clue what it means," I grumbled.

"If I'm Watson, that's my line."

"This is not fiction; this is real. You're not Watson; I'm not Sherlock." As I said it, I remembered Sherlock had some sort of an addiction problem that kept cropping up at inopportune moments. The parallel wasn't a comfortable one. "Let's go." I opened my door and levered myself out, then looked at her across the roof of the car. "We're not trying to catch a killer. Remember that. We're just looking for information. If things get wonky, run. You got that?"

"Sure." The word adults used in place of "whatever."

I felt *so* much better. "I mean it."

Miss P joined me at the front of the car. "What's our plan?" She handed me a copy of the insurance claim. Thankfully, although fully valued, it was short.

"You take the first seven items, I'll take the rest. Memorize them and let's see if any are at the shop. I'll take the lead."

The night had turned cold—not a surprise in the high desert in January. The sun could warm the days, but when it dropped behind the Spring Mountains to the west, the temperatures plummeted. And the ground, with only limited hours of weak sun, didn't hold any heat. I pulled my sweater tighter around me—one day I'd opt for a cute bomber jacket or something. With his impeccable taste, Teddie had been in charge of my wardrobe. The wardrobe that had vanished in the fire. Now, I was a new me with no Teddie to make sure at least my fashion choices wouldn't make the year's worst dressed list.

Yeah, every facet of my life was circling the drain, and I felt powerless to stop it.

The neon sign over the shop was larger than the storefront—appearance over substance. Appropriate for a pawnshop. And Vegas. Growing up around games of all types, I should like them. I didn't. But I was good at them.

Some sort of cosmic joke, for sure. I thought we found our

passions by doing what we were good at and then getting addicted to the adulation. Silly me.

When I pulled open the door, a bell pealed somewhere in the back. The place smelled like desperation. To be honest, the pawn thing had always bothered me. Taking advantage of those on the ropes didn't strike me as a Golden Rule construct. But then, lately, everyone seemed to be abandoning such archaic virtues in droves. I tried not to think about it.

Despite our recent run, tonight luck had swung our way. Nobody else was shopping for a deal tonight, at least, not here. We had the playing field to ourselves.

Behind the farthest counter, a man stepped through a door hidden behind a gun case of rifles lined up like soldiers at attention. None of them had orange circling the barrel, which made me frown. But the man who stepped into the light turned that frown upside down, in a masochistic sort of way.

"Well, if it isn't Frenchie Nixon."

Frenchie sported a painful thinness and an air of quiet terror, like the guys selling their own plasma to get by. His hair was still stringy and unwashed. The tats looked the same, too, at least as much as I could make out peeking from under his sleeves which were a couple inches too short. Gone was the open, approachable manner I remembered. Now, he wore a facsimile of his sister, Gracie's, closed, wary look. Gracie owned a pawnshop out on the Boulder Highway where Frenchie cut his teeth in the business working his way up to becoming one of the least skilled ten-finger guys around town. He'd done some time after I'd caught him pilfering from one of the Big Boss's downtown properties, but none of that stuff had ended up in Gracie's shop. No, he'd kept it all in several storage units. Televisions, radios, towels, you name it, but he kept it all. Said he stole it just to see if he could.

At the sound of my voice, he backed against the wall. If he'd been a dog, he would've rolled over on his back. I have that effect on folks I've fired. "Have you seen a young woman around here tonight? Seventeen, long hair, alone?"

Behind the roll-over-and-play-nice game, Frenchie's wheels were turning, weighing the odds, analyzing the angles, determining which one might yield the best outcome. That was the only way to get the truth out of him—make it impossible for him not to play. Long ago, we'd established who was the Alpha, so he didn't take long to make up his mind. "Looked like she needed a few good meals?"

"Yeah." I kept my interest hidden. If he knew Bethany was important, that would change our bargaining positions a bit, and I didn't feel like breaking any bones tonight, not really, and certainly not Frenchie's. He'd be way too easy. "What'd she want?"

He angled his head. A hint of shrewdness peeked through the give-up. "What's she to you?"

"A pain in the ass. Promised a friend I'd ask, that's all." I traced a finger down the edge on the glass case, pretending to be interested.

He licked his lips. "She was looking for a rifle."

"Damn kids. What is it these days? Everyone thinks a bullet is a good way to solve a minor skirmish."

"Overkill," he deadpanned.

I resisted a smile, but beside me Miss P giggled. I elbowed her in the ribs.

"Did you have what she was looking for?"

"She combed through them all but didn't find even one that appealed to her cultivated tastes. Now, I'm going to have to wipe them down. Don't want no fingerprints."

"Always a good plan." Anticipating Miss P's retaliatory elbow, I braced for it. "She left?"

"I told her to scram. She had jailbait written all over her." He rubbed his cheek. "Got a slap for my efforts."

A slap. That sounded personal. My anger uncoiled, a snake

sensing prey. "Guess you didn't have what she was looking for." Way to go, Bethany. Not smart, but feisty.

And that would get her in trouble.

His bloodshot stare settled on me for a moment. Something feral and angry lived there. Big dreams, no power or ability to achieve them—that would make anyone angry.

What do they tell you to do when you meet a bear in the forest? Make yourself big? I pulled my shoulders back and stretched to my full height—a height Frenchie Nixon had only dreamed of. I had him by several inches, thirty pounds, and a whole lot of pissed-off.

He didn't back down.

Was he pretending, or was I?

I made an exaggerated glance around the shop. "A step down for you. Your sister finally wise up and boot your ass out the door?"

"No, you're the only one who canned my ass." Simple words. The emotion they rode on, not so much.

"You stole several hundred grand worth of electronics." Logic never trumped emotion, but it was one of the windmills I couldn't resist tilting.

A bit nonplussed, he crossed his arms. "Rules. Sometimes you just gotta see if you can break them and get away with it."

I totally got that. In fact, it was becoming a bit too strong a theme in my life at the moment. But, I was so not going to bond with the likes of Frenchie Nixon over a shared authority issue. James Bond, maybe, but not Frenchie Nixon. Not ever Frenchie Nixon.

With one arm, I made a sweeping gesture, taking in the stained and flaking linoleum, the paint so old it held shadows of previous items that had hung in the sun. The dusty inventory held little value—electronics so old they probably were sneaking up on being collectibles, some abandoned jewelry dotting the cases, guitars with broken strings, playing cards, and other things of no discernable value unless a rare painting lurked underneath a velvet Elvis. Pawnshops always seemed like businesses hanging on the savvy and smarts of their owners. If that was true, and I suspected it was, this place didn't stand a chance.

Nobody was tending the store and, by the looks of things, they hadn't in a long while.

"How'd you end up in this lovely establishment?"

"My sister and the owners here are tight. I'm on loan to get their operation running smooth." He kept the counter between us as if it would deter me should I become violent. I was a bit insulted—some puny little glass case would never stop me.

If I had more time, I'd love to get him to expound on his definition of "smooth." Even as wise as I was to most of the tricks, I bet he could teach me a few.

Miss P leaned in and whispered, "We'd like his help."

"There are many ways to elicit help," I reminded her. Intimidation was my go-to.

Her frown told me what she thought of that. "Okay, we'll try it your way." I turned up the corners of my mouth. My smile wasn't totally devoid of feeling, assuming homicide was a feeling. "Frenchie, I'm looking for a gift for my father. His birthday's coming up and I'd like to get him something special."

"You're a rich gal. I'm sure you can buy him anything he wants."

"Maybe. But I'm looking for something unique, original. Something I couldn't get at a gallery or a department store."

"Like?"

Even selling to a willing customer was beyond Frenchie's scope. The last time I'd seen him, he'd scored some decades-old dynamite that was ready to explode. Perhaps my expectations—hell, *any* expectations—might be too high. "The Marauders coming to town has everybody going crazy over football. Got any memorabilia or something that might be one-of-a-kind?"

"Got some new stuff in tonight. Stanley doesn't even know we got it yet. It's fine and one of a kind. Value's gonna skyrocket what with all the local interest in the NFL and all."

I elbowed Miss P in the ribs, making sure a grunt covered the gasp I knew she wouldn't be able to hide. "Sounds like just the ticket. My father's a fan. I'd like to see what you have."

As expected, Frenchie started his backpedaling. The guy never did anything without a negotiation. "Thing is, with all the stuff in the safe, I'm not supposed to touch it unless Stanley's here."

"I'll give you an extra twenty percent to pocket if you show me what you've got."

He licked his lips, parched by the flames of greed, no doubt. "I gave him my word."

Which, with a nickel wouldn't buy a piece of penny candy. For once, I actually managed to keep my thoughts to myself. "The line's out the door at the Pawn Star's place. I'll take my business there." I guided Miss P toward the door.

"You won't find stuff like this at that *Hollywood* store." He didn't even try to shade that with contempt, only longing. Even Frenchie Nixon wanted his fifteen minutes.

I let my pace slow slightly. "So you say, but I haven't seen it."

"Thirty." He breathed the word, infusing it with the hope that he'd lived to pocket the profit. Living at the edge—that's what Frenchie Nixon liked. And, given his relatively limited repertoire, this was as close to the edge as he got.

I stopped and turned back around. "What?"

"Thirty." His voice was stronger now, riding on a conviction that the risks were worth it. "Thirty off the top and you've got a deal. And you owe me."

"Thirty flat. And only if it's worth it." No way would I mortgage my soul to Frenchie Nixon, well, not if I didn't have to. And, since this was my first push back, I knew he'd cave. "And I'd say it'd take you three lifetimes to get close to even with me."

He flashed the grin of a guy who knew his place and merchandise, then disappeared into the back.

I gave Miss P a self-satisfied smirk.

Could Frenchie be our thief? Was he that smart? Maybe he was smart enough to know how to hide behind playing dumb? My pea brain acknowledged the possibility but resisted it out of hand. I'd been wrong before—once, maybe twice—but not quite at this magnitude. To think Frenchie Nixon bested all of us and the FBI defied possibility.

No, if he was our thief, he had to have had help.

Miss P peeled off to pretend to be fascinated with the meager offerings in one of the cases on the right wall. A guitar hanging on the far wall caught my eye—an old Gibson. Teddie had one a lot like it. Not sure what had happened to it, but it had disappeared. I presumed it had perished in the fire along with the me I used to be, or at least her wardrobe.

He might like a replacement.

I stepped on that thought. Even I was becoming disgusted with me. Why couldn't I let go? Pathetic. The road to self-loathing: hang on to someone who rejected you.

Just as I was starting into serious self-flagellation, Frenchie backed through the door. He held a large black velvet tray, which he maneuvered as if it held the crown jewels and a tumble would dent a centuries-old, priceless tiara. With one forearm, he swiped the top of the counter clean then presented the tray for my amazement. From the look on his face and the larceny in his eyes, not drooling was a huge victory, although he did dab at the corner of his mouth with a knuckle.

One look at the tray and I understood why. "Whoa!" Diamond-encrusted gold covered the thinning velvet from corner to corner, edge to edge. "Where'd you get this stuff?"

"I'm not at liberty to say."

"You got them tonight?" I glanced up and held him with a serious gaze.

"Yeah." His eyes slipped from mine. "Courier was above reproach."

Above reproach. While I'd entrust the fortune spread in front of me to a few of those closest to me, I wouldn't characterize anyone as above reproach. I'd love to ask who Frenchic considered as occupying that lofty perch, but that would be the one tick that told him the cards I held.

I poked at the rings—yes, they were mostly rings, Super Bowl rings, each worth a fortune even when divorced from who owned it. And when attached to the previous owner, the value would skyrocket. Some of the rings had tags, many had inscriptions presumably identifying the owner, but I couldn't read the fine print.

"These aren't hot, are they?"

"Depends on your definition."

I narrowed my eyes, hoping for clairvoyance. "Did you steal these?" I motioned Miss P over, so she could compare the stash against her mental list. While my memory was a sieve, I was pretty sure that I was looking at a large portion, if not all, of the missing jewelry. But Stanley and Godwin couldn't be that stupid, could they? Hide the loot virtually in plain sight? Hell of a risk.

"Technically, no." He pressed a blue-veined hand to his chest. "Since our last run-in, I've taken the high road as you said."

The high road, my ass! Scared straight was more like it. Our last run-in, as he called it, involved enough old dynamite to level several square blocks. I pretended like he'd earned the benefit of the doubt. "Good to know. So where do you get this stuff?"

"Beats me. Stanley and Godwin show up with most of it, except like tonight, when they use a courier. I don't ask no questions. Figure if I don't know, it can't hurt me, right?"

"All depends," I said, staying on the sidelines on that one. Normally, I couldn't resist cannonballing into the moral quicksand. Maybe I'd changed. More likely I was tired and running out of time. A glance at my phone. I needed to wrap this up, but I had no idea how to do that. Even my platinum AmEx wouldn't cover a down payment. And they'd probably get a bit testy over the whole stolen goods thing. "Godwin and Lipschitz are feasting in my hotel as we speak, so who showed up with the goods tonight?"

Frenchie backed up until the wall stopped him.

"Tell me."

As he opened his mouth, the door behind me burst open. "Everybody down!"

CHAPTER THIRTEEN

THAT VOICE sounded familiar. Miss P and Frenchie hit the floor as I slowly turned, my hands held in front of me, waist high, palms out. "Seriously?"

Marion Whiteside, brandishing a pistol pointed at my chest, stopped when he recognized me. "Shit, what are you doing here?"

"Same thing as you, I suspect—looking for stuff that doesn't belong."

He lowered the gun slightly.

Now I'd only lose a knee should his finger tighten. I side-stepped a tad. "What are you thinking, barging in here with a gun? How long did O.J. spend at the invitation of the state for a similar escapade?"

The gun lowered even more. When a man got a good mad on, every logic circuit shorted out. Women weren't immune, but it took us longer to drive the long road to insanity.

"The two losers who run this joint, they cornered me at the party spouting some bullshit about I had a debt to pay. Debt? Shit! What I was paying was usury." He clammed up, biting down on words threatening to expose a secret.

One step too far and he'd given me an opening.

"And now your things are gone?"

"Yeah, stolen last night."

Oh, I saw a connection coming. "Let me guess, from Bungalow 7?"

His sheepish look was all the answer I needed. "The stellar owners of this fine establishment offered you the bungalow as part of your payment for headlining the signing last night."

Now he looked ashamed.

"Why were you pushing Boudreaux about your stuff at Babel? Is this what you were talking about?"

"Caught Boudreaux lurking around in front of my room. Made me suspicious. Sure enough, somebody had lifted my stuff. I figured he was a good place to start."

"Was this when you left the signing and were supposed to go straight to the party?" Brandy had said something about making a detour through the Bungalows.

"Why didn't you report the items as stolen?"

"When you got a secret to hide, your options are limited." A bit of Marion's anger took the hangdog out of his posture.

"So, you decided felony armed robbery, which is a serious offense by the way, was a good option? Must be some secret."

He stared over my shoulder at Frenchie—a ruse to avoid looking at me, I'd wager. But he had Frenchie shaking out of a most-likely-stolen pair of Air Jordan 4 Retros that retailed for 1,600 bucks or so. I could only imagine the street price.

"What were you in debt to those two idiots for?"

"Look, man, don't ask me that. They were just the muscle." He extended the pistol to me butt first. "Stupid idea. Glad you were here."

The muscle? Marion bulged in all the beach-muscle places. They must have something really big on him.

I tugged Miss P to her feet beside me. Somewhere behind me, Frenchie didn't make a sound. "Watch him," I said out of the side of my mouth to my right-hand man as I handed her the pistol.

"Shoot him if you have to, but don't let him move, much less touch those rings."

A smile twitched as she took the gun. "As you wish." In my absence, when Jeremy was on a case, she'd taken to watching old movies with Teddie. Now, she quoted them. The guy was getting on my last nerve.

I turned my frustration and a hint of badass on Marion. "So, have you gone all stupid or something? You want to tarnish a stellar career and reputation with one idiotic vigilante gambit?"

He squirmed under my dressing-down. "Man, you know what football does to you?"

"I think I have an idea. It lures you with promises of fame and wealth, and you might get both, but at a physical cost that can be devastating."

"When you're a young stud, you think you're invincible. A few concussions, a broken leg, one ACL and an MCL on the other knee, along with the normal beating." He winced. Even he knew it was an explanation, and not an excuse.

"What keeps the pain tolerable?"

"I started on Hydrocodone."

"And when that stopped working, you moved to higher and higher doses, then stronger and stronger drugs?"

"Go figure, I'm one of the goddamn opioid epidemic. Ain't that rare. I didn't know what the hell those drugs were—still not all that clear on it. Football was my way out—out of the hood, away from the drugs and stuff." A low rumbling chuckle vibrated through him, punctuating the irony. "But, I can hold onto some pride. I don't do the drugs to get a high. I use them to live."

"And watch all you worked for go down the drain. Once they have you over a barrel, they bleed you dry." A story that played out so many times it had become almost trite—until you witnessed the carnage up close. "Most of the guys hock their jewelry to pay for the drugs?"

"Yeah, but I'm not sure how it works. The stuff never shows up in the places you'd expect. It just disappears." He ran a hand over his close-cropped hair as if pressing it into place.

Habits. Hard to break.

"They can have my stuff. That's our deal. But I was holding stuff that wasn't part of the deal for fellas who didn't get the high-rent digs."

Usually, at least in Vegas, the pawnshops paid a small percentage of the value to the owners, and then, after a bit of time, they sell it on the open market. Super Bowl rings bring high-dollar prices and media attention. And this didn't sound like the usual deal, not if what Marion said was true.

"What's the deal?"

"They get the goods; I get the drugs." He shrugged. "They said they wanted it to look like a theft."

"But you didn't report the goods as being stolen?"

"No, that wouldn't be fair, would it? I got compensated, so to speak."

Godwin and Lipschitz weren't hobbled by the same morals. "When did you start using?"

"High school."

My voice went deadly. "Who gave drugs to kids?"

He looked at me with a mixture of pity and incredulity. "You don't watch much news, do you?"

"Please, I work 24/7 in Fantasy Land."

"That sounds nice."

"It has its moments. But, seriously, high school?"

"Most big careers are made or broken in high school and maybe the first year or two of college. But you get hurt, then you can't play through the pain, or you need some meds to mask a concussion or something. Man, some of these kids come from lower than nothing—their talent is their ticket out."

"Which leads to bad decisions."

"The coaches juice them up, knowing what they have riding on it. You get shunted off to a second-tier college, and getting to the

NFL gets that much harder. The coaches aren't stupid—they know the raw talent when they see it."

"Keeping the studs playing doesn't hurt the coaches' careers either." Thinking about Lake, I wasn't sure the same held true for him.

"No, but I'd like to think they started out with a more philanthropic approach."

"Like a misguided Florence Nightingale? I got news for you—your Fantasy World is even more removed from reality than mine."

I wanted to trot out the what-about-getting-an-education lecture, but for the ones with physical gifts, professional sports offered the lure of potential millions. The only other option with that kind of payout was dealing drugs—similar riches, similar physical Russian roulette. I'd not made that connection before. Talk about a cost-benefit conundrum. An education, even a professional one, offered much less unless you had a penchant for graft or an incredible skill with AI.

So many things were wrong with this picture, but, as long as the money was there, the kids would keep sacrificing themselves on that altar and we'd end up here with former greats of the game hocking their wealth to be able to function without screaming in pain…if their brains hadn't turned to Swiss cheese.

Marion's gaze drifted to the tray of sparklies behind me.

"Take a look. Let me know if you see anything that belongs to you or your friends."

Frenchie had plastered himself against the back wall. His shirt stuck to him; his face had paled.

Marion fingered through the rings, stopping to pick one up and hold it to the light occasionally. "Man, I know all these guys."

"Any of those rings stolen?" I asked as I looked over his shoulder.

"No way of knowing without asking, not that any would come clean."

An interesting choice of words, but I'd dive down that rat hole later—once we solved the current problem. As it was, my list of problems was full to overflowing, not that that was unusual or anything. "Any of yours there?"

"Yeah." He pointed to several items. "These are mine."

"Is that all of them?"

"No. MVP ring is missing, but other than that, my stuff is all here."

Miss P let the gun sag a tad.

"But not the rest?"

"No."

"Keep the gun pointed at his heart." Miss P jumped at my bark, then did what I said. "We've got some connections but no answers. If Frenchie so much as blinks, perforate him, but let him live. And let me think."

I eyed Frenchie. Habits. Hard to break.

"Give me the gun," I said to Miss P. When she handed it over, Frenchie looked like he was ready to faint—he knew I'd use the thing, and without much provocation. "Check the back," I said to Miss P. "In his zeal to show us the goods, I bet Frenchie left the safe open."

He pulled in a deep breath, confirming my suspicion.

Miss P didn't take long. When she pushed through the door she held a bag high. "Bingo."

Maybe this *was* turning into the stupid criminal night I was hoping for.

"You can't look at that. It's not supposed to be here. They'll shoot me for sure." Frenchie's knees buckled slightly as he reached for the bookcase next to him to steady himself.

"Then why are they here?" With my thumb, I slowly racked the slide, cocking the hammer and chambering a round. Even though I'd already done that, the sound of a round being chambered, the unspent one arcing away, sure raised the dramatic tension. If Frenchie Nixon thought I was bluffing, at least now he knew I had the ability to follow through. "You lifted the stuff even though Lipschitz and Godwin gave you specific instructions to take only what belonged to Mr. Whiteside. Then you brought it here. Am I right?" Frenchie had a habit of hiding stolen goods on other people's property. Our last encounter involved a stash of dynamite on the top of my hotel, no less. He was lucky I let him live. Right now, I was rethinking that choice.

"The courier was supposed to stash the extra stuff for me." His eyes widened when he realized the trap had slapped closed on him.

Like I said, habits. Zebras and their stripes and all of that. "The courier?"

"Detective Reynolds." Frenchie found a smirk. "Always nice to have a cop working for you, isn't it?"

A veiled reference to Romeo I ignored. The fact that Reynolds was the bagman didn't surprise me at all. "Marion, you do the honors."

Marion poured out the contents of the bag onto a tray Miss P had found under the counter. One look and his shoulders bunched.

"All of it there?" I stopped him as he reached toward an exceptionally gaudy bit of gold and precious stones. "Don't touch it. Let's see whose fingerprints show up."

His finger paused over each item as he worked through a mental checklist. "Yep, it's all here."

He pulled his hand back reluctantly as if he was thinking about sweeping up his property in one swipe and making a run for it.

Running from bad decisions and difficult future ones—I was the poster child. "You got this. There is a solution."

"Not a good one."

"Yes, a good one," I corrected. "But perhaps not an easy one." Preaching to the choir who didn't want to sing the song. Was I trying to convince him or me? "Is this all of it?" I asked again to be sure.

"All this was in the safe in my bungalow and the door was locked." Relief eased the hunch in his shoulders and they relaxed. "You got a problem."

"Indeed. I'm just glad it's not a four-million-dollar problem. When I'm done, there won't be enough left of Godwin, Lipschitz, and their inept cat burglar to scrape off the sidewalk." Before I did, I needed to find who helped them. Reynolds would show up. But someone on our staff had to help with the lock on the door, maybe even the safe, although, given enough time, Frenchie could probably have handled that.

"What does inept mean?" Frenchie asked.

Marion answered for me. "Look it up. Next to the word you'll find your mug shot."

"What code did you use on the safe, if you don't mind me asking?" I asked Marion.

"My jersey number, twice." He'd made it easy. Most people did.

"Even you could figure that one out, Frenchie." I felt a smile bloom as I steadied my aim at his heart.

He lifted his chin in an ill-conceived hint of defiance. "You're not going to shoot me."

"Depends. I'm having a really bad night on top of an abysmal day."

"Headache?" Frenchie gave me a leer.

Terrific.

Bad news traveled fast in the city. Especially when I'd managed to take myself out of the game, thereby providing a window of opportunity. Bad, and I felt a twinge of guilt, but not that much. Life had taught me being a fallible human was far easier than pretending perfection.

"You don't want to piss me off, Nixon."

"I second that." Squash Trenton strode through the door. He shouldered in next to me and took in the situation with one glance. "You buying or selling?" he asked me.

Jesus, was somebody handing out invitations? "Oh, no, no. You go away. The last thing I need right now is some attorney to go all by-the-book on me."

"Never been accused of that before." Squash tried the camaraderie route first. "Glad I'm in time."

"Bet you've never been in quite this situation where a client or two are concerned. And don't try to play me—I'm wise to your game and immune to your charms." Okay, that last part was completely untrue. The lawyer was smart and far too clever for my own good. On a good day, I felt confident pitting my skills against his. Today was not a good day. "And, need I remind you, we work for opposite sides at the moment."

"A matter of opinion."

If I read his tone right, he was leading me down a path, so I circled back. "In time? In time for what?"

He lifted his chin toward all the bling. "This the stuff Lipschitz and Godwin filed the insurance claim for?"

"Yep."

"Cool." Not the answer I expected from their attorney.

I gestured to the bling with the gun. "I have your new clients stone-cold." I pointed to the second tray. "We found all of this in their safe, which Mr. Nixon here was kind enough to open for us."

"With a bit of encouragement." Squash lifted his chin, gesturing toward the pistol. "So, Frenchie, time to come clean."

"He already said he lifted the stuff. Godwin and Lipschitz told him what and where. Like I said, your clients are toast."

"Lots of legal hoops to jump through before we throw Stanley and Godwin on the rack." Squash sounded like the lawyer he purported to be.

"Well, you play by one set of rules."

"I am licensed by the state. And the Grievance Committee takes a dim view of legal vigilantism. While I can push the limits, I can't exceed them."

An interesting gambit, but I wasn't ready to throw my lot in with the lawyer. "What are you doing here, by the way?"

"When I saw all that food and high-end booze you had delivered to their bungalow, I knew you'd either caught on or had a strong hunch. I followed to make sure no one caused you any trouble and you got what you came for."

You could fool some of them, some of the time. "That obvious, huh? And your clients?"

"Busy as you intended. And they're not my clients."

Everybody had an angle, and I lie, not that I'd expected straight shooting from the hired gun. "You represented yourself as their counsel."

"Technically accurate at the time, and self-serving. But, since then, we've quibbled over compensation, so I have withdrawn my representation."

"Do they teach you guys how to talk out of the side of your mouths in law school?"

"A third-year elective."

"Which I'm sure you aced."

"They're no real grades in law school."

"*That* explains a lot."

"And you're no criminal despite how this looks." Squash loved letting folks assume an answer to their question. I gave him grudging respect for his aptitude—a worthy opponent and a fickle ally.

"Observation and obfuscation, another third-year elective?"

"No, those I learned from you."

The guy could really dish it. In my diminished state, I was finding it hard to keep pace. "Flattery will get you what you deserve." A veiled warning I had no intention of delivering on, but bluffing I could do.

"I can handle it."

He tossed me the ball, expecting me to run with it, but I hadn't a move left.

Marion saved me. "Flirting with her and she's holding a gun. You're either one brave dude or an idiot."

"Guilty on both counts." With no apparent effort, Squash shifted to handling us both.

I regained my verbal footing. "You lied before, Trenton." Frankly, expecting a lawyer to resist the call of the game was beyond even my level of delusion, but I wanted to believe him—I wanted to believe *somebody*. "How do I know you're telling the truth?"

"I'm here, aren't I?"

"Pretty weak for a professional liar, Counselor. But, I don't have the stomach to put you on the rack and stretch the truth out of you." I chose to cut him some slack, or at least reserve judgment. I could be accommodating—especially when holding a gun, looking for answers, and running out of time. I turned my attention to the klepto. "Frenchie?"

He jumped and then wilted under everyone's attention.

A moment to let him sweat, then I dove in. "Your bosses are going to be pissed. Storing it in their safe puts them in the bullseye." He shook his head so vigorously I thought his eyeballs would fall out. Even the guilty couldn't resist professing their ignorance. I raised the gun a tad higher and he stopped. "With your already lengthy record, your upside doesn't look too good."

Frenchie turned to the lawyer, pleading his case. "Seriously, Mr. Trenton, are you going to let her scare me like that?"

This would be where I'd know which team Squash Trenton played for, other than his own.

He shook his head, milking it. "Looking bad, Frenchie. I'd play ball with Ms. O'Toole if I were you."

Okay, a good sign, but he could still be using me to get information he wanted for his own purposes.

Frenchie wrapped himself in a hug. Too short to begin with, his sleeves hiked to show a sleeve of tattoos from his wrist and disappearing underneath the threadbare cloth. One was new, or at least looked it.

I didn't make a habit of remembering tattoos—they just

confused me. Since I spent my life vacillating on everything, the concept of permanent ink kept me awake nights...well, permanence of any kind had me counting sheep. "Want to tell me how you got past the door lock?"

With his back already against the wall, he had nowhere to run. Frenchie looked among all of us. The look on his face made me feel practically clairvoyant—he was weighing the chances of running.

I didn't bother to add my two cents. Curing stupid wasn't in my vast repertoire of unparalleled skills.

"Okay," he deflated under the weight of give-up. None of us in the room actually thought he had an upside, just a different angle of sliding into the abyss, leading to either a soft landing or a splat. Either way, he was going down, whether he deserved it or not. And this would be a third strike. I really didn't like that result—he was a menace and an irritation when he plied his trade in my backyard, but, in the whole horror of the Universe, he was a bit player.

He'd spent his time in local and county facilities. But as a habitual offender, Frenchie Nixon would be eaten alive in the Big House.

I leaned into Squash and whispered, "You're going to do something, right?"

He took a deep breath. "Sure. But you might consider using that marker you have from the DA." Daniel Lovato, our District Attorney, owed me big time. Everybody knew it; they just didn't know why, which was a good thing.

Frenchie Nixon wasn't exactly who I'd been holding onto that marker for. "I'll see how this plays out."

"Time's getting short, Nixon," I prodded.

"You gonna help me?" Finally, Frenchie was looking with a clear eye at his predicament. Or at least he knew he needed to deal to get the help he would need to save his ass. The jury was out as to whether he needed me and my penchant for playing outside the lines, or whether he needed Squash to navigate the system.

I wanted to assure but not over promise—such a fine line. Leaving him hanging, though, wasn't something I could live with. I think he knew that. "You do your part; I'll do mine."

He took me at my word. "I stole the stuff as we established." He made it sound like it had been his idea to come clean. "Stanley told me where it would be and then gave me the cover while I got it."

"Boudreaux?"

"Yeah. Jesus, when I heard him jawing with Mr. Whiteside here," warming to his story, he lifted his chin toward Marion, "I about stroked out. Had to dive out the back."

"How is Boudreaux mixed up in all this?"

"Man, they don't trust me with that kind of info." Frenchie scratched at an itch on his left hand, drawing blood.

"Yeah, I know. If you knew, they'd have to kill you."

Frenchie jerked as the concept hit home. Murder was so far removed from his normal petty, and now not so petty, theft.

I didn't blame him for being twitchy. This whole thing had me wishing for a new life and a new identity, in a place far from Vegas. "And the door lock? Did he also give you a key?"

"A key?" Frenchie scoffed. "You've got those electronic locks. Everybody who's got a lick of sense can bypass those. Hell, the how-to is all over the Internet. And for a couple of bucks, you can buy all you need."

"All the locks at the Babylon had been changed to cure that defect."

"Not that one. They told me it'd been changed back to the old stuff."

And that opened a whole new Pandora's Box. "You got in, so it must have been."

No matter how much I wanted to deny it, this reeked of an inside job. My staff was like family—a betrayal would cut deeply. "How did they know the lock would be one of the old ones?"

"Somebody in Security told them."

Security? What had Jerry not been overseeing? Or better question, who? "Okay, then what? How'd Reynolds get roped in?"

"He's on their payroll. Hangs around here all the time. But he wasn't the one I was supposed to hand off to."

"Really?" I sensed a bit of bravado building in Frenchie Nixon and I didn't like it.

"Your friend, that kid, you know the one? He was supposed to be the bagman."

"Detective Romeo?" I tried to keep my voice steady and my hands distracted. I couldn't tell if he was lying.

"That's the one. You and him are tight, right?" He enjoyed poking me with that goad.

"I know him, yes." I kept any emotion out of my expression and tone.

I raised the gun higher, my finger tightening on the trigger.

His eyes widened.

"He's been playing on the Dark Side. I don't know what game he's got going. He's not a bad dude, not like some of the others, but running with that crowd, the kid is going to get burned."

Well, that was the second thing Frenchie Nixon and I agreed on this evening.

"You do know we're going to have to call the police, right?" My comment was meant for everyone. No one argued. I turned to Miss P. "Get Metro here. And tell them no Reynolds and no Romeo."

I left Miss P with the gun, holding court and making sure Frenchie Nixon didn't so much as blink. Marion backed her up. When I was sure everyone was resigned to his fate, I pulled the lawyer aside.

He let me lead him to the back of the shop. "Why Ms. O'Toole, so forward."

I whirled on him. "Cut the crap, Trenton. Tell me what you're really doing here."

The façade of bullshit disappeared. "I represented Lipschitz and Godwin in an insurance case. I sued the insurance company on their behalf. We won. The company paid. Then it turned out all the goods they claimed had been stolen from them had, in fact, been stolen from the original owners. None of it was this sort of thing, this memorabilia, which would be so easy to trace. But, they've got insurance scams going every which way."

"And your carcass roasting over the coals for filing the suit on false premises. Is the insurance company turning up the heat?"

"What do you think?"

"Well then, Mr. Trenton, it looks like we both have a problem. How do you think they're playing this memorabilia gambit?"

"I can tell you." Frenchie poked his head through the door.

Miss P's voice filtered in through the opening. "Sorry."

"She's not the shooting type." Frenchie shrugged, then slithered his thin frame through the opening. "I'm here cuz I wanna help you."

I hated being played. "Don't think that gives me any warm fuzzies. You want to help me so I'll help you."

"So, it works for everybody. A good deal, right, Mr. Trenton?"

Squash sent me some amused side-eye. "Seems like. Long as you deliver. Do you know how this scam works?"

"Sure. Pretty sweet. The clients approach one of the dealers with some goods to trade in exchange for their supplements, you know."

"Supplements. Cute." I scoffed under my breath, but apparently not low enough to keep from being heard.

Frenchie took that as a compliment, puffing up like a rooster parading his wares for the hens. "The dealers report that to the boss. The boss arranges to have the stuff lifted. The clients report it stolen, which it was. Insurance makes them whole."

"It's not stolen if you are paid for it."

"See my problem," Squash said.

"They did this to you? Wanted you to sue the insurance company to pay up without letting you in on the details?"

"Close enough."

"I'm surprised you let them live."

Squash cocked his head to the side and gave Frenchie Nixon a hard stare. "Once I get my ass out of the crack, all bets are off."

I didn't doubt him for a minute. Frenchie Nixon's Adam's apple bobbed several times as he paled. Looked like he didn't doubt the attorney's resolve either.

"Who's the boss?" I asked Frenchie.

"You think somebody like me is going to be trusted with that kind of information?"

I kept my no to myself.

"Even if I was privy, you know. I wouldn't want to know. They kill folks with that kind of knowledge just to keep them from squealing to cops and pushy hotel types."

"I notice you left attorneys off your list."

"I can talk to them, and it can't go anywhere."

I didn't think this was the time to enlighten Mr. Nixon as to the limitations of his theory. Since Squash didn't step in, I assumed he agreed. "So," I continued, "the *clients* get the drugs from the dealer and the insurance proceeds?"

"Sweet deal, huh?"

More like a felonious deal. "And the dealer has hot goods. What happens then?"

"Sold on the black market. There's tons of folks who just want to own a piece of greatness, you know? They don't care how they come by it."

Yeah. And somewhere out there in this world of two-bit hoods and major players all looking to score, my young cousin was looking for a gun.

I needed to find her before the bad guys got a whiff of her scent.

CHAPTER FOURTEEN

NOBODY HAD heard from Bethany. I'd called everyone I could think of while my not-so-happy little gang waited for Metro to show up.

Of course, Mona had to have been right—Bethany didn't have her phone.

When the cops arrived, I gave my statement, corroborated by all present, and took my leave, but only after threatening Squash with bodily harm if he didn't deliver Miss P safe and sound and intact when all the excitement was over.

Out of ideas, I waited until I knew a black-and-white had been scrambled to pick up Stanley and Godwin. With half a mind to stay and watch them sweat, I fought the urge. I couldn't, not with Bethany unaccounted for and an invitation burning a hole through my imagination. The guest list alone would be worth the price of admission. With his new ankle jewelry, Mr. Ponder wouldn't be there. And, without supervision, Mrs. Ponder would be fun to watch.

Despite my anticipation, I had a feeling Teddie and Jordan were going to enjoy it far more than I.

But I wouldn't enjoy it at all if I couldn't get a bead on Bethany.

Fairly confident she could handle what came her way—she'd already fielded a lot in her few years—I still worried. Somehow, I felt a responsibility that truly wasn't mine, once again proving that if there was an emotional minefield, I could not only find it, but charge right in without a dog to sniff the way through.

Now there was an idea! A dog to ferret out the bombs of life and help you avoid them. But the problems helped you grow. Okay, so a terrible idea—avoiding life was never a good long-term strategy. Sort of like the guy who sold pieces of his life to investors through the Internet. They all got to vote on the life decisions he made. Last I heard, it hadn't worked all that great, despite his initial euphoria at offloading responsibility for his decisions.

Life by committee. Just shoot me now.

Not feeling at all in the party mood, I headed toward the Ferrari. With Squash Trenton in the middle of the melee, I felt pretty confident justice would be served, although perhaps not in the expected way.

The lawyer piqued my interest. A bit of a conundrum, he kept me off balance. I liked that, and yet I didn't. A challenge always intrigued me. Part of that was the juvenile in me—just tell me I can't have it or can't do it and my resolve hardens and my focus pinpoints. The more adult side of me knew that not every challenge needed to be met and not every interesting man was worth the attention, in fact almost none were. But…

Didn't they say keep your friends close and your enemies closer?

A rationale for questionable behavior—and that would be painting it in the best possible light.

If I was my own worst enemy, how exactly did the adage play out? Not sure I could keep myself any closer. Of course, I'd twisted the logic into a worthless tautology, leaving only the kernel of truth it grew from.

Romeo sprang to mind—or really moved to the front as he'd

taken up permanent residency in the worry lobe of my tiny brain and its counterpart in my heart.

My thumb found his speed dial number.

After the twelfth ring, I hung up. Out of ideas, with no destination, I just stood there on the sidewalk, in a not-so-nice part of downtown, after dark.

And I gave up.

I couldn't do it anymore.

Years ago, I'd met a criminal defense attorney at the height of his game. Shortly thereafter he dropped off the face of the earth. Several years later he resurfaced as the manager of an Italian joint in one of the ubiquitous, cookie-cutter strip malls dotting suburbia. His words haunted me still.

You spend too much time with the bad guys and you become one.

But I'd spent my life training to be who I'd become—I wasn't competent to be anyone or anything else. Me, the great hedger of bets, and I hadn't left myself an escape route out of the life I'd let pick me.

All I'd wanted to do was save everybody.

And it dawned on me that some folks didn't want saving. Others didn't deserve it.

Something whizzed by my head. Lost as I was, it didn't register at first.

A voice out of the darkness shouted, "Get down!"

Paralyzed, I didn't move.

A body hit me from behind. The air went out of me as I face-planted on the cement. My nose took the brunt of it. Whoever hit me landed on top, then held me there with his weight.

"Silencer," the body said in a muttered curse.

Another shot ricocheted off the storefront. Then another shattered glass.

"Yep, silenced," I reiterated because that's the one thought I could muster. "Get off." I tried to rise against the man's weight, gaining little ground.

Maneuvering under him, I worked my hands under my shoulder. Gathering strength and some air, I took several deep breaths and only succeeded in making myself madder.

"I said, get off!" With my palms under my shoulders, I levered myself with all the force I could muster.

The body on top of me rolled to the left. He placed a hand on my shoulder. I couldn't make out his face with the light behind him. "Stay here, okay? Get behind something solid."

Jeremy! The accent finally registered on my diminished consciousness.

"Just this once, don't do anything stupid." He pushed off and disappeared into the darkness before I could tell him stupid was all I had left.

I half crab-walked and half crawled to the car, then, with my back against solid metal, took a moment to gather myself. I tasted the metallic tang of blood. With two fingers I pinched down the bridge of my nose, working gingerly toward the tip. Halfway down, it wiggled where it shouldn't. I bit down on a gasp of pain. My hand came away wet—blood. *So this is what a broken nose feels like*. Cosmic payback?

Nothing I could do about that…except deliver some payback of my own.

The shooter was mine.

Like I said, stupid was all I had left.

Reaching up, I popped the door then risked brief illumination by the interior light as I rooted for the Glock I'd started keeping under the driver's seat. Thankfully, the Italians weren't big on bright lights inside fast cars. The gun was where I'd left it, and it felt good in my hand. I didn't have to check the chamber. What's the point of having one if the thing wasn't loaded?

I cocked an ear to the wind, listening. No shots. No shouts.

Jeremy had run south. The pawnshop was north. Using a dark spot between the weak glow of the streetlamps, I crossed the street.

North was my bet.

Frenchie said he was supposed to hand off the goods to a cop.

A cop could connect the dots.

A cop would know where to look.

My give up gone, I fought the urge to hurry. Miss P was back there. Marion and Squash, too.

Frenchie could handle just about anything...unless the shooter intended to shoot him, which didn't raise my blood pressure overmuch. Eventually, we all got what we deserved—or what we couldn't out-run.

Keeping to the shadows, I broke into a lumbering trot as I limped to protect my injured calf. The warm trickle of blood oozed down to my upper lip, then sideways to the corner of my mouth, then down my chin. Nothing I could do about it, so I ignored it.

Up ahead, somebody else had the same idea to use the shadows as cover. I slowed as I watched, keeping pace but not closing, not yet. Hard to tell in the darkness, but I'd say male, not large enough to be Jeremy. And he held one arm down at his side as if he had a gun. He ducked behind a car across from the pawnshop, giving me the opening I needed.

Crouching, I moved between the cars parked along the curb and into the street. Hugging the cars, I kept them between the figure in the shadows and me. Seven cars separated us, and I counted them as I moved as quickly as I could.

From his vantage point, the guy had a clear view through the front glass windows into the shop. Given a modicum of skill, he could pick off anyone he wanted.

That thought alone made me want to kill him.

At the sixth car, my breath coming in short gasps, my legs screaming to straighten, my back joining the chorus, and my calf on fire, I moved back between the cars toward the curb. Afraid to make a noise, I moved slowly, methodically, an inch at a time, fighting myself. *What if he shot through the window? What if he shot*

Miss P? My heart hammered. I held my breath. Seconds turned into eternity.

One more car to go. He was at the other end, between this car and the next, eyeing the pawnshop. The light through the window dimmed the shadows. I felt exposed. Sweat slicked my palm. I adjusted my grip on the gun.

A car rounded the corner up ahead, then gunned in our direction. My heart skipped a beat. I held my breath. I tensed. The car accelerated past.

I eased my breath out in a silent sigh.

The man was close. A matter of feet.

So close I could hear him breathing, smell his sweat.

I could shoot him. But if I missed, the pawnshop was behind him.

I set the Glock on the ground, then I coiled myself and counted to three.

On three, I launched myself around the car and tackled the man still taking cover there. Taken by surprise, he had no time to turn or even raise a hand or gun in defense.

I rode him to ground. He landed with a meaty thud and a groan.

His gun—I'd been right about the gun—skittered under the car.

"Shit." A ragged gasp for air. "Lucky?"

"Romeo?" Now I knew why he hadn't answered his phone—he'd been skulking around in the dark…with a gun. I held him down as relief and homicide coursed through my veins.

"How'd you know it was me?"

"Your perfume. Could you get off me? I can't breathe." He expelled his last bit of breath with the last word.

"I don't wear perfume." Sympathy eluded me. I didn't give voice to any of my worst fears. I let him up but stayed behind the cover of the car after retrieving my gun. I wasn't willing to even admit the possibility that Romeo could've been shooting at me, so there had to be another shooter out there. Another shooter with a silencer.

"Female. Large. Pissed. And with a limp. You sorta stand out."

"Don't hold any punches, okay?" A bum calf, a broken nose, and now a bruised ego. "You knew I was back there?"

"You got skills, but skulking isn't one of them."

I could live with that. "What the fuck are you doing out here?"

Romeo joined me crouched behind the car. He kept an eye on the pawnshop. Inside the shop, Marion sat on a Honda 250, dwarfing it. The detective who had grilled me now had Frenchie in the bright light. Frenchie hadn't moved—he remained rooted to the same spot behind the counter. Uniforms swarmed the place.

I couldn't see Miss P.

"Who's the cop?"

"Somebody new, on loan from Reno."

On loan. That meant something internal was going down at Metro.

"Friend or foe?"

Romeo took a moment as if weighing dice before throwing them down the table. "Depends on how smart he is."

Didn't everything? Nothing like having your life in somebody else's hands and hoping to hell the guy was smart enough to figure the score. Not as unusual as it should be.

While we watched, I felt under the car for Romeo's gun. My hand touched metal. "Since when do you use a silencer?" I retrieved it and handed it to him.

He stuffed it in his coat pocket. "Since I started trying to beat them at their own game."

I shook my head. A dangerous game. "You don't need me to tell you how stupid an idea *that* is."

"I think you just did."

"No, that was my pitch to join the team, your team."

"Well, I appreciate the noble gesture and all, but I haven't a clue what game we're playing." His sigh held a hint of desperation and a resignation that wouldn't be helpful and could prove deadly.

"Buck up, Grasshopper. We'll figure this out. We always do." I hazarded another glance over the hood of the car. Still no Miss P anywhere in the shop, at least, not that I could see through the front window. "Were you shooting at me?"

"Of course. Anybody else would've hit you standing there like the wide side of a barn."

"I think I'm insulted."

"I wasn't the only one out here with a gun. I wanted to make sure you hit the concrete. Lots of people would love to take a crack at you."

"Now I feel honored."

"You are the weirdest person I know."

"Flattery, so beneath you. If you have a plan, now would be a good time to tell me. I have a party to go to." I glanced at my phone. Plenty of time—if I didn't dawdle too much. Just in case we got hung up, I took a moment to text Teddie.

You got us all costumes?

I held my breath for the answer.

Got them. It's going to take a while to talk you into yours, so leave me a window, okay?

He wouldn't…oh, but he would. Even though unsure of my transgression, I knew, somehow he'd make me pay.

"You're going to the party?" Romeo sounded like he didn't believe me, but he knew better. "What, and miss all this?"

"The guest list will be most interesting. You said so yourself."

"Need a date?"

"A cop would dampen the frivolity."

He let out a long sigh. Even though I couldn't see him very well, hidden as we were in the shadows, I knew he was shaking his head, his face scrunched into his best disgruntled look. "Why I wanted to be a cop." Romeo sighed into the night—a sigh full of subtext. I didn't even know that was possible. "I should be you."

"Me? Well, *that* would come with all sorts of complications."

"I'm adaptable."

"Funny, I never pegged you as a switch-hitter."

"What?" The kid wasn't following. Of course, he was concerned about life, and, apparently sex, or making a joke about it, was foremost in my pea brain.

So helpful. I'd left him somewhere near his own goal line. "Never mind." I leaned my head back to rest against the metal.

"Is that blood all over you?" Romeo switched from banter to concern.

"When you started shooting at me, Jeremy tackled me. My nose took the brunt of it."

"Jeremy's gonna have hell to pay." Romeo sounded like he wanted a ticket to the face-off.

"Can't blame a dog for being a dog. He was just doing what any guy on testosterone overload would do."

Romeo angled a better look at me in the light.

"What?"

"Just making sure you're really you. You don't sound like you."

"A loaded statement full of wiggle room. So, what are you doing here?"

"I could ask you the same question," he deflected, buying time.

"I was following some stolen goods and Bethany, on a suicide mission looking for a gun. She ran away from Mona who is not pleased."

"Bethany. That kid has a strong streak of you in her."

"That's what worries me."

"Nothing to worry about—she's smart enough not to cross the lines you leap over. I saw her get in a cab about fifteen minutes ago."

I thought I'd faint as relief opened a flood of blood from my brain. "Where'd you see her?"

"Being escorted out of one of the pawnshops a couple of blocks over. She'd given the guy one hell of a time."

"Any idea where she was headed?"

"I heard her tell the driver to take her to the Babylon."

By my calculations, fifteen minutes should be enough to get her home. If the driver knew the back roads, she should be in the bosom of her family once again. As if on cue, my phone vibrated—I'd turned it to silent. Mona. Since I knew the news and didn't have time for the drama, I declined the call.

"Is there anything more irritating than a teenager who thinks she knows everything and wants to rub everyone's nose in it?" Romeo sounded like he'd had experience.

"Oh, a few things." Young, wet-behind-the-ears detectives going all Lone Ranger and playing a dangerous game ranked a bit higher than stupid teenagers, but with no upside, I didn't push it. "Did you see if Bethany had a rifle?"

"She's seventeen!"

"And this is Utopia where we all live on love and happiness and play by the rules." Frankly, that sounded like Hell—I'd have no purpose, no reason to get out of bed in the morning. "Some things are not self-evident, Romeo. By definition, law-abiding citizens do not break the law. That leaves the rest of us, Bethany included, who will bend all the rules to see the good guys win. So, I showed you mine, now your turn."

"No gun."

"What brought you out to this fine neighborhood after dark? Are you looking for the rifle as well?"

"No." Romeo sounded like he wished it all was that simple. "I was following Reynolds."

"Did Jeremy come with you?" Romeo popped the magazine from the handle of his pistol, then added enough rounds to bring it up to maximum.

"No." With everyone doubting Romeo, I didn't tell him I had Jeremy following Reynolds. Instantly, I felt horror at my waffling on Romeo's virtue. But I didn't tell him. "You said you shot at me. Did Reynolds also take aim my direction?"

"Yep. Stupid fuck. He should know that does nothing more than piss you off."

"Damn straight. I get first dibs." A panicked giggle burbled up so fast a little leaked out before I clamped a hand over my mouth, smothering the rest.

"Oh no. Reynolds is mine."

The way Romeo said it left no doubt he'd save me the trouble of killing Reynolds. Of course, that meant I'd probably have to save them both, which ran me smack into that whole some-folks-didn't-deserve-saving thing. If Romeo couldn't save his own bacon, I'd step in. But, as to Reynolds, I'd be more interested in turning up the heat.

"You let him shoot at me?"

"He'd already gotten off the two rounds. I saw Jeremy land on you, so I figured you were enjoying the ride."

"Thanks for that ringing endorsement of my stellar character."

"Hey, if I remember my Bible studies class correctly, coveting is the only thing expressly off limits. But, you were okay. Reynolds took off. So, I chased him."

"An interesting interpretation of one of the Ten Commandments. Since when did your principles become so malleable?"

"Not being so restricted just evens the playing field. Survival of the Fittest is the only rule the bad guys play by."

"That's not a rule; that's a theory. Brains over brawn, Grasshopper."

"Do you have an unlimited supply of those things?"

"A bottomless pit. Seriously, without principles, we become who we're fighting."

While not exactly brushing me off, the young detective didn't exactly embrace my theory either.

"Where'd Reynolds go?"

"He hopped a ride in a Babylon limo."

Before I could process that, my phone vibrated once again for my attention. This time it wasn't Mona. "Trenton?"

"O'Toole! Shit. Don't you answer your phone?"

"I've been busy being shot at. It's on vibrate anyway." If he'd called, I hadn't felt them. A quick check. Yep. He'd called twice. Shit. "Where's the fire?"

"That ass Reynolds bolted in here, grabbed Miss P, and ran."

Fuck. Not only had he taken a hostage, he'd taken her in one of my limos. If I found Reynolds first, Romeo would be denied his wish.

~

BEING A VEGAS RAT HAD ITS ADVANTAGES. WORKING THROUGH THE maze of side roads, back roads, and alleys, pushing the car and my skills, I pulled in the rear entrance to the Babylon's parking garage in record time. Brandy had confirmed only one limo was out and Paolo was driving it. I'd called him several times, redialing the minute each call rolled to voicemail.

He hadn't answered.

Somehow, I managed to avoid the picket lines in front of the hotel. I bypassed the line of cars snaking its way up the driveway. Throwing my proletariat leanings out the window, I wheeled into my reserved space, which I rarely used. Something about parking a Ferrari in a gold-level space right by the door reeked of an entitlement I found repugnant. But, tonight, I shelved my delicate sensibilities in favor of expediency—Romeo wasn't the only one slipping from black and white to gray when it was expedient.

By design, the back entrance routed everyone directly into the casino. We wouldn't want to deprive folks of the opportunity to deposit some money in various machines on their way to dinner or a club. The longer we kept them gaming, the better we were at our job.

Most people thought mischief was our main industry. Not so. Our focus was actually separating fools from their money. But, according to the marketing gurus, putting it that way would be a hard sell. Instead, we sold sex and silliness and an escape from the mundane—an incendiary mixture that kept them flocking to Vegas where most couldn't resist the Siren call of a chance at hitting it big.

Some days, I found being in a "sin" industry hard to justify. The argument that I wasn't responsible for my guests' bad choices only went so far. The rescue gene ran strong in me; but, once again, not everyone deserved to be rescued, even some who did remained out of reach.

Every now and again, the ugly underbelly of my town messed with my magic.

Tonight was one of those nights.

Reynolds had Miss P!

Despite knowing I'd attract attention and perhaps incite a riot, I ran, a lumbering, limping juggernaut hell-bent on doing damage to Reynolds.

People filled the casino. Most of the stools in front of the slots were occupied, and players two-deep ringed the most popular table games. Other tables that catered to a special clientele still sat idle. Even though we knew the economics, changing out the games and the tables required a run through the Gaming Commission that rivaled the FDA drug approval gauntlet. Often the payoff didn't justify the price.

Few paid attention as I flew past. One man called out. "Lady, is that blood? Do you need help?" I waved him away and kept running.

Nobody else seemed to have heard him.

Excesses barely turned a head in Vegas, I guess.

The music, barely audible above the excitement, had an upbeat tempo to keep the energy high. Young women and men, barely clad, wove through the throng with free beverages of choice.

Alcohol as a loss-leader.

Everywhere else that was frowned upon. In Vegas, it passed as a great business plan.

I hit the door to the stairs so hard it bounced off the wall and I had to hit it again. Two stairs with the good leg, one with the bad. Repeat several times. My breath sandpapered my throat until it was raw. The hallway was clear.

With my hand on the knob to my office and still puffing from the climb up one friggin' flight of stairs, I worked to find some courage. Brandy would be waiting, and, for once, I didn't have the answers she'd want. I couldn't save Romeo. I could try, and I'd give it my all, but the final decisions rested with him.

For the first time ever I felt useless.

Totally on empty in every way, I couldn't face her now—her fear, her recriminations that she wouldn't mean but would voice in her powerlessness. But that was my job.

Ready to handle what hit me, I pulled open the door.

She jumped when I burst through the door. Her face pale, her eyes big, she held the receiver to her ear. When she saw me, she extended it to me. "Jeremy."

I grabbed the thing. "Please tell me you know where Reynolds is."

"I was following him," Jeremy said.

"And?"

"I lost him."

"Shit. He has your wife in the back of a Babylon limo."

"How?" One word with razor sharpness to cut deep.

"Trenton said he burst into the pawnshop. And I would hazard a bet that because your wife fancies herself some kind of vigilante and because I'm losing my grip, she didn't resist and is now a pawn in this game rather than a player."

Jeremy muttered a few expletives, some of which I caught and some of which I deserved. In large part, this was my fault. Playing fast and loose with my own life was one thing.

"This one's on you, Lucky. You took her there; you invited her into a world she knows almost nothing about."

Guilty on all charges.

I started to cop to a plea, but Jeremy had hung up.

Brandy stared at me. My office shouted silent recriminations. No laughter. No love. All gone. "What happened to you?" she whispered.

"What?"

"Your nose. All that blood."

I felt the caked blood and some still viscous on my face, then looked down to see it splattered across the front of my sweater set. "It's been a night."

"Romeo?" This whisper was choked.

"He's fine." I tossed the words off, a bit more harshly than I'd intended.

"He didn't come with you?" She acted as if that was a huge transgression on my part.

"We both had cars." I squeezed her hand and gave her a tight smile. "It's okay." I had no idea if it was or it wasn't, but I lied for both of us.

Then I tried Paolo one more time.

This time, he answered. "Paolo" was all he said. He didn't use my name, and his voice sounded tighter than a high-c wire.

I was amazed Reynolds had let him answer this time. "Paolo, don't say anything. Just listen and say yes or no to my questions, okay?"

"Yes."

I planned the path I wanted to lead him down. This was my one shot to save Miss P. "Are you *en route* to the Babylon?"

"Yes."

"Is Miss P with you?"

"Yes."

I let out a breath I hadn't been aware I was holding. "And a detective with the police department?"

"Yes."

"Detective Reynolds?"

No answer.

"You don't know?"

"No."

"Are you to go to the front of the hotel?"

"I think so."

"Do as you've been told. I'll be waiting." I killed that call then called Romeo.

"Yo."

"Yo?"

"I'm feeling like you sound."

"Guilty yet hopeful? Good. How soon can you get to the entrance to the Kasbah?"

"I'm half a block away. Been circling. Didn't know where else to go."

I filled him in, then I disconnected and called Jeremy, hoping he wasn't mad enough to ignore my call.

"Any news?"

I should've known worry would trump anger. That would come later. "Miss P is in the back of the Babylon limo. Detective Reynolds is with her. I'm not sure which team he's playing for if you get my drift. I'm taking the front. Romeo is taking the Kasbah. Can you take the garage entrance?"

"Two minutes."

With the men in place, I headed toward the only other entrance at the front of the hotel. The valet shack hid in a copse of large imported trees on the other side of the six-lane driveway from the front of the hotel. From somewhere cool and rainy, the trees were having their troubles adjusting to the temps in Vegas, but right now the cooler days of January seemed to bring them out. Judging by the foliage, the trees thought it was spring. Being perpetually a bit off and misreading all the signals myself, I felt empathy and an odd connection.

Thankful for the shelter, I hunkered in the shack amid the trees. No one would see me there, but from that particular vantage point, I had an unobstructed view of the traffic climbing the circular drive toward the hotel.

With the sun long gone and the glare of headlights, I had to wait until the cars passed underneath the first of the lights at the foot of the drive before I could see them clearly. The valets, running with the night's business, didn't even give me a second glance as if it was normal for me to be skulking in the dark. As the seconds ticked by, the windows started to fog—one hot body shut inside on a cool evening turning to cold night. With the sleeve of my sweater pulled over my palm and grasped firmly, I swiped my forearm across the window, clearing the fog temporarily, and I tried not to breathe.

The parade of cars never thinned. Lambos, Porsches, Mercedes, and the ubiquitous Land Rovers, dotted among the cabs and Lyfts and Ubers.

But no limo.

According to my phone, nine minutes had passed. They should have been here by now. And I hadn't heard from Jeremy or Romeo. In case my calculations had been off, I gave it two more minutes, then abandoned my post and scurried inside, hiding in the crowd exiting their cars and moving toward the entrance.

Halfway across the lobby, stymied as to whether to run to the garage or the entrance to the Kasbah—the limo had to go to one of those entrances since it didn't roll up to the front—I paused under the glass hummingbirds and butterflies taking wing high above. Barely a day went by that I didn't want to join them in their flight to somewhere else.

Right now, I wished someone would call me and tell me something.

I didn't have to wait long. Just as I was dreaming of where I would fly to, my phone jarred me out of it. "Tell me." I didn't even pause to look at the caller ID.

"Lucky?" Miss P's voice, breathless and worried.

My knees went weak. "Where are you?"

"The Kasbah entrance."

"Thank God you're safe."

"I'm fine, but you need to come quickly. Reynolds took off. I think Romeo is going to kill him if he catches him. Jeremy just got here. He's gone after both of them. If you don't get here quick..." She let a whole list of horribles hang in the silence.

CHAPTER FIFTEEN

As I raced through the lobby, over one of the bridges that crossed our little stream, I startled a momma duck and her brood. The momma splashed into the water, squawking her displeasure, while the babies peeped in fear. A little girl who had been watching them gave me the stink-eye. If she wanted a piece of me today, she'd have to get in the back of a long line.

As I hit the casino, I spied Temperance, my MMA fighter moonlighting as a security guard. "Come with me." An order she couldn't refuse.

"Jesus, you look like hell," she said as she fell into a sprint on my heels.

Adrenaline muted the pain in my calf. I ran with only a slight hitch. "Mad as hell, too."

We pounded past startled gamblers and dodged revelers just getting the party started—I barely saw them as I put my head down and ran. The guard at the entrance to the Kasbah rose to stop us as we rounded the corner and headed toward him. When he saw it was me with security in tow, he stepped out of our way. I thought about yelling at him to call more security, but that might involve Fox—I had no idea where he was or what game he played

—which only muddied the waters and increased the odds I might kill someone before the dust settled, so I flew past without a word.

The entrance was on the far side of the cluster of bungalows in the middle. Technically, we could wind our way through, but the fastest route was around one side. I chose the left—no reason other than I thought it might be the road less traveled.

Miss P paced the curb when Temperance and I skidded to a stop in front of her. "Thank God."

"How did you…?"

"He let me go, then took off when he saw Romeo. But you need to hurry. They went that way." She pointed through the entrance into the dark.

The gate was closing.

"You wait here," I said to them both.

Both objected, but they were too late. In five strides, maybe less, I slipped sideways out the gated entrance, which was within three feet of closing, then stopped in the alleyway.

As with most hidden entrances to hidden treasures, this one was unmarked and down a long, dark alley far from the lights of the Strip and the front of the hotel. One light illuminated the gate to serve as a deterrent to anyone intent on stopping one of our guests to relieve them of their personal goods. We'd doubled-down with a guard with a gun just to the left of the gate.

With hands on my knees and gasping for breath, I managed to ask, "Which way did they go?"

The guard pointed down the alley, away from the lights.

Of course, they went that way.

"Your gun."

"You look like you've found enough trouble already. Why don't you walk it off?"

"Give it to me, or I'll take it from you. How'd you like to explain being shot with your own gun to the guys around the water cooler?"

He couldn't get it out of his holster fast enough. With guards like him, security became a wish rather than a promise. "If you shoot anybody, I'm screwed."

"That would make two of us." I chambered a round, thumbed off the safety, and ran.

My footfalls echoed off the buildings to either side—tall walls of concrete. Graffiti decorated the lower half of most of the walls —swirls of color I could only half-see and mostly imagine in the dim light reflected off the cloud deck above. The light was just enough to keep me running down the alley and not veering off into a wall or a dumpster. Every now and then, I'd splash through some standing water—not ideal for my new Ferragamos.

Romeo would pay. Reynolds would pay.

Creatures scurried in the dark to either side—rats or worse. But they'd have to run fast to catch me, so I pushed them out of my thoughts and focused ahead. A mile stretched between each of the major intersecting streets on the Strip. Whose bright idea was that? Sucking wind, my throat raw, my legs burning, I willed myself on. Up ahead, I could see the lights and passing traffic of Desert Inn. Giving the men more sense than they regularly exhibited, I doubted they would dart into traffic. As I approached the cross street, I slowed. The walls on either side gave way to fenced employee parking lots, then the maze of small buildings underneath the D.I. flyover hurling traffic over the Strip.

Romeo, Reynolds, and Jeremy could be anywhere. Man, I'd invited them to this party and none of them chose to return the favor.

At the end of the alley, with too many choices in front of me, I stopped. Where was Dorothy's scarecrow when I needed directions to the Emerald City?

A shot rang out to my right. Okay, not exactly a straw man, but I'd take it.

Drawing a deep breath, I once again willed my legs to run.

Romeo's gun had a silencer. Jeremy could be armed or not—he

ran hot and cold that way depending on the job. With too few brain cells left to process that, I parked it, trusting all would be made clear.

Keeping my ears open, my head on a swivel, I trotted now, and my legs and lungs thanked me. Running full tilt-into a firestorm wasn't on my list of acceptable evening activities—even if Romeo was up to his ass in badness.

The pounding of the blood in my ears told me my adrenaline levels still spiked, yet my calf started to burn. With the end of my sweater sleeve over one palm and caught with my fingers, I rubbed my face, careful not to bump my nose. Without a mirror, I felt sure I was making the whole thing worse, but I couldn't help it.

The rabbit warren under Desert Inn always gave me the creeps at night. Dark, with the stench of too much alcohol and too little hope, this was one of the places the bright, shiny dreams brought to Vegas went to die.

Another shot in front of me. This one closer. I pressed myself against the wall to my right, listening. My heart pounded; blood whooshed through my ears.

Not helping.

I willed my body to silence and, for once, it complied.

Craning my neck, I hazarded a peek around the corner. Thirty feet, no more, a man moved from shadow to shadow. A long coat hid his form. I slithered around the edge of the building and followed.

One weak bulb cast a tight shadow around a doorway—the painted sign long since faded to illegible. The man skirted the light, but I could see just enough to make out his outline. The coat looked like Romeo's. The man was thin, angular, perhaps a bit taller, but it was hard to tell. Romeo or Reynolds? His walk gave him away—he shuffled rather than walked on his toes.

Reynolds. But it was hard to tell in the darkness.

Left to my own devices, I'd just point and shoot—sort of like sailing past asking for permission to simply ask for forgiveness later. But in this case, forgiveness would probably involve incarceration, so I needed to make sure it'd be worth it.

Reynolds.

I knew I'd shoot him someday, or I'd break his nose then choke the life out of him. But I could wait. Like buying a car, the anticipation would be way better than the fulfillment.

Keeping a decent distance, but ready to shoot should the need arise, I followed the man using the deeper darkness of the shadows. The fact that I accepted this as normal, just a part of my usual day, should have me worried. Or, at least, I thought it should. I knew other people's lives were a bit more mundane and usually didn't involve the regular use of firearms, or so the media would have me believe.

But, these days, that wasn't entirely true.

There was something wrong, very wrong, at the heart of our country. An anger that seethed and sometimes exploded. And while it was my problem to help solve, it wasn't what was driving my current situation.

Maybe Reynolds was angry; most likely he was—folks with the least talent often expected the greatest rewards. Misplaced arrogance of epic proportions—not unusual, but always distasteful. One thing I did know: Reynolds was going about it the wrong way.

Bad guys posing as protectors offended me on every level.

As quickly as I could without drawing attention, I closed the distance, but it took time, dodging from shadow to shadow, pausing when Reynolds did so he didn't hear me behind him.

Games. I hated games—even of the cat-and-mouse variety.

Twenty feet. Stop. Don't breathe. Breathe. Fifteen feet. Stop. Don't breathe.

At ten feet, I was timing my leap when Reynolds pounced on someone I hadn't seen hiding in the shadows.

The two men fell to the ground. Rolling. Fighting.

I stayed hidden, waiting, biding my time.

As they tumbled and rolled, I strained to see. Which one was Reynolds? Who was the other guy?

I squinted. Moving in the dark, I worked for a better view.

Tangled together, the men stopped rolling. One had gained an advantage, pinning the other with his weight.

He raised a fist, bringing it down hard.

It landed.

The man on the bottom went limp.

The guy on top pushed himself off and staggered to his feet. Reaching down with both hands, he fisted fabric and pulled the dazed man up against him.

Together, they staggered into the light and I could see.

With an arm around his throat, Reynolds held Romeo against him. Two bodies glued together by desperation.

I'd waited too long.

Life, nothing but a timing issue, and mine sucked.

Romeo's knees were weak; his body sagged, but his legs held his weight.

Reynolds didn't seem surprised to see me when I stepped out of the shadows.

"I'll let you have the kid here, but I walk." Reynolds's gun hovered, ready to shoot either me or Romeo.

Where was Jeremy?

While I didn't think he would bring me an advantage as Reynolds held the trump card, I still wished for the moral support. Holding the pistol at the ready, I eased around to see better, moving imperceptibly closer. The kid's eyes stopped rolling around in his head, a bit more light returning.

"What makes you think I want the kid?" I asked Reynolds.

"Right. He's like your own personal butt boy." He thought I was bluffing.

"You're crass but consistent, Reynolds." With a steady hand

and a cold heart that surprised me, I raised my gun. My heart tripped along at a lazy pace. My vision telescoped.

"Lucky, if you turn me in, I'm toast," Romeo said. "Let him walk. We'll get him next time."

I closed one eye, my arms straight in front of me, the gun steady.

"Are you bloomin' crazy?" Jeremy's voice—the voice of reason—sounded so brittle it would crack with a slight blow. Better late than never, he lurked somewhere behind me.

"Crazy?" A slow, growing grin spread across my face. I doubted anyone could see it, which didn't matter. The grin was for me. "You have to ask?"

My finger tightened. The gun jerked in my hand. The sound of the shot echoed off the buildings surrounding us, reverberating as if I'd shot a fish in a barrel after crawling in after him.

Reynolds yelped and fell to the side. He clutched his foot in both hands. Pain pulled his face into a grimace. He clenched his teeth, fighting it, which saved me from hearing his true opinion of my Annie Oakley skills and probably my heritage and character as well.

Romeo staggered. Without shifting my aim, I leaped to grab his arm and steady him.

Jeremy rushed to contain Reynolds as I kept the gun trained on him.

Romeo pulled himself together. "You turn Reynolds in, he'll take me down, too."

"Not even a thank you? Kid, you really are getting on my one last nerve."

"Dead would be preferable to prison. Do I need to remind you that I'm a cop?"

"No, but clearly, you need to remind yourself." I lifted my chin toward Reynolds, who was still dancing around holding his foot. "He's got answers we need."

Sometimes, by our own actions, we become collateral damage

or caught in the trap, or whatever cliché worked. Romeo had stepped in it, and it was my luck that I was the one to deliver the *coup de grâce.*

Lucky me.

"So, you were the one that put the brass onto me?" Romeo hid his emotion in a flat tone.

"The brass? What're you talking about?"

"Somebody put the Chief onto me. He knows just enough to want me on a water-board."

Now it was my turn to be hurt. Seriously? *Me?* "I don't have any idea what you're talking about. I don't know jack."

"Everyone says that. It's like the first sure sign of guilt."

Somewhere in this conversation I didn't understand lurked an insult. "Says what?"

"They pretend not to know what the cop is asking. But you know enough."

I gave him a look from under my eyebrows. "Pretend?" As I drug the word out, anger whittled my voice to a sharp edge.

"Look, the Chief knew all of it—the stuff we talked about in the bar. I didn't share that with anybody but you. You're the only one who could've squealed."

"Squealed?" That one word, a register lower, held homicide and hurt.

He spread his arms, and his expression closed. "When there's no other possibility..." His conclusion screamed in the silence.

I swept my free arm toward Reynolds. "There's another possibility."

"Seriously? He's in way deeper than me. He couldn't have known that stuff anyway."

I couldn't argue with the logic, only the fallacy of his assumption. But, to be honest, I couldn't come up with anyone else who would have ratted him out, so I shut my mouth. Somehow, the truth would rear its ugly little head; it had to.

Jeremy pulled Reynolds to his feet—a red stain grew as

blood leaked out of his shoe. He gave me an appreciative nod, sort of a professional acknowledgment. "Nice shot. Impressive, actually."

Most days I'd preen at an attaboy like that. Not today. Used to people taking pot-shots at my character, I was surprised that Romeo's hurt more than I expected. Was he mad at himself and deflecting his anger onto me, or did he really think I'd sell out my partner?

"The shot went through my pant leg." Romeo bent down and stuck a finger through the hole. "Tiny margin of error."

"Just lucky, I guess," I said, not that I would've minded shooting him.

Tapped out, I turned toward home. Family, as toxic as they were, held some comfort—they couldn't turn me away. Okay, not much, but it was something, and right now I'd take anything that might make me feel human.

Romeo had given me an impossible choice. I'd had to turn Reynolds in. We needed answers and we needed them now. Hell, Romeo himself had confirmed that Reynolds was up to his ass in something that had gotten a state senator killed. Somewhere in all of that, there was a line between accomplice and bystander that I didn't intend to cross. Knowing what I knew, would letting Reynolds walk cross that line? Since I didn't know the difference between what I knew and what I could prove, I couldn't answer that.

I'd leave that to the cops.

I'd waited until the cops had rounded everyone up, and I watched them go. Too late, I realized I had no car, only foot power, which, while unpleasant, wasn't a bad thing. I took the time to gather myself.

My thoughts had settled a bit, and the walk had soothed the

sting of my frayed emotions and Romeo's betrayal when I strode back to the back gate, stopping in front of the guard.

"Felt weird being without my piece," he said, apropos of nothing.

If he was trying for a guilt trip, he'd have to try a lot harder. "Yes, since this gate is regularly stormed by the marauding hordes, I'm sure you felt horribly under armed." I handed him the gun, barrel first, but pointed it at the ground. I never saw the wisdom of handing a gun to someone butt first so all they had to do was grab it and squeeze. Even an accident could result in a nasty gut-shot. That would actually be an improvement over the rest of my evening up to now, but I couldn't take the time. "I didn't kill anybody, although the night's still young." Of course, I'd perforated a cop's foot, but, with no time to call the EMTs should the guard stroke out, I left that tidbit out.

It took him several tries to secure the thing in his holster. "At least it won't be with my gun."

As I watched him, my blood pressure spiked, and I thought the jury was still out on that. "Let me back in. I have a family firing squad to face."

As he opened the gate, he plucked a crumpled box of smokes from his breast pocket and shook one out. "Might as well face them with style. You got the bruised and bloodied part already."

I took the cigarette with a smile and a nod, then he let me back into my carefully controlled little bit of fantasy-land.

Miss P wrung her hands as she wore a trench in the sidewalk, pacing back and forth in front of the entrance to the Kasbah. I saw her before she saw me. "Jeremy's fine. No one died, but Reynolds took a bullet to a foot."

"Who shot him?"

"I did." I gave her a quick and dirty as I escorted her through the large bronze doors, then around to the hall leading to the casino. The Kasbah was quiet. Someone had removed the yellow crime scene tape that had draped the front of Bungalow 7, returning it to stately glory. It dawned on me that the bit of titillating tawdriness provided by the CSIs wasn't all bad—being close to a bit of criminality amped the chatter and the excitement.

We both fell silent as we entered the casino. Worried and scared, I thought the revelry sounded a sour note. Miss P seemed to feel the same as she crossed her arms and lowered her head, plowing through the crowd.

Lost in thought, I let her lead. To be honest, I was tired of being the one everyone looked to, the one everyone counted on to fix everything. Yes, I was pathological in my need to help, so it stood to reason. Then it dawned on me: fixing everyone's screw-ups only perpetuated the behavior. They didn't learn from their mistakes—and they kept making the same ones over and over. Case in point—Mona.

Next chance I got, I vowed to abdicate the throne of Chief Problem Solver.

I needed a life.

But, one more major ass to save and then kick across Clark County.

Romeo. The kid was sending signals so mixed even a CIA decoder couldn't make sense of it.

What did he want me to do?

No doubt, Reynolds would barter the kid's complicity in exchange for his own escape. My job was to see that Romeo didn't take the fall. Trouble was, I had no idea how. Or how the kid would work against my best efforts. It's like he had an incarceration wish. If he hated his job, this was not the best way to change careers. I mean seriously, making license plates had gone the way of the buggy whip. Wouldn't it be nice if you really could knock some sense into young males? That would save all of us a world of hurt.

Miss P and I stopped in the middle of the lobby under the soaring birds with joy and excitement whirling around us. I didn't feel any of it as I sought my safe place in business-mode. "Vivienne's on her own in Security."

Miss P looked at me with wide eyes and a blank stare. "What happened to your nose?"

"Your husband broke it."

She reeled back. "What?"

"Not on purpose. He was being noble; don't worry. Why did Reynolds bring you here?"

"He didn't explain. In fact, he didn't say much, just that I'd be all right."

"I see." My standard response when the opposite was true. "Anyway, find Temperance or someone else you trust to back her up. We need to figure out who's doing what to whom and quickly." I started for the elevator then turned back. "Oh, and call the Sheriff. Ask him…never mind. Perhaps it's best if I talk to him myself. The Sheriff loves to play cowboy. I need info on Reynolds and Romeo and exactly who is pointing at whom and what they are backing it up with, and hopefully where they got the info. As the head cop in town, I expect the Sheriff to give me his best John Wayne little-lady routine. I need some ammo to blow a hole in his bullshit before I get in the ring with him."

And I knew exactly who to ask.

"I know that look," Miss P said.

I didn't ask, but I suspected I looked a bit like a death-row resident waiting for a call from the Governor. "Sometimes, high people love to roll around in low places."

"Mona." She shook her head as if to say, "You know better." I knew better; I just didn't have better. "This is going to cost you."

"Romeo's worth it." At least the Romeo I used to know was worth it.

"I'm not sure about Reynolds," Miss P said with a frown.

"Me either." We parted ways at the stairs. She headed up to the office while I would take solace in the flagellation of my family. What can I say, I'm a glutton for punishment. And it was time I dished out a bit of my own.

Bethany had some answering to do.

Ten o'clock. Time flies and all of that. But now I barely had enough time to debrief my newest family member, then go find Teddie and Jordan and deal with whatever horrible costume they planned to parade me around in. With my life devolving into a deep morass, at some point things would come to a head and my tenuous thread of control would snap.

Best I could hope for was a light sentence.

Chase Metcalf caught me lost in the development of an escape plan. "Just the lady I was looking for." He didn't sound happy.

I glanced at his reflection in the elevator door. Serious with a hint of mad replaced his normal smile.

Turning to face him confirmed that. "What's going on?"

"Whoa. Guess I'm not the only one you pissed off tonight."

I narrowed my eyes at my reflection. Perfect for Halloween. And, as I suspected, I'd made it worse, wiping the blood around my face. "Pissed off. I haven't even talked to you since I left you in Babel."

"You been talking to my wife then?"

"Your wife? No. I don't know her, nor would I know where to find her, why?"

"Well, somebody told her about the episode in the elevator. Man she's seeing red."

"You're the second person who has accused me within the last hour of doing something like that, which, for the record, I would never do."

"Well, only you, me, and the ladies knew about it. And I don't think the ladies had the wherewithal to get ahold of my wife's cell number."

I had to agree with him there. "Her cell?"

"Would it be part of your registration information?" He'd tried and convicted me without giving me a chance to defend myself.

"You provided whatever information we have on record, so

that makes your question rhetorical. To be honest, I don't have access to guest information." That shaded the truth—I could get it if I needed it. I hadn't, but once again, without facts, I had no ammunition with which to defend myself. "I'm really sorry. I didn't tell your wife anything, but I promise I will find out who did. In the meantime, I will send her some Champagne and a nice spread, on me."

"She's partial to Beluga and Cristal." Still no smile.

"So noted." I pulled a card from the pocket on the back of my phone case and extended it toward him. "Would you forward to my email whatever information was passed on to your wife? If you can send me the original email, text or whatever, that would be great."

He pocketed the card without looking at it. "Sure. It was a video."

The elevator doors opened, and I practically leaped inside, but, at the last minute, I managed to retain a modicum of dignity.

My mind whirled as the doors closed on Chase's unhappy face.

First Romeo, now Chase. Both conversations occurred in the hotel.

My heart fell. Someone had been listening in. And, at least in Chase's case, they'd also been watching.

This had Fox's handiwork all over it—indicting videos. But, if Fox was behind this, he was operating outside of his blackmail sandbox. For what purpose? I dialed my direct access to Vivienne.

"Yes?" She sounded guarded.

"Kill the video and audio to this elevator."

Five seconds, no more, then her voice returned. "Done."

"Have you seen Fox? Is he there?"

"No. He didn't show for his shift."

"Are you filling in for him?"

"Yes." One thing that had gone right tonight.

"Has anyone been paying a lot of attention to the video feeds?"

"Hard to tell. We all do our own thing up here."

In the darkness in Security, with everyone focusing on their own job, their own bank of monitors, someone intent on doing dirty could probably pull it off, especially without Jerry there. "True. Now that you're manning the helm, wander a bit and report anyone doing anything they shouldn't or asking questions that seem beyond the appropriate scope of their job, okay?"

"You got it."

I reholstered my phone as the elevator slowed.

Romeo, I could understand, but why Chase? What did he have to do with anything?

CHAPTER SIXTEEN

AS I'D both feared and hoped, the family had convened on the couches in front of the windows in my parents' apartment. When the elevator spit me out, three heads turned in my direction.

"Help yourself to a drink," my father said, raising his voice to be heard across the vast expanse of the great room.

As if I needed an invitation.

Was I a guest in my own family? Was that possible? Or were we redrawing boundaries with all the new additions? Or maybe I was trying so hard to hang onto what was that I was losing a place in what is. Nothing made sense, and the harder I thought about it, the less sense it made. All I knew was my life was abandoning me one person at a time.

"In a sec." I charged through the swinging door to the kitchen. With a handful of paper towels and some water, I went to work on all the blood. The stuff was everywhere, crusting on my face and neck. The cleanup took me longer than I thought. After turning my sweater inside out and pulling it back on, I felt like perhaps I wouldn't scare anyone too much.

I was wrong. When Mona got a look at me, she gave a little yelp and went all maternal…a very unusual state for her.

"*Lucky*?" Worry pinched her face even though it didn't propel her off the couch.

"I'm fine, Mother." Making a beeline for the bar, I gave the hand-knotted silk rugs a wide berth—something about stepping on handcrafted art bothered me—as if the knotters would feel the disrespect. I didn't even want to think about the animals that had given their hides for the sake of interesting furniture. The exotic trees that had been sacrificed didn't bother me quite as much—although someone once told me that scientists had recorded lettuce screaming as it was harvested. Whoever that was, a pox on their soul—the visual of my salad fighting for its life would never leave me.

The lesser works by the Masters that graced the walls, each exquisitely lit to perfection, added class to the carnage. At least no lives had been lost in their creation. Well, Van Gogh took his own—a loss to humankind I still mourned. And he'd never known what his talent meant to so many.

But I guess the purpose of the giving is not in the getting back.

Somehow, I managed to wade through all that guilt and finally arrived in front of the bar. Medicinal beverages called from three shelves eight bottles wide and three deep. If the Big Boss didn't have it, it wasn't worth having.

I poured a healthy dose of my favorite poison, Wild Turkey 101, then fisted the Steuben tumbler and joined my family at the windows. Despite Bethany curled in the corner, Mona moved over, clearing a space on the couch, but I chose to join my father at the window.

"You smell like a plumber." My father wasn't one to mince words. "And you look like a prizefighter. I hope you won."

"Well, my day has included lots of running through old garbage and being shot at. But, I'm here and still breathing. I'd call that a victory."

He accepted that as coming with the territory, which spoke volumes. "A shower..."

"Next on my list." Another glance at my watch. Time was running out.

My phone dinged. Another text.

Where are you? Party is about to start. Teddie knew better than to prod me. He did it anyway.

I'd like to go on record as someone who abhors texting. Whatever happened to calling? But, on second thought, hearing Teddie's voice right now...

My reply was pithy *"Not without me. I have the invite."*

And I have your costume, such as it is.

I let that go. Either Teddie was kidding, or he'd be dead, simple as that.

You and Jordan at your apartment? It wasn't really Teddie's apartment, but I didn't have the patience for accuracy. Since the fire, he'd taken up residency in the small apartment next to my parents'. Even though the repairs to his own unit in the Presidio, one floor above my former home, had been completed several weeks ago, he showed no signs of decamping to a more comfortable distance...for me. He seemed fine with the tripping over each other coming and going.

Yep. Waiting on you.

I'm next door contemplating homicide. Be there shortly.

Need help?

Good friends brought the weapon and the shovel, no questions asked.

And Teddie and I were good friends. We'd failed at being good lovers. Well, the sex had been smokin', so not a complete failure, but ultimately unsustainable. I felt warmth flood my cheeks and shut out those memories, focusing instead on my father and the view out the window. "What'd you do with Ponder?" I asked as I sipped my brew and drank in the lights of the Strip as they unfurled at an angle to my left.

"They gave him an ankle bracelet and left him in my care. He's sleeping the last of it off in the spare bedroom."

"Caught bloody-handed and he gets out on bond? And on your recognizance, I'm assuming. Took some doing, I bet."

He stared out the window. Even his reflection refused to look at me. "A couple of phone calls."

Only part of the story. "How much?" Normally, I didn't get into my father's wallet, but he hadn't been making the best choices lately. One bullet had aged him decades. Would he ever be who he used to be? Would the rest of us? Rhetorical questions—the answer was a two-letter word that began with an N and ended with an O—but just because I knew didn't mean I could live with it.

"Five-hundred-thousand."

As bonds for murder went, that one was so light it floated. I didn't want to think about how many markers he had to hand out for the favor. A future price, a future problem. Right now, I willed my worry to quiet as I absorbed the shimmering dance of neon radiating down the Strip. Nighttime in Vegas—nothing like it.

"And Mrs. Ponder? Why didn't she fork over the dough?"

"They went all in to move the team, so it's a bit complicated."

"It always is. Where'd you stash her?" Frankly, I half-hoped he'd sent her packing, but on an answer quest, I needed to gather everyone so I could light a match, toss them in hot water, and see who jumped out of the pot first.

"I gave her a suite on the twenty-sixth floor. She said something about having a party to go to."

Pursing my lips, I nodded. "She say which party?" There were several tonight, but Boudreaux indicated she would be at his.

"No."

"She did say she needed to do some shopping. The theme is black and white and she needed something new," Mona chimed in behind me.

Mona sounded a bit miffed at not being included. Somehow, I

had a feeling that, by the end of the evening she'd be glad she warmed the bench on this one.

My luck held—now, if only for a wee bit longer, then perhaps I could pull Romeo's delicates out of the fire and put a killer where he belonged. "Sky would rather party than comfort her husband?" Sarcasm dripped from every word. For some reason, I found Sky Ponder easy to hate—and that was all the more reason to reassess.

"He loves her," my father said as if reading my mind. Maybe he held her in low regard as well—not that either of our opinions mattered. His words held simple wisdom, and pain—he knew the price exacted by loving a difficult woman.

"And he's divorcing her."

Love wasn't worth that kind of pain.

Teddie had taught me that.

"It's complicated. Lots of money involved."

I had nothing to say to that, so I let it go. With one arm crossed across my waist, the other elbow resting on it and my glass held high, I turned and surveyed my cousin.

If a human could make themselves smaller, she did it, shrinking into the couch.

"What a damn fool, stinking stupid, asinine, juvenile, selfish—"

"I think she understands," my mother said, cutting me off.

"Yes, well, considering only someone with a single-digit IQ would do what she did tonight, I thought giving her lots of options might improve her comprehension."

"She *is* going to veterinary school at Cornell this fall."

"Only if I let her live." I eyed my mother. In fighting trim, she'd lost all of her baby weight. Her cheekbones were now as sharp as her normal tone. Her hair, caught at her neck in a gold clip, trailed down her back. A few tendrils softened her face, but not her bark. I knew Mona missed being relevant in the same way she had when she ran her own business. Granted, it was a whorehouse in Pahrump, but she had been a lobbyist for the Prostitution Industry, and, in many circles, that made her someone. Even though I could acknowledge her frustration, I still took the bait every time. She'd made her bed. And happy was a choice, so she'd better get over the whine. And while she was at it, she could kick me down that road as well.

A fight would keep me from ruminating on what I'd done to Romeo. Yes, he'd done it to himself, but I'd helped him along. No choice, really, but my heart still broke and I beat myself up for not finding a way out of an impossible situation.

Mona—she was the counterbalance to an otherwise decent, reasonably happy life.

Apples and trees were fine when it came to my father, but I balked at claiming too much shared DNA with my mother.

"Would you like in on this? I can roll you in if you need a good dressing-down."

She stuck her nose in the air and studiously turned away. She'd traded her pearls for a large-link gold chain with several links encrusted with diamonds. My father must've done something epic to have to buy his way back into her good graces with that. It was their thing—not that I was comfortable with it.

Frankly, my price was a good bit higher than an impressive piece of "important" jewelry, as Mother called it. Each generation had its own rules of the game. Problem was, I had no idea what the rules of my generation were. It seemed like men took advantage of women, women let them, and the anger ran deep.

As a generation, we sucked.

Another problem on my long list of to-solves. Any more problems and I'd go around the bend and never come back. I guess there were worse things.

As the anger leaked away, curiosity and fear replaced it. "You do know what you did tonight was beyond stupid, right?"

Taking a sheet from my playbook, Bethany fortified herself behind a wall of silk pillows. "I know."

"What were you thinking?"

When she glanced up at me, her gaze was unwavering, her eyes focused. "I was trying to find where a cop would get rid of a rifle."

"What?" It felt as if the air around us all had frozen solid. "Which cop?"

"Detective Romeo."

She started to shake. I squeezed into the tiny section of couch Mona had vacated and wrapped the girl in my arms. Skin and bones, she resisted at first, then tucked in tight as sobs shuddered through her. "He's...your...friend."

"That won't change. Tell me what you saw. Romeo was at War Vegas last night before we met up with him and saw the body?"

She nodded and took in expansive gulps of air, working for control. "Much earlier. It was just dark—a little light on the horizon, making it hard to see. I couldn't see him well, but that coat, it stands out, you know?"

"His Columbo impersonation."

Too young to get the reference, she gave me a quizzical look. "Not important."

She pulled into herself and took a deep, steadying breath. "I was on patrol, monitoring the game. My job was to keep out of sight as much as possible but to make sure the players were following rules, that sort of thing."

"An on-site referee."

She nodded. "The football players actually cause the least trouble, which I thought was funny given how big they are, and super scary competitive."

"They're used to referees. Are all the players told there are people on the playing grounds watching?"

"Everybody gets a mandatory safety and rules brief before they gear up."

"And where did you see Romeo?"

"I heard a shot, a real one. It's very different than the pfftt of an air rifle. With all that was going on, it was hard to figure the direction, but having been raised around guns and having done a lot of hunting as a kid in similar terrain, I made a pretty good guess. I saw Romeo heading the other direction."

"Away from where the body was found?"

"Yeah. He carried a rifle. Of course, that wasn't unusual—everybody had rifles."

"What made you think his might have been real?"

"I didn't, not at first. Not until after we found the body with the gunshot to the shoulder."

Smart kid. She'd noticed.

"And the videos? Any luck confirming any of this?"

"I've found a few who will let me see what they recorded. Not too many, as you might suspect. It's against the rules, and somebody got killed."

Mona unfolded herself. "I'll get you a cup of hot tea." She patted Bethany's knee before disappearing toward the kitchen.

My mother never made tea; she ordered it.

"Don't go too far," I called after her. "When I'm finished with Bethany, I need your help."

"It's my life's calling to do your bidding." She threw the words at me, then scurried through the kitchen door.

"Look no further to see where I inherited my penchant for sarcasm," I said to no one in particular.

Mona surrounded herself with an emotional wall. The maternal thing always had chafed my mother like a wool shirt on a sweltering day. When I'd been seven, the stress of motherhood resulted in an itchy rash over 90% of her body. The doctors were amazed. I was less so—pretending to be what you weren't took a heavy toll.

I'd been doing it my whole life.

"When she returns, I'd be careful," I said to Bethany, feeling all protective like an older sister, surprising myself. "Her culinary skills are limited."

Bethany pushed at a lock of hair that had fallen across her face. "I know, but she means well."

I wasn't sure. The milk of human kindness barely trickled through Mona's veins. "So, the videos?"

"The ones I saw—I'm cataloging them, marking the tape locations, and getting them ready for the police."

"For the M.E.?"

"Yes, but Detective Reynolds is the go-between."

"Really?" Add another powerful man to my call list—first the M.E., then the Sheriff.

The sharpness of my voice caught my father's attention as well. "Yeah," Bethany answered.

"She doesn't leave here. You got that?" I said to my father.

He gave me a quick nod and shut down Bethany's forming argument with one of his patented scowls.

I softened my voice as I turned back to Bethany. "Okay, I'd love to see the videos, but I don't have time right now. Can you give me the high points? Who else was there that night?"

"Lots of NFL types—I didn't know all of them, although I think my boss has a list somewhere." She pulled Mona's silk pillows into a barricade around her slight frame, her legs tucked up close to her body like a stork.

"If he does, the police should have it." So far, Jeremy and Dane hadn't uncovered any other player with a beef against Senator Lake—not that anyone would advertise that sort of thing in neon, but if Jeremy and his team couldn't find it, it didn't exist.

"Boudreaux was the big draw. He's quite a shot."

Hand-eye coordination—the stuff of great athletes and snipers. "Just what I need, a big shot with a big shot." But it did pose some interesting questions. "But no gun?"

"After I finished showing the CSI the video room and all of that, I went back to the scene. Romeo was waiting. We scoured the scene looking for a rifle stashed somewhere but didn't find anything. After looking at the tapes later, I realized Romeo had taken the rifle long before we all converged at the scene, and he was just stringing me along." She stared past me out the window. "He was good at it."

"Did you ask him about that? Why he ran?"

"Not directly. I didn't want him to know I knew he'd been there." She twisted the corner of one of Mona's silk pillows, which would've gotten her a bark and a bite had my mother seen her. "That made me sad, you know?" Tears welled.

"I know." I'd passed sad and was well into mad. Not for one minute did I believe Romeo had sold his soul to the Dark Side. What made me mad was being deliberately left out of the loop. "What did you say?"

"I asked if he'd ever been to War Vegas before."

I didn't even have to try to guess his answer. "And he said no, that arriving at the scene was his first time."

"Pretty much."

"Anybody else in the game who looked out of place or was acting odd?" In a game that required a serious murderous streak, what would be odd? Looking through my Rogers and Hammerstein rose-colored glasses, I was at sea.

"There was this other guy. Bogie hired him on the spot. He suited up, but I don't remember him hanging around for the intro course."

"It's not required?"

"Not for staff. And really not for anyone else, but it's strongly encouraged." Bethany unwound the tight little knot of silk and tried to smooth it out. "Don't tell, okay?" A flash of fear.

"You've got a free pass with Mona. She's working through some heavy guilt right now. But I won't breathe a word." Bethany, my cousin, was Mona's niece. Mona and her sister had suffered an assault when they were kids. Mona, the stronger one, had found a way to move on. Her sister had not. Through one of those political plays that often hid the guilty, the assaulter had not only escaped punishment, but also his guilt had been hidden. But two young women knew the truth—an accusation would ruin his newfound legitimacy as a country vet. He'd found Mona's sister at the sanitarium. Realizing her word would never be believed, he did what he'd started years before. Bethany resulted. Recently, he'd sniffed out Mona and had come after her. He'd died. I'd taken a bullet in the calf for my troubles.

Justice had been served.

While I'd inherited Bethany, essentially a kid sister, my mother staggered under a load of guilt. Misplaced, for sure, but she wouldn't listen to reason.

Guilt, a bazooka in the war against self-respect. Wasn't most of it borne by those who lacked the responsibility?

Bethany flicked a glance at my father. He raised his hands, palms out. "Mona won't hear it from me. Last thing I need is another thing to keep that woman on the warpath."

I tried to focus as I glanced at my watch. Was stylishly late a good thing when it came to this Privé party? Who knew, but I was going to find out. My phone dinged the arrival of a text, which I ignored. Teddie, I felt sure. As if pressuring me was going to improve anything. A caveat to the Curse of the Y-Chromosome: control it or kill it.

"So, even if you don't go through the little rules thing, you can still play?" I asked Bethany, cutting to the chase.

"It's just legal overkill. We use air guns that shoot plastic pellets. Nobody gets hurt."

The irony hit us both.

"The new guy, the one Bogie hired, where'd he go? Did he play? Was he a referee?"

"I don't know. I didn't see him again, and he wasn't on the few tapes I got." She started to rewind the delicate cloth.

I didn't stop her. "What'd he look like?"

"Big. Like the players but a little soft. You could still see the muscle, but not in a ripped, pro athlete sort of way. Blond hair. Angry little eyes and lips that look good on Angelina Jolie, but only highlight a man's shortcomings. And he had this way of walking; a bit sideways like a rabid dog."

"As long as he wasn't foaming at the mouth."

"I didn't get that close." Realizing what she was doing, she smoothed out the silk, then tucked the pillow under several others. Then she picked up the unadulterated pillow on the top of the stack and clutched it to her stomach. This one had fringe, which she started to braid.

Mona was going to need some new pillows if she didn't die of apoplexy first.

I turned to stare out the window as if I'd find an answer in all the flashing lights and silly come-ons. An answer probably lurked there, but not to the questions I asked. Romeo had my guts knotted, my brain spinning, and my heart bleeding. I'd love to kill him if whoever was gunning for him didn't get to him first.

If I could just figure out who was gunning for him. He'd made enough enemies; it'd take too much time to sort through them all. I needed a break.

"Back to Romeo. You're sure it was him? Did you see him on any of the other feeds?"

"No. Like I said, they were spotty. But it looked like him: thin, angular, hunched shoulders, the raincoat thing."

"You didn't try to stop him?"

"I stepped out of the shadows and called to him. He glanced my direction, then ran."

Staring out the window, I chewed on my lip as I struggled to come up with a plausible excuse. My father, who had turned his back on the lights, gave me a look that wasn't hard to read.

"Not good, right?" Bethany gave voice to my father's fear.

"No, not good."

"That's why I went downtown tonight. A pawnshop seemed like the place a cop would ditch a gun he didn't want found. You know how on TV the cops always have snitches and guys they work with at all the seedy places."

Make-believe wasn't reality—only a kid would equate the two. But tonight it came closer than I was comfortable with.

"There's one other thing. I'm not sure if it's important or not."

"All this is critical." I hoped to a defense and not a prosecution, but things weren't shaping up exactly the way I'd hoped.

"Romeo wasn't part of the game. He hadn't been at the safety briefing."

"So, he hadn't known he'd be watched."

Waiting in the wings, Mona breezed back in as if responding to a cue from a director.

Life is but a play...

She carried two steaming mugs. One she handed to Bethany, then she took a position by her husband's side, offering him the second mug.

He took a sip, then grimaced. "What is this?"

"It's tea. It's supposed to be calming."

My father tried another taste, this time without the grimace.

Bethany cupped her mug in both hands, a climber clinging to a safety rope.

"We all ought to mainline the stuff, then," I offered, wishing I had my own mug but knowing it would have little effect on my frayed nerves. Alcohol would soften the hurts, but it would exact a price, one I could no longer pay.

Mona sniffed at me, unable or unwilling to discern honesty from bullshit.

"Mother?" I bit down on my grin when she actually jumped. I'd made an effort to keep the bark to a minimum, obviously to little effect. "I need your help. Can you give me some dirt on the Sheriff?"

Her shit-eating grin bloomed slowly like a flower after a soaking rain. "The Sheriff? Oh, honey, he and I go way back. How much dirt do you need?"

Mother might be a pain, but she had her uses. "Enough to

encourage him to do something he won't want to, but not so much that I piss him off."

Mona drummed her fingers on her chin as she rolled her eyes skyward in thought. After a few moments, she settled back with a look. "I'm a little worried. The Sheriff might not take to me giving out his secrets. Do you think maybe I could wheedle the information out of him?"

She looked so desperate and sounded so pitiful. Having been a somebody in the world of commerce, if prostitution fit, being relegated to diaper duty would be a blow. "This is really important, Mother. Life and Death important."

"The Sheriff and I were..." She flicked a glance at her husband. "Close. He trusts me. And he'll believe me."

I looked to my father for help, but he stayed on the sidelines. I glanced at my watch—the sand had run through the hourglass. "Okay, Mother. I appreciate your help." I stifled a smile at her relief, but her gratitude made me uncomfortable. "Here's what I need."

CHAPTER SEVENTEEN

"YOU WANT me to go as a cow?" I eyed the two men who had met me at the door of the apartment next to my parents'.

Teddie, standing directly in front of me, with Jordan next to him for moral support, held up my costume—yes, a cow, complete with dangling udders.

Teddie looked like he was gargling rocks as he fought a guffaw. "You said black and white. This is a Holstein, a very noble cow."

Fun at my expense—nothing made me grumpier than being the butt of the joke. "You're not making any of this better for yourself."

"My *mea culpa* act wasn't working, so I thought I'd just go back to being me."

The subtext in that statement made my gut instinct stand up and salute.

Just being himself.

"You used to think I was fun." He tossed off the line with the practiced ease of a consummate performer.

Like my mother before, I found myself struggling with the line between truth and bullshit.

"That says more about me than it does you." Getting nowhere with Teddie, I nailed Jordan with a glare. "Just so you know, you're not off the hook. Under the law, accomplices earn the same punishment as the trigger man."

Jordan had the sense to look sheepish. "Guilty as charged. But, Lucky, think about it this way. You believe many of the suspects in this whole drama will be at the party, right?"

Except for the cops—a fact I glossed over. "Everything is pointing to that." Out of ideas, options, and the will to fight, I let him lead me down the path even though I knew where we headed.

"So, dressed this way, you can get close to them, and they won't know it's you."

He was right, but I wasn't yet ready to cave, despite knowing pride often led to a scraped ego, at best.

He could sense my vacillation and honed in for the kill. "Look, I've played a lot of cops in both television and film, hung around with the real deals who were there to keep us as close to reality as Hollywood would allow. I've even hung out with the writers who had to research the stories and make sure they were accurate, so I know how this sort of thing works."

"You're trying to convince me by using people who make stuff up for a living as your foundational sources?"

"Weak, but hey, it'll also cover up that nose, which looks ghastly by the way. What's the downside?"

"I look *udderly* ridiculous." Working hard to keep up with taking the blows of Romeo's recent behavior, then segueing to the absolute idiocy of going to an invitation-only party in a cow costume with two jokers, I had little resiliency left. Laughter would have to do.

The men looked at me bug-eyed for a moment as the joke settled in, then they both laughed, relief washing over them and wiping away the worry.

I joined in, and the rest of my resistance evaporated into give up and give in. I reached out, snapping my fingers. "Ten minutes."

~

WITH OUR ENTRY UNDERWEAR, USING THE TERM LOOSELY, TUCKED in my left udder, I took my escorts through the labyrinthine maze of back hallways. Before we'd stepped out of the sanctity of the apartment and, desperate to hide my embarrassment in anonymity, I'd donned my mask. Pride came at a price—the last guy who'd donned the costume had eaten a potent garlic dinner. The smell, which, trapped along with my hot, moist breath inside the headpiece, threatened to grow to puke-inducing strength, almost had me diving for cover back in the safety of Teddie's apartment. Curiosity kept my stomach contents where they belonged and me forging ahead.

Romeo needed me. I still wasn't sure whether he needed rescuing or a swift kick in the ass, or both. Even though I had no idea what tonight would bring, I had an idea I'd know more at the end of it than I did now.

Teddie flanked me on the left. Short on subtlety and long on confidence, he'd chosen a court jester's costume that hugged every curve, leaving nothing to the imagination—not even his identity concealed poorly behind a tiny mask. His spiked blond hair and sparkling baby blues were dead giveaways. Those of us who knew him best only had to take a look at his ass, which I studiously avoided doing on principle. Besides, seeing out of the tiny cow eyeholes was more difficult than I imagined. Cows had wide-set eyes—I did not, enough said. Tonight would be spent looking first out one eye, then the other. If anyone wanted a piece of me, I'd never see them coming.

Jordan, in his inimitable style, had chosen a perfectly tailored tux, his smile his only mask. Often lauded as the pinnacle of male pulchritude, he needed no adornment—something I both loved and hated about him, depending on the level of my self-confidence. Complicit in the cow costume, Jordan wasn't eliciting feelings of love from me tonight.

And, adding insult to reality, he'd also been right. As we stepped aside periodically to let the housekeeping and food service staff by, the men got the attention and the recognition. But, if anyone even bothered to glance my way, a grin was the best I got.

Every one of them knew me, but they didn't recognize me.

Hiding in plain sight. This could work.

I amused myself with the game, growing ever bolder as we wound our way to the bank of service elevators in the opposite wing of the hotel.

"Having fun?" Teddie gave his reflection in the metal doors the once-over, angling for the light.

I nodded, which seemed to make him unhappy.

All the more reason to play it up. I nodded again and gave him my best silent sports-team mascot impersonation. He rewarded me with a tight grin. He had to—I looked ridiculous.

I leaned into Jordan, well, as close as I could get given my bovine exterior. "That's the angle. I'm not talking. I'm the proposed new mascot."

"The Vegas Heifers?"

I bristled, but then realized I had udders—at least on the outside—my balls were hidden. "A joke, but let's run with it as long as we can."

"Do you have any idea what kind of party this is?"

The doors slid open. We had the car to ourselves—I guess even Jordan and Teddie weren't sufficient inducement to get someone to ride up with a cow.

"It's by some group called Privé."

He choked, then swallowed hard. "I told you," Teddie said with a smirk.

"What?" I looked between them as my heart sank. My bad feeling about all this came home to roost. Sometimes I hate it when I'm right.

A glance passed between them. "This is going to be fun." Jordan opened his jacket, then, after untying his bow tie, he unbuttoned the two top buttons on his shirt.

"You both know?" The doors slid open depositing us in the hallway between the bar at Babel and the Secret Suite. Another night of revelry at Babel was ramping up, the music thumping, the voices shouting over it, excited.

Couples, attired in tiny bits of black and white, filtered through the hall toward us. Interest flared on the faces of both the men and the women when they spied Jordan and Teddie. As they raked the men with their gazes, their interest turned to thinly disguised lust.

My initial comfort at the partiers coming two by two fizzled, replaced by a very bad feeling. "I'm not going to like this, am I?" As I thought about the doors-locked-masks-off-at-midnight thing, the horror of what I'd gotten myself into washed over me. "Oh, this is one of those…"

"Polyamorous parties," Teddie finished my question with the answer.

We'd touched on this subject before, but I never thought… "Arrive with one, cum with another? Is that it?" My skin threatened to crawl off on its own.

Jordan gaped at me. "Well. I've not heard it described quite that way. A little class, Lucky, a little class."

"Class? *Please!"* I pressed a hand to my chest. "Give me a moment here. I'm presiding over the death of love. A little respect, could you?"

Teddie opened his mouth to argue, then snapped it closed. He knew an argument he couldn't win.

When did everything from orgasms to attachments become so expedient?

"In for a penny," Jordan offered up a platitude as if it would do anything positive.

One tiny-assed, long-legged, blonde sashayed past me. "Oh, I think far more than a penny. More like 150,000 pennies…per hour. Maybe a slight discount for a blow job but doubtful."

Teddie cocked one eyebrow at me. "I'd heard everybody had a price."

Even though he couldn't see the murder in my icy blues, I leveled them at him anyway. "But to sleep with a cow is priceless."

That knocked his smirk into next year—a minor victory in a night lacking many, so I took it and summoned a bit of backbone. I could do this. But, if worse came to worse and I couldn't contain my hurl reflex, I pitied the poor guy who rented the cow costume next. "I can't believe you two brought me here."

"*You* invited *us*." Jordan clearly thought the whole thing worthy of a Hollywood farce.

I couldn't disagree. Once again, I'd miscalculated. At least I was consistent, but that was about all I could say about my recent level of performance.

Billy the Boilermaker had been billed as the bouncer, but it was Beau Boudreaux who blocked the door to the Secret Suite. Blood from his broken nose blackened the half-moons under his eyes like that black smudge the players wore to minimize glare or look stupid. I wasn't sure of the exact goal and thought either equally plausible. Personally, I thought it was just acceptable war paint.

Now, I had my own broken nose, so I knew what it felt like. It wasn't too bad, actually. Men were such whiners.

The outline on Boudreaux's cheekbone had faded into a rectangular purple shadow. If he kept up his battle with the world, his face would be one huge bruise. Of course, given all my damaged body parts, I wasn't one to talk.

I rooted in my udder for the filigreed underwear, but with a hoof for a hand, I failed. Finally, Jordan rescued me. Poking around in my cow privates, he found the entwined bits of thread and handed them to Boudreaux.

"That'll get two in."

Jordan motioned between himself and Teddie. "We're together."

"Invite is good for one couple. No cows allowed." He didn't even look at me.

"Mr. Ponder's orders." Jordan's Oscar win had not been a fluke—even I believed him. "Something about a team mascot."

That got a cursory glance, then Boudreaux's face flushed. "That asshole. He swore he'd get even."

Get even? For what? The words screamed through my brain. My father had said something about an affair with Mrs. Ponder. Oh, how I'd love to hit him in the face with that. His reaction would be enlightening, if I lived. With questions burbling, I chomped down on my tongue. Even though not the brightest bulb, Boudreaux would recognize my voice.

But, dear God, couldn't one of the two men with me have the brainpower to ask the next question, please?

"'That who you've been fighting with?" Teddie asked.

Wrong question! *Why? Ask him why Ponder wanted to get even!*

"Hell, no. I ran into the bitch hotel boss lady, Lucky somebody. She has a wicked elbow, but that's all she's got."

"Oh, she grows on you." Jordan pressed against me, then grabbed my arm, hiding his restraint behind the skirt of his jacket. "Especially when you might find yourself needing someone in your corner."

Boudreaux opened the door to the suite, then stepped aside, allowing us to pass. "A fucking cow," he muttered as I squeezed past, my udders grazing his crotch.

With a wicked elbow, asshole. I half-thought he'd hit me or pinch me on the ass, but he didn't. If he had, we'd find out if it were possible to break an already broken nose.

My phone sang out. Secured in my right udder, the ringtone was a bit muted. Sirens—Mona's ringtone. I ignored it. After a few moments of wailing, a moment of silence, then it started again.

The only way to shut Mother up would be to pretend to listen.

The door to our left led into the service areas. With an exaggerated shrug, hands lifted in my best mascot imitation, I tilted my head toward the door. Once I saw a glimmer of understanding, I motioned for Teddie to dig out my phone.

"Always wanted to milk a cow," he said with a smile that barely held the weight of his emotion as his fingers brushed places they used to roam freely. "I guess I can cross that off the bucket list." He handed me the phone as it stopped ringing.

The men looked ready to engage in battle, so I motioned for the two of them to join the party, then, with Boudreaux focusing on two nubile young things whose costumes left little to the imagination, or perhaps fired imaginations, considering the venue where inhibitions ran unfettered.

Thankful for a respite from the visuals, I ducked through the door.

Mona answered before the call even rang through from my end. "*Lucky*! We've had a *disaster!*" my mother reserved speaking in italics for only the worst problems.

My heart did a dead-fish flop. "What?"

"A *detective* is here. He wants *Nolan*."

"A detective? Which detective?"

"God, Lucky. How can *that* be important? They all work for the *police*." Her voice dropped to a theatrical whisper.

Right. And Glinda the Good Witch didn't actually make Dorothy risk her life several times before telling her she could've gone home right from the start. Frankly, I'd always felt I'd have a better chance with the Wicked Witch of the West—at least all the cards were on the table with her. None of that passive-aggressive benevolence Glinda wore like a crown of righteousness.

But I didn't waste time on a life-is-like-a-fairy-tale conversation with my mother. If she hadn't admitted it by now, she never would. Sometimes clinging to life as you wished it to be was the only way to live through life as it was.

"His name, Mother?"

"Lucky, your tone." She sighed dramatically as if I couldn't be a bigger disappointment—she knew better. Finally, she gave me what I demanded. "Reynolds."

I wondered how a bad cop would fare in prison among the inmates he'd helped send up and I smiled. "Is he there to arrest him?" Hadn't Romeo said he'd already been booked on Murder One?

"How can he arrest him?"

Mona's questions always staggered me a bit, as if I was spinning at a slightly slower speed. "Well, a dead man, a knife, blood, a few public threats..."

"Oh, for *Heaven's sake!* I know all of that and we've been over it, Nolan and I. He said he didn't do it."

"Well, that settles it."

"Lucky!"

"Mother, I've got to go. Why don't you call the D.A. and have a little chat. I'm sure he'll take your word as to Ponder's innocence. I don't have the time to run interference." Nor any intention, but I didn't say that. "I have a party to attend."

"Of course you do, dear." Her words dripped with a subtext I'd developed an immunity to decades ago—or that's what I told myself. And if I couldn't believe me...

"Mother!"

"He couldn't arrest him even if he wanted to because he's *gone!*"

"Mr. Ponder is gone?"

"Didn't I *say* that?"

"Mother, given there are several interpretations of "gone" and there are two men involved in your side of the conversation, can you elaborate? Who is gone, and what does gone entail actually?"

A dramatic sigh barreled through the line as she composed herself, or whatever she did before lambasting me with an explanation bordering on hysterics—that subtext cut right into my soul. "I went to wake Nolan up. He'd put pillows under the covers, and he was *gone*!"

"Gone? Like disappeared? Like running from justice?" Why did men run from everything? Their chromosomal defect, namely trying to replace an X with a Y, could explain some of it, but you'd think eventually they'd grow a brain. "Any idea when?"

"In the last hour or two."

"Running from arrest is so stupid." Teddie had done exactly that, and we'd both nearly died trying to put it right.

"Who's going to be arrested?" Mona's voice dropped to a conspiratorial tone. Since I knew better, I'd say she was enjoying the game of misdirection.

With no real choice, I bit. "Isn't Reynolds there to arrest Mr. Ponder?"

"Of course not!"

"A social visit, then?" Two could play this game.

"Don't be silly. He wants to let him go."

Her ace trumped anything I held in my hand. I folded. "Mother!"

"Lucky, don't use *that* tone with me! *You're* not listening—as usual."

Every moment of every day, with a few slips, Mona kept insisting I was the idiot—at some point she was bound to be right.

The only gambit I had left was to accept defeat now to have a chance to gain victory later. A long shot. My normal odds. "You're right, Mother. I'm sure." I let her harrumph in surprise until I figured I'd breached the wall. "So, tell me, why does Reynolds want to release Nolan from his ankle jewelry?"

"Nolan has an alibi, and it checks out."

"Who says?"

"Detective Reynolds."

~

The boy who cried wolf—the truth had not set him free.

With all the angles he played, and all the strings he pulled, Reynolds made that kid look like a piker. But they both had a similar problem—no one believed anything they said.

Least of all, me.

Ponder was covered in blood and holding what was presumably the murder weapon—and he had an alibi?

I'd stepped through the looking glass for sure.

What angle was Reynolds playing this time? Trying to spring an accomplice?

As I pocketed the phone and stepped back into the public part of the hotel to face down Boudreaux, this time without my two Galahads, I knew the truth would set someone free—I just couldn't fathom who.

Luckily, Boudreaux was occupied with a scrum of scantily-clad couples—I didn't have the restraint necessary to resist breaking another bit of cartilage should he give me any more lip Using several representatives of the Beautiful People with Wandering Eyes to hide my heifer-self, I managed to slide past and melt into the party. Slipping in unnoticed was far easier than I expected. Dressed as I was, I developed a new appreciation for those who walk the globe in relative obscurity, no one throwing anything more than a brief bit of amusement or pity their way.

Teddie and Jordan clustered together at the piano, back-to-back like animals sensing predators. Teddie eyed the instrument with undisguised yearning. If he could sit on the bench and let his fingers fly over the keys, he'd be transported, and the world would fall away.

Boy, what I would give.

I closed within ten feet when one of the women we'd seen in the hallway slithered up to Teddie. "I don't care who you came with or what your sexual predilections are, you're mine at midnight."

He swallowed hard and gave her a nod and a smirk worthy of James Bond. Only I saw the fear.

At midnight, the masks come off. Reality slapped me upside the head. Murder or mischief? Frankly, I preferred the former. But if I was in the game it'd be nice to know what the rules were. I leveled one eye out the peephole at Jordan.

Even he could read the thought there. "You stake your claim, then trade when you're done."

I shuddered. Shit! When I was done? The thought of swapping made this one-guy-gal nauseous. Now I had to pretend to play—well, no one would want a cow, so I had to watch my best friends—okay, one best friend and one first love—barter themselves to the bidders with the most intriguing assets.

It was one thing to know Teddie had slept with someone else; it was another thing altogether to witness it. My courage failing and bile rising, I turned toward the door.

Again, Jordan's iron grip staked me to the floor. "Trust us. We got this."

While leaving me out in the cold, they'd come up with a plan. As I tried to work up some mad, I realized they really hadn't thrown me to the wolves.

They'd hidden me in a cow costume.

Jordan and I waited while Teddie threaded his way through the crowd toward the bar at the back of the great room opposite the wall of windows. Through the windows, several mermaids and mermen, both genders dressed only in flowing locks and green tailfins from the waist down, swam in the pool. Intertwining, fondling, kissing, they were a high-class substitute for porn to get the partier's juices flowing and lust on.

Gauging by the pawing and drooling, I'd say the strategy was spot-on.

While Jordan and I chose to keep to ourselves, we watched the other invitees as they visually measured each other, checking off the requirements. Occasionally, someone would lean into another and whisper. At a nod, they'd both make notes, in pencil, on an individual form or something; it was hard to tell without acting too interested. At a shake of the head, they'd move on. Everyone was stunning. I was the bovine adrift in a sea of pulchritudinous perfection.

I had no idea how they made their choices.

The odd man out, I was happy to be hidden.

"The evening's dance card, if you will." Jordan knew my problem with swappers and took a perverse delight in sharing the details.

Karma was a bitch, but he knew that. He just loved the game. Next move would be mine.

Teddie returned, weaving through the crowd. His face red, he carried three very large plastic mugs with lids and long straws. "Sippy cups. Each holds an entire bottle of wine. I got you Veuve," he said as he handed me mine—a plastic jug with a top and a long straw. "I guessed you'd be a meaty Cab kind of guy," he said to Jordan, pegging him perfectly. Superficial thoughtfulness had always been one of Teddie's strengths.

While I'd been known to sip Champagne from a Flintstone's jelly jar, I'd never had the good stuff from a sippy cup. Tonight would be a night of many firsts. I took a long pull. Same exquisite taste. Same millions of tiny bubbles of happiness. Same warm glow.

After lightening my sippy cup by half, I felt fortified enough to face the evening. As if Jordan sensed my readiness, he said, "Let's mingle."

He pulled me over to the nearest couple. "Hi."

Both dark-haired, sultry, and interested, they gave him an appraising look. He waited until they both looked willing. "We're throwing something a little different into the mix tonight." He motioned to me, which elicited lukewarm smiles. "We've hidden a prospect in this silly cow costume. Male or female, you don't know. Beautiful or not so much, you don't know that either. The only thing we know is the skill level is high." He gave a wink and a knowing nod, almost overplaying his hand. "So, view your cards as draft choices, if you will, the top line being your top draft choice. You need to decide what draft choice you're willing to trade to play with what's under the cow costume."

"Kinky," the woman said as she licked her lips and angled, trying to see through the peepholes. "Blue eyes. I'm in."

I snapped my head around intending to give Jordan the stink-eye, but the cow headdress spun a half rotation more until I was looking out the back of my head. I swiveled it back into position as I worked to regain a modicum of dignity.

"What if some of us give the same draft choice?"

Jordan tapped her on the arm and leaned in, "You negotiate," he said, his whisper laden with every possibility a warped mind could conjure.

My skin crawled; I felt like shedding it like a snake. Good thing I had a thick black-and-white hide. Sweat trickled down my sides as heat and humiliation rose. As I let Jordan lead me from one cluster of over-amped partiers anticipating the night's fun to another, I scanned the crowd and pretended I wasn't being auctioned off as the evening's secret toy.

One advantage of being tall was I could usually look over most crowds I found myself mired in. Not tonight. Everyone matched my height or exceeded it.

The two women I'd braced in the elevator, our panty pushers, were holding court in the corner by the bar. The taller one, Olivia, wore one of the G-strings they'd been handing out and a sheer black lace bra, six-inch Lou-bous and a crystal-encrusted dog collar with matching leash. The other one, Stella, carried the whip. The extracurriculars they not-so-subtly advertised gave me the willies. Puns arrived with panic, what can I say?

Two men and another woman clustered with them, but the girls weren't engaged. Each of them cast looks toward the door. Were they planning an escape or afraid someone would show up?

Whoever or whatever, it had them worried, shifting like gazelles sensing a lion. One nudged the other with an elbow and their faces brightened.

I turned to look at what shoved their worry aside.

Brandy.

Even without the black-and-white uniform, she turned every head in the room as she elbowed her way through the crowd. Her youth shouted, “Fresh meat,” which lured the seasoned party participants.

Ignoring those who reached out to stop her, she shrugged them off like a horse shaking off flies. Tall and lithe, she walked with feral grace. Lethal skills to match hid behind her innocent exterior. As a former cage dancer she’d acquired the black-belt skills to defend herself.

Like the others, she let her gaze roll over the cow costume. Nothing jumped out at her, not one flicker of recognition. I think I felt good about that, although, at this point, I was confused enough to be perpetually conflicted. She turned her attention to Teddie and Jordan. “Have either of you seen Lucky? I was told she was with you.”

I leaned into her as close as I could get. “Does Romeo know where you are?” Shit, I sounded like my mother. I took another drag on my sippy cup straw.

Brandy focused and maneuvered to see through my eyeholes. “Are you in there?”

I nodded dramatically so the cow head actually moved up and down.

Her lips pinched, she looked at me long and hard, then shook her head. “I got nothin’.”

“Yeah, me either,” I said with a snort.

“Jean-Charles came by looking for you.” She kept her expression flat, her voice free of recrimination.

“I think I’m sorta glad he didn’t find me, not like this anyway. Right now, I’m safe. He’s cooking. Keeps him out of trouble. Wish

I could say the same for myself." An itch bloomed on my right thigh. With my hoof-encased hand, I tried to scratch through the matt of faux fur.

"You don't cook," she said it as if not cooking would earn me a platinum-level man card.

I already had one—a few noses broken and balls busted was all it took. Pretty easy when you considered the gauntlet women had to run each day in the workplace. "I have a professional kitchen replete with a French chef to satisfy my every desire, so what's your point?"

"I should know better."

Several men and one woman sidled over, their interest aroused. "Who's the new chick?" the woman asked.

Jordan stepped in next to Brandy and curled an arm around her shoulders. "My daughter. And she's just leaving." He gave her a sharp look. "Right, honey?"

"Sure. Right after I tell this cow something important." She pulled me into a corner. Once out of earshot, she hissed, "Have you talked with the M.E.?"

I shook my head.

"Well, he's looking for you."

"Two men looking for me—this could be either really good or really bad." I tilted my head and gave her as much wide-eye as I could—we still attracted too much interest.

She swiveled; then, satisfied no one could overhear, she leaned in. "The blood on Ponder? It was Lake's. You know that already, but here's the kicker," she lowered her voice. "Best as Doc could tell, Lake's body ended up a gallon shy, even taking into account the blood that had sprayed everywhere and had seeped into the sand."

I chewed my lip, which Brandy couldn't see, and thought about that.

She touched my arm. "There's more. The knife? It was the murder weapon, but he had a hard time establishing that. Some of the wounds were shallow, some deep, some angled one way, some another. Hard to tell which one was actually the lethal blow. Lake must've put up one hell of a fight." Brandy's eyes drifted over the crowd, lighting briefly on a few of the men.

"Great." The tumblers were spinning. With the handprint, murder weapon, and phone call, it seemed like they had Ponder cold. Yet, he kept insisting he was somewhere else. I couldn't prove it, but no one had placed him at the scene yet either.

Brandy pulled a slip of paper out of her pocket, her eyes going back and forth as she read down the list. "Oh, yeah, the lock on Bungalow 7 had the old electronics in it. But there were scratches indicative that it had been replaced, then the new stuff taken out, and the old put back. And the chip you found in the Secret Suite was one of our active ones. Last time a game was set up there officially was two weeks ago, but Jerry called, said he was on it and he'd found whispers of a set-up game, all under the table, as it were."

"Interesting. I need to think. I'm missing something."

"It's all a jumble."

"Anything else from Jerry?"

"Oh, yeah. He said you were right about Chateau Marmont. Fox and Boudreaux were regular visitors." She folded her paper and tucked it away. "Any idea what that means?"

"It means I'm on the right track, it's all coming together. And," I waited for her complete attention, "we've got someone on the inside helping the wrong team. Any idea how we can figure out who?"

"Half of Security was working on the lock project. I checked."

"Good thinking, but not the answer I hoped for."

"A bit too tidy, don't you think?" Stupidity knew no bounds, but a smart guy like Ponder sure was making a lot of mistakes. Yeah, he was so high he didn't know where he was, but still.

She turned to go, then turned back around. "Oh, and Ponder had enough Fentanyl in his system it should've killed him."

"Self-administered?"

"Couldn't say." She wore a mask of worry under her bravado.

I rested a hoof on her arm. Not exactly the reassuring squeeze I was going for. Would the indignities never cease? "Romeo? How is he?" I didn't know how much he'd been able to tell her. What would she think of my choices? Would she think me a traitor as well?

"Jeremy told me Romeo was with Reynolds at the station. Do you have any idea what is going on?"

I wanted to lie, to tell her I had all the answers, but there were times to bluff and times to show all your cards. Laying my hand out, I folded. "Clueless."

Like a young shoot in the desert sun, she wilted.

"Go home," I said using my indoor voice, keeping it low and light.

"I can't. Too many memories and fears all shouting in the silence."

"Then go to work. The night is just getting a start on crazy."

I watched her until she had safely exited the suite. Since she'd gotten rid of the horrid boyfriend she came to the job with, I hadn't seen a hint of stupid in the girl. But rarely was so much temptation, all free for the taking, gathered in one room, although I felt certain her opportunities on any given day far exceeded mine.

Jordan tugged my arm. "Anything interesting?"

Since he'd pulled me back within earshot of our panty pushers, who would recognize my voice, I didn't answer, sipping from my sippy cup instead, but the Champagne was getting warm. Even Veuve didn't have the same pop without the proper chill. Jordan pulled me to a stop, and he launched into his spiel once again to anyone within earshot.

"Not interested." The sharp words shut Jordan down.

I knew that voice.

Fox.

I whirled, scanning the armada of the scantily clad that pressed in around us. Fox had to be the guy in jeans and an attitude. As he swam his way toward us, pushing people out of the way with each stroke, his scowl grew deeper, his face redder.

He wasn't what I expected. Tall, hard muscles bulked beneath his black Babylon Security uniform—he was every bit the measure of a could-be NFLer. He even had his game face on. As he came closer, I stood my ground. His cologne arrived before he did—a nauseating overabundance of Aramis and anger. Some of the partiers caught his scent. Perking up, they honed in. One, a very handsome man, even had the audacity to reach out and squeeze a butt cheek. He got slapped for his interest. He seemed to like it.

As if Fox sensed me under the silly costume, he gave me a stare—hard eyes, too. I hadn't liked his attitude or his voice, and now the rest of the package gave me a very bad feeling.

I raised my hooves and backed away.

He lifted his chin and moved on, snaking through the crowd until I could track his progress only by the parting of the human sea to let him pass. He headed toward the kitchen—there was a service entrance there. I jiggled my cow head that direction. Jordan ignored me. I looked for Teddie. He'd bailed. The soft notes of a piano sounded from across the room, accompanied by a smooth, melty tenor.

Great. Not exactly the stick-by-my-side Galahads I thought they'd be. Of course, I hadn't voiced any expectations, so, when invited to a party…party.

Or not.

Trying not to call any more attention to myself, I eased through the crowd. I didn't hurry—Vivienne could track Fox once I could get out of this extra skin. For the whole of my life, I thought our brains separated humans from the rest of the animal kingdom, putting humans on the top rung of the ladder. I was wrong—it was our thumbs. As a cow, I couldn't grab my phone much less dial it.

I'd about run out of "excuse mes" and "I'm sorrys", and I'd only been able to fight my way as far as the bar. The amused looks were getting old and if one more person, male or female, touched, fondled or pinched without permission, I refused to be responsible for what happened next.

"Oh shit," Stella whispered as I passed by.

For a moment, I thought she'd figured out my ruse, but instead she looked over my shoulder toward the front door.

"He's looking for us, I can tell. And he's got the bitch with him."

I swiveled to get a look—it took some adjusting as I was scanning the surrounding area through two tiny holes too far apart. When I caught sight of who she referred to, even my heart tripped, and I knew he wasn't looking for me.

Beau Boudreaux with Mrs. Sky Ponder hanging on his arm, clinging like a lover, looked over the crowd with a serious case of furious. Perhaps my father's assertion of an affair was true. Lust coursed between the two of them like an electrical current from one of those globes that made your hair stand on end and sent bolts of static electricity arcing toward anything with a positive attraction.

His beady eyes, like tracers, looked for targets. They landed on the girls next to me.

Stella gasped. "See?" She could barely get the word out.

"He's pissed and coming this way." Even Olivia's composure cracked, a tiny fissure, but the crack was there.

"Why? We did exactly what he asked." Stella had found a squeak of a voice.

"That bitch, O'Toole, must've told him we ratted."

Offended to my core and without one erg of restraint left, I whipped off the cow head before I really considered the ramifications. "Seriously? I let you two skate, and you think I'd give you up to *Boudreaux*? For Chrissake, the guy laid out his girlfriend with a left jab! A colleague in another hotel caught it on tape. Next time, you better think a bit more carefully who you get in bed with."

The two hookers seemed confused at my rather epic analogy as they stared open-mouthed.

"You three. Stay right there!" Beau shouted. "You bitches are mine."

CHAPTER EIGHTEEN

GREAT, ONE cow lumped in with the collar-and-leash girls. Nobody could say we lacked animal magnetism.

The girls gave me their best deer-in-the-headlight impersonation.

That was my cue. "Follow me!" The gig was up, so I dropped my head and bolted for the kitchen. Beau blocked the front entrance—I only hoped Fox or someone his size wasn't guarding the rear. Anyone else I felt sure I could take. The girls waited a fraction of a second—enough time to kick off their heels and then grab them by the sling straps.

The door swung out, almost hitting me. A server carrying a large tray backed through the service entrance. I dodged—thankfully he was young and nimble, with fully intact reflexes. His eyes wide, his mouth forming a silent "O," he went to his left, and I went to mine. A head fake and I felt my hair brush the underside of the tray. The waiter, with both hands on his prize, whirled out of the way, slinging only a few cold shrimp and a crab claw.

At the back hall, I took a hard right; then, seeing the light through a crack in the elevator doors, I dove. My hoof made it, holding the doors open. Only a few inches, but they were enough.

The girls gathered me up, then the three of us pried the doors open and dove inside. On my knees, I pressed the button for the basement about a million times. With my heart stopped, I stared through the open maw, expecting Boudreaux to burst out of the Secret Suite any millisecond. Finally, the doors started to close.

None of us moved until the elevator started its descent. I sat with my back pressed against the sidewall. The girls offered me two hands. It took both to lever me up.

"You didn't sell us out?" Olivia said as she adjusted her G-string, then gave her breasts a plump. My mother had always preached the gospel of presentation. Maybe she had a mother like mine dishing the same advice, the daughter applying it liberally, unlike Mona's daughter. But I doubted she had a mother like mine.

Mona was a one-off—one of the few graces the Fates had bestowed.

But now was not the time to vilify my mother. We didn't have long, and we needed a plan. First safety, then explanations. *Think, O'Toole. How do we get out of here?*

A voice filtered down from above. "Ms. O'Toole?"

For a moment, my heart stopped. Had God answered? She never answered. Then oxygen hit my brain and focus returned. Tonto had ridden to the rescue. *Vivienne*! "Lock the elevators on the top floor now!"

A couple of seconds, maybe three. "Done. One car left before I could hold it. Should I stop it?"

"Who's on it?"

"One of the football players."

"Does he have a broken nose and two black eyes?"

"Yes, he's pounding the walls. Looks pretty mad. There are a couple of customers, not players. They look terrified."

"Damn." I couldn't leave them trapped with Boudreaux, his anger redlining. "Let it go. But try to get security to meet him in the lobby."

"A team is on its way, but the timing might be tight."

There was that timing issue thing again. At least mine was getting closer. "You can't leave him locked in an elevator with innocents." The lawsuit would arrive at my desk before I did.

"Agreed. I've been looking for you. You haven't been answering your phone."

"I thought I felt my udder shudder." My world settled; my focus returned. The me I used to be had finally decided to put in an appearance! About friggin' time! My shoulders went back as I pulled myself to my full dignity, even though I was dressed like a cow. I had this. I extended my right hoof to the girls. "I could use a hand."

Stella showed her pluck with a weak smile. "I'd be delighted." She managed to peel back the hoof to reveal all five digits, my thumb now being my most favorite.

Even though she watched through the eye-in-the-sky, Vivienne, showing stellar potential for the management-training program, did not comment on my attire. Whether that was worth a raise or my undying appreciation, I had yet to decide.

I rummaged in my udder while Stella worked on releasing my other hand. My phone eluded me. Finally, my hand closed around it. The elevator slowed for arrival. "Vivienne, Beau Boudreaux, the football player with the anger management issues, is following us. Please do everything in your power to slow him down. Throw him in the drunk tank, but it'll take several details. Then, if you can locate Mr. Fox, kindly do the same with him. But try not to let the two of them kill each other, although, I wouldn't be totally opposed."

She didn't respond.

"I'm kidding about that last part. I'd like the opportunity to kill them both." As the doors started to open, I stepped to the door as it eased open.

The garage level. One floor down from the lobby where Boudreaux would end up.

The lights buzzed and flickered. Rows and rows of cars stretched from where I stood toward the garage entrance, which was protected by a sliding metal gate I'd been told even a tank couldn't penetrate. Exhaust fumes lingered, just strong enough to identify. Other than that, the place was a tomb—a tomb with no real means of escape and nobody to come to our aid should we need it.

Bad choice. Too risky. I punched the button for the lobby level. At least we'd be surrounded by people, not that they'd be much help, not at this time of night and its normal level of required inebriation. Security would be close but perhaps too few. How many security guards would it take to contain an out-of-control pro-football player? That sounded like one of those lightbulb jokes. And just like when confronted with the jokes, I didn't have an answer this time either other than more guards than we'd have, which was answer enough.

My escape route, such as it was, would take us by the elevator bank from Babel and the Secret Suite—the one currently carrying Boudreaux.

The only upside was, from there, it would be a straight shot to the front door.

"You guys ready for one more dash to safety?"

Both women nodded, not that they had a choice or anything.

"When the doors open, we'll be in the service hallway, but we'll have to make a run across the lobby to the front doors. We need to get away from here and stash you somewhere safe. Got it?"

Once we got out the front door, that's where my plan ended.

Once again, the doors slid open. My heart hammered. What would be waiting on the other side? This was the live version of a game show where choosing the right door meant escape versus capture like something out of *Hunger Games.*

Not sure where Boudreaux fell on the IQ bell curve, I paused and looked up and down the hallway before motioning the girls to follow. Servers pushing carts, housekeeping staff balancing towering piles of crisply folded linens, a symphony of customer coddling with nary a misstep.

In two strides, we shot through a gap in the stream of service personnel and crossed the service hallway. At the double doors leading to the area behind the reception desk, I crouched, bending at the waist. "Make yourselves small. These doors will put us behind the reception desk. Keep behind the desk as best you can. If someone looks, they could see us from the lobby. There won't be much room, but we'll need to move quickly."

Unless the elevator had stopped at multiple floors, Boudreaux had to be in the lobby. The question was, had security been in time and in sufficient numbers to detain him? Security, assuming they had made it, wouldn't pull their guns—not so quickly and not in the lobby on a crowded weekend night. An unruly guest or risk shooting an innocent? No contest.

Like a sick conga line, the girls and I snaked out into the small space behind the desk. Four stations to make it past then around the end of the desk, then a streak across the lobby and…I didn't know what, but it would come to me—I was a pressure performer. Lately, my skills had been slipping, but I ignored that fact.

Consumed with excited guests, all wanting to get into their rooms and then jump into the fray, the reception staff didn't notice us. Sergio worked the last station—yes, I'd let him stay on the job. Innocent until proven guilty and all of that. And, with the way Romeo had been skulking around pretending to play for the other team, Sergio could well have been unwittingly recruited. Why wouldn't he believe Romeo, detective *extraordinaire* and one of my inner circle?

Once again, an excuse, not an explanation. He should've checked with me. Yeah, Miss P was right: I'd gone all soft and squishy.

We'd made it past the first two stations unnoticed, and I was starting to breathe normally when a voice froze me. A bellow of anger. I cringed and hunkered down. One of the girls behind me reached out and grabbed my cowhide, fisting her hand in it.

"Boudreaux," Stella whispered. I didn't ask how she knew his bellow, but the answer would prove interesting and most likely appalling.

"Don't you touch me!"

Boudreaux all right.

"I'm looking for three bitches, one of them your boss. Those three owe me. Get out of my way."

I wondered how I'd gotten on his shit list. Despite the broken nose, last time I'd seen him he'd been all sweetness and light, or his version anyway. I'd be willing to bet he'd gotten wind of my little chat with Frenchie Nixon.

For now, luck beamed our way—he hadn't seen us, and someone was trying to slow him down. I started breathing again. Security must've made record time. Reinforcements. This plan of mine that wasn't a plan just might work.

But the savage in his tone had a primal effect accelerating the heartbeat, and raising the hackles. That whole fight or flight thing steered dangerously toward fight. Out of answers, hurting and pissed, my ass backed into a corner by everyone, I wanted a fight; no, I *needed* one.

But first, I needed an exit strategy—the girls would not be collateral damage. This was my fight and mine alone.

Sergio worked the last reception terminal, Ginger the one between us. Boudreaux and his drama had captured Sergio's attention. I tried to attract Ginger's attention instead—she remained focused on her guest. Nothing worked so I crab-walked my way close enough to tap her on the leg, a fairly exceptional leg in sheer hose.

Startled, she yelped and jumped back. Not the desired effect.

With a finger to my lips, I shushed her and motioned for her to bend down. She nodded as she put two and two together to get at least close to four. "Call Paolo. Have him meet us out front immediately."

She grimaced. "Your nose is bleeding."

"Paolo. Now!" I inched behind her, leading my conga line toward the end of the counter and a short dash to safety, in theory.

Sergio sensed movement. Thank God, he didn't yelp as he swiveled a look in our direction. His eyes widened, but when I shook my head, he got the drift. Returning to his job, he pretended all was as it should be. With a lift of his chin and a worried grimace, he tried to convey what was happening and, from his expression, it didn't look good. The sound of a scuffle. Angry voices. Interested onlookers.

I preferred to think positive. Any distraction would provide a bit of cover…if we could get as far as the front door unnoticed.

We snaked past Sergio. Feeling pretty good, I risked a peek around the corner.

Behind me, a voice rang out. "Ms. O'Toole! What are you doing?" The voice seemed louder than necessary, or maybe I wanted more quiet than usual.

I looked up, following the voice to its owner—Ginger.

Frantically, I waved her to quiet. Sergio leaped toward her, then clapped a hand over her mouth.

She slipped out of his grasp. "Ms. O'Toole!" She paused for effect and a glance across the lobby.

The crowd quieted as her raised voice drew attention.

"What are you doing here behind the desk?"

"Let me at her!" Boudreaux.

"Run for it," I hissed over my shoulder. The girls didn't hesitate. I wanted to stop and beat the truth out of Ginger. That would be suicidal, but so tempting. Even without confirmation, I'd bet my virtue I'd found Boudreaux's and Fox's inside man—and she'd just cycled out of Security.

My feet slid as I rounded the desk. I staggered. Stella grabbed my arm and steadied me. I pushed her in front of me, Olivia too, then, bringing up the rear, I put my head down and ran for the doors.

Boudreaux jumped toward us. He wasn't that close, but too close for comfort—and he had the angle. I pushed the girls, propelling them toward the front doors.

I turned and braced for the fight.

As I feared, Boudreaux, his face an unnatural red and contorted with rage, his fists clenched, moved toward me with the uncanny grace of a feral animal—Security hadn't been able to hold him. He was wise to my elbow-to-the-nose trick, which left me with few others and none as effective. As I clenched my fists, I glanced at the girls who had slowed in the doorway and were now staring at me in horror. "Go!" I shouted, then I whipped back around. I couldn't stop him, but I could slow him down.

As he barreled my direction, closing the distance alarmingly fast, my life flashed before me. Not really, I made that up to be overly dramatic. But I did see a long stay in the hospital and maybe a new job.

I cringed, bracing for the blow, but I held my ground.

Ten feet.

I clenched my stomach.

Five feet.

From my left, a hurtling ball of human fury launched herself into Boudreaux. A flying leg kick, then a flurry of punches, fists and elbows flying.

Temperance! Security had arrived with all her MMA skills. Already bloodied, she must've been the Security personnel heeding the call, and she appeared to be alone unless we had wounded in the lobby. Had any one of my employees actually read the handbook? Two by two was the rule for Security. But right now I wasn't going to quibble with her choice.

Boudreaux had her by well over a hundred pounds, but she took out his knee and landed a punch to his nose. I cringed as he staggered back. "Go," she ordered. "Get them out of here. I got this."

I took her at her word and didn't waste a nanosecond. As I hit the doors, I glanced back in time to see Boudreaux stagger to his feet. Favoring his knee, he circled her like a prizefighter. He dodged, but she landed a glancing blow to his already busted knee. He yelled and moved in and flattened her with a left jab to the jaw. With his longer reach, that was his signature gambit with women.

She fell like a stone.

Boudreaux, standing over her body like a victorious gladiator, gave me his slitty eyes and an overconfident grin. He stepped over the inert form of my security guard. Conflicted—I should help her. Standing in the doorway, I looked for the girls out front.

They huddled at the curb, unsure and afraid.

To help any of us, I had to stay alive. One sweep of the cars and I had my plan.

Paolo, his megawatt smile at full brilliance, held the back door of the limo open for a man, his back to me. Several nubile young ladies wearing tube tops pulled to barely cover the important stuff, staggeringly high heels, and long blonde extensions clung to the man's arms and harbored dreams of avarice, no doubt.

In one leap, I grabbed the girls, shoved them in front of the group moving toward the limo, and pushed them into the back. They scrambled onto the forward-facing row seat. Following, I dove after them.

An iron fist circled my arm jerking me up short. "Not so fast."

My heart about leaped out of my chest, but the growl wasn't quite right.

Not Boudreaux.

Fox!

Anger flared. Adrenaline spiked. I let him jerk me toward him. Using his strength and my momentum, I drove my bulk into his. He grunted in surprise. Stepping to the side, I twisted his arm behind him. With one hand on his elbow, I pushed, hard, stretching tendons to the breaking point. His knees weakened. As I felt his muscles slacken, I shoved him into the limo head-first. My anger propelled him most of the way; the girls did the rest. Head-first, I launched myself after him, using his body now wedged between the two rows of seats. Then I rolled to my right, onto the backward-facing bench seat.

Paolo had bolted around the car and now slid behind the driver's seat as I pulled the back door closed.

"Go! Go! Go!" I shouted at Paolo. I pushed to a seated position, putting my feet on Fox's chest and applying all the leverage I could.

Stella had the heel of one stiletto pressed into his neck. Wisely, he didn't move.

Boudreaux shoved his way through the throng, some waiting for a car, and others moving toward the entrance. He skidded to a stop not five feet from me. Even though metal and glass separated us, I reared back—one of those involuntary self-preservation things that left me feeling sheepish, but victorious.

A phalanx of Security swarmed Boudreaux. True to his IQ, he turned to fight.

"Drive!"

Paolo threw the car in gear and stepped on it.

Tires screeching, fishtailing a bit, the limo clipped a car waiting for a valet to usher it around back. Thankfully, not some exotic iron, but still, my expense account would take a hit.

A small price to pay to cheat death one more time.

"I'm not going to be happy about who we pushed out of the way to commandeer the limo, am I?"

Paolo's dark eyes stared at me in the rearview until I started to get a bit queasy. "Eyes on the road."

"Yes, Miss Lucky. And, no, not happy, Miss Lucky."

"Serious suck-up to fix it?"

"Yes, Miss Lucky."

I raised a hand. "Don't tell me. In my weakened state and already sagging under a heavy load, I couldn't take it."

His smile lit his eyes. The man was wise to my bullshit but smart enough to know when it held the truth.

When he hit the end of the driveway, Paolo wheeled around a tight turn. I grabbed for the handhold as centrifugal force pulled at me. I did not want to give Fox any opportunity to turn the tables, so I hung on with both hands. The girls rode it out. Fox did the same.

Once established heading north on the Strip, I leaned back a bit and eased my death grip, but I didn't let go. "Don't slow too much, but make some turns, so if anyone is trying to follow, it'll be difficult."

"Yes, Miss." Paolo pressed his cap down on his head, then gripped the steering wheel with both hands as he hunched in concentration.

"Oh, and don't kill anyone and try not to get us arrested."

"You take away all the fun," he threw over his shoulder as he wove through traffic.

"Opinions differ."

"Do you know where we are going, Miss Lucky?"

"No destination until I'm sure we're not being followed." I looked down at Fox. "And we get some answers. For that, it's best to stay in the car where his screams can't be heard."

Fox tried to move, but his shoulders were wedged between the seats.

Stella would have none of it. She pressed her advantage, drawing blood. "Next time, Big Boy, I puncture your windpipe."

"I heard that." The amused voice of Vivienne emanated from my phone at my hip. Somehow, in the scuffle, I must've answered it.

"You need context to fully appreciate my situation."

"Just one thing," she asked. "Whose screams?"

"Fox's."

"Sweet. The guy's a douche." She sucked in a breath. "And I'm on the speaker, right?"

"Not to worry. Mr. Fox, should he live, will no longer be in our employ. And you will get a promotion and a raise due to your exceptional character-judging skills. And, for the record, I agree, he's a douche."

"And Boudreaux?" she asked, a hint of relief in her voice.

"He's a douche, too."

That got a chuckle. "I'm sure. But what exactly would you like us to do with him?"

"How many people did he hurt?"

"None badly. Brandy jumped in and took him down with that Aikido or whatever it is she's like a super black belt in. With his broken nose and damaged pride, he started making nice. Detective Romeo was here also, but she didn't need anyone's help."

"And Temperance?"

"Pissed but fine."

A fact that helped me feel a little better about abandoning her. "Romeo was there?"

"Yeah, looking for you."

I bet. And I had no idea what to make of that. I figured he'd be singing like a canary down at Headquarters. The guy had as many layers of Teflon as a politician. Who knew?

"Is he there now?"

"No, I told him about your adventure, and he left."

"Okay." He didn't arrest Boudreaux. "Take Boudreaux back to the party."

"You mean like let him go?" Vivienne tried to maintain a lack of emotion in that comment—she almost succeeded.

The girls across from me did not. Their displeasure was easy to read.

"Yeah, let him go. He threatened us, but that was it. Besides, everybody in this farce has guilty written all over them. I don't know what game they're playing, but let's give them some rope and see who hangs themselves."

"Yes, ma'am."

"Watch them all. If you need to bring in more sets of eyeballs, do it."

"On your authority?"

"No, yours. You're in charge. Can you handle it?"

"No worries. I got this."

"Let me know if any one of those idiots moves even a muscle."

"I can't see inside the Secret Suite."

"I understand. Just let me know if Boudreaux or Mrs. Ponder leaves. And I want you to hold onto one of our own." I told her about Ginger, our suspected traitor, and we discussed what to do with her. Vivienne disagreed with my suggestion of firing squad. I deferred to her suggestion—drunk tank, not that I was happy about it.

"Can you take me off speaker?" Vivienne's voice turned serious.

I hit the button and pressed the device to my ear. "Done, but speak softly." Somewhere, I'd lost my earbuds.

"I heard a female voice. Would that be one of our panty pushers?"

"Yes."

"Are both of them there?"

"Yes." I pretended to look out the window, but I watched the girls' reflections.

Stella kept her focus on Fox, but Olivia watched me.

"I did some digging on them. I don't know what it means, but they show up at a ton of NFL events. They could just be working, that's what they do, so I don't know. Just thought it was interesting and you should know."

"Thank you. Great job. Any sign of Mr. Ponder?"

"He's not in your parents' suite?"

"According to my mother, he's gone missing. No sign of him?"

"Negative."

"Okay, let me know if he shows up or any of the other jokers move. I'll be a bit busy giving Mr. Fox the treatment he deserves and putting the ladies somewhere safe for tonight, but I'll be available. After that, I'll head right back. Something's going down. I just wish I knew what."

"Roger." Vivienne signed off, and I made sure the connection didn't stay open.

My self-control hanging by a thread and relishing homicide, I glared at Fox. For some reason, I wasn't even bothered by the fact that my thoughts alone had probably earned me another black mark next to my name on St. Peter's ledger—assuming he hadn't crossed me off already. I mean, if Jimmy Carter had sinned simply by having lust in his heart, well, it wasn't looking too good for me. "Ladies, I'd be willing to bet my virtue that you're looking at the guy who sold you out to Boudreaux." Of course, I didn't have much virtue, but I felt pretty sure he had to be the one. He'd been listening in on all of us.

My little pronouncement landed with the desired effect. Stella put a bit more pressure into the heel on Fox's carotid. Blood welled around the delicate heel. Olivia drew a derringer out of the front of her G-string, leaving me rather speechless.

Where had she hidden it? It was small but not *that* small. My perspective, my experience, of course. I shut my brain to examining the possibilities—one thing I did know; I wasn't touching the thing.

I leaned back, abandoning any impression that I would ride to his aid. "Fox, I'd fess up here pretty quick, but the choice is yours. You gave a video to Boudreaux, one you took of the three of us ladies chatting in the elevator, didn't you?"

He glanced at the women, then gave me a nod. We all swayed with Paolo's maneuverings, although he had slowed down.

"Why?" I let go of the handhold but didn't let my guard down.

His wide eyes took my measure. "I'm doing the same as you, stirring the pot."

"Because of Lake?"

"He was my boss." Emotion choked his words.

"And something else, I think. You two go way back. Am I right? To Ely?"

"I met him there, yeah. He gave me a job on his security detail. Guess I had the muscles for it. Then he learned I had the smarts for more."

Curiously, he left out the football connection. "So you were promoted."

"The Golden Boy, as they say." Fox would've preened except for the stiletto pressed to his carotid.

"I bet the senator didn't know about your little sideline—the whole blackmail angle."

"Know about it? Hell, it was his idea. A way to get political leverage, he said. There wasn't anything illegal in what we did. We simply traded knowledge for favors."

"Nothing illegal." It wasn't a question, just a statement that left me reeling. That kind of thinking messed with everything—it subverted the whole political system, and it messed with my magic. I couldn't decide which sucked the air out of me faster. "Politics is a dirty business, so why not wallow in the mud with the rest of the swine. Is that it?"

At the insult, his hands clenched.

"Careful, your ego is showing. Don't let it make you do anything stupid."

"Yeah," Stella lowered her voice to a not quite growl that still sounded impressive enough. Of course, she had the advantage at the moment.

As the car swayed, Stella's stiletto made alternating deeper then shallower indentations in his neck. Wince on a right turn, breathe on a left. He was probably wishing we were on a NASCAR track. "I also figured it would get you off my back."

As answers go, that one was unexpected. "You ran them over to get to me?"

He flicked a glance at the two women, both of whom looked intent on returning the favor.

"Boudreaux's a loose cannon. He's got everything we all wanted, and he's just pissing it away, screwing the wrong women, hanging with the crowd that is interested in only his money and reflected fame...as long as it lasts." Fox lost himself for a moment, a distant look clouding his eyes. Stella gave him a jab and he returned. "If you had your hands full, I could do my job."

The light dawned. "Romeo and Chase?"

"Got you running in circles."

"I'm beginning to see how this all went down." And I was. A few tumblers dropped into place. Not enough to open the lock, but a good start. "Romeo's not in trouble, then."

It wasn't a question but Fox answered anyway. "Oh, he's in trouble. That guy Reynolds has him on a short leash. I just turned up the heat. Easy to do since you took an instant dislike to me."

"You didn't pass my gut-check. Something was off, but I couldn't prove it. Had to goad you a bit to see what you'd do."

Even though his shoulders were wedged tight, he managed a shrug. "I played you wrong."

Played me. "I kicked you the ball, and you didn't even get it out of the end zone." Boy, the guy was pricking my ego as well. I needed to let that go, or I'd end up wedged in the back of a limo with three people intent on doing me serious bodily harm.

Ego, always there, and most of the time making you call the wrong play.

He forced a grin. "Well, it didn't turn out all bad. I'm in the company of three beautiful women."

"When bluster doesn't work, resort to charm? Seriously? With this crowd?" I skewered him with a slitty-eyed look. "You're in the big leagues here, Fox."

His eyes narrowed and his face flushed.

"I'm making a mess of this, aren't I?" Fox switched to a half-humble gambit.

"You started off on the wrong foot and have been leading with it ever since. Tell me about the videos."

"Easy to manipulate and, folks usually cave rather than fight. Easy pickings."

"Because there's always a hint of truth in there that needs to be concealed."

"If you do it right." Fox could've been talking about hopscotch or any other kid's game.

"And the Ponders' video?" I tossed the hook, hoping to catch something.

His eyes widened for a fraction of a second, then narrowed. "You are so fishing. Better be careful what you catch."

"If the fish I've caught so far are any indication, I'm good."

"The problem with me, Ms. O'Toole, is you've got to get somebody to press charges. How many folks with big secrets want all of that a matter of public record?"

He had a point, but I wasn't about to let him win.

"Miss Lucky," Paolo said from the front, saving me from making not-so-idle threats, homicide being the last resort.

"If they are following, then Paolo lost them." My chauffeur who had a rather awful habit of slipping into the third person when referring to himself sounded triumphant—Patton marching into Paris.

"Good. Let me think." My adrenaline levels had returned to allow a hint of rational thought. Only one place to stash the girls that would be impenetrable. "Take us to the French Quarter, private entrance. We're going to call on my aunt."

CHAPTER NINETEEN

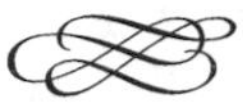

THE FRENCH Quarter occupied one of the lesser locations in town—a "local's" casino, it was close to the Strip but far enough away to lose the cachet and the foot traffic. A perfect metaphor for its owner, my aunt, Darlin' Delacroix. She wasn't really my aunt, and Darlin' wasn't really her name. Just as Vegas was a creation of fantasy and wishful thinking, so was Darlin'.

Her real name was Matilda. But she'd left Matilda back in Ely.

Years ago, when I'd been too young to complain, Matilda had moved to Vegas, changed her name, enlarged her bust, dyed her hair, and become one of the family, thanks to the poor taste of my mother. An honorary family member, Mona called her. To me, she was what she'd always been—a pain in the ass.

When she'd trekked south to Vegas, Darlin' had brought with her a family fortune made from mining a variety of minor minerals in northern Nevada. With a fraction thereof, she'd bought a very down-on-its-luck property. With the rest of her money, she'd exerted her influence, making the French Quarter the most profitable off-Strip property by a long shot. In doing so, she'd also become the first female owner of a Vegas casino and managed to navigate the local topography of cheats, wiseguys, unions, and outright thieves. Yes, she earned major respect points from me for that, grudging as they were. Still, that didn't mean she wasn't a total pain.

Continuing in stealth mode, Paolo had worked his way back toward the French Quarter, making several turns through the dark neighborhoods on the wrong side of the Fifteen. Dotted with warehouses surrounded in chain-link and topped with concertina wire, it struck me as a bad choice for eluding bad guys until I spied all the security cameras recording every movement, our license number, and the faces they could capture.

Vegas was nothing more than a citywide set for a modern version of *Candid Camera.* Most days that fact had me checking my teeth for green stuff, and half-expecting someone with a camera to jump from behind a statue or a street performer. Tonight, the fact that someone was recording all of this let me not be quite so concerned about looking over my shoulder.

The four-story pink, blue, and yellow sign out front, flashed and danced. Tonight was an extra fight night—a special card to meet demand, according to the smaller text. A has-been singer from the seventies was also "Back by Demand" to headline in her small theater. My aunt, catering to a slightly different crowd than the big properties on expensive real estate like the Babylon, knew her crowd and appreciated the fact that their money was just as green as the fancy-pants, as she referred to the glitterati and those wanting to bask in their glow. The Quarter's largest drawing card besides loose slots was a slate of prizefights held every Friday night, which always attracted a huge, rabid crowd.

In an effort to avoid squandering even a single opportunity to separate patrons from their money, the Quarter also boasted a bowling alley, a twelve-screen movieplex with reclining chairs and two-dollar buckets of popcorn, and a kid zone where parents could deposit the next generation, sometimes forgetting to collect them.

No wonder the parking lot was jammed as we cruised by. "On second thought, Paolo, let's go in the front. More people. Pull right up front like we're important." In order to deal with my aunt, I needed to get my game-face on. Getting my swagger on would help, too.

"Can I get up now?" Fox asked, his voice a bit choked—Paolo had made a quick right.

"Ladies?" I cocked an eyebrow indicating a question. "I believe Mr. Fox's excuse for putting you in harm's way was that you were expendable."

"Hey, that's not true!" His voice cracked in the lie. "Nothing bad was going to happen at the party."

"Weak, but it's up to them. What do you say?" I asked Stella and Olivia. "Death or dismemberment?"

That got everyone's attention.

Paolo eased the big car to the curb, and a valet jumped to open the back door.

"Allow me." A voice I wasn't expecting but wasn't surprised to hear.

Romeo elbowed the valet aside and then extended a hand.

I let him lever me out of the car. "Ah, my bad penny."

Like a karate fighter, he gave me a shallow bow but cocked his head to keep me in sight in case of a sucker punch.

As if.

The kid's face had aged another decade in the last hour or so. "What is it?"

"Marion Whiteside was injured in a drive-by. Somebody shot up the pawnshop. They got Frenchie, too."

"How bad?"

"Whiteside took it through his right shoulder. Not life-threatening."

"Not his life, anyway. If Whiteside gets the shooter in close range, all bets are off. Any idea who that might be?"

"Not yet. Non-descript car, witnesses with bad memories,

license plates covered. Weird, they peppered the place with a rifle. Got the slugs, .30-.30, but they're no good without a gun." He raked a hand through his sandy hair, which, in the odd multi-colored light, looked gray. His light blue eyes picked up the purple, his skin, the pink. The kid was fading into the background.

"Did you get a slug out of Lake?"

"Yeah."

"I'd compare the two," I said, leading him down a path he should've seen.

"Same shooter?" Romeo considered the possibility.

"I'd be surprised if it wasn't." The kid should've seen the synchronicity. But, trying to save his own bacon could be distracting, though, so I cut him some slack. Each of us had his or her limit. "Any idea who they were gunning for?"

"Don't know for sure. They used the scatter-bombing approach—kill everything and you'd get your man. But, my bet's on Frenchie."

"Is he alive?" Not that my heart would bleed, but I didn't need to lose a key witness to all these fun and games.

"Last I heard. Even though Frenchie squealed like a pig, the docs didn't seem to share his concern."

"You have a detail on him? I have a feeling he has some numbers we'd like to plug into the equation."

"Around the clock, two of my best. Are you any closer to figuring this out?"

I glanced around Romeo. Fox glared at me from under Stella's heel. "Yep. Pieces are fitting; I'm getting the picture."

Romeo pulled in a deep breath. My comment was water to a man lost in the desert. "I knew I could count on you."

We would discuss his "faith" in me later. But I'd be the first to admit that, given my distracted state, he could've played me, too. Any chump could do it, and had.

"What should we do with him?" the girls asked, indicating Fox.

Guess I'd drawn the short straw, and the decision was mine. All manner of painful prospects crowded my pea brain, none of them legal, but all of them delightful. I turned to the detective. "Since you're standing here and not under house arrest or something, you clearly are many moves ahead of me in this chess game, so your call."

Romeo brightened a bit at Fox's predicament. "He's a bit player. And with the heat up on Ponder and Boudreaux, Fox'll keep his nose clean. He knows they're playing in a whole different league, and murder is part of the playbook."

The girls let Fox up, then scrambled out of the car after him.

Fox glared at Romeo. If I didn't know better, I'd say Romeo was rubbing salt in an ego wound on purpose. Also, his zeal to let Fox go concerned me.

"Thanks, Paolo. I owe you." I shut the door but not before I heard, "No, you owe Mr.—" The door slammed on his words, cutting him off. Perfect timing. Tomorrow's problem. "Fox, go with Detective Romeo to the station. He may think you're a bit player. I intend to prove otherwise."

Romeo didn't fight me. "And what am I holding him on?" The detective might be a few moves ahead, but he was having trouble keeping up.

"Protective custody?" Not too quick on my feet—that was so lame. "Haven't you heard? There's a killer on the loose."

"That's only in the movies. I need something solid." Romeo wanted nothing to do with Fox; he made that much clear.

"Fine. Blackmail." I turned to the women who waited just beyond Fox's reach. "He confessed. The ladies here and I heard him. Right, ladies?"

"If you say so," Stella waffled. Olivia looked over my shoulder, avoiding my question.

Hookers and police—water and oil. I got it, but I would win. "See?" If they crossed me, the water board wasn't out of the question. No way would I let a hooker's reticence to cooperate with the police undercut a solid felony.

A gloat slipped over Fox's piggish face.

But my sly grin shot his gloat out of the water. "And attempted murder."

"What?" he squealed. "Of whom? You got nothing. "

"Fine." Romeo motioned to a uniformed cop I hadn't noticed. He whispered in the guy's ear, then relinquished Fox to him. "Twenty-four hours to get me something solid or I'll have to let him go."

"You'll get it."

"Who'd he try to kill?"

As we watched the large man leave with the much smaller cop, a sense of foreboding settled over me. I brushed it off.

Courage, don't fail me now.

"Frenchie Nixon, for starters." I raised a hand to fend off the questions. Frankly, I didn't have all the answers…yet. But I was close, so very close. "Work with me. Have I failed you yet?"

"No, but I'd sure like to be in the loop."

I gave him a pointed stare.

He hung his head. "Okay, point taken. What can I do to make it up to you?"

"Protect me from my aunt."

Resigned to his fate, he reached out to guide the girls toward the door. "Top floor, right?"

"Yeah. You go ahead. I need to make a quick stop." I pulled him aside and whispered. "Make sure you get the girls there and keep them in your sight. I'm not done with them yet."

With their shoulders back, the girls threw haughty looks at Fox's back as the crowd swallowed him. The girls took a moment to rearrange their dignity. The crowd did dart a few looks our way—three women, two looking like they were on their way to a BDSM party and one dressed as a cow. Even for Vegas we pushed the envelope.

"You do know how to make an entrance," Romeo said, then turned and disappeared into the French Quarter. Mired in dread, I gathered up the ladies, then trailed behind.

Once inside, we dove into the crowd. Like Mardi Gras throngs on Bourbon Street, most of the patrons wore ropes of beads and clutched tall glasses of Hurricanes as they ogled each other. Dixieland jazz pumped over the crowd, keeping the energy just short of explosive levels. At the French Quarter, every night was like Fat Tuesday.

An almost nauseating mixture of aromas filled the air—deep-fried beignets, strong Cajun spices, chicory coffee, last night's excesses, and tonight's to come.

An eardrum-shattering trumpet blast high above announced the aerial show. Perfect timing. Now the mass of humanity that had been creeping along at a glacial pace would solidify while everyone watched the show. Every hour, on the hour, the French Quarter put on its own version of a Mardi Gras parade. Wisely, Matilda hung it from the ceiling rather than trying to navigate the throngs in the casino. A bit of brilliance, really. She and my father, they each knew their market and how to pack them in. On a track over the crowd, buckets decorated like floats and filled with costumed revelers tossing beaded trinkets into the crowd meandered as carnival music blared.

"Keep moving," I shouted to the girls in front of me. We snaked single file, letting the cop cut a path. "Follow Romeo. I'll be right there."

Aunt Matilda had two vices, handsome young men and cheap gin.

Romeo would have to sub as the young man even though he was a bit too buttoned-down for her proclivities and wore too many clothes. Good rotgut, to the extent that wasn't an oxymoron, would balance him out.

Cheap men and a cheap drunk—my aunt's idea of a perfect evening.

~

To make things easy, Darlin' had made sure to have a tiny liquor store tucked into an inconspicuous corner of the sportsbook at the French Quarter. No hotelier wanted their guests to buy by the bottle when by the drink was much more lucrative for the house. But, Darlin' knew her crowd, and most of them weren't the Cristal type.

Only one customer stood at the counter. A tallish gal, her brown hair tastefully gathered at her neck, her face showing only hints of makeup, she had the pinched look of the terminally underfed with traces of Southern insincerity. She wore a simple cotton dress, no hose, and espadrilles as if she'd stepped out of the pages of Southern Style. In deference to the chill, she'd also donned a tailored jacket—white leather with "designer" written in each silver rivet.

Nolan Ponder's money gal. And she owed me a favor.

She was waiting to pay for an identical bottle of gin.

Guess her tastes weren't as high-brow as her presentation. Or we were both running with the same crowd.

In Vegas, a book could never be judged by its cover. Strippers were English majors at UNLV, dancers were their professors, and hookers were schoolteachers from Iowa. Not one to judge, that didn't mean occasionally some stories didn't get to me.

I set my bottle down next to hers. "You're a long way from the Babylon. Ever find who you were looking for?"

She shot me a glance, then did a double-take. "Your evening has clearly been more colorful than mine. Is a Furby convention in town?"

The world clearly conspired to offend even the few sensibilities that remained after decades in Vegas. I'd managed to avoid the Furby conventions, so I wasn't intimately familiar—a good thing as they had something to do with having sex with people dressed in fur costumes. I couldn't imagine being violated as a cow. The whole idea presented a Pandora's Box of legal, ethical, and moral questions best left unopened.

The cashier, a tall, greasy guy with a last-meal look about him, slipped back behind the desk. He eyed us, then, apparently finding us worthy, gave us a yellow-toothed grin. From the cloud enveloping him, he'd been out for a toke.

"I'll pay for both," the gal with the changing costumes pushed a twenty across the pockmarked counter. "Not every day I get to buy cheap gin for a cow."

That analogy actually held water when it came to my aunt as well, although I'd never tell her that. Matilda took herself very seriously, while the rest of the world hid their smiles.

I'd love some of that moxie, not that I'd ever admit that to her. Admitting it to my badass self was hard enough. "I can pay for my own, but thank you. Rarely do I impersonate a farm animal, but tonight it was expedient and far better than the alternative." Just the thought of my oversized body in a G-string, bedazzled bra, and dog collar, and carrying a whip was enough to send me to bed for a week.

"You make a good cow." The gal lifted her chin at the cashier as she pushed across a twenty.

"Insulting people you don't know. Is this a new approach to winning friends and influencing people?"

She gave me the side-eye. "You don't remember?"

The cashier held up the bill. "This'll pay for one. I'll need a two spot from you too, Ms. O'Toole." The cashier gave me a look that captured indifference and unimaginable sadness.

I guess, either way you looked at it, one bred the other.

While a twenty wasn't a two-spot, correcting him wouldn't do a thing to improve my current situation. "Twenty bucks for a ten-dollar bottle. Welcome to Vegas." She'd dangled the bait. Question was, did I really want to know what I'd forgotten? But even I knew that would be an impossibility. Curiosity killed the corporate cow—unanswered questions, my Kryptonite. "What don't I remember?"

"We were seven. You had a pony. My parents sent me to visit my older sister. They had no idea she was a hooker working for your mother."

The dim bulb of a childhood barely illuminated the dark corners I'd worked hard to forget. "You stayed with Trudie just off the kitchen."

"You sure I can't buy your booze? I owe you. You never told my mother what we were doing. She would've shit a brick. I got to ride the pony and shoot a gun. You even taught me how not to get pushed into a corner by some guy and then how to break his nose if I miscalculated. Can't tell you how many times that saved me through the years." She had a bill ready to slap down for my bottle.

Yeah, me too.

"At least you got a summer of being a kid." As life went on, I came to appreciate how much being let to roam free as a kid had shaped my personality. "But somehow, letting the seven-year-old I vaguely remember buy me gin cheapens the whole memory. Appreciate it, though." My pride intact, there was just one problem. Zipped into the cow carcass, I couldn't reach a pocket without a knife or some help. I didn't have a knife, and I so wasn't asking for help, so I took the path of least damage to my pride. "My credit is good here?" I asked the cashier.

"Sure thing. But it'll cost you a ten-spot to bring the bill to your office for collection."

That one he got right. My pride and the sanctity of my memories were worth ten bucks. "You have me at a disadvantage."

My implication as to his lack of chivalry fell on deaf ears as he drew up a handwritten chit and made me sign it. Thirty bucks—perilously close to any value my aunt might have, even taking into account the value of the gin. "What are you doing back in Vegas? Reliving good memories?"

"As much as I'd like to wander down memory lane with you, I'm trying to find Nolan Ponder."

"And you think he might be here?"

Clutching her bottle of gin by the neck, she gave me the once-over, a smile playing with her lips. "No. He wouldn't be caught dead in a place like this. I'm looking for answers."

"Maybe I can help? Inside the cow costume lurks a fearless corporate drone with access."

"Good point. And I'd hardly call you a drone. Only a fool would underestimate someone who can tame Darlin' Delacroix."

After dropping that little bomb, she turned on her espadrilles and headed toward the door.

We met again at the elevator. Our reflections were pure irony. Many times, I'd felt like a cow next to some skinny, petite thing, and now I was one.

A New Age metaphysical bit of manifesting gone way wrong.

One thing the cow suit was good for was keeping people at a distance. Nobody joined us in the elevator. My finger hovered over the buttons. "Floor?" I asked unnecessarily.

"All the way, as you suspect."

Darlin's apartment occupied the whole of the top floor, or at least this wing of it. "You do know what you're in for, right?" I punched the button, then leaned against the side wall. I tried to cross my arms, but my hooves got in the way.

Finally, that broke her reserve. "How do you do that?"

"Do what?"

"Manage to look in charge even when dressed as a cow with your privates showing and all."

I glanced down at my udders. A bit of overreaching, but a fantasy. "Bullshit and booze."

"Seriously?"

"Remember I said bullshit..."

"Right."

"There was this party and the costumes had to be black and white. And my ex is being all passive-aggressive."

"Privé." She reached into her breast pocket and pulled out a card. "Brinda Rose. You knew me as Thorn. After law school, I decided something a bit more grown-up might help."

"Did it?"

"It's the South where a woman in business has always been considered unbecoming."

"In Vegas, the sexism is much more overt. Women are commodities." I scanned the fine print. "You're a money manager? From Dallas? Honey, you're a long way from home. Don't the Ponders live in San Antonio?"

"They did. Dallas is not far."

"They're moving to Vegas?"

"Mr. Ponder will be. The Mrs. will be staying in L.A. where she's happy." Ever the loyal employee with a legal background, she held her cards close, giving nothing away.

"I know they're divorcing." On the theory that push only got you push back, I left it at that, laying the foundation. "Weren't you from New York?"

"My ex took me to Dallas." There was pain there, and something else. Revenge?

"Dallas? That's grounds for homicide right there."

She sagged against a wall. "You have no idea."

"I've never lived anywhere but Shangri La, so you're probably right. But the Dallas folks, when they stay at the hotel..."

"Pretentious, I know. Some are okay under all the big hair and insincerity. The trick is figuring out who is good and who is downright evil."

"It's the same everywhere." I thought about the evil I chased and fought the urge to chuck the whole thing and run until I dropped. But where would I run to? From what I'd seen of the folks who ran to Vegas to escape, their problems came along for the ride.

"And you know about Privé?"

"It's my job to know."

"You're not the normal money manager, are you?"

She wrinkled her nose. "A bit more hands-on."

"Ah, a keeper. My condolences." I stuck out my hand. "We're in the same field, sorta. Nice to meet you, again."

We shook while juggling two bottles of very cheap gin. Not sure what that meant, but it had to be some sort of sign. "I assume we are both buying presents for the same person, and hoping for answers to the same questions."

She waffled. I could tell she wanted my help, but, in her profession especially, being able to keep information private was a large part of what she was paid to do.

"Look, your boss is facing life in prison, if not death. We take murder pretty seriously around here, despite popular opinion. He had the murder weapon, his handprint was in the middle of Lake's jersey, and Lake's blood was all over him. And a call from his phone to Lake right before the murder presumably to set up the lethal encounter doesn't look great either." Of course, we'd placed everyone else at the scene except Mr. Ponder, and the Mrs. hadn't yet arrived in town, but it wasn't in my interest to say so. So, swine that I am, I didn't. I needed to know what she knew and what she was looking for.

"We've got about twenty more seconds," I said, watching the floor counter wind up. Darlin' didn't have cameras with audio in her elevators. Appalling, but right now, I was profoundly grateful. Having a private conversation—who would've thought that would be considered a luxury? "Would you mind going first? Give me some background: what brought you here? What do you suspect, and what do you know? Then perhaps I can connect some of the dots for both of us."

Brinda gave me an appraising look—being the first to show your cards required some trust. I kept my mouth shut. I doubted anything I had to say in my defense would be taken seriously. The cow suit detracted a bit from my gravitas, as it were.

Apparently, that was the right tack as she started in. "I've got money disappearing from Mr. Ponder's private account. All cash, so I have no idea where it's going."

"Paying off a blackmailer?"

Brinda looked surprised. "I know everything about the man down to the anchor he has tattooed on his left ball." She held up a hand, again shutting my half-formed question down. "No, not from personal experience. I'm good at what I do."

The whole tattoo visual was a bit nauseating. "I wish you'd stop doing that."

"I have two law degrees and a couple of decades of asking questions." She thought I was referring to the anticipating question things, which, I was, sorta.

"Does Ponder have any enemies?"

"You don't claw your way to the top of the heap without acquiring a few, but nobody who is involved with moving the team to Vegas."

"What about Senator Lake?"

"As far as I can tell, they were normal sparring partners in the money game. Lake playing to his constituency. Ponder angling for a profit. If anything was between them, it was a grudging mutual respect."

"Why, then, do you think Ponder staggered into the Babylon, drugged out of his mind, covered in blood, and holding the murder weapon?"

"I have no idea. And I can't find him, so I can't get his take."

Ponder. His disappearing act didn't help his claims of innocence. "What about Mrs. Ponder and the divorce. A bitter pill to swallow?"

"Hard to tell, but I would assume losing her position would rankle, although Mr. Ponder has made a generous financial offer. She doesn't much care for San Antonio."

"If her background is indicative of her character, Vegas would be more her style."

"She's cleaned up her act or taken it underground, but I have no evidence of anything."

"And that's why you're chasing the money."

"The only thread I could find."

I felt the elevator slow for arrival. "Time's up."

A frown wrinkled her brow, then it was gone.

"What?"

"Boudreaux. He's in tight with the Mrs., and he's got a lot to lose."

"I agree. He's in this up to his tight little ass." I hit her with my don't-fuck-with-me look. "Boudreaux told me you two were tight, that you were working together."

As the elevator's doors opened, she gave me a skeptical look. "Do I look like his type?"

"Too smart by half." I held the door and let her step through before I followed.

"Even if I felt like rescuing a puppy from the gutter, I'm married." There was a wistfulness and hurt to the assertion.

"Not an impediment, I assure you. Mrs. Ponder is married as well. So are half the folks who come to Vegas looking for some excitement."

That seemed to steal her moxie. "I know," she whispered. "Boudreaux is scum."

"Scary, too. That whole anger thing."

She relaxed—two women bonding over shared abuse. A sign of the times.

"What I'd really like to do is to catch who perforated Lake, nicking all the relevant arteries and veins to kill him. What they did took a certain kind of hate." I shivered at the visual. That one would never leave me. The horrible ones never did. "Boudreaux had motive and opportunity. But Ponder had the means and the murder weapon." I was a little light on motive just yet, but I kept that to myself.

"Have you figured out where Ponder was at the time of death?" Just like a lawyer, she honed in on a critical omission.

"Not definitively. I'm chasing a theory. Not sure I can prove it, though. Ponder was covered in a white powder which we suspect was Fentanyl. Got any insight into that?" The buzzer sounded its distress. A few more moments and I'd have to let the doors open.

"Between you and me, right?" Brinda Rose confirmed.

I crossed my heart with a dangling hoof. "Scout's honor."

"Mr. Ponder had some back surgery a couple of years ago. Painful stuff. Been addicted to opioids ever since. He's been tapering off. I really thought he was getting control of the addiction."

So, she knew. His addiction wasn't quite the secret my father thought it was. "Yeah, I know. And my father knows. And you know. Who else knows?" I let the button go and the doors slid open with an audible sigh, echoing my frustration. "Did he share his problem with his wife?"

"No. As far as I know, nobody in the organization knew."

Interesting, her depiction of Mrs. Ponder as being in the "organization" like the water boy or something. "Except you."

"I handle the money. And the payments I'm chasing aren't for the drugs. Those come from a different account, one Mrs. Ponder doesn't know about."

"She knows about this one?"

"Yes, but she doesn't have access. All the transactions are triggered through his phone, a fingerprint-protected app. If his addiction got out, well you can imagine the ramifications, not only with the NFL but in business as well."

"Well, somebody damn sure knows." And our lawyer/money manager was super naïve.

Lifting a print was child's play.

CHAPTER TWENTY

DARLIN'S PARLOR boasted flocked red wallpaper, dainty Queen Anne couches covered in purple velvet with frayed edging and crushed under the weight of the kaleidoscope of young men draping themselves suggestively, skirted end tables boasting lamps of fish-netted legs topped with fringed shades, and enough creep factor to scare off all but the most desperate.

A telling comment as to where I fell on the spectrum.

Nothing moved as if we were all on a set awaiting the opening curtain. The only things showing signs of life were the potted palms weeping in the corners. Frankly, if I had to live here, I'd be weeping too. When I was a child, Mona had not been happy when I'd taken a peek and dug in my heels, refusing to venture past the threshold.

The stuff of nightmares, the place wasn't the only thing that gave me the creeps—and made me sad. Darlin' was the poster child for aging ungracefully. Tonight's choice of music was "Fly Me to the Moon," a far sight better than the groaning and wailing she shot out of speakers at decibels not even reached by jet airplanes.

Four-foot-ten and eighty pounds dripping wet, Darlin' commanded attention from her perch on a raised chair, her legs stretched in front of her, her feet resting daintily on a footstool. The two girls who I'd sent on ahead sat on either side, like acolytes at an altar. Olivia had stashed her derringer—I didn't speculate as to where. Quick studies, both women had figured out their place at Darlin's. Romeo, arms crossed and looking a bit shell-shocked, held up the wall in a corner.

For a woman sliding toward eighty, she pushed the fashion envelope. She normally wore her hair long and blonde. Tonight she sported a shorter, sassier look in flaming red. Not a good look, although she had softened her lipstick to a shade of pink rather than the usual volcano red—a bit less garish, but not much. In keeping with her aging ungracefully, she sported sheer black hose with a perfect seam on her still-thin legs ending in a pair of red stilettos. She'd traded Lycra for leather, but her skirt was still black and still so short it had decency on the run. Given the season, she'd opted for a figure-hugging sweater, in black, of course. She'd abandoned her leather jacket with the Elvis mosaic on the back, choosing instead to have her idol immortalized in velvet and hung on the wall above one of the couches.

Her toes reaching for the floor, she slithered off the faux-throne. "Lucky! Brinda!"

"You two have met?" I raised an eyebrow.

Matilda gave me a look that, had she been capable of empathy, would have verged on pity.

"Honey," she took a hoof in both hands, "your mother told me you've been under a lot of stress and haven't been yourself since coming back from Asia. I had no idea—Mona's never been known as one to undersell anything." She plucked at my black-and-white hide. "My therapist is a doll—young, handsome, he makes me feel more like me than ever."

So many possible comebacks, none of them appropriate. But, if I ever laid myself out on Darlin's therapist's couch, I hoped my friends would put me out of my misery. “You’re so kind.” I half-squatted, then bent down to give her a hug—four-foot-ten is a long way down from my six feet. “Aunt—”

“Don’t you dare.” She gave me the stink-eye. “Now I know you need that empty skull of yours cracked open under a bright light. But, given your current attire, I’m thinking you need a heavier hitter than Dr. Damien.”

She gave Brinda a quick hug, then gave a heavy sigh as she blessed me with a once-over. “I had my money on Mona going daft before you did.”

“I’m overcome.” The snark did a complete fly-by, racing over her head unnoticed as I knew it would. “But, in my defense, lumber-sexuals are all the current rage, and I hear the next big thing will be agri-sexuals. Farm animals will be their focus. I’m getting a jump start.”

That one got her. She grimaced in distaste, a shudder racking through her.

With her back to me as she retreated to her throne, I let my victory shine through in a sly smile, which Brinda caught and returned. I resisted a fist pump to rub it in.

The young men, hired to be unctuous and apparently good at their jobs, rushed to give her a boost.

My turn to shudder, an involuntary spasm that shook my udders.

Darlin’ seated herself, arranging to present her best parts forward. Once settled, she gestured to the women at her feet. “Now, what’s this I hear about somebody coming after these beauties?”

With a glance at Brinda, I filled her in.

Darlin’s expression hardened. “I’ll keep the girls with me. Mind you, not because I have any love for Justice Lake or Beau Boudreaux. Justice tried to take my daddy down back when mining around Ely resembled the 1849 Gold Rush. And Boudreaux, he’s been feathering his own nest since he was a toddler. When his best friend got busted for the drugs all of the football team were taking, thanks in large part to Lake, he rolled on them all in return for keeping his resume spotless. A huge scholarship and the NFL beyond were on the line. Guess I can't blame him."

"His best friend was a guy named Fox?"

"That's the one."

"Did Daisy Bell know the two of them?"

"She went to school with those boys." Darlin' was a championship prevaricator from way back—she'd had to be to get this far in a white-boy world. I hadn't the time or the patience, or, quite frankly, the skill, to parse the truth out of her.

"I'd like to talk to her."

"It's a free country." Something in the way she said it didn't ring true.

"She keeps a low profile. I don't know how to find her. I'd like your help."

Darlin' pursed her lips and shook her head. Her smile weakened, as did her bravado. "We haven't talked in a long time."

Liar.

"Is she in trouble?"

Darlin' glanced between Brinda and me. "I got this, Lucky. Don't worry."

This case was completely crazy—my lead horse, Mrs. Ponder, hadn't even made the starting line by the bell. Still, she was a comer—I just had to prove it. "Is Daisy Bell okay?"

"I told you. I've got this." Jesus, just like my father. The two of them handling their own problems the old Vegas way. Didn't they know this was the new Vegas? Yes, it was grown from the seeds of the old way, but now burying a body in the desert didn't earn you respect—it earned you a spot on Death Row.

"Can you send your staff away? We need to have a private chat with your two guests here." I motioned to the girls who bracketed Darlin'.

"I told you she knew," Stella hissed.

Olivia didn't answer. Instead, she eyed me coldly. "Shut up, Stella."

Darlin' gave a dismissive wave and the young men draped all over the room peeled themselves off the furniture and disappeared one by one through the swinging doors that led to the kitchen.

After the last of her males disappeared, I watched the doors swinging while I gathered my thoughts. "Okay, ladies, I want to know what you were doing handing out "invites" to the Privé party and riding up and down in my elevator. I know you show up at a lot of the NFL soirees all over the country. I also know you dropped by to see two pawnshop guys who run a black-market business in stolen sports memorabilia."

They glanced at each other but didn't offer any info.

"Romeo?" At my summons, he levered himself off the wall. "Want to deliver these two ladies to Boudreaux?"

"Boudreaux," Stella spluttered. "He'll kill us."

"You can't do that!" Olivia added. "Put us in jail."

"For what? You told me yourself you weren't guilty of anything. And you weren't hooking in my hotel. You also said that." I resisted a smirk.

They knew what I wanted.

Stella gave Olivia a pointed look. At her nod, she turned back to me. "Look, we just talk to the guys, find out who's got problems that need a solution. Not much different from scouting johns. Money's almost as good."

"So, you are the marketing department for this little drug, memorabilia, insurance scam?"

"We just find the guys. What happens after that isn't on us."

I didn't think now was the time to educate them on accomplice culpability. "And what were you supposed to be doing last night?"

"Making sure Marion Whiteside stayed at the party."

"Who asked you to do that?"

They clammed up.

"I'd be willing to bet Fox did."

"But he was blackmailing us," Stella said.

"He wasn't blackmailing you. He was working with you and Beau. And he heard you two sell out to me and he sold you out to Beau, ruining a great gig for you."

"Why was Fox so mad at the party?"

They stared at me owl-eyed. Stella started to shake.

"This is bad, Stella. You know how to make it better—tell me what I want to know."

"Okay. Okay."

"Don't!" Olivia barked.

"We're not getting out of this without her help." Stella turned back to me. "I didn't get it all but it was something about a football jersey."

Romeo looked to me for clarification. Instead I gave him a grin. "Thanks, Stella." I turned to my aunt, who was riveted. "Keep them here. It's important. I've already had one witness shot up. I don't want these two to end up a pile of bones bleaching in the desert." Overselling, but terms my aunt understood. "I'm going to need your car and driver. Where is he waiting?"

"Side entrance."

"Romeo, you and Brinda are coming with me. We each know pieces of this, and I bet it might take all of us to finish the puzzle."

As we fled toward the elevator, my phone dinged.

A text message from Vivienne: *Mrs. Ponder and Boudreaux are on the move. They've called a car. Not one of ours. Still no sign of Mr. Ponder.*

I still had Dane on speed dial. Not sure why or what that was about, but right now I was happy for my indiscretion.

"I was just going to call you." His voice plucked some chord.

The whole Texas twang was overdone—of course, he was from

Texas, but I always felt like he overplayed that card—like he wanted us all to think he was stupid when he was far from it.

"Do you have any news on Mrs. Ponder's plane and when it landed the night of the murder?"

"If it landed, it didn't land at McCarran, not until much later that night. But you'd seen her in Vegas before that."

"Did you check North Town?" North Las Vegas airport took the corporate jet overload when McCarran ran out of landing slots and parking spaces.

"Not there either. What kind of Citation is it?"

His question exposed the itch that had been bothering me. "Hang on." I lowered the phone. "Brinda?" She jumped at my tone. "You came in Mrs. Ponder's plane, right?" She nodded. "Exactly what kind of plane is it?"

"Citation Sovereign. Why?"

"You normally go into McCarran?"

"Yeah. More services and so close."

I returned to Dane. "A Citation Sovereign. Let me guess; it has short landing capabilities."

"Yep."

"Try Henderson."

I cut him off and pocketed the phone. Punishing men for my conflicted emotions about them was getting to be a problem to solve. I added it to the list. The Lucky O'Toole Self-Improvement Program was off to a rocky start.

"Where'd you land when you came in?"

"McCarran."

I had one shot and a fifty-fifty chance of being right.

~

Bentley skidded Darlin's Prius through the gate and onto the ramp at the FBO at McCarran Airport.

Yes, her driver was Bentley, so she could say she had one,

which appealed to her Champagne tastes. The Prius was a nod to reality.

"You're sure they're headed here?" Brinda asked.

"I'm not sure of anything. Sometimes running for your life is the only option left. For Sky and Beau, I'd say they're about there. The case against them is pretty significant."

"The case for what?" Romeo didn't try to hide the scoff.

"Murder and several other lesser felonies."

"You can prove it?"

"Most of it. The rest should shake out, though." I sounded cavalier because I was. I was pretty sure I knew who was doing what to whom, why, and how to prove it. A few pieces still eluded me, but they'd show up.

The last in, Romeo unfolded himself first, and rather ungracefully, landing on his ass. Brinda next. She managed a Princess Grace exit. Of course, she did.

Now my turn. I'd wedged myself into the corner of the tiny back seat. I hadn't taken the time to extricate myself when it would have been easy. Now I'd pay the price.

Now *there* was my epitaph.

The hooves covering my feet were stuck on something up under the driver's seat. Hung higher and tighter than a pretty boy's balls; they wouldn't come free no matter how much I tugged and yanked.

Unable to move, I stuck my hands out. Bentley, ever the gallant, got out of the car and moved his seat forward. That only meant I could breathe. I was still stuck. Brinda grabbed one hand, Romeo the other, and they pulled.

"I'm thinking we should kill the fatted calf," Romeo said to Brinda. He even kept a straight face so no grin to slap off.

Not that I would. Although… "Cute." Was everyone starting to sound like me or was I imagining it? And just when I'd lost my own voice?

"You could've ditched the costume." Brinda took the higher road. "You do have clothes on under there?"

"Jesus!" Romeo seemed alarmed at the thought of me in my skivvies.

"It's been so long I've forgotten. But I'm game if you are." I leaned forward. Bentley leaned in our side and worked the zipper down. From the front, Romeo grabbed the neck and pulled as I wiggled my arms loose. We freed my upper half.

The cold air hit me like a slap.

Using both hands, I got the thing over my hips. "The rest should be easy. Hold my hands to steady me, and I'll step out of this thing." Not quite as easy as I thought, but eventually I broke free. Losing my balance, I fell half in and half out of the car, taking Romeo with me.

My face ended up in his crotch. Surprisingly, my nose didn't yell in protest to yet another assault. Matching every other part of me, the thing was numb.

Pushing myself up, I smiled at him. "You've missed me. I know you have."

His grin was the first I'd seen since he'd stolen a very pricey, one-of-a-kind watch out from under the nose of a master jewel thief. Basking in his radiance was worth the indignity. "Your nose is bleeding again. If you got blood on these pants, they're yours."

"We've got to go!" Brinda said, her voice taut. "I think that's the Ponders' plane taxiing out."

Romeo eyed the tower in the distance. "We're too late to stop it."

"Out of the box, Grasshopper. Brinda, can you get the pilots on their cellphones?"

"Not now. Once they get their clearance, they would've turned them off and stowed them."

"What about the Unicom?" Thinking out loud, I knew the answer to my own question. "Never mind, they switched to ground frequency. Unicom wouldn't be able to raise them." I glanced over my shoulder. "Bentley, bring the car."

"Oh, you so are not doing whatever it is you're thinking of doing!" Romeo shook his head and backed away.

"Brinda and I are indeed. You know the pilots, Brinda? They'd recognize you?"

"I sign their paychecks, a status I think will override any argument from Mrs. Ponder."

"Even better. Let's go."

Bentley skidded the Prius to a stop, and we both climbed in as the plane eased off the ramp onto the active taxiway. Romeo put a hand on my arm. "This is serious. If you're wrong…"

I shot him a smile and climbed in. "I'm not!" I shouted at him before I shut the door. "Bentley, follow that plane!"

He accelerated across the ramp and onto the taxiway until the ass end of the small jet loomed over us. "We won't have much time, Miss Lucky. The police and the Feds will be all over us."

"Then I suggest you pull alongside or in front or something to stop the plane."

"Yes, Miss." He hunched over the wheel. "I've always wanted to do this," he muttered, making me smile.

"You do know what you're doing?" Brinda looked comfortable either way.

"I have contingency plans. We should be fine if we can get them to stop before they hit the main taxiway, which is up ahead and perpendicular. The traffic here is light and mostly private or local tour operators. And, technically, we could still be on the ramp, I'm not sure."

"Which would make the Officer-I'm-so-sorry-here-have-a-look-at-my-cleavage thing much easier." She didn't have any buttons to unbutton or she might have.

The sex angle disappointed me. "That might work in Texas, but this is Vegas where cleavage is a yawner."

"Good. It's much more fun to go toe-to-toe."

Innuendo in the heat of battle. I liked it. "But the power is still theirs."

"Hence, the cleavage comment you didn't like."

Would I always be an open book? "After that intersection up ahead, things get gnarly, and we'll have to cross an active runway. Bentley, it would be ideal if we didn't have to do that. Good news is the plane will slow to turn and may have to stop to get clearance." They could've been cleared all the way to the active runway. Either way, they'd have to slow down.

Bentley stepped on it.

"Hit the inside lights so they can see who we are." The interior lit up like a stage hit with all the kliegs at once.

"Bentley, are you having a Butch and Sundance moment? Give them a target they can't miss? I do not intend for us to go out in a blaze of glory."

"It's a fantasy of mine, Miss Lucky."

"*Now* you tell me."

We'd pulled even with the cockpit. Brinda, sitting next to me in the rear, rolled down her window. Even though throttled way back for taxiing, the jet engines whined, making communication a hand-signal thing. Brinda mouthed, "Hold my legs," then thrust her upper body through the open window. Waving wildly, she tried to get the pilot's attention.

The airport remained free of flashing lights other than the red and green position lights on the tips of the airplanes' wings—eyes winking in the darkness.

I tapped Romeo on the shoulder to get his attention. Motioning to his inside pocket, I tried to get him to pull out his badge. He did, then he turned and held it up for the pilot to see. Next, I tapped Bentley, motioning him forward and closer to the plane.

He gave me a grin, then did as I asked.

That worked. The engine spooled down to idle. Shouting was now a viable communication option.

"Motion them over to the ramp!" I shouted to Brinda.

A helicopter operation with a large expanse of free space, it would get us back into at least having an argument that we hadn't strayed from private tarmac. The engine's whine didn't rise. The plane stayed stopped.

"Bentley, be prepared to cut them off." Beau Boudreaux with his muscles and fury might be Mrs. Ponder's trump card.

He eased the car forward, giving him an angle.

I tugged on one of Brinda's ankles. "What are they doing?"

"Can't tell."

Brinda wiggled her way back inside. A grin split her face. While she was pretty with a scowl, she was stunning with a smile. I wanted to hate her, but I couldn't. "Thumbs-up from the pilot. He's moving the plane off the taxiway to the ramp."

Romeo's phone rang. He answered with one word, "Romeo." He glanced back at me, his face darkening to a deep scowl. "Status?" A few more seconds. "Roger. Put a BOLO out and keep me apprised."

"What?" I asked knowing bad when I saw it.

"Fox escaped. Damn near killed my man."

"Is he okay?"

"Going to be."

The engines spooled up, and the plane eased into a hard right-hand turn. Bentley whipped around the front of the plane, then parked the car, leaving the plane just enough room to stop on the ramp and go no further. As we piled out of the car, this time with a bit more dignity, the plane's door opened, and the steps unfurled.

A young man stuck his head out as the engines shut down. "Brinda, you, and your friend, and the cop."

Brinda started up the stairs. Romeo stepped in next to me. "This could be a setup."

No could be about it. "We're reading from the same playbook."

"Would you stop with the football analogies?"

He knew mental gymnastics, as simple as they were, helped offload my panic. He also knew the answer would be no. "Let me quarterback this. You still got your piece with the silencer?"

"No, Chief took it from me. Told me to keep my nose clean and not hanging out with you would be a good start."

"Harsh. And so unappreciative." I'd helped solve a lot of cases for the man. "But you should've listened." I motioned him to go in front. "Youth before beauty."

"Lamb before the lion." He stepped in front. "And your Glock?"

"I put it back under the seat in the car. Tonight, I couldn't trust myself."

"You need to work on that."

Second-guessing, one of my best things.

As we inched up the stairs, I felt like the condemned doing the midnight walk. The whole thing felt like a trap, and I had no fight left. "Before I die, I'd like to know one thing."

"The key to eternal happiness?"

"No. I want to know how you got out of being thrown in the Gulag. You made it sound like the cops had you cold and Reynolds was going to nail you."

"He didn't." Romeo ducked through the low doorway before I could ask any more.

"Really?" Pausing on the tiny top platform, I leaned down and stuck my head inside. "Reynolds let you walk?"

Mr. Ponder stood at the rear of the plane. He waved me inside with the pistol in his hand. "Join us, Lucky. You're late to the party." Still attired in one of our Babylon logoed velour tracksuits, he looked like he hadn't had a hit of his joy juice in some time. Pain etched deep grooves in his face, bracketing his mouth. His hand shook. Sweat beaded. His smile stretched only as far as a grimace. Still, he had the overbearing attitude of a man used to getting his way.

His wife, her feet tucked under her and her arms lashed across her chest, made herself small in the crook of a couch that lined one side of the cabin. In a red sweater set and tan jeans, she looked like a wilted flower against the white leather upholstery.

Brinda had taken a seat next to her with Romeo hunching uncomfortably as he straddled the arm of the couch.

"Take a chair." With the gun, Ponder motioned to the club chairs opposite the couch. "This is my wife's plane. Sorry the accommodations are a bit tight. We've been expecting you."

"Where's Boudreaux?"

Sky sobbed, then cowered at a glare from her husband.

The young man who lowered the stairs, presumably one of the pilots, stood to my right wedged in the tiny galley. "He shot him," he whispered. "Really just winged him. He's in the back bedroom. I had to tie him up." He showed me his hands. The blood was still red. "You might want to run for it."

Mr. Ponder brandished the gun, his veneer slipping. "I didn't kill Lake. It looks bad, I know. But somebody is framing me." He stared me down, his eyes a bit wild. "You have to believe me."

"I do. And, better yet, I can prove it."

All eyes settled on me, most were disbelieving, but Sky Ponder's were murderous. "What?" Mr. Ponder whispered. "You believe me?"

"And I can prove it."

"How?" Romeo asked.

I heard sirens in the distance. Strobing red lights flared across the field and flashed through the side windows. "Better make your case quickly," Romeo hissed.

"You really were at a private game. One Boudreaux fixed up in the Secret Suite. My Security head is gathering the witnesses."

"He told you that?" Romeo mouthed.

I ignored him. Brandy had said Jerry had heard whispers. With Jerry, that was as good as gold. The chips, the one Ponder had and the one I found, were a good start. Somebody had to have been there—dealers, waitstaff. Someone would talk. "Then, a call from your phone arranged the meet at War Vegas with Lake."

"War where?" Ponder's confusion seemed genuine.

"But you didn't have your phone. Your wife did."

"I did not!" With the indignation of the guilty, Sky gathered the last of her fight-back.

"His phone is gold. Everyone else's is silver. You handed his phone to him in my office. I saw it."

"But I wasn't here." She settled back, sure she'd just thrown down the winning card.

"You landed at Henderson, not at McCarran. And I'm sure, if someone were to search this plane, the water, the shower, hiding places, they'd find the clothes you showed up in. Nobody wears Lilly Pulitzer to Vegas, much less in January."

Her fight faded. "You can't believe him." She pointed at her soon-to-be ex. "He was drugged out of his mind."

"And that was your biggest miscalculation. You thought the Fentanyl you gave him and covered him in so none of us idiots would miss it would be enough to kill him."

"It should've been." She clapped a hand over her own mouth. "That's what the Medical Examiner said," she mouthed through her fingers.

Ponder lowered his gun. If a man could shatter, I was witnessing it. "You tried to kill me? I thought we'd worked all this out."

"Do you think I'd give up the throne and accept a house and a stipend from you? I had it all. Why would I take less? If you were gone, it all would be mine."

So captured by the story and so focused on the gun, I failed to realize one of the key players was missing. "Where's Fox?"

"Fox?" Ponder either didn't know him or didn't know why he would be there.

"Yeah, Boudreaux's and your wife's flunky. He carried the rifle used to shoot Lake into War Vegas. And I'd be willing to bet he tried to take out one of the witnesses to the full breadth of this whole little operation."

"What operation?" Mr. Ponder again, this time not so confused.

Why wasn't Fox here? "You know. That's why you're divorcing the woman you love. She couldn't resist keeping a fallback plan, in case you decided you'd tired of her. So she stayed with what she knew: dealing. Then Boudreaux and Fox, both needing their own exit strategies, figured out a plan that was a bit more nuanced which provided a bit of protection from the legal system, if you will. A few more layers to work through."

"You love me?" Sky Ponder whispered as the realization dawned.

Too late. Way too late.

Love forces you to be all in. If you're not, if you hedge your bets, it'll bitch-slap you to Hell and back...if you make it back.

Even though Sky Ponder was a snake, I felt horrible for her. You grow up having to protect yourself, to scratch and claw for every penny and you never learn how to let go, how to trust. Her path and her fall—I needed to pay attention.

"Kid," Mr. Ponder addressed his comment to the young man who'd given me the best advice of the evening, to run for it. "Encourage Ms. O'Toole to step completely inside, then pull up the stairs." Red lights strobed through the window. "Do it now!"

Tires screeched as several cars skidded in around the plane.

Shit! I knew why Fox wasn't here. I kept my spot in the doorway. "Don't shoot anybody, Mr. Ponder. You're free and clear, and broken hearts, while extraordinarily painful, are not lethal. Trust me. I know." I motioned the young pilot back, and he stepped into the shadow behind the bulkhead. "Get some help for Mr. Boudreaux, although, if he dies, the world would be a better place." But having Ponder take the fall wasn't something I wanted to see.

I knew what I had to do. If I thought about it, I wouldn't do it, so I didn't. Instead, I reached in, grabbed Romeo, then threw myself backward down the stairs.

CHAPTER TWENTY-ONE

WITH ONE hand fisted in Romeo's coat, I only had one other with which to grab the railing and slow our fall.

Landing on my back, the air left me as I slid down the last two steps. Romeo landed on top of me, forcing the breath left out with a whoosh.

This time it was his face in my crotch. He looked up at me and managed to blurt out, "I do miss you," before we both scrambled off the stairs, ducked under the plane, and crouched behind the stairs. Little protection against the Feds with guns, but it was something.

"Don't..." I sucked in air. "They tell you..." More air. "To never go..."

"With your captors? Yeah."

Romeo and I risked a peek. Looking out at all the people with guns, I reevaluated. Ponder was only one man with one gun.

"First time for everything. Never imagined you doing what *they* say." He put a hand on my back. "Are you okay?"

"Tomorrow I will hurt in places I never knew I had. But we have one more person to save before I fall apart."

"Who?"

"Reynolds." I grabbed my phone and hit Jeremy's speed dial.

"Remind me to work for you more often. I'm sipping some fancy cocktail at a high-brow place, waiting for your bloke to do something, and all on your dime," he said without preliminaries.

"You're still on Reynolds?"

"He got a phone call. I followed him to Hyde at Bellagio. He's waiting for somebody." He listened while I filled him in. "Got it."

"Be very careful. And, if it's a choice between you and Reynolds--"

"I let the dingo get the cop." A weird phrase, loosely translated I think it meant, "no way in Hell."

Knowing arguing with Jeremy was a waste of precious time, I pocketed my phone. "We've got to hurry," I said to Romeo.

"Reynolds?" Romeo shuddered in revulsion.

"He's been playing us. He's been pretending to be the bad cop, playing it to his advantage. You showed up in the middle of his gig, threatening to ruin it all and blow his cover in the process."

Romeo sat back on his heels. "And he put me under the gun to keep me from interfering." Skepticism infused every word. "I don't believe it."

"You don't want to believe it." I took a breath, fighting my need to hurry. Fox had a huge head-start, and Jeremy was in the middle—we needed to hurry. "Think about it. He figured a way to keep you out of it. He cold-cocked you to prevent you from being the bagman for Lipschitz and Godwin. He kidnapped Miss P and took her out of the pawnshop before Fox, most likely, shot up the place."

"Why didn't he go back and rescue everybody else? Marion Whiteside was there."

"I shot him in the foot and he had to go to the station with you." My fault, but understandable, knowing what Romeo had seen fit to share with me. "Let me ask you a question."

"Fire away, even though you seem to have all the answers." He wasn't grousing, even though it seemed a lot like he could be.

"Were you at War Vegas before I called you and sent you on a treasure hunt for Lake's body?"

"No."

I sighed. Just as I thought—in the dark, Bethany had mistaken Reynolds for Romeo. Even I'd had a hard time distinguishing them in a dark alley. "Reynolds had the rifle used to shoot Lake—he clocked Boudreaux in the face with it."

"Boudreaux killed Lake?"

"No, Mrs. Ponder, but that's where I need a bit more evidence. She was here and she shook sand out of her shoes in my office. But, that's all I got on her. Either Reynolds saw her do it, as Fox probably thinks, or we'll need the clothing she wore or some other physical evidence."

"What if we have her on tape at War Vegas?"

"Do we?"

"No." The kid deflated.

"Don't give up, kid. Get a warrant. Search the plane, including the wastewater. She had to have cleaned up after she offed Lake. She could get on the plane without being seen—she'd had them park it at Henderson Airport. Much less traffic. And then swab-down the Secret Suite. That's where they drugged Mr. Ponder, doused him in Lake's blood, and gave him the murder weapon. As he was trippin', they took him down the back staircase—the secret entrance to the Secret Suite, and shoved him into the lobby. Their only miscalculation was the Fentanyl. The Mrs. didn't know her husband had a fairly serious habit and it would take a more than fairly serious amount to kill him."

"And Fox?"

"He does the dirty work while Mrs. Ponder and Boudreaux keep everyone's attention. Right now, he's on his way to clean up that last little mess."

"Reynolds." Romeo was starting to buy in.

"What if Mrs. Ponder is smarter than we think?"

"One of these idiots will roll." I squeezed his shoulder. "We got this. But now we need to return the favor to Detective Reynolds. And we need to hurry."

"Are you sure about all of this?"

"Yes."

Romeo dusted himself off. Hard to do crouched behind the stairs, but he made a valiant effort.

Covered in blood, I didn't even bother.

"Where are we going?" Romeo asked.

"Hold it right there." A female voice.

"Airport Police."

"Are they the Feds?" I asked Romeo.

"Beats the hell out of me, but I think they're the law around here."

The stairs started to ascend, leaving us rather exposed.

"Someone's buttoning up the plane." Romeo couldn't resist the obvious, but that meant he'd scraped the bottom of the I've-got-a-plan barrel.

"Works for me as long as we keep the bird on the ground. They won't be leaving." I nodded toward the Prius.

When we had headed for a showdown in the plane, Bentley had parked the car directly in front of the plane as close to the nose wheel as he could get without bending metal. I could just see the hood. The airport cops had him sprawled across it. He looked up to see me smiling at him. He gave me a thumbs-up and a shit-eating grin.

"You want to take the lead in explaining all of this to the local constabulary? And make it quick. We've got to go."

EVEN THOUGH WE WERE WELL INTO THE NEW DAY WITH SUNRISE not too far, the normal nighttime gridlock packed the Strip from

Tropicana to Flamingo, slowing us to a crawl. Strolling pedestrians sped by us. Sipping from yards of daiquiris and margaritas and carrying buckets of beer, they leaned down to peek in at us, raising a glass as they strolled past. Some had lost various bits of clothing; others had lost all inhibition.

"Come on." I popped the door before Bentley had time to stop. It didn't matter. I hit the ground in an easy stride, Romeo on my heels.

"Do you know how far we are?" Romeo sounded like he had no run left.

"Hours if we stayed with the car." I scanned the sidewalks. As luck would have it, a pedicab was parked under the portico of NewYork-NewYork. "This way." The pedicab sat alone, the driver nowhere to be seen.

Romeo, who'd fallen behind, arrived winded at my side. "You think he'll be back soon."

Guess all the chasing bad guys recently paid off—I'd never been able to outlast the kid before. Or I was already dead—my calf didn't hurt; my nose, even though I couldn't breathe through it, didn't leak blood. Only explanation was my heart had stopped. "Not waiting to find out." I straddled the seat; my feet found the pedals. "Get in back."

"You can't be serious."

I showed him serious, then pushed down on the higher pedal. He dove into the back, then righted himself. His hand found a loop, and he held on like a toddler in a crowd. "I'd use both hands."

This time, he didn't argue.

"Where is the little bell? And what are you supposed to shout? On the left?" I wheeled down the driveway, ignoring cars coming at me. The traffic parted except for one large black SUV.

"Shit!" Romeo shouted.

At the last minute, I closed my eyes and pedaled as fast as I could. Tires screeched. Brakes smoked—I could smell it. A few invectives in a female voice and a language I couldn't identify. Two breaths and I sneaked an eye open. We were still alive! At the sidewalk, I paused pedaling. "To the left!" I shouted at Romeo as I threw my weight into the left-hand turn, fighting centrifugal force. Behind me, I felt Romeo shift. The inside tires went light on me, but we hung on, thrusting our bodies as counterbalance like sailors on an America's Cup boat.

Once headed north, I hit the pedals again. Scattering pedestrians, I stood up and pumped furiously. At the Monte Carlo, construction in front forced me to veer into the street, against traffic. I hugged the fence and, for once, thanked the Powers that Be that the traffic was at a virtual standstill. The cars left just enough room to squeeze past. One cab took his share of the lane out of the sidewalk as well. I clipped him and thought, as awful as the cab drivers can be, it was cosmic justice. His shouts dwindled as I pedaled north as fast as I could, which, hyped on adrenaline, was pretty darn fast. Three young darlings clad in tubes of Lycra and balancing on stupid-high heels, scattered like a flock of geese as I wheeled around the front of The Cosmo, the hanging-out place of the beautiful twenty-somethings.

Bellagio loomed in front of me. A crowd had gathered, spilling onto the Strip. They stood five-deep along the rail as I wheeled up the long, curving driveway, the fountains to my right. Tonight was Andrea Bocelli night—the first chords of "Music of the Night" sounded through the speakers lining the drive. The first salvo of the fountains drew a collective *oh* from the crowd. Billed as one of the Seven Wonders of the Modern World, the fountains always drew a crowd and a vigorous response. Last time I was in Geneva, their lone fountain shooting into the sky seemed pathetic in comparison. One compared to twelve hundred, lit by forty-five-hundred lights and they all dance to music?

Nothing like it.

But tonight, the crowd slowed me down. Coasting to a stop

under the *porte-cochere,* I pulled out my phone and hit Jeremy's number. "Where are you?"

"Still at Hyde, but your guy is paying up. He'll be on the move shortly."

I dismounted and took off at a run. Romeo was right behind me, his coat flapping, his breath coming in gasps. We dodged and darted through the crowd, hanging a right into the casino. Sticking to the right wall, we avoided most of the gambling crowd. Up ahead, I could see the door to Hyde on the right, with a bouncer out front.

He didn't even slow me down as we charged by. I heard him shouting behind us as he chased us inside. Beautiful people draped across the wicker furniture, basking in the glow of heaters, hip cocktails, and attention. Most weren't startled as we ran into their presence. Instead, they looked at us with a bit of disdain as if we were beggars crashing a society soiree.

Skidding onto the patio, we stopped. The bouncer roared behind us. "Romeo, take care of that. Do your badge thing."

He gave me a wide-eye but did as I asked. No more bellows. Easy as that. I needed a badge.

Where was Jeremy?

In the background, the fountains danced, booms announcing a spectacular launch of water into the night sky. Lights added an almost-daylight brightness to the lake. Underwater lights pointed toward the sky at each water nozzle.

I spied Fox by the balustrade, the fountains dancing behind him. He saw me at almost the same time.

"Fox!"

A boom from behind him. Water shot into the sky.

When I looked back, he was gone.

Reynolds, three tables over, whirled when I shouted. I pointed to where Fox had been. He glanced below. With one hand on the balustrade, he vaulted over and he, too, disappeared.

A body flashed by me. "I'm on this." Jeremy!

"Wait!"

My shout didn't even slow him down. With Romeo on his heels, the two of them vaulted into the darkness. I stepped to the railing and shook my head. Talk about jumping without thinking. Fox in front, the fountains still dancing, the three men following him—they formed a human wedge as they struggled through the knee-deep water. One misstep and they'd be singing soprano at the very least. In all likelihood, the force of the water being shot into the sky was probably lethal, but I wasn't sure. Impossible to watch; impossible to look away.

Men. Always opting for brute when brains would do nicely.

I scrolled through the contacts on my phone. Finding the one I wanted, I pressed send. A crowd gathered around me, watching the show and the men dodging through it as I waited for an answer. This crowd used perfume and cologne as weapons—like a gas, the nauseating mixture enveloped me. One of the mating rituals I'd never understand, it fell on the spectrum of why waste time on the subtle art of seduction when one can hit them with a stone and drag them back to the cave? And look where that had gotten us.

Finally, a voice on the other end saved me from my random mental walk. "Fountain Room."

I had to stick a finger in my other ear and strain to hear over the music, the excited chatter, and the booms and bursts of high-flying water. "Is Iceman around?" Iceman ran the fountain choreography. He'd come by his nickname when he helped solve an icing problem with the fountains—some bit of esoteric physics I didn't understand, but apparently it almost caused Steve Wynn to stroke out. All those millions and the nozzles would ice over in the middle of a show? I'd stroke out, too.

"He's busy."

"It's important."

"Call back. But you can't have a private tour of the room nor can you play with the fountains. Not even for a blow job."

That flipped a switch. I lowered my voice to corporate bitch mode. "You put him on or I'll have your ass. Come to think of it, your ass is a grape when I talk to your boss."

A pregnant pause. "I miscalculated. I'm sorry, sir." Too little, too late. I knew his boss, and he'd take a dim view.

He fumbled the phone, then a voice came over the line, one I recognized. "This is Walt." Walt didn't cotton to his nickname. Told me his mother had hung Walter on him. He loved his mother, so that's what it would be. Gotta like a guy like that.

"Hey, Walt. Lucky O'Toole."

"Hey, Lucky! Long time no see. You want to play with the fountains again?" We'd spent several hours in a dinghy in the middle of the fountains with a bottle of bubbly choreographing a Vegas commercial for the Visitor's Bureau one fine summer morning in the wee hours when magic lurked in all the nooks and crannies. And to think, a blow job had not been on the table at all.

"Of course. That kind of power goes right to my head. But not now. Right now, I need a favor." I kept my eyes on my little band of merry men. Progress was slow.

"Sure thing. What can I do you for?"

He always said the same thing, the same way—he thought it was funny. I was pretty sure he didn't realize he left himself wide open to all kinds of misinterpretation.

"See those four idiots running through the fountains?" I watched them zig and zag. Jeremy, Reynolds and Romeo had fanned out behind Fox, trying to outflank him. A good strategy, but nobody was making much headway. The water and a healthy respect for water pressure slowed them down.

"Yeah, we get them a lot. One wrong step and one of those fountains could cut them in half or at least do some serious damage to the delicates. The pressure is pretty intense."

A here-hold-my-beer-moment if there ever was one. "Yeah, well the one in front is wanted for murder. The three behind are with the authorities trying to corral him. Think you can cut him off at the pass for me?"

"Song's just ending. Let's give the crowd an encore. What do you say?"

"My thoughts exactly. Let's run them around and tire them out."

Keeping the line open and the phone pressed to my ear, I watched as the three men and one idiot, to the extent that wasn't redundant, staggered through the water, the fountains firing, then dancing around them. An eight-and-a-half-acre lake was a big corral. This could be fun.

As the song hit its final high note, like the fireworks finale on the Fourth of July, all the fountains burst skyward. The water rained down in a soft sizzle, melting into a fine mist as the music trailed away. A roar and clapping erupted from the crowd.

Fox made a beeline for the nearest exit point—the far side. The shops at Bellagio loomed over him. At this time of night, they'd be closed. If he made it, his only entry point back into the hotel would be Prime or Picasso—the two restaurants on the lake level. They both would still be open.

Walt was good, but I hedged my bets. Security at Bellagio assured me they were all over it.

"Can you turn them back around without killing them?" I shouted into my phone.

"I'm timing the lag time—it takes a bit to fire up one of the nozzles."

I waited. Fox drew closer to the side. He was almost past the fountains and into the clear when a jet of water erupted in front of him.

"Woo-hoo!" Walt shouted in my ear.

Fox stopped, then bent forward, fighting momentum that threatened to throw him headfirst into the column of water.

"Shit!" Walt again. "If we have brains spread all over the fountain pool, the boss man will have my head. Timed it too close. Sorry."

The men behind closed the distance.

"Looked perfect to me. I got your back and I'll pay for the cleanup." Frankly, given Fox's lack of brainpower, I didn't think there would be much to clean up.

In the lead, Jeremy lunged for Fox. He darted to the right. Now he headed toward the Strip with Jeremy on his heels. Romeo worked his way out to the right, Reynolds to the left, leaving only one path.

"One more time, Walt? Same timing?"

"This one's dicey. I might take out your man, too."

I swallowed hard. Was getting Fox worth losing Jeremy? Stupid question. No.

"Your call. If we can't get him now, we'll get him later. He can only run so far. My man is too important to lose."

"Got it. I think I can do it."

Life and death, a very slight margin for error, and Walt had his finger on the button, not me. My worst-case scenario—well, one of them. My heart in my throat, I watched, stymied as to whether I should shut Walt down or not.

Go big or go home. "If you see an opportunity—"

A single salvo from one of the fountains cut me off.

My heart stopped. Romeo and Reynolds pulled up short. I stared through the mist. Nobody around me moved. Those gathered on the driveway who had stayed to watch fell silent. The water fell.

Two men appeared through the mist.

I sucked in air, and my heart restarted.

Jeremy had an arm around Fox's throat. Reynolds and Romeo closed quickly.

"Walt, you are a friggin' genius."

"I nearly died pushing that button."

Him and me both.

~

I'd read Reynolds right, in the end.

When the excitement was over and the danger passed, the cops had shown up and taken Fox into custody. After confirming my suspicions, Reynolds had taken Fox away. Still not buying into the whole Reynolds-is-a-white-hat thing, Romeo went with him.

Jeremy, wrapped in towels, his hair standing on end after a good rubbing, found me standing in front of the hotel watching the fountains. An hour had passed, and they were doing their thing again. Andrea Bocelli's soothing tenor filled the night. "I should've listened to you. Who knew you had a direct line to the guy controlling the show?"

"Someday, you're going to stop underestimating me."

"Brilliant idea, actually." He didn't sound surprised, which told me he already had.

"I could've killed you."

He put an arm around my shoulders and pulled me into a squeeze. "No. When under the gun, you make the right decisions. Trust yourself."

I patted his arm. Everyone had more faith in me than I did. Maybe there was a lesson in there.

I'd misjudged Reynolds and learned another good lesson: just because I didn't like someone didn't mean they were bad. Books and their covers—I knew better.

Life. The lessons were coming at me hard and fast these days. Like bullets to the gut, they left me staggering and on the verge of losing myself.

Who was I really? And what did I want?

I needed to step out of my life to figure that out. A quiet place and a quiet mind where nobody expected anything from me.

"Go home. I'm sure your wife is worried sick."

"And where are you going?"

I hadn't a clue. My phone vibrated at my hip, and I gave him a smile. "Life calls."

"No, duty calls. Shut it down. You'll find your life where duty ends." With a smile, he stepped away, turning toward life, his life.

With a sigh, I glanced at the caller ID. Mona. "Hey, Mother."

"Lucky!" She sounded breathless, excited. She had a life and wanted a purpose. Would any female in this family get the balance right? "I finally got the Sheriff."

"He told you the video was patched together, Romeo is in the clear, and he skirted the issue when it came to Reynolds."

"Oh." She deflated, and instantly I regretted trotting out my competence, and my dumb luck. "It's great you confirmed all that. I really appreciate it. I never would've gotten squat out of the Sheriff—he's always looking for a reason to arrest me."

"You think?" I couldn't tell whether her enthusiasm was over my appreciation or my possible arrest, not that it mattered. I'd helped her feel good about herself, added a little magic to the Universe. At the end of the day, that's what it was all about anyway.

"Have you wrapped things up, then?"

"Yes."

Infused with maternal concern, her sigh wrapped around me like a warm blanket. "Come home, then. I want you to tell me all about it."

"I will, but not now."

"Where are you going?" Despite my best assertions otherwise, she knew me well.

As I watched the fountains dance, I decided a man, a very good man, deserved his shot. "Paris."

"What?"

"I'm going to Paris." Maybe, just maybe, I'd find myself there.

THE END

Thank you so much for going on a Lucky adventure with me. I hope you enjoyed the ride.

As you may know, reviews are SUPER helpful. They not only help potential readers make a choice, but they also help me win coveted spots on various advertising platforms.

So, if you would please, do me the favor of leaving a review at the outlet of your choice.

NEXT UP FOR LUCKY…

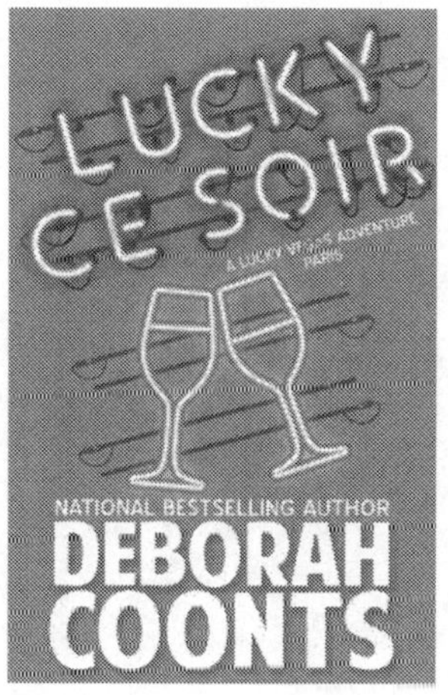

Read a short excerpt below

CHAPTER ONE

"SHE'LL TURN me to stone." Panic rooted me where I stood as I stared at my nemesis. All four feet and eleven inches of impeccable…Frenchness, she worked her way across the room, stopping periodically, greeting people with a smile, a nod, a quick word. Yet, somehow, she kept the dagger of her attention buried to the hilt between my ribs.

The party in my honor whirled around me—a kaleidoscope of well-heeled French fashion and feigned disinterest. However, the woman headed my way left no doubt I was very much the American *plat du jour.*

Chef Jean-Charles Bouclet, my perfectly presented fiancé in his bespoke tux, cultured manners and delicious accent, pressed close, his shoulder touching mine. His favored cologne, *Eau de* Seared Beef and Browned Onions, wafted around him, telling me he'd been calming his nerves in the kitchen before my last-minute entrance. A single bead of sweat trickled down the side of his face. "What?" He'd been only half-listening.

"Stone. One look from your mother and I'll be a permanent fixture in this ancient ossuary." I made a sweeping gesture that included all the statuary lining the room. Tucked discretely into individual alcoves they lorded over the festivities. "Maybe that's where all these marble figurines came from, former guests who were found wanting."

He raised an eyebrow. "At least three of them were gifts from various kings. A bit gaudy, but one never says no to a king." Jean-Charles gave me the hint of a smile.

I followed his gaze which was locked onto the oncoming human missile, then I leaned in and whispered, "Don't look her in the eyes."

Sheathed in expensive one-of-a-kind couture that hugged her every curve, she advanced on us with an expression worn by those intent on vanquishing their enemies. Before I looked away, I took a bit of delight in the few extra pounds that expanded the middle of what might have been an hourglass figure. And her shoes were...sensible, a French fashion faux-pas. Her hints of human frailty lent me courage, albeit fleeting, but enough to stiffen my backbone.

Jean-Charles shook his head and finally gave me his attention. "You are making no sense. What do you mean she'll turn you to rock?" His Adam's apple bobbed as he swallowed hard, then ran a finger around the inside of his collar, tugging it to allow blood to get to his brain, apparently without the desired effect.

"Not rock. Stone. Like Medusa." As I braced for the imminent encounter, I let my gaze wander over the gathered throng, looking for friends in the crowded ballroom. No joy. Not a friendly, recognizable face in the lot. In fact, they all looked pinched and judgmental, with a hint of fear, making me feel like I was guest of honor at my own evisceration.

Okay, overly dramatic, but the whole meeting-my-well-heeled-very-French-future-in-laws had me on the verge of apoplexy. Once I did the I-do thing, my options would be gone. How was I supposed to know if I'd picked the right one? God knew Teddie had been an epic fail.

Epic.

My heart still bore the scars, but it had healed. My confidence, not so much.

But who was it I didn't trust exactly? Jean-Charles? Or me?

"Medusa?" Jean-Charles angled his head and looked like he was entertaining my analogy for a moment. Then he dismissed it with a quick shake of his head. "Don't be silly," he said, but he didn't sound convinced. Instead, he adjusted his bow tie and swallowed hard. The usual robin's egg blue of his eyes had turned dark and moody. Emotion pulled the skin tight over his cheekbones. Even still, with his full lips and soft brown hair curling over his collar, and that body hugged by the Italian cut of his tux, he was delish. He could be kind, sensitive, demanding, churlish, enigmatic—a dizzying array, which I currently found endlessly entertaining, but worried might wear me out. Time would tell...if I survived.

Seriously, death-by-mother-in-law is a thing—I know it is.

"You're scared, too," I whispered to Jean-Charles, still unable to focus an unwavering gaze on my future mother-in-law.

"She's my mother." Repeating the obvious was his go-to when avoiding telling me something I didn't want to hear. "And terrified would be more apt."

I swiveled a wide-eyed look at the man I supposedly knew better than anyone.

His eyes caught mine for a fraction of a second before his gaze skittered away. His smile was tight and thin. "You and I, we share difficult mothers."

"*Now* you tell me?" Despite whispering, my voice held a shrill note.

Jean-Charles sidestepped my accusation by focusing on a face in the crowd. Following his gaze, I found myself staring at a balding man, his sneer his only distinguishing feature. Jean-Charles looked a bit surprised and put out at seeing him.

"Who is that?"

"Someone who was not invited."

"Gotta have some steel *cojones* to crash your mother's gig. Personally, I would not tempt death that way."

"He would've been wise to stay away."

Christophe, Jean-Charles's son, moved from clutching his father's leg to tugging on my vintage Bob Mackie gown.

Five years old, blond curls and large baby blues like his father's, he most likely sensed our discomfort and needed reassurance. The kid was an emotional weather vane. My mother, Mona, a new mother to a set of twins, had told me that many things about dealing with children were instinctive. My disbelief had drawn a knowing smile. I hated it when Mona was right. Thankfully, it didn't happen that often.

After carefully disengaging his fingers from the delicate fabric, I squatted as much as I dared in the tight sheath, then lifted him. "Ooof! You've been eating too many happy-face pancakes." Christophe still fit on one hip, but he would soon outgrow that perch, and my ability to fly him there. I nuzzled his hair which smelled of baby soap and warm memories.

"*Grand-mère,* she looks...different," he whispered, one hand fisted in my hair.

"A woman on the warpath," I muttered, then braced for the elbow to the ribs I knew would be coming. Jean-Charles didn't disappoint. A soft nudge of displeasure which I ignored. "Girding her loins for battle to protect her sole and sainted son," I explained to my future stepson despite his father's glare. The hint of laughter in Jean-Charles's eyes told me I was on safe ground. The laughter dimmed when I turned on him. "I thought your mother lived on a farm and named the cows." Even with my limited functionality at the moment, I distinctly remembered that was how he'd described his mother—a charming story about his father's irritation at not being able to butcher and serve the cows which, in the naming, had become pets. The woman advancing on us with the purpose of a bullet fired from a rifle could have killed the cows with her bare hands and thought nothing of it. My opinion, but the look on her face did little to convince me otherwise.

Jean-Charles shrugged. "The vineyard. The farm is more of a hobby. How do you say it, their men's farm?"

"Gentleman's farm?" Usually his trouble with American idioms, which I had a strong suspicion was slightly feigned for my benefit, charmed me. Today, not so much.

"*Oui.* This." He seemed far too pleased with himself.

I resisted the urge to wipe the smug off his face. Probably bad form at a fancy French *soirée.* Instead, I narrowed my eyes. "Lying by omission." Was that a capital offense? Punishable by death or just slow, delicious torture? Either way, it was still a big check in the "con" column.

Yep, I was straddling the commitment fence. Uncomfortable to say the least.

And Jean-Charles's mother was just more of what I didn't need.

As she drew closer, the partiers formed a circle of interest, their intensity wafting off them like cheap cologne. Activity and conversation stopped.

My future mother-in-law, Madame Jeanne Marchand Bouclet, stepped into my space. I resisted the urge to step back, reestablishing my boundary. The more I traveled, the more I realized the American concept of personal space translated about as seamlessly as our humor. The English were equally amused and appalled by it, the Italians ignored it, the French invaded it, and the Asians missed the concept entirely.

I held my ground as Madame Bouclet gave me a rheumy-eyed once over. The pale bow of her mouth scrunched in only slight distaste—I took that as a win. Her brown hair, the color softened by invading gray, was cut in a stylish bob. Her gown, a golden chenille that changed hues where it wrinkled and flowed, was fitted and tasteful, yet provocative in its off-the-shoulder design. A long cocktail length, the dress exposed her ankles and the color-coordinated ballet slippers adorning her feet.

My shoes were French, but my gown shouted American chutzpah and not a little bit of Vegas showmanship, no doubt considered a bit bourgeois by this crowd. I envied the effortless style with which French women carried themselves. I also envied their figures. Of course, they didn't have to ignore the Siren call of In-N-Out Burger, animal style, every day.

Jean-Charles's mother said nothing, so I clamped my mouth shut, too, thinking then it would be impossible to stuff my foot in it. We faced off, her appraisal and my fear a chasm of silence between us.

Jean-Charles leaped into the breach. "Mama, may I present Miss Lucky O'Toole."

She flicked one stenciled eyebrow skyward and extended a hand, palm down.

I hadn't a clue what to do with it. Kiss it? Not a chance.

"Mama!"

Using his exalted-son status, Jean-Charles competed with the raised eyebrow thing. I could beat them both but now was probably not the time. The crowd eased even closer. I felt certain they'd drawn a collective breath and held it. The air didn't move, hanging instead thick and stifling with emotion.

"Jesus," I sighed, the dregs of my patience dried on the bottom of my empty flagon previously filled with the Milk of Human Kindness. I took her hand in both of mine. "It's a pleasure to meet you. The men in your family have been singing your praises nonstop. Thank you so much for inviting me to your lovely home and having this amazing party. I am incredibly honored." What can I say? Suck-up is my best thing—a skill well-honed through years in customer service at the Babylon, Las Vegas's most over the top strip resort. And before that, at lesser properties in the wild and wooly parts of Vegas most well-heeled folks never see. When I began life at a whorehouse in Pahrump, who knew I'd end up here, in Paris, feted by those at the upper end of the upper crust? Certainly not me. This was so far from my normal that all I could do was make it up as I went...and apparently use too many superlatives.

Madame Bouclet inclined her head slightly.

The room filled with expelled air. The mood brightened. The fear skittered to hide in the corners. Jean-Charles visibly relaxed, and the lady in front of me gave me a smile. "My dear, please ignore my son's lack of manners. I've been looking forward to meeting you. You have captured my son's heart and have enraptured my grandson—both challenging tasks. I must learn how you have done such a thing." Her English was flawless—infinitely better than my high-school French, which I had yet to trot out. In this crowd, being six feet tall, curvy, and American was enough of an embarrassment. "Let me introduce you to my friends." She turned on her heel.

Jean-Charles motioned for me to follow, then fell in behind me. Christophe gladly rode my hip, bobbing along high above the fray. Being tall was my cross to bear, but I figured it was infinitely better than staring at everybody's thighs. So I took pity on him, and on me, and let him ride into the fray, a human shield as it were...but he didn't need to know that.

"Where's Desiree?" I tossed the words over my shoulder as I followed in Madame Bouclet's wake.

Jean-Charles rested a hand lightly on my shoulder as he leaned closer to catch my words. "*Pardon?*"

"Your sister?" I was counting on her to be my wingman. Her absence left me flying solo. Of course, I'd been complicit in the death of her estranged husband, Adone Giovanni, who, with his mistress had conspired to steal Desiree's business. So maybe expecting her to greet me with a buss on both cheeks might be overshooting.

Frankly, I thought my assistance in taking him out of the gene pool was a good thing, but love could be super-complicated. Maybe Desiree was planning to plant a dagger between my shoulder blades. To be honest, I didn't have a clue what transpired between her ears, nor what she held in her heart.

"She would not miss Mother's party." Jean-Charles made the prospect sound like doing so would mean the guillotine.

"Hope she's okay."

"*Pffft*," he puffed in French derision. "It will be a man. It is always a man."

"Rather evolved of you. Your man card is in trouble. Don't you Y-chromosome types always blame bad things on women?"

"I am not saying she is not at fault. She chooses the men." He tugged a bit with the hand still on my shoulder. "What is this man card?"

"Only thing that keeps you guys in the game."

Madame Bouclet yanked my attention back to the terror at hand. I so should've brushed up on the rules of French decorum. Vaguely, I remembered something about not touching anyone, and for sure not smiling very much—the French think it makes Americans look like fools, and perhaps a bit insincere. Spot on, in my book.

She stopped in front of a couple waiting with expectant expressions. Tiny, perfectly turned-out, they gave her a thin smile. "This is Miss Lucky O'Toole, Jean-Charles's fiancée."

I painted on what I hoped was a pleasant expression that wasn't a smile and tried to remember my fancy manners.

The names, unusual in their pronunciation, faded as one overwrote the one before on my mental hard drive. Christophe wriggled on my hip and my arms ached from corralling his weight as a starched and unctuous liveried member of the staff hurried to Madame Bouclet's side. If the interruption bothered her, I couldn't tell. Composure was something I strove for, failed at, and consequently strongly admired. Jean-Charles's mother's was impeccable. I wondered if she also had the royal wave down.

As the man bent and whispered in her ear, Madame Bouclet's hand moved to her throat, her fingers intertwining with her pearls, twisting them like expensive worry beads. Her face paled. Her jaw slackened, revealing her age and her worry. The man stepped back, and Madame Bouclet motioned to her son with a fluttering hand held close to her side, a subtle move to not draw attention.

Jean-Charles touched my elbow with a gesture of understanding, and I relinquished his son, my arms screaming their thanks. In one fluid movement, Jean-Charles took his son, lifting him high, then dropping him on his shoulders. "What is it, *Maman*?"

"It's Papa." She wilted as her knees buckled slightly. With a flawless segue, Jean-Charles caught her arm, steadying her. "He's not well. His heart."

Jean-Charles skewered the butler with an unmistakable look. The man turned on his heel and disappeared through the doorway. Jean-Charles, now holding his mother's elbow and his son, inclined his head, indicating I should follow him. I dug in my heels. "I should stay here."

"*Non!*" His tone brooked no argument.

This was not the place to make a scene—I could feel the heat of the partygoers' stares.

Jean-Charles ushered us through a doorway hidden in the paneling of the front hall, then down a hallway with multiple intersections with other corridors. The back of the house. As a hotelier, I was familiar. As a gal from Pahrump, this was home.

Worry propelled Jean-Charles. I had to hurry to keep up.

At the third intersection, he turned right, then burst through swinging double doors. I followed, catching the doors on the backswing. Blinking at the light, I found myself in a cavernous, white and stainless kitchen, the workstations spotlighted by commercial-grade overhead lights. Delicious aromas wafted from ovens and bubbling pots. My stomach growled. I cringed as the family clustered around me, afraid they might have heard.

But something was wrong.

Jean-Charles pushed into the kitchen. "What is going on here?" He kicked at a pot rolling on the floor. Utensils were scattered on the tile like grown-up Pick-Up Stix. A pool of something that smelled drool-worthy oozed from under a prep table. "Where's my father?"

"Over here." A voice, indignant but weak, answered in a timbre that held hints of his son's.

Jean-Charles kicked at a pot as he hurried toward the voice. His staff remained rooted. In full French bluster, he turned and shouted at them. "Back to work. And clean this up, now!"

They all jumped. Hell, Jean-Charles's imperious tone had me wanting to reach for a spatula. Instead, I followed him while the others held back. While food sizzled and steamed, they clustered together, staring at the man slouched in a chair someone had pulled into the center of the kitchen. Long, lean, all angles and anger, he pushed away a young man pressing a cloth to his head, pressing it to his head himself. When he lifted it slightly, I gasped at the long, red gash in his forehead. The man let loose a long stream of French I didn't understand yet understood perfectly. His other hand drifted to the center of his chest where he pushed, then winced in discomfort—from the gash or his heart, it was hard to tell.

I glanced at Jean-Charles, then again at the man in the chair. That apple hadn't fallen far.

Jean-Charles shifted Christophe to his hip as he knelt by his father's chair. Christophe, his eyes glistening, patted his grandfather's face. Children and their empathy.

Why do we lose that as we grow?

"The pain? Is it bad?" Jean-Charles asked his father in a whisper.

Looking at his father, I could answer that one. The man was so pale his skin held a hint of blue. His cheeks hollowed below too-wide eyes. He panted as if running a race, perhaps against Death himself. My father, with a bullet in his chest and blood leaking out so fast, had been as close to death as one could get without stepping into the afterlife. Jean-Charles's father was right there, toes curled over the edge of the abyss, his features donning a death mask as he sank into himself, his life force depleted. The man was way past "not well."

"Should I call the doctor?" Jean-Charles had seen the same as I had. Without waiting for permission, he nodded at his mother who eased away to summon help. "Did you take the nitroglycerin?"

He pushed his son's concerns aside. "It will go away."

With two fingers, Jean-Charles fished around in his father's breast pocket extracting a small tin. With a thumb, he popped it open and extracted a tiny white pill. "Take this."

One of the kitchen staff appeared with a glass of red wine. "It is the Lafite."

Jean-Charles nodded his thanks as he took the glass, waving it under his father's nose. As ammonia does for a fainter, the wine brought back the elder Bouclet, focusing him. "That's the '82," he gasped, then sucked in more air. "One of the best vintages," another gasp then pull-in of air, "a rare cult wine. We set aside a case for a special day. We wanted to toast your engagement," a gasp, a wince, then a deep breath, "with something special."

"And that is very special." Jean-Charles held the glass to his father's lips. "Take a sip. See if it is aging well." Christophe, his eyes wide with worry, clung to his father.

A little nitro with your rare Bordeaux. Not a great pairing but a terrific bribe. One that worked as the old man did as his son insisted. Jean-Charles's mother returned. Her slight nod let her son know she'd found the doctor. I assumed he was on his way since no one made any move to relocate the elder Bouclet.

"How is it?" Jean-Charles asked after his father had taken a few sips, savoring each of them. A touch of color returned to his cheeks. He breathed easier now, easing the force with which he pressed on his chest. "It helps. The pain is lessening."

"The wine?" Jean-Charles asked as if that was what he'd meant. "How's the wine?"

A smile passed between them. His father bestowed a look of love. "Not as special as you, but it is very good."

"Papa? What has happened?" Jean-Charles used a soft, measured tone. "Are you sure you're okay?"

"The pain is almost gone." His father waved his hand, a human flag of surrender. Jean-Charles had his father's hands, long and narrow—artist's hands that could concoct a variety of delights.

Jean-Charles pushed his father's hand away from the cloth he held to his head. "Permit me." A demand framed as a question, one of his best things...and most irritating. He snuck a peek under the now-red cloth, then let loose a stream of low, guttural French.

Madame Bouclet swooped in, snatching her grandson to her chest. "Jean-Charles!"

Her offense was justified. If I were more of a lady, the bit I caught would have made me blush. One of the staff rushed to do his bidding, returning quickly with a first-aid kit. Jean-Charles set to work. His hard expression brooked no argument. His father sat motionless, as if carved from stone, his hands on his knees, his back erect, his face flushed with emotion. "The wine," he gasped.

His son brushed the comment aside. "Who did this?" He dabbed at the cut with cotton soaked in alcohol drawing a few epithets from his father, which he ignored. A quick glance around the kitchen. "Did you fight with someone? Who was here?"

Most of the staff turned from his question—apparently, they knew what happens to the messenger.

"Laurent." The word sounded like an epithet.

"Here? In our home? What did he want?"

"The wine," his father repeated.

"He wanted the wine?" Jean-Charles closed the cut with two butterfly closures.

"He had a crazy story. I didn't listen. I didn't let him finish," his father managed, then convulsed into a fit of racking coughs that he caught with a white napkin pressed over his mouth. His skin turned an alarming shade of red. "Uninvited in our home," he managed between coughs and gasps.

Still a bit iffy on French protocol, I assumed from his inflection that was almost as grave a sin as disrespecting the women of the household, maybe more.

"Easy, Papa. Slowly." Jean-Charles helped his father take a few more sips of the Lafite between spasms.

This stress, both physical and clearly emotional, only put more pressure on a bad heart.

"Enzo did this to you?" A hint of incredulity subtexted the question.

From Jean-Charles's inflection, I took it Enzo Laurent might be scum, but he was no blackguard, and as an honorable man he wouldn't ever do such a thing. Men came in all types and sometimes shifted from one to the other with the proper motivation. I guessed we all could. My mother often had me seriously considering homicide. I mean, the idea of three-squares, a cot, and no Mona was almost irresistible at times. But jail would probably be incompatible with my serious authority issues, so I'd restrained myself…so far.

"No. A man. In the tunnels. I surprised him. He ran out through the kitchen. I couldn't catch him. The swine ran right by Enzo. At my shout, he tried to stop him as well. His jaw may be broken for his efforts."

"What did the man in the tunnel look like?"

"Young. Dark hair. I never saw his face. He and Enzo tussled, and then he was gone."

"Where is Enzo?"

"I threw him out!" The elder Bouclet seemed offended at the

question that, in its asking, suggested there was another course of action. "The wine," he gasped as he grabbed his son's lapel.

"What about the wine?" Jean-Charles asked again, looking at his mother who bracketed his father on the other side. Holding his hand in one of hers while securing her grandson with the other, she eyed her son, her eyes dark with worry.

Monsieur Bouclet sat up straighter, his face clearing as he stared at his son with a look of pain and disbelief. "The wine, it is gone."

This time it was Jean-Charles's turn with the raised eyebrow trick. "What do you mean it is gone? The cellar is full. We even transported the entire winery library from the winery to show our guests. I checked it myself last evening."

The truth in his father's stare could not be denied. "It's all gone."

End of Sample

To continue reading, be sure to pick up *Lucky Ce Soir* at your favorite retailer.

ALSO BY DEBORAH COONTS

The Lucky O'Toole Vegas Adventure Series

Wanna Get Lucky? (Book 1)

Lucky Stiff (Book 2)

So Damn Lucky (Book 3)

Lucky Bastard (Book 4)

Lucky Catch (Book 5)

Lucky Break (Book 6)

Lucky the Hard Way (Book 7)

Lucky Ride (Book 8)

Lucky Score (Book 9)

Lucky Ce Soir (Book 10)

Lucky Enough (Book 11)

Other Lucky O'Toole Books

The Housewife Assassin Gets Lucky

(Co-written with Josie Brown, author of the Housewife Assassin series)

Lucky O'Toole Original Novellas

Lucky in Love (Novella 1)

Lucky Bang (Novella 2)

Lucky Now and Then (Novella 3)

Lucky Flash (Novella 4)

The Brinda Rose Humorous Mystery Series

90 Days to Score (Book 1)

The Kate Sawyer Medical Thriller Series

After Me (Book 1)

Deadfall (Book 2)

Other Novels

Deep Water (romantic suspense)

Crushed (women's fiction)

ABOUT THE AUTHOR

Deborah Coonts swears she was switched at birth. Coming from a family of homebodies, Deborah is the odd woman out, happiest with a passport, a high-limit credit card, her computer, and changing scenery outside her window. Goaded by an insatiable curiosity, she flies airplanes, rides motorcycles, travels the world, and pretends to be more of a badass than she probably is. Deborah is the author of the Lucky O'Toole Vegas Adventure series, a romantic mystery romp through Sin City. *Wanna Get Lucky?*, the first in the series, was a *New York Times* Notable Crime Novel and a double RITA™ Award Finalist. She has also penned the Kate Sawyer Medical Thriller series, the Brinda Rose Humorous Mystery series, as well as a couple of standalones. Although often on an adventure, you can always track her down at:

www.deborahcoonts.com
deborah@deborahcoonts.com

facebook.com/deborahcoonts
twitter.com/DeborahCoonts
instagram.com/deborahcoonts
pinterest.com/debcoonts
bookbub.com/authors/deborah-coonts
amazon.com/author/debcoonts
goodreads.com/DeborahCoonts

Manufactured by Amazon.ca
Bolton, ON